BLACKENED

SEEDS
&
SHADOWS
BOOK 2

K.W. BERNARD

Cover by Atra Luna Design.

pISBN: 979-8-9986678-2-4

eISBN: 979-8-9986678-3-1

CONTENT WARNING

B lackened is darker and dirtier than the first book in the series. Please, take care. For content details and a list of potential triggers, visit kwbernard.com.

CHAPTER ONE

It was too cold for proper snow but perfect weather for ending a species.

The icy splinters stinging Dagmar's cheeks beautifully complemented those that lodged deeper in her chest with each stride toward the lorkai's extinction.

Yet, the storm was a comfort.

Winter's long-lost bite gripped her stiff and deadened fingers like an old friend. Ancient memories swirled with the whipping wind, howling that her newfound humanity didn't make her helpless. It reminded her who she'd been lifetimes before an impossible spell stole her immortality—an elite Northland warrior. Fearsome and fatal.

She was that woman again, with centuries more experience.

And a gut full of foreboding.

She had a daughter, after all. One bound and determined to kill herself along with the lorkai.

"Sarlona."

The young woman spun, raising her brows over the most enchanting oceanic gaze Dagmar had known in all her years. Gods, the girl was beautiful. She'd stay stunning forever if she abandoned her foolish quest.

"Keep the Council out of this. I'm begging you." Not really. Dagmar had yet to get on her knees. Though if doing so might have changed Sarlona's mind, she'd have dropped into the snow that moment.

Sarlona sucked on her lips. "I have no choice."

With every plodding step toward her daughter, Dagmar broke the thick rime a few inches below the powder and sank to her knees anew. She stood taller, even with Sarlona perched atop the crust, but her size was meaningless.

To the two superior beings before her, Dagmar was small.

She'd never speak or act like it, though. "You could choose to embrace your destiny. To carry on your grandfather's legacy." She glanced at Benton, who waited a few paces ahead and stared through her father's stormy eyes, no doubt aching to put his hands around her throat. "You could listen to your mother instead of destroying our people."

"You're not my mother," Sarlona said, words colder than any blizzard.

They landed like an axe to the ribcage, striking harder than ever now that Amenduil's wicked spell had made them true.

"There are some things even magic can't erase, Sarlona." *Nothing* could erode Dagmar's brutal brand of love. "I am and will always be your mother. No matter what you do."

Smile muted, Sarlona slipped off a glove and rested silky fingertips along Dagmar's jawline.

The Northlander peered into her boundless blue gaze and waited for the soul-deep tug on her Marrow. It didn't come.

Instead, heat bled from Sarlona's hand and spread over Dagmar's skin, thawing her fingers, toes, cheeks, and thighs. The touch brought the warmth of a tavern fire and a sweet, tender glow that urged Dagmar to squeeze the lovely girl in her arms.

After everything Dagmar had done to her, Sarlona showed her mercy and kindness. She was so understanding. So forgiving...

So fucking infuriating.

Sarlona's empathy would kill them all. She'd trust the wrong mage. Again.

Dagmar recoiled. "I'm fine. We're almost there." The realization twisted shards of anxiety in her viscera. This would go poorly.

"We woulda been there and back by now." Benton glared with the wrong eyes and folded arms that didn't belong to him. "If you hadn't slowed us down."

"You *need* me to translate the Council's double-speak," Dagmar sneered. "And feed you. So you don't grab the first spellcaster you see and get tossed atop a pyre before you're even through the door."

Benton had gained some control since he'd been rescued from the Abyss and stuffed into Glaucus's body, but he was even more of an animal as a lorkai than he'd been as a man. In a tower full of casters, where everyone *dripped* with Marrow... Dagmar doubted he could keep himself from draining someone for long.

"You two better feed."

She ripped off her gloves, wishing for the hundredth time in the last few weeks that she had a greater capacity for Marrow. At her peak, she didn't hold enough to throw a spell. She couldn't sustain a newborn lorkai and an ancient who acted like one.

Skipping a few paces ahead, Sarlona bunched up her sleeves. "I can take from the forest." She ejected her carpal blades with a flick of the wrists. "I'll be okay."

Dagmar might have believed her if the two monsters weren't about to have dozens of Aven's most Marrow-rich casters dangling before them. "That won't be enough."

Plopping to her knees, Sarlona drove each claw through the snow and into the frozen ground. A wispy, blue-green glow gathered in her arms and wound up her body, painting bliss across her face. The snow evaporated around her, and every living thing—saplings, shrubs, and chunks of moss—withered into ash. A few nearby trees, the roots of which she must have nicked with her claws, flagged and blackened to charcoal before dissipating on the icy breeze. Their remnants cast a sooty stain over the pristine snow.

Desecrating the land like that killed Sarlona. If she accidentally drained someone to death, it would destroy her. So would the Council, should that someone be a mage.

Sarlona opened her eyes, and her euphoric expression faded. Her brow knotted at the small patch of utter devastation. A hollowness bled into her gaze when she yanked her claws free and retracted them like folding knives into the undersides of her forearms.

The fact that she wanted to rid herself of the serrated, ivory daggers cracked Dagmar's granite heart. It broke when she turned to Benton.

He beamed at her with his shittiest grin. "I've gotta have a drink, though."

Her father's smiles had always been soft, small, and warm.

Dagmar held out her pale hands, and Glaucus's aged, rich brown ones closed on her freezing fingers. Dread seized her chest when his fingertips lit up manna-blue and tapped into her Marrow. His eyes flared yellow, and he drew in, groaning with her maker's voice.

She winced more from the unbearable sound than any pain. He'd gotten better at feeding. After the first raw, rough tugs, numbness swept over her. A tingling warmth followed. He was figuring things out...

Soon, he'd *really* be dangerous.

He winked when her gaze drifted from the snow-blasted tree trunks to his storm-cloud eyes. "Kinda likin' that, ain't you, Daggy?"

Her stomach flipped, and her nostrils flared at the nickname alone. "I don't need you to—"

Hot pleasure shot through her thighs and abdomen, stealing her breath and swallowing her words. Every muscle tightened with anticipated ecstasy. Biting back a moan, she fought to keep her eyes from rolling.

Her daughter's snarl saved her. "*Benton.*" The orange glow in Sarlona's glare cast hellfire across an otherwise angelic face. "Don't do that. Not without permission."

He released Dagmar's fingers, and her insides cooled. "She's done a hells of a lot worse to me."

That was an understatement. Given how Dagmar had treated him, it was a wonder he didn't use his new dominion over mortal biology to rot her teeth, give her kidney stones, or start tumors in her lungs. He should have tortured her like she had him.

But his gaze sank into the snow. "Yeah, okay."

Despite the dissolution of their supernatural bond when his body had drowned in the Abyss, Sarlona's influence on him hadn't waned.

Fortunate for Dagmar.

He peeked at her with a fresh grin. "Sorry, Dags. The next time you want me to warm you up, you're gonna have to ask me for it."

Rage heated her face and corded the muscles in her neck. She shoved her aching fingers into her gloves with a snort. "You'd better pray no one can make you mortal again."

It wasn't much of a threat, but she couldn't afford to waste her wrath on Benton. Not when she might need it to save her daughter.

CHAPTER TWO

The metallic tang of magic hung thick in the air with the brutal cold. Sarlona's preternatural sense of smell and whichever organ now detected magical energy told her they were nearing a great source. In the past, a spell of her own would have deciphered the wards protecting Apogee, the Society of Progressive Sorcerers' Council tower. But Dagmar had stripped her of the ability to cast one when she'd forced the lorkai quick down her throat and turned her into a monster. Resentment chewed at Sarlona with each step closer to the political hub of the power she could no longer wield.

That didn't stop her from worrying about Dagmar.

The air was icy enough to freeze damp clothing into stiff sheets within seconds. It didn't bite Sarlona like it had before, but she tasted its intensity along with the magic.

If anyone could endure that eye-watering cold, it was a Northlander. But Dagmar hadn't had to worry about exposure for centuries. Even swathed in her usual hide and fur, with the addition of a cloak made from a great white bear, she appeared underdressed.

When she caught Sarlona glancing back, her voice could have passed for a bear's growl. "I'm *fine*." She adjusted the pelt around her head and shoulders. "It's just up ahead."

Sure enough, a gleam of polished black stone appeared beyond a swirl of sugary snow and dense evergreen. "I see it."

Benton squinted. "Hey, me too."

Well-known for being magically hidden, the trio had half expected they'd never find it. The heavy-duty community spell concealing Apogee prevented individuals from going there if they'd never been. One had to be led to the tower on their first trip.

And while Sarlona and Dagmar had visited before, they'd both been different species then. Benton had never been—but Glaucus's body had. It seemed the spell recognized faces, not what lurked behind them.

"Tread lightly," said Dagmar.

Easier for a pair of average-sized lorkai than a three-hundred-pound human.

Sarlona waded through the neck-high fir at the edge of the tree line and into the vast clearing. A sneaky blast shoved snow down her shirt and blew the hood from her head. "They just had wards of warning and repellents of ill intent last time I was here."

Dagmar burst from the brush, and the north wind buffeted her, perhaps punishing her for abandoning it all those years ago.

Winter's last throes.

The air, the afternoon light, and the restlessness of the creatures beneath the snow all whispered to Sarlona of the changing seasons. At least the land still spoke to her. Even if she couldn't touch its magic without deadening it.

Dagmar shielded her face, pushing ahead, and Sarlona let her lead the way.

With Apogee looming—a hideous obsidian scar jutting from the wilderness to cut into the white sky—going there seemed less wise. Spells Sarlona couldn't sort out saturated the grounds, and the scent of more than a hundred mortal casters rode the wind. It grabbed her just as her mother's fresh-baked bread and simmering stew had after a day of working in the fields or forest. Except this hunger grasped at her soul instead of her stomach. She'd known the tower's residents would rouse her thirst in ways Dagmar and Ashmore's guards did not, but she hadn't expected it to hit her before a single mage came within reach.

Benton drifted closer, grimacing, and Sarlona grabbed his shoulder, hoping to steady him. Bringing him along seemed foolish now. In the short time he'd been stuck in a lorkai body, he'd struggled to master himself under the best circumstances. Apogee would test them both. If either lost control, there'd be consequences.

Executions, according to Dagmar.

The flurry of activity behind Apogee's walls—scrambling footsteps, the crack of rushed spells, and urgent whispers—started before the trio had crossed half the clearing to the tower. When they arrived at the entrance,

Jasper, the SPS emissary to lorkai and other monsters, awaited them. He stood center of the massive arch that marked the magical door, flanked by two elven warcasters.

His chestnut gaze fixed on Benton. "You sent no notice of your visit." His tone and smile were warm even if his words weren't. "What business brings you to Apogee, milord?"

A magical shield kept the wind from mussing Jasper's mahogany hair or spotless brown coat. His face was pure calm, but his anxiety leaked into the air. The fact that the scent of it added to his appeal formed a lump in Sarlona's throat. At least the desire to devour him didn't shake her bones as it had at their first meeting.

She hopped in front of Benton. "I've come to request the Council's aid."

Jasper cocked his head. "What—"

"Dagmar made me a lorkai," she blurted.

The Northlander crossed her arms. Her face was stone.

Jasper gaped, retreating when Sarlona neared.

Her chest tightened. All she'd lost swelled and tried to swallow her. "I—" Her voice broke. "I need them to change me back."

Recovering his composure, he straightened the coat that already hung flawlessly. "How awful." He glared at Dagmar, then Benton. "I'll—"

"And that's not Glaucus." Sarlona threw up her hands, bidding the bristling guards to stop before they seized her companions.

Jasper narrowed his gaze at Benton. "Who is it, then?"

"One of Ashmore's guards." A twinge of grief for the old lorkai almost brought a tear to her eye. All of it did. "Benton." Her voice wavered. "Amenduil put his soul in Glaucus's body."

A shadow crossed Jasper's face. "*Amenduil?*"

"And turned Dagmar human," she said, spitting out the last of a much shorter and coarser explanation of the situation than the one she'd rehearsed.

Her hackles raised when Jasper's stare roved over Dagmar too long. The former lorkai wasn't just at Benton's mercy. Sarlona would have bet on her against any warrior, but against a gifted mage, the Northlander might not fare so well. And no doubt Dagmar had rubbed a few the wrong way. Not physically, Sarlona hoped.

Jasper opened his hand, and a slip of paper materialized in his fingers. His glance put ink to it. "I'll send word to the Council."

"Thank you," Sarlona said.

He tossed the note, and it vanished with a golden flicker.

She gestured at Dagmar, whose cheeks had gone from bright pink to leathery white. "Can you at least let her in?"

"Yes, of course." Jasper waved, and the guards faced the tower wall and slapped their hands to the polished stone. Below the arch, the wall faded, becoming hazy, then transparent. Jasper beckoned the trio through, and with a loud sigh, Dagmar led the way.

A dozen guards waited for them inside.

"Brace yourselves," Dagmar warned.

Despite the lorkai's resistance to magic, the hindering spells hit Sarlona like a cartload of bricks. She and Benton grunted in unison under their unexpected weight.

"We'll have to confirm the details of your predicament independently," Jasper said. Guards slid between the trio and bumped them apart with their shielding. "I'm sure you understand."

She did. But that didn't diminish her uneasiness when the guards pointed their glowing blades, staves, and fingertips at Benton and Dagmar, urging them in different directions. Benton gazed at her over his shoulder as the tower guards led him away, his haunted eyes lingering like they might never meet again.

Dagmar glared.

Sarlona followed Jasper as bade, surrounded by four stoic guardsmen, ahead to the tower's winding central staircase. "Benton hasn't done anything wrong." That may have been the biggest lie she'd ever told. But, unlike Glaucus, he hadn't sinned against the SPS.

"He won't be harmed," Jasper said to the endless onyx steps. "Just examined and questioned."

He brought her to a spacious chamber on the fourth floor, one of several reserved for visiting mages, and evaluated her himself. She showed him the glowing lorkai irises and carpal blades with escalating apprehension. His dour countenance and somber tone as he cast on her—benign scanning spells as far as she could tell—wore at the vestiges of her hope.

The questioning was more her recounting the nightmare of the last few months than anything. A quill floated behind him, scribbling in a blank book while she spoke, and he sat across from her, attentive and doe-eyed.

She burst into tears the second he and the guards left. It hit again, the cold emptiness where her Gods-given gift once dwelled. The talent that had defined her, that she'd spent the last fourteen years honing at the expense of companionship and normalcy, had been ripped out by the lorkai quick. The paths in her through which the Gods had once threaded Their power had been warped. Tainted. She could only wield it now by stealing it from other beings. She was cut off. Separate. Not only from nature but from the Gods.

Never mind that she couldn't go home. Not without provoking her old mentor. She'd never see her family again. Unless she was willing to endanger them with her thirst.

She'd run out of tears by the time the door reopened. Two guards took up posts on either side of the doorway, and a raven-haired, emerald-eyed, middle-aged woman entered. Behind her strode a tall man with golden skin and a glowing hilt peeking over his shoulder.

Sarlona bowed her head at the woman. "Councilor Talvianna." Then the man. "Council Leader Kyran."

"Oh, Sarlona..." Talvianna rushed forward, brow knitted and full lips in a pout. "I'm so sorry." She almost grasped Sarlona's hands but recoiled at the last second.

The shred of relief the councilor's sympathetic tone and motherly bearing provided drowned in that flinch. Even Aven's most powerful sorceress feared Sarlona.

She shouldn't have been surprised.

The council leader folded his bare, muscular arms across his black leather cuirass. "Let's see it."

Sarlona raised her eyebrows for a second, then slipped her gloves off. Both mages winced as her fingertips flared with cyan light and her irises burned, vision enveloped in a violet aura. She rolled her sleeves above the elbow and flicked her wrists to eject her carpal blades.

They gawked, faces crinkled. Was she truly such a horror?

"And you can't cast...*anything*?" Talvianna's pale skin, flawless but for the traces of crow's feet, blanched.

"Nothing." Saying it aloud was an extra punch to Sarlona's heart.

Talvianna shook her head. "I can only imagine... How tragic."

Kyran scratched at his goatee. "Well, welcome to the Society of Progressive Sorcerers. I assume they told you about the treaty?"

Sarlona stifled her frown and ignored the void opening beneath her feet. Was there no question she'd remain a monster? "Glaucus told me the lorkai are conscripted members." Due to their biological 'magic'—and the threat they posed to casters were they to become enemies. "I would have joined before..." She searched his cold, dark eyes for any sign of forgiveness, but his face was unreadable, and his scent was bland. Except for the reek of Marrow. "I was following Sylvanus's lead."

"We keep it in the library," he said. "You should read it before you go."

Sarlona's hope withered into a husk. "There's nothing you can do to reverse this?"

He shrugged, then looked at the ceiling flickering blue with the reflection of the chamber's magical torches. "It seems quite impossible. There wouldn't be many monsters if magic could unmake them."

"Amenduil managed it." Sarlona gazed out the window. Speaking the Abyssal mage's name made her crave sunlight, but there was none—only a white rectangle.

"We don't practice Abyssal magic here." Kyran's tone was matter-of-fact. Absolute.

Of course not. Sarlona had prayed there were other ways.

"The Council will convene tonight about your situation," Talvianna said. "We'll discuss any possible solutions."

Sarlona met the councilor's long-lashed gaze, forcing her eyes to cool to the deep blue she'd been born with. The light in her fingertips died, and she retracted her carpal blades. "Thank you." She allowed a seed of hope to sprout once more. "I'd forever be in the Council's debt."

"Yes. You would." Kyran shoved his hands into the pockets of his leather pants, relaxing his posture. His voice softened with it. "This was a terrible crime committed by our members against you. We'll attempt to set it right."

"Thank you," Sarlona said again, but the instant the heaviness in her heart began to lift, a new one settled in. "I... I don't want Dagmar harmed or imprisoned."

"Well, that's not up to you, Sarlona." His cheeks blew out with a puff. "But we'll take it into consideration."

"She's non-magical. If—" Sarlona's thirst struck like a snake, sinking its fangs into her throat and choking off her words. The pair before her teemed with Marrow, and the scent of it, the hum, threatened to swallow her. She had all she could do not to seize his bare arm.

Dagmar. Dagmar had put this vile need in her. This black tide of violence trying to drown Sarlona with every swell. The whisper that told her to take everything, all that the thrumming vessels before her contained, and leave them cracked and hollow. Must she defend a monster simply because it no longer had claws? What was this instinct to protect the creature who had inflicted this evil on her?

"That should spare Dagmar of any consequences," Talvianna said. "As for the guard…"

"Benton doesn't want to hurt anyone." Sarlona saw that in him, however deep he sometimes buried it. "But temperance isn't a strength of his. He *can't* stay like this…"

The councilors exchanged dour glances.

Kyran cleared his throat. "Retrieving his body would require extraordinary blood magic. If it's even possible." He latched his gaze onto Sarlona's. "We don't do that here, either."

"I know…" Sarlona whispered, hope draining from her. They could remove Benton's soul from Glaucus's body, she had no doubt. Where to put him afterward was the issue. Soulless human bodies were hard to come by, and stashing him in an object or animal was no answer. Gods, this never should have happened to him. It wouldn't have if she hadn't run… If she hadn't trusted Amenduil…

Talvianna half reached for Sarlona's arm. "Maliculius is scouring the library for a solution."

"There are also the ethical implications." Kyran clasped his hands behind him and drifted toward the window. "To restore you both would mean the end of the lorkai."

It would. But few knew better than Sarlona how wretched the species was. Their extinction would trouble the world no more than losing a tick or intestinal worm. All they did was take, contributing nothing to the web of life.

Yes, she could preserve the lorkai by turning Dagmar. But an immortal Dagmar would try to remake Sarlona and open the Northlander up to imprisonment or worse. No… If the lorkai went extinct, so be it. She couldn't care after everything Dagmar and Glaucus had put her through.

Given how threatening lorkai were to casters, she doubted the SPS did either.

CHAPTER THREE

The tower guards cramped the circular chamber where Sarlona waited for the councilors. Their rich, sweet scents hung like a fog, inviting her to do terrible things to them.

Dagmar's orbiting of the massive, round table in the center shrank the space further. At least her movement distracted Sarlona from the itch to pounce on the quivering prey that lined the wall.

Benton stared into space, eyes glazed over and hands locked on his thighs to keep them to himself.

The room felt like a test. One that the lorkai were meant to fail.

When the door at last cracked open, Sarlona yanked Benton from his seat on the glossy tabletop, heart racing. This was it. The councilors would either cut a path from this nightmare or extinguish the last sparks of hope.

Dagmar wandered to her side as Kyran, Talvianna, and Maliculius filtered in. They took seats closest to the door, opposite the lorkai, with Kyran in the middle.

He cleared his throat. "Again, Sarlona, I would like to apologize on behalf of the Society of Progressive Sorcerers for the crimes committed against you by two of our members and welcome you to our organization."

"Thank you, Council Leader." Her voice shook, strangled by dread. She prayed his words only implied that they expected her to join as a druid after restoring her magic.

Kyran glared at Dagmar. "It may be unjust, but given Dagmar's current state as a non-magical being, we have no authority to sanction her."

A strand of the tightness unwound in Sarlona's chest. "I understand."

Acrid irritation rather than mellow relief leaked from Dagmar's pores. She gripped the back of the chair before her, knuckles bleaching. "Are you going to exterminate the lorkai or not?"

"Perhaps." Talvianna's melodious voice rang out in contrast to Dagmar's rumble. "Since you transformed so recently," she said, addressing Sarlona. "We believe changing you back might be possible within the confines of legal spellwork."

Sarlona released the breath she'd been holding. Light seeped into the world. She could have her life back. The shreds of it. She'd stitch them into some sort of future. One far less desolate than what had lain before her moments ago.

The strip of dark-stained hickory in Dagmar's grasp split along the grain and came off in her hands. "You *can't*," she growled and tossed the chunk of wood onto the table, sliding it three-quarters of the distance to the councilors. "You'll—"

With lightning speed, Sarlona ripped off a glove and snatched Dagmar's wrist, stopping the Northlander from pounding her fists on the table. She slackened the former lorkai's every raging muscle fiber.

Dagmar's arms fell limp, and the remaining protests died in her throat.

The guards, who'd raised hands and fondled weapons, sank to attention.

Sarlona couldn't contain her smile. "Thank you, Councilors. You can't know how grateful I am."

Kyran smirked. "Well, you can show us." A wave of his hand summoned a piece of paper that floated, slaloming, in front of Sarlona like a falling leaf.

She plucked it from the air—a list of chores. All members had 'jobs' to complete for the good of the SPS each year, commensurate with their abilities. Dagmar claimed that, in the case of lorkai, they were deadly.

Sure enough, the first and third items on the list required her to kill other monsters. But it was the second that drained the blood from Sarlona with a cold rush. "Sylvanus will never listen to me…"

Benton stiffened at the name, and Dagmar stormed beneath her surface.

The paper trembled in Sarlona's fingers. "He—"

Talvianna put up her hand. "If there's anyone he will listen to, it's his former apprentice."

Benton scowled, shaking his head. Sylvanus had almost killed them both when Sarlona had gone to him for help. How would she convince the ancient druid to join the SPS after he'd refused for almost two hundred years?

"They are difficult tasks." No sympathy dwelled in Kyran's tone. "But so is the spellwork you're asking of us. And the time and energy of the Council is precious."

Sarlona bowed. "Of course. I understand." Apprehension and elation battled for room in her core. Impossible as the assignments seemed, the three councilors had granted her more hope than she'd had in weeks. She'd find a way to complete their tasks. She had to.

"It's important work," he added.

"Can you help Benton?" She prayed the Council could grant him a little hope, too. If they couldn't... At least she'd be able to keep him well-fed with her magic restored.

Tenting his wrinkled hands on the table, Maliculius leaned forward. "*We* can't. But someone proficient in blood or Abyssal magic could. If you have blood or flesh from his old body." He spread gnarled fingers at Benton. "I know a few mages in the Westveld Circle who could help, but their prices will be high."

"We'll find a way to pay," Sarlona said as Benton slumped. The coin for the spell wasn't the real problem—the reagent was. There were old, dried drops of him around Ashmore, but whether that would be enough for blood magic...

Another slip of paper materialized with a slight wave of Maliculius's hand, and Sarlona snagged it. It bore two names and cities in the neighboring kingdom of Westveld.

Kyran rose from his chair, and the two other councilors followed his lead. "We'll work out the spell while you complete your assignments." He marched to the door but paused before exiting. "One more thing—we'll need your quick to power it."

A wide-bottomed vial manifested on the table.

Dagmar raged against Sarlona's control, roaring telepathically.

Sarlona shut her out. "Okay."

CHAPTER FOUR

The rasp of her knife tip between stones in Ashmore's dungeon scraped at Sarlona's ears as much as the grime. All her magical training told her the gory dirt where Benton's blood had dripped wouldn't be enough.

Its scent comforted her, though. Even old and dry, his fluids smelled like home. And like her. Infused with her quick, his human body was partly hers.

How she missed that deep connection they'd shared. Never mind his face. The way that stupid grin spread between his stubbled cheeks...

He still grinned, but far less often, and a short, silver beard surrounded the smile.

"This ain't gonna work, is it?" He set a weathered hand on her shoulder as he hovered over her.

She peeked up. No sign of his grin. "It depends on the spell... But I don't think so."

"I can't handle the hunger, Sar..."

Heart sagging, she took his hand and let him tap into her. "I know."

He drew on her Marrow, but she had little to spare. The dingy stone wavered with his tug at the magical energy. Weakness washed through her. It had been lapping at her bones since she left her quick in Kyran's vial.

Dagmar stopped pacing. "Enough." Despite the cold of the disused dungeon, sweat beaded on her forehead. "She needs to regenerate."

He let go, his blissful expression contorting.

Sarlona toppled from her crouch to her knees. "I'm okay."

Dagmar snarled. "You're not. You almost killed me this morning."

Though Sarlona's lorkai vision penetrated the deepest night, the dungeon seemed to darken. "I'm sorry."

Grabbing Sarlona under the arms, Dagmar hauled her to her feet. Even deprived of her supernatural strength, she could lift a woman without a grunt. "Not half as sorry as you'll be when you do kill me. You can't keep feeding him."

Dagmar was right. Sarlona's hunger swelled, begging her to spin on the Northlander and drain her now. Ripping herself free, Sarlona retreated into the lengthening shadows.

"I—" Dagmar shivered and paled while sweat trickled from her hairline. Staring at the jar of brown gunk, she scratched her throat. "I can get his blood."

Benton squinted at her. "How?"

Dagmar ran a hand over her wild, brassy blonde hair. "I know who would have some."

Sarlona's nerves prickled with alarm. She could think of no good reasons to keep human blood, but there were plenty of bad ones...

"Why would someone have my blood?" His voice was low and his eyes flared red. "*Who?*"

Dagmar winced, pinching her shoulder blades together like that would stop another shiver from working up her spine. "Al— The Baron of Gulway."

Benton shrugged and opened his hands, features twisting.

Sarlona cocked her head. The tangy reek coming from Dagmar was unmistakable, but Sarlona hadn't believed the Northlander could produce it. "You're...scared."

"I'm uncomfortable." Dagmar puffed, then took another breath. "He's a vampire."

Benton shoved her just enough that she stumbled. "How the cock—"

"You don't want to know." Dagmar locked gazes with him.

"The lord baron is a vampire..." Sarlona had never met the man, but with Ashmore part of his barony, she'd have to before long. "Why would that frighten *you?*"

Dagmar swiveled away, her upper body writhing as though she tried to shed her skin. "He's not *a* vampire. He's *the* vampire." She spun back, fixing her stare between Benton and Sarlona's boots. "No. He's...his own...thing." Taking a deep breath, she shook her head. "We can't talk about him. I don't want to summon him here."

"We can't *talk* about him?" Benton folded his arms. Gooseflesh broke out where he'd rolled up his sleeves. "If he's got my blood—"

"I'll take you to Gulway." Dagmar flicked a finger between her chest and Benton's. "You and me. I don't want him here. I don't want him within a mile of Sarlona."

Dagmar had lost her mind. Or she was up to something. Sarlona mimicked Benton's body language, minus the gooseflesh. "I think I can handle one vampire."

Dagmar laughed, but no amusement lurked in her expression. "You can't. No one can. But at least I know his games."

Benton wiggled as though someone had dropped a fish into his pants. Sarlona stared at him. "You too?"

He shook himself out. "I—"

"I'll take him. You," Dagmar pointed to Sarlona, "kill the enveloper and talk to your teacher."

All the warmth leached from Sarlona, leaving icy tendrils where veins had been. Nothing sounded more daunting than confronting Sylvanus. He'd broken her heart and almost incinerated her when she'd gone to him for help.

Benton's hands tightened into fists. "Sar ain't goin' near that ancient prick."

"She has to." Dagmar's dull blue gaze fixed on Sarlona's face. "If you're dead set on destroying our people." She closed in, wrapping unyielding fingers around Sarlona's upper arms.

Though she towered no lower now than when they'd first met, nothing was imposing about her anymore, especially with the scent of her fear stinging Sarlona's nostrils. All the terror Dagmar had inspired seemed a distant memory. All the pain...forgivable.

Sarlona still couldn't conjure much sympathy for her. "*You* destroyed them. When you brought me here."

Dagmar massaged circles into Sarlona's shoulders. Her sprawling hands could have splintered bone mere weeks ago, but they hadn't always been rough. "You're not okay," Dagmar repeated. "But you will be." Her touch couldn't manipulate like it had before—couldn't control. Yet it threatened to knead Sarlona from stiff, cold clay into something more malleable. "If you weren't funneling your strength into Benton and wasting your quick, you would be already. Give it time..."

Sarlona cut off the growl rising in her throat. Whenever the Northlander took on that motherly tone, part of Sarlona raged. If not for Dagmar, she might have been helping her real mother with supper at that very moment. Instead, she stood in a dungeon with a jar of blood-dirt and a seven-hundred-year-old Northlander, trying to figure out how they'd get a vampire to help retrieve her ex-highwayman lover's body from the Abyss.

Still, earnestness infected Dagmar's voice, and the hard lines in her face melted for no one else.

"I know you miss your magic... Your parents and brother..." Dagmar's eyes twinkled, brightening from muted, blue stone to the surface of a deep lake. "But you'll come into your new power soon if you stop wasting it. You'll master the hunger in no time." She glowed with a rare, mirthful smile. "We'll retrieve Benton's body. He'll be your Bound again. And in a few years, when you're stronger, you can turn me back. We'll *all* be okay—together, as a family."

Sarlona pried Dagmar's powerful hands from her arms without a word. The former monster knew why Sarlona couldn't remain how she was. She'd heard all the arguments on those nights when she'd held Sarlona down, drained her, and forced the poisonous lorkai quick down her throat. She'd seen them all when she'd broken into Sarlona's mind, violating her in ways a mortal never could.

Everything that mattered to Sarlona was in her old life. Everything but Benton.

Sarlona glanced at him, longing for the mortal man she'd known. For his gorgeous, electric blue eyes and shit-eating grin, his gruff voice, narrow, muscular hips... She even missed his dark, unwashed hair and the ale on his breath. "I'm going with you to Gulway. If the lord baron is as dangerous as you say, you'll need my help."

Dagmar crossed her arms. "Your help won't make an ounce of difference. If you go, you risk being trapped there for centuries." She wriggled with another shiver. "The blood of the most powerful virgin lorkai female in millennia? He won't want to relinquish that. I'm unbuttered bread to him now. And he had his fill of Glaucus's blood centuries before my father spent himself on me."

Sarlona breathed deeply, craving air she didn't require. The notion of being imprisoned and fed upon again... This time, not for weeks or months, but years. She shuddered.

And the longer she stayed a lorkai, the more impossible it would become to free herself of Dagmar's curse. The current councilors might die before she escaped. Her family, too.

Sarlona's heart thrashed. The idea of Benton walking into the den of a creature so dangerous without her inspired no less dread. "What do you want to do, Benton?"

He wiped his sweat-less brow. "I can't stay like this, Sar. You know that. I'll risk anything to be human. Anything but you..."

Sarlona spun on Dagmar. "What if he kills you?"

"The lord baron doesn't kill," Dagmar said, shaking her head. "He doesn't have to."

Sarlona's gaze hopped between her two companions. "I mean Benton." He snorted.

Dagmar shrugged. "It's a short journey. We'll bring potions and stop to feed at every opportunity."

Something in Sarlona's gut squirmed in warning. She rubbed her chin and speared Dagmar with her stare.

The Northlander didn't flinch.

Maybe she should have forced her way into Dagmar's mind to sift through her motivations, but she didn't have the stomach for it. "Why risk your life to help Benton?"

The light left Dagmar's eyes, and her scent grew heavy. "Because I can't stand looking into my father's face when he's not here."

Sarlona's suspicion fractured with her heart. Despite knowing he'd been the architect of her doom, she missed Glaucus, too. He'd always had warm words and gentle touches for her. It hurt to meet his stormy stare, knowing he wasn't behind it. And he'd been her captor, not her companion of seven centuries. "All right... Go without me."

CHAPTER FIVE

B enton leaned against a tree with his back half-turned to Dagmar, who couldn't find a trunk wide enough to hide behind. "Didn't you just piss?"

"The baron is best met with an empty bladder," Dagmar grumbled.

Her aromas tugged harder at his hunger with her pants down, inflaming one appetite and triggering another. He couldn't indulge either without disappointing Sarlona, though. A fact that made Dagmar's increasingly sweet scent over the last couple of days frustrating, to say the least.

"Un-*fucking*-believable..." A growl rumbled from the far side of the tree.

"Heh." He chuckled when she marched toward him, shooting slush from beneath her boots, with the front of her pants still unlaced. "Are you bleedin'?"

"*Yes.*"

She was sweating, too. And while the air had grown heavy and foggy, and the last storm's snow dripped from the forest canopy, the weather was far from balmy.

"Do you have Glaucus's handkerchief?" She shoved her hand into his breast pocket before he could answer. "Sarlona's insane to want to be a human woman."

Snickering while Dagmar stuffed the silk square into her pants, he shook his head. "Who'd've thought a Northland warrior would go all to pieces when she's gotta admit she has lady parts."

She glared at him. "The baron is a *vampire*, Benton. The last thing we need is to chum the waters..." After tying her pants, she rubbed her temples and took a deep breath. "Gods be good to me." Puffing, she strode onto the packed-ice road.

Gulway's towering white spires came into view above the treetops just as the sky began to dim. A dusky-eyed woman in golden plate armor met them at the city gate, addressing Benton with a familiar tone. "Your business is with the lord baron, I presume."

Dagmar doffed her horned helm and wiped her brow. "Is he free?"

"He will be by the time we get up there," the guardswoman answered. She turned on her heel and strode through the gate, displaying the gilded broadsword holstered over her crimson cape.

Dagmar followed, and Benton tailed her, his heart light with hope and muscles tight with wariness.

Even amid the winter's grayest dregs, the city was beautiful. Carmine flags and banners bearing golden stags flapped bright and un-tattered over clean, clear streets. Buildings stretched straight and high without a block out of place.

Benton couldn't help marveling while they zigzagged up the switch-backing cobblestone to the castle on the hill above. The impressive palace overlooked the city on one side and the sea on the other, its bleached, gull-spotted spires reaching far into the darkening sky. He'd never seen anything like it.

Yet it felt familiar.

Without a word, the guards threw back the doors to the short curtain wall surrounding the castle, then to the palace itself. Silence hung like the mist until the guardswoman opened half the ornate double doors to the main hall, revealing a crimson runner over gray marble.

"The Lord of Ashmore and Lady Dagmar, milord," the guardswoman called and gestured inside without entering herself.

"Thank you, Wrenwyn." Tinged with an eerie, unplaceable accent, the melodic voice from the main hall sent cold water spilling down Benton's spine.

The guardswoman retreated, and Dagmar crept into the hall as if she wore twice her weight in armor.

Reminding himself that he inhabited an immortal body, Benton shadowed her. His hand itched to jump to his hilt while he scanned the cavernous chamber, but the room was neat and bright for a monster's lair. Gulway's crimson standards adorned the walls, a long dining table stood to the right, and twin stairways swept up behind the dais.

The baron sat upon a marble throne at the platform's center with the red strip of carpet ending at his feet. "Ah, my old friend." His ice-blue stare fixed on Benton as he rose. He flashed a fanged-but-disarming smile, and some tension drained from Benton's shoulders. "And his Northland princess." The vampire beamed at Dagmar.

"Lord Baron," she replied, tight-jawed.

Standing on the taller side of average with a muscular but far from bulky frame, he didn't appear too intimidating. The preternatural grace with which he floated from the dais was what prickled Benton's skin. That, and the worn grip of the sword dangling from his hip. A well-used blade always raised Benton's hackles.

"We're all immortals here." The baron opened his hands as he neared, the tails of his bloodred, gold-embroidered coat trailing him. "We can dispense with the pretense, can we not?"

Dagmar jerked, stiffening into stone.

"I can unwind a bit, yes?"

"Please don't." Her grumble just breached a whisper.

The baron's eyes laughed, and with his next blink, everything changed.

The torches and chandeliers blew out, leaving the slate sky to light the room from the windows high above the dais. The air condensed until it became too thick to breathe and so heavy Benton's knees threatened to buckle. And the baron grew massive—too large for the castle. For the city.

He wasn't a man. Or a monster.

He was a tempest. A hurricane bottled in flawless, pale skin.

Yet he stood at the same height, wearing that soothing smile, while his haunting, glacial eyes flickered with amusement. "What brings you to visit, my friend?"

Crushed under the weight of his aura, Benton collapsed to his knees at the vampire's feet.

"Glaucus... You don't often kneel so readily..." The baron stooped, peering into Benton's eyes. "There's something different about you..."

Benton froze like a cowering animal in the grass. Had his voice worked, he would have screamed, not explained.

The vampire stretched one manicured hand at his face, and Benton thought his heart would rupture.

Dagmar choked, then cleared her throat. "He's not—"

"And *you*, princess." The baron swiveled his head to her like a reptile. "You are *very* different."

She didn't breathe when the creature stalked toward her. Didn't twitch.

Standing on his toes, he inhaled beside her throat. "Kneel," he whispered in her ear.

She trembled as though straining to lift a gigantic weight, then fell to her knees. Her helm banged to the marble.

He slid behind her, lips hovering near her neck. "But you still smell exquisite..." After skimming his lips over her ear, he brushed her hair aside.

Her eyes softened, and her cheeks flushed when he kissed her throat. "Please, Aldamon, this is important..."

The vampire straightened, and some of the oppressive heaviness leaked from the room. Though still terrifying, he became less omnipresent.

Frowning, he gazed at her. "You didn't bring me your beautiful daughter?"

She stood with a scowl. "We need your *help*."

He raised his eyebrows. "She is well, yes?"

"Yes."

The vampire spun, and Benton wanted to curl into a ball when the monster's stare cut into him. "Where is Glaucus?"

"Destroyed. Utterly," Dagmar answered, her voice rising above a whisper. "If Amenduil can be believed."

The amusement bled from the baron's face. "I am sorry. *Truly*." He extended his hand to Benton. It might as well have blazed with hellfire. The vampire dropped it to his side. "Rise."

Though fear threatened to freeze him to the floor, Benton didn't dare disobey. Shaking, he climbed to his feet.

The baron pivoted to Dagmar. "I don't have the power to restore an obliterated soul."

She cleared her throat. "Can you pull Benton's body from the Abyss? Do you have his blood?"

The baron smoothed short, jet-black hair that already appeared immaculate. "Probably. And, of course, I do."

A knot in Benton's chest loosened. He could have his body back—his humanity. His relief did nothing to return his voice or mobility, however.

Her posture slackened. "Thank the Gods."

"You may thank *me*." The vampire swiped a wayward blonde strand from her face. "I've yet to decide how."

Inching rearward, she shook off a shiver. "Thank you, Aldamon. You'll do the spell to put him in his old body?"

"I'd love to." The vampire flashed Benton a warm smile.

So much weight slipped from Benton that if the baron's presence hadn't been grinding his insides into the rug, he might've floated off.

Dagmar retreated when the baron closed in on her. "I don't suppose you know a spell that could make me a lorkai again?"

The baron grinned. "I can make you a *vampire*."

Blanching, she shook her head. "That's all right." Her gaze stayed glued to the floor.

"A pity." Mischief danced in the baron's eyes. "What is it, princess?" He cocked his head. "Why have you come?"

Dagmar puffed and cracked her knuckles before her gaze left the swirling marble. "I need you to change Sarlona's mind."

The baron shot her a disapproving look and scooped up her helm. "Literally, I suppose."

She followed him to the table, where he set her horned helmet. "She's willing to *end* the lorkai. And she may well get herself killed..." Her voice strained. "Remove her memories of her magic or her family. Make her embrace what she's become."

A spike of rage unfroze Benton. "You gods-damned bitch." *That* was why she hadn't wanted Sarlona to come along. So she could go behind her 'daughter's' back and ask a primordial monster to alter her thoughts. To erase her hopes and desires. To steal her memories—the parts of Sarlona that made her who she was. He tried to draw his blade, but his fingers slipped from his grip, and a glance from the baron stilled him.

"That would be rather cruel of me," the vampire said, burying his hands in his coat pockets. "No... I shouldn't interfere with Sarlona. Or any like her."

Dagmar ran her fingers over her scalp. "Then, will you destroy the Demon of Zelule so my daughter doesn't get turned to ash attempting it?"

The vampire raised his brow. "I...think my price for that would be higher than you're willing to pay, princess. Higher than Sarlona is willing to pay, I'm sure."

Dagmar bit her lip, deflating.

"Tomorrow..." Aldamon said, smiling. "Go home and convince her to remake you."

Benton's skin iced over. *Tomorrow...*

"The three of you, together—as immortals—can defeat the Demon of Zelule." The baron swiveled to Benton. "Once that's done, then I'll retrieve your body and restore you to it." His voice, while soft, made Benton's bones vibrate. "But you must return to me alone. *And...*" he glanced at Dagmar, "I'd like to borrow him for three nights."

She shrugged. "I don't care what you do with him. I just want him out of my father's body."

"Are those terms acceptable, Benton?" the baron asked.

Benton wanted nothing more than to have his body back, to be human. But three nights alone with that monster? As a mortal, woefully helpless? That nightmare might rival the smoke, flames, and warm, wet tendrils. "Yes," he whispered, more in fear than agreement.

"Wonderful." The vampire beamed. "If that concludes our business..." His wicked smile bared fangs that appeared more prominent than before. "I believe it's around dinner time... Care to join me, princess?"

Dagmar's gaze sank to the marble. "Of course," she said, brushing her hair away to expose her throat.

"Princess..." Disappointment laced his tone. "You know me better than that..." He took her hands one at a time and slipped off her gloves. "Why would I want to pierce your lovely skin when you're already bleeding?"

She cursed under her breath and set her axe on the table before tugging at the straps on her armor.

The frigid claw in Benton's chest stifled his snicker. He forgot she existed when the baron pivoted and fixed a predatory gaze on him again. "Are you hungry?"

If he was, terror smothered the sensation.

The vampire floated nearer. "Perhaps we could trade..."

Benton's bones froze, and his skin caught fire. Touching that monster... Sipping at the energy of a star... Ice ripped through his veins. Paralyzed by the creature's stare, he couldn't answer.

The vampire's eyes blazed without changing color. "My Marrow for a little blood?"

The notion of the creature's lips on him sucked the air from Benton's lungs. He was too afraid to say no but far more horrified of answering yes.

The baron rushed forward faster than he could track, standing an inch away with the sides of Glaucus's open coat pinched in his fingers. His breath heated Benton's throat, and its warmth trickled into every recess, melting his insides. The desire to rip free battled with the urge to lean into the terrifying and tantalizing monster.

"The power of eternity and a gentle kiss?" the baron whispered in Benton's ear.

Those words hit him low. Marrow like that... No. He wouldn't survive it. Shutting his eyes to avoid gazing into the enchanting ones before him, he rasped, "I can't."

The baron retreated. "Perhaps later."

Alone with that creature...for *three* nights.

The vampire spun to Dagmar, who stood naked with her shoulders back and head held high. "Please don't forget that I'm mortal now, Aldamon."

The baron appeared before her, his hands on her chiseled waist. "When have I ever been too rough for you, princess?"

She didn't answer, but the spicy-sweet scent of arousal leaked into the air, battling the acrid reek of fear. With a glare at Benton, she jutted her chin toward the door.

He took that as his signal to slip out but couldn't lift his boots. Or help staring. He'd never caught more than glimpses before...

Had she clutched a lance while standing over broken bodies, he might've mistaken her for the ancient Imperial god of war. Except rounded, creamy flesh hung high on her broad chest—just enough to fill his hands... The ache to test its softness spread through him like a disease. She might be hiding other tender areas, too... In her mouth... Beneath the shock of blonde... Between her iron ass cheeks...

The baron guided her rearward until her hamstrings hit the table's edge, and she had to lean onto it. Glancing over his shoulder, he offered Benton a devious smile. "Won't you join us?"

Her eyes widened, and a heated claw snatched Benton's groin.

He pictured spinning her around and bending her over the table—then pounding into her until she roared his name, and he spilled inside her. With the tricks he'd been learning, he could make her love every second of it. Beg for more...

But unless Dagmar granted him permission, neither she nor Sarlona would forgive him for that. Besides, he didn't want to risk being bent over the table himself.

Shaking, he forced his boots backward across the marble to the doors. Days seemed to pass before he reached them. He slipped out just as the monster pushed her down on the table.

Her cry followed him from the room, unlike anything he'd heard escape her—high-pitched and feminine. Gods knew why it made him lurch.

Wrenwyn waited for him with a blank face. "I'll show you to your chamber."

He trailed her with lumbering steps instead of the supernatural agility Glaucus's body allowed.

"You get used to it," the guardswoman said, glancing at him. "Sort of."

With the steady pulse of the baron's heart still pounding faintly in his ears and the creature's overpowering scent clinging to his clothes, he didn't see how. The noise at least faded when Wrenwyn led him down the pristine stone halls and up the brass-railed stairs.

She took him to a bed chamber on the sea-facing side of the castle and ushered him in. With a four-poster canopy bed draped everywhere in scarlet silk and a balcony overlooking the ocean, the room was much too fancy for the likes of him. He gaped at the golden sconces, embroidered, stuffed chair, and the mirror etched along the margins with leaves and birds that took up half a wall.

The click of the latch on the door behind him snapped him from his stupor.

Wrenwyn pulled off her gilded helm to reveal satiny black hair that hung in a messy ponytail and framed her face in sharp angles. "The lord baron asked me to feed you, milord." She set the helm on the long, dark-stained bureau under the mirror. Tossing her gloves aside next to it, she continued, "I have some magical ability."

Benton grinned, hunger peaking again and feeling more like himself. Inhaling deeply, he leered at her. "You do, don't you, darlin'?" He stalked to her and snatched her by the hips, drawing her close. "You smell good, too."

She sidestepped him when he tried to pin her against the door. "I'd like to lie down."

He grinned wider and let her withdraw to sashay to the bed. As she unstrapped and laid aside her sword and chest piece, he almost forgot about the horror that lurked downstairs. She removed her belt and the golden plates that hung over her muscular thighs last. Reclining on the bed, she gazed at him, dusky features stone but not jagged like Dagmar's. "I'm ready, milord."

He chuckled. Glaucus's neat, stately appearance and title had its advantages. Strange, beautiful women had never climbed into bed for Benton. Not without a lot of cajoling. Or a down payment.

"Trust me, sweetheart, you ain't ready, and I ain't a lord." He gave her his hungriest stare, aching for a hitched breath, a racing heart, and trembling hands to add a tanginess to her Marrow. The monsters inside loved that.

He didn't get any of it.

She smiled with smooth, pouty lips. "The lord baron told me who you are."

When?

Amusement wilting, he floated toward the bed. Much as he wanted to smother his fear with someone else's, he wouldn't shake the woman before him. "And you don't mind if I—"

"Drink my Marrow, milord." Her tone was respectful, forceful, and crystal clear.

His thirst for her magical energy drowned all other desires anyway. Sitting beside her, he allowed his fingertips and eyes to flare to life. She lay back as he slid fingers under the hem of her shirt to rest on her waist and cradled her jaw in his other hand. "How good do you want it to feel, darlin'?"

Her coy smile revealed the lines of midlife and, for a second, that more familiar hunger spiked.

It vaporized when he knitted his energies into hers using that strange organ in his fingertips. Only the Marrow mattered.

She tasted—felt—like heaven. Drawing hard, he repaid her with the warmth of a hot bath, whiskey, and a lover's embrace. She moaned while he drank, writhing each time he jolted her with a shock of fiery pleasure. Once he'd had all he dared take, he built a tingling wave in her, stalling it at its crest.

She panted, trembling. "Please, milord—"

The wave broke, crashing through her. She arched and cried out, her sweet scream echoing through the night.

Neither of them said a word while she donned her armor and weapon, but she twisted as she slipped out the door. "Sleep well."

He might never sleep again, knowing that the primordial monster haunting Gulway's shadows wanted a taste of him. "Thanks, darlin'."

Flashing a smile, she disappeared beyond the crack.

Too afraid to crawl into bed or roam the dark castle halls, he crept onto the balcony and gazed at the black, angry sea. The icy winds yanked at his hair and clothes while he sought the magic in it that Sarlona lived for.

Dagmar's cries rose above the pounding surf every so often, bouncing down the marble corridors. Each made his skin crawl, but whether pain or pleasure generated them, he couldn't tell.

"The perfect combination, Benton," the baron purred in his ear.

Benton jumped halfway out of his boots and choked on his next breath. Habit hopped his hand to his hilt, but he froze with the blade half-sheathed.

The vampire's warm breath tickled the skin below his earlobe. His chest heated Benton's spine. "Shall I show you?"

Mouth dried and stuck like it was filled with cobwebs, Benton couldn't say no. His whole being screamed it, though, as hands alighted on his shoulder and hip.

"Come to bed."

Leaping from the railing and into the storming sea sounded safer, but the baron's unyielding grasp pivoted him to the bedchamber. Fingers clasped Benton's frozen hand and helped ease his blade into its sheath.

"My best smith forged this weapon." Aldamon peeled Benton's fingers from the grip one at a time, thickening the rime in his veins. "You helped me with the enchantments." Sweeping him inside, the baron leaned close. "But you don't recall any of that, do you?"

No. It couldn't have happened. Benton couldn't have met a collapsing star and forgotten. And Marrow-rich or not, he had never cast a spell.

The vampire turned him around and gazed into his eyes. That stare, all blue ice and mist, held Benton captive. It numbed his racing thoughts.

Groping for his mental defenses, he found his walls intact. But those ghostly eyes peered into his depths regardless. The monster saw right into him.

"That's okay, Benton. It will be fun getting to know each other all over again." The baron smiled, squeezing his arms, then shepherded him to the bed. "Call me Aldamon."

Benton couldn't call him anything. Speech was impossible. He just gaped at the bed like it was the Abyss. *Caught*. Trapped with no way out. Doom caged him with the chamber's walls.

"I've been thinking about you. Missing your scent..." The vampire's honeyed tone dripped with thirst.

Benton didn't blink, heart thundering as the emptiness of infinity nudged him until he retreated onto the mattress.

"And the blue fire of your eyes... Your *taste*..." The baron's snow-white fangs peeked from behind full lips with every word. "I can't wait to retrieve your body for you..."

Benton lay back, yielding to the hand that pressed on his chest. The fear gripped him too deep in his being to do anything but tremble and comply. All Glaucus's lorkai strength was meaningless in the face of that monster. He had to appease the baron or suffer obliteration.

The vampire's warm fingertips kissed his jawline with the gentleness of a moth's wings, and Benton shut his eyes. He just had to endure. Survive to the next moment without letting the universe unravel. He was good at that.

But as Aldamon's breath caressed his ear, carrying the saccharine copper of Dagmar's blood, Benton disintegrated into the soft touch on his cheek. The next moment would never come. He'd be stuck in this one forever.

"Sleep well, Benton..."

CHAPTER SIX

S arlona knelt in the wet snow and peered at mucus-coated bones worn to resemble sun-bleached driftwood. The acidic slime burned her nostrils, smothering the earthy must of moist forest and the chalky odor of skeletal remains.

No tracks led to or from the grisly midden. Envelopers didn't contact the ground while in motion. Instead, they hugged it, their legless, undulating forms skating inches above the earth. But the etheric aroma of preternatural power tinging the monster's leavings would reveal its path. The same smell clung to low-hanging boughs nearby.

With a trail to pursue, Sarlona skipped through the mist, boots silent in the slush, stable even atop smooth, wet rocks and skinned logs.

The traces led her deep into the wilderness. To places unfamiliar yet home. She'd spent hundreds of cold nights on mountainsides like this one, miles from the nearest road or marked trail. Most of which were with Sylvanus sitting in silence opposite the low-burning fire.

He would be the real challenge.

Not that destroying an enveloper would be simple. Without magic, she couldn't just end the creature with an inferno.

She'd have to put flint to kindling to fell it—after she'd hacked it into pieces.

Reminding herself what envelopers did to their victims, she took a deep breath. Depending on the stage of their life cycle, they drained the blood from their prey or dissolved them in acidic, needle-toothed gullets. Four children and two women had gone missing that winter, believed to have been taken by the one she hunted.

And now, another boy was missing, gone just last evening. He might still be alive.

The thin trail intersected with another thicker track of balding and frayed fir branchlets. This met a third, fresher trail. She followed uphill, where the sparse forest dwindled to scrubby pine and the snow hardened.

Her ears pricked up when she neared a rocky outcrop. A faint heart-beat thumped from underground. No, *two*. One small, muffled, and rapid—weak. The other was strong and loud but diffuse like the heart had no chambers.

She supposed she'd get to do a full anatomical investigation if she was successful.

The enveloper's scent grew overwhelming as she slipped between boulders and homed in on a hollow concealed by overhanging juniper.

She crept to the side of the burrow, careful not to make a sound or block the gray light leaking into the hole. Wriggling down the narrow tunnel after the enveloper and trying to drag it out feet first seemed like a terrible idea. Yet the missing boy it had swallowed couldn't afford for her to wait in ambush.

"Come out." Perhaps calling the enveloper wasn't the wisest move. "Or I'll fill your hole with fire."

Easier said than done these days, but doable. The enveloper must have sensed the threat wasn't empty.

An ebony, faceless 'head' poked out—the end of a smoky, man-sized leech. It craned its vague neck at her. *What are you?*

It couldn't smell her. Only other lorkai could. "Your doom. If you don't release your prey."

She backed off as it slipped out of the hole like an eel swimming in air. Then, it towered over her, a seven-foot-tall, diamond-shaped monolith.

What are you? it asked again.

She should have lunged for it without another word. Dug her fingers into its flocked, sable skin, and ripped out every wisp of energy that flowed through the obsidian, man-eating chrysalis. Instead, she answered. "I'm a lorkai." Saying so threatened to cave in her chest.

The enveloper twitched, and she scented a pungent change in its chemistry. A pulse of fear, she hoped, but she had no reference to know what odors matched what reaction in a creature so foreign.

You're real?

"Release your prey." She spoke with the monster's voice, burying the girl she'd been in Mast Landing beneath the black hunger of Ashmore.

The enveloper squared its pronounced, armless shoulders. It stood, staring at her with neither feet nor eyes. *Why? So, you can drain the life out of him?*

She parted her lips to reply, but the words caught in her throat. The question was reasonable. Each time she passed within sniffing distance of a mage, she burned to tear open their robes and grope their bare flesh until she sucked out their last magical morsel. Then start on their life force. The yearning, which had once drawn her to a pot of stew after a hard day's work in the cold, raged to leave humanoid husks behind instead of an empty bowl. She hadn't drained the life out of anyone yet, but she'd come close. If not for Glaucus's intervention, that gnawing hunger would have claimed Benton when he'd still inhabited his own body. That was one of the many reasons she had to become human again.

"I'm going to return him to his parents."

The enveloper slithered through the air, half-smoke-like, half-snake-like, taking up a position over her shoulder. *Will you?*

Whispering near her ear when the words were in her mind didn't have the effect it no doubt intended. She pivoted to look in its...point.

"Yes." She couldn't drink from *a child*, no matter how ravenous she became or how loud the monster inside roared. Ashmore's guards and any men she found in camps or alleys were who she worried about.

But Glaucus's warnings echoed in her memory. Madness would take her if she denied herself for too long. The monster would snatch control and feed. She hadn't even realized she was killing Benton that night. The man she *loved*. She'd even fought for the satisfaction of finishing him off...

She shook her head. No. She wasn't like the sentient maw hovering at her side. Her needs were satisfied with little fear or pain. Outside of Ashmore, she was no more than a strange dream to her victims. She'd never be like the enveloper. If she had to traverse hellfire, she'd solve this before she killed an innocent.

"You can spit out the child. Leave this mountain. Devour animals," she said. Gods knew why. Her task was to kill the enveloper, not convince it to behave itself. She had to end it to appease the Council.

An acrid scent wafted from the enveloper as it straightened. *Is that what you do? Feed on animals?*

The monster in her depths slipped its chain. Yes, she drained animals. Weak, lesser things who should be eager to feed her the energies they squandered.

She circled back toward the hole. If the enveloper tried to flee, it would have to go elsewhere. "I feed from the wicked." Unless, of course, there were none within reach. "I don't kidnap and torture children until the life leaves them," she said, reminding herself why she had to kill the ebony monolith before her.

How fortunate for you that you weren't made into a fanged pit.

For a second, she felt fortunate. She couldn't imagine being transformed by an enveloper. Punctured by a hundred thin fangs and drained and dissolved for days, only to reform as an unrecognizable entity. Limbless, faceless, sexless, just a floating vertical mouth and unrelenting hunger.

Her gut clenched. As it had on the farm when an animal was born too deformed to survive to market. The urge to put it out of its misery swelled.

I'm too small to engulf a grown man.

Most human men, anyway. The enveloper could swallow adult goblins, halflings, and smaller women. There were options other than children.

I was a woman.

Sarlona's stomach flipped. She wondered when that had been.

Do you think I want to do this? Be this?

Which was mercy? Letting the creature live or executing it? No one chose to be an enveloper. Of that, she was certain.

She cleared her throat and steeled her gaze. "Then I'll leave the choice to you." Stupid. "Give me the child, and you can live. Feed on adults and release them alive from now on. Or I can send you to the Otherrealms."

In a blink, the enveloper collapsed into a velvety ribbon, undulating through the air toward the forest. It slithered far faster than an animal, but to Sarlona, it lumbered. A burst of four steps put her in front of it. Instinct ejected her carpal blades. She'd mourn how accustomed she'd gotten to them later.

The enveloper reversed direction without turning, leading with its tapered posterior as agilely as it had with its front. She cut it off again in half a second, and it darted left, then down, skimming across her thigh and gliding along the ground. Its lack of hips and seamless transition from forward to backward made predicting each of its movements difficult. It couldn't outrun her, though. If she'd had the resolve and no concern for the enveloper's prey, it would've been in pieces already. She blocked its next pivot with her right claw, and it shot for the sky.

Leaping, she caught downy flesh in her crushing grip. It dragged, sinking with her, then bent, wheeling on her and morphing from a long, kite-shaped eel into a manta ray as it split down the middle. It parted the flaps of its mouth, revealing a gape of onyx mucus membrane studded with three-inch-long, translucent needle teeth, then spat its victim at the ground.

Reflex snatched the pink, slime-coated bundle.

A little boy.

Her hand trembled around his raw upper arm and her heart rocketed into her throat. His lidless, eroded gaze held her paralyzed.

Until the black thing rose from her depths. With Sarlona broken, it was free—to feed, kill, and take control. Her wicked grasp tore into the velvet mouth-demon, groping for any trace of magical energy. She ripped at it as she dropped the boy into the snow and seized the sentient maw with both hands. Desperate, the enveloper hinged, snapping its boneless jaws over her. The world darkened and exploded into pain. Dozens of acid-coated, venomous fangs pierced her flesh. With the air squeezed from her lungs, her skin stinging with corrosive mucus, and her veins seared with toxins, the monster inside stormed. Adrenaline, rage, and her lorkai metabolism counteracted the subduing effects that the venom should have had. With a growl, she punched forward and sliced upward, rending the enveloper's inky flesh like delicate fish skin. It shrieked in her mind, spitting acid and writhing.

She slashed with her other claw, and they plummeted to the ground. After tearing herself free, she descended on the sundered abomination, shredding it to the chorus of its mental screeches while it flapped like sentient bat wings on the snow. The screams stopped, but she kept cutting, snow red not from blood but from the light of her scarlet gaze.

Until a soft groan called Sarlona back, and the monster receded.

The boy.

She raced to him and grabbed his tiny fingers. Zipping into his mind, she tried to block out his thoughts—the relentless plea for his mother—as she fumbled for the cords that would render him unconscious.

Mercifully, he faded out.

But his small body still lay in the snow, weeping blood, and his unseeing eyes stared at the universe in righteous horror.

"It will be okay. It will be okay," she whispered to herself, not the boy. Her mind raced, and her heart thrashed as she searched for the right threads to weave herself into. Healing him would have been simple if she'd still been human. He was weak and near death from blood loss, but his injuries weren't catastrophic. She knew half a dozen spells that would regrow an epidermis and replace blood within seconds.

"He *won't* die." She'd figure this out. It was her own suffering that she scrambled to end. "He won't die." The ghastly sight of him, not the hopelessness of the situation, caused her panic.

She found the correct levers to pull deep in his bones and forced whatever strange power dwelt in her own to seep into them and fill his veins. The increasing strength of his heartbeat soon stabilized hers, and she remembered to breathe. She worked on the puncture wounds next. None were life-threatening. Each fang had been positioned to avoid piercing organs and killing the victim before the enveloper had taken all it needed.

She knitted the thin wounds together, then moved onto the skin. Layer by layer, she grew it back until the boy was whole.

Hyperventilating, she scooped a handful of old snow and pressed it to her forehead. The true horror had gone—that pink, oozing bundle—but her work wasn't finished. She had to burn the enveloper, or it would reform to terrorize and consume more innocents. And before she returned the child to consciousness, she'd have to tread into his nightmarish memories. If she wanted to wipe away his trauma, she'd have to live it with him.

He wouldn't remember anything. But she would.

She took a deep breath, focusing on the icy point pricking into her skull and the cool trickles dripping down her face. The cold air seemed to pass through her lungs and into her veins.

First, the enveloper.

She tore off her cloak and swaddled the boy with the clean side of the thick wool to protect him from the cold, then pivoted to the tatters of the diabolical orifice sullying the snow.

The dampness of waning winter would make a fire difficult to start without a spell. She ached for the simplicity of gathering her focus and willing flames to roar from her fingertips as she collected kindling—bits of dead juniper caught up in the living branches, birch bark from down the hill, rusty pine branchlets hanging in the crooks of limbs. At least the scavenging didn't take long with her lorkai speed. And creating the friction between sticks to produce a few minuscule embers was easy enough with quick and tireless arms. Her muscles itched, though, when the wood dust repeatedly sputtered out with an unconscious child lying in the snow and the shreds of black velvet snailing closer together. The wet air snuffed out every flicker. Shaking, she peeled apart the thinnest layers of birch bark she could with her nails and placed them in the sawdust. Finally, a spark set upon one. It curled in on itself, blackening and passing its flame to the next. After a few minutes of coaxing and coddling with dried needles and strips of bark, a fire came to life in earnest. Before long, she stood beside a blaze as the last shreds of flocked obsidian skin and needle-shaped teeth crumbled to dust with the boy cradled in her arms.

Her finger brushed his cheek when she adjusted the cloak around his face to ensure he could breathe, and her hunger spiked. Shame peaked after it with the gnawing dread that hadn't left her since she'd turned in the waves and spied Glaucus waiting for her on the beach those months ago.

She imagined chunks of herself burning, blood sizzling, skin charring, and fat bubbling. At last, at peace, having been dispatched by some holy warrior.

Leaving the fire to burn out unsupervised, she sprinted down the damp mountain with her cloak bunched between her hands and the child's skin.

CHAPTER SEVEN

B enton paused, waiting for Dagmar to catch up. Trekking slow enough
for her to keep pace had been a challenge on the way to Gulway. On
the walk home, she trudged at a glacial pace.

"You all right?" Benton asked. Gods knew why.

Dagmar snorted. "If I'm not?"

A pang shot through him. That had to be Glaucus, lurking with some
buried memory or affection in the gray matter Benton occupied.

She grumbled at the ground. "I'm fine. Just...drained. In more than one
way."

Her naturally pale complexion was chalk white, and the vampire's reek
coated her.

"You want me to try..." Healing wasn't something he'd practiced much,
but restoring a little blood might not be that complicated.

"No." She threw him a glare. "The last thing I need is you fumbling with
my insides."

He didn't know why the hells he'd offered. "Well, by the sounds you was
makin' last night, you don't always mind a man fumblin' inside you."

Laughter followed her flush. "Aldamon doesn't fumble, believe me."
Her muted grin lingered. "His deftness makes you forget your name."

The vampire's mere presence had made Benton forget how to breathe.
How Dagmar's heart hadn't given out in the monster's arms, Benton
couldn't imagine.

"I'm sure you'll find out when you return to him," she said with a wink.

Benton's skin iced over, and his heart thrashed. "He... He knew me
already?"

"You trained in Gulway with him for weeks," she said, beaming.

Frozen a moment ago, now Benton's skin burned. His chest heaved.

She clapped a hand on his shoulder. "Did you think all your talent came naturally?"

A lot of it. That's what had saved his life at fifteen when highwaymen had ambushed him outside of Ironhill. He'd snatched the sword from the bandit who'd been determined to get something out of Benton, no matter how empty his pockets were. Pure instinct and animalistic fear had stabbed the asshole's throat. And had guided the blade long enough to impress Randolph and earn him the place of the man he'd killed.

Stick the other guy first—or die. It wasn't that complicated.

What hadn't come naturally came from Randolph, experience, then Glaucus. Not...

She drew close, putting Benton in her shadow. "Glaucus had to wipe Gulway from your mind to keep your night terrors at bay."

He shoved her harder than he intended, and she slid in the wet snow, barely keeping her feet under her. "Well, why the cock didn't he do somethin' about the other shit?"

Because nothing would be left of him with all the darkness extracted.

Just like there wouldn't have been much left of Sarlona if Aldamon had done as Dagmar requested. "And how could you ask that monster to cock up *Sar's* mind?"

Dagmar stalked toward him, nostrils flaring. "I want what's best for my daughter, Benton. I want her to live for millennia." Her voice lacked the nightmarish reverberation that once shook windowpanes but still dripped with rage and conviction. "To come to her true potential. What I asked Aldamon to take is inconsequential in comparison."

"Her damned memories?"

"She'll make millions more. Eternity, Benton, is what she wants to throw away." Dagmar growled in his face. "I just needed him to stop her. And I want her to be happy. Don't you?"

He shoved her again. Enough to get out from under her. "I want her to be *her*."

"So do I. But I'll do whatever it takes to keep her safe." The veins in her throat bulged. "I won't let her destroy herself."

"If you cockin' cared about *her*, and not just the cockin' lorkai, not just Glaucus's bullshit, you'd help her get her life back." He met her glare with a red glow tinting his vision. "You wouldn't have done this to her."

"I don't expect you to understand what I've given her. I don't expect her to understand. Not for decades. Because she's a child, Benton. You're children." Her voice quieted, but her tone remained steadfast. "And children don't always know what's good for them. They may even scream and cry at how unfair their circumstances are. That doesn't mean their parents aren't making the best decisions for them."

Benton snarled. "What the cock would you know about it?"

A plume of vinegar hit the air and her face reddened. He'd struck a nerve.

"More than you," she grumbled through a wall of teeth.

He thanked the gods for that. If there were any children out there with his electric blue eyes, they were better off without him. Nevertheless, the sweetest shiver overtook him when he contemplated creating life with Sarlona.

"Yeah, well... Watch how fast I fuck a kid into Sar once we're human." He chose his words to irritate Dagmar, but the sentiment made him glow. He and Sarlona—human and happy... A family...

The universe wasn't that kind to him.

More vinegar seeped into the air. "Why bother?" Dagmar snapped. "You'll probably burn that kid to death, too."

Benton threw her against a tree before the brunt of his rage even registered, forcing her low enough that they were face to face. She snarled, wrath roiling in her eyes, and a growl rumbling low in her chest. Her muscles knotted into steel.

Awash in her scent, his hunger spiked. He crushed her forearm across her chest to hold her still while he sought the flesh of her jaw and throat with his free hand. His glowing fingertips met delicate skin. All that ferocity... It couldn't protect her from his need.

Grinding his hips into her, he drew on the sparse but sweet threads of Marrow that wound deep into her being—and slipped.

In another time and place, he lay on top of her, holding her as he trapped her now, with his forearm throbbing and dripping where she'd bitten him. Her plain blue eyes burned with a fire that threatened to consume him. She roared like a demon but tasted of divinity. A sea of determination and fearlessness greeted him as he slid into the shallow waters of her unprotected mind. She was beautiful. Not in feminine allure but in the way of a perfect warrior. Enthralled and drunk on the ambrosial morsels of her Marrow, he waded deeper. And met an abyss of loneliness. The ache to smother it forever stole his breath.

"*Benton...*" She thrashed. "Fuck. Don't look at me that way."

She was pinned to the tree again. He was him. Releasing her, he backed away. He *had* to get out of Glaucus's body. Soon.

CHAPTER EIGHT

Infinity stretched from the catwalk built into the manor's roof. The stars were endless. Maybe Sarlona should've been grateful for her supernatural vision when she stared farther into the celestial realm than mortal eyes ever could.

Yet with her magic, she'd traveled there, projected. She'd never view it from that perspective again if the Council failed to undo what Dagmar had done.

She tried not to think about that, holding all the attention on the stars themselves she could. Beautiful crystalline lights hung over her and all the worlds, always. She thinned, opening herself until she was nothing—everything—and imagined those distant orbs burning in her soul.

Her being tingled with cool, bright pinpricks while the stars shone in her. She was made of them, and they of her.

A creak on the catwalk steps flung her back into a monster's body.

The uncharacteristic timidness in Dagmar's footfalls told Sarlona the Northlander tried to approach quietly.

There was no quiet for Sarlona anymore.

She offered a final prayer to the Gods above before addressing the woman who'd stolen her life and still sought to take more. "Have you come to apologize?"

Dagmar snorted. "Benton didn't waste any time tattling."

Unable to bear the granite conviction Dagmar's expression no doubt conveyed, Sarlona kept her gaze soft and on the heavens. She tried to hold one spiritual tendril out there, where her problems didn't matter and no one could hurt her. "He *warned* me."

"I won't apologize for trying to protect you from yourself." Her voice held all the assuredness her face might have displayed, anyway.

"What will you take next if you manage to steal my memories and desires? My soul?" Sarlona refused to let tears fall, but they crept into her throat. "When will you be finished destroying me?"

Boards groaned nearer before Dagmar answered, "I'm saving you, Sarlona. So your light will shine forever."

She stood too close. Sarlona half expected huge hands to fall on her shoulders and half missed the days when they did so without hesitation. Dagmar's musky-sweet scent wrapped around her like a fog, triggering a hungry twinge.

"What do you want, then?" Sarlona peeked rearward for a glimpse of a dour expression.

"It's time for you to make me a lorkai."

Despite lacking a shred of amusement in her heart, Sarlona laughed. She spun on her haunches to glare at Dagmar with glowing yellow eyes. "Oh, it is, is it?" The Northlander looked like a giant from Sarlona's reclined position on the walkway, yet she seemed tiny. Impotent. That's how Sarlona wanted her to stay. "Why would I *ever* do that, Dagmar? Especially after this latest betrayal..."

The Northlander's scent turned acidic, but her face was a mask of stoicism. "You have no choice."

The fire in Sarlona's veins shot her to her feet. "*No.*" It felt phenomenal to say. "I won't do it." She hadn't realized she'd yearned for that revenge. To condemn Dagmar to exist as a creature she wasn't meant to be. To lose what she was and be told she could never regain it. But despite how sweet that vengeance tasted, Sarlona didn't believe she'd enact it.

Neither did Dagmar. "You will, Sarlona. I know you."

Better than anyone. Dagmar had forced herself deeper into Sarlona's heart and mind than she permitted even Benton to tread.

"You can't end a species," Dagmar said, voice placid. "No matter how much you hate what you are or what I've done to you."

It ate at Sarlona daily. Knowing that if she succeeded in her mission to free herself and Benton from preternatural need and restore her magic, she'd take something from the universe that could never be retrieved. Even if that thing was a monster that preyed on innocent casters.

But knowing how many people she might hurt if she failed, or how many more Dagmar would prey upon if given the lorkai quick weighed on her, too.

"The lorkai are a curse, not a species," she told the Northlander's fur-lined boots.

Dagmar picked her nails as though the response bored her. "You and Benton will die in Zelule without me. If you want to change back, you must change me back."

There was a reason the Demon of Zelule had haunted the pits outside Southpeak for generations. If the Council wanted the creature destroyed, and they hadn't done it, then taking on the fiend was close to impossible.

Sarlona gazed at the stars rather than at Dagmar and crossed her arms. "Yet if I'm successful at both, you'll force this affliction on me again."

"If I can," Dagmar admitted.

"Then why the hells would I do it, Dagmar?" Sarlona stopped herself from grabbing the Northlander and shoving her from the roof. "So I can relive this nightmare?"

Dagmar shrugged. "I was never like you, Sarlona... You know how little Marrow I have. And I'm not asking to be well-made."

Sarlona's anger slipped into the dark where the monster lived. "You don't think you'll be able to make another child in my lifetime?"

"You're so strong," Dagmar said, a smile creeping onto her face. "I'll be more powerful as your newborn than I was as Glaucus's, but nothing like I was before I turned you. It will be years, maybe decades before I can pass on my quick."

"Then you'll...leave me alone for a while?" However much Sarlona dreamed of living her old life, she had trouble picturing it. She'd have her old power and her freedom. But what would she do with either? She couldn't pick up where she'd left off with her apprenticeship. Not after Sylvanus had tried to kill her. Neither could she move home to her father's farm with a highwayman who'd been sentenced to hang.

She stiffened when Dagmar's hands swallowed her shoulders. "No matter what becomes of either of us, we'll always be family, Sarlona." Though Dagmar's eyes couldn't glow anymore, the light poured into them with her smile. "And I'll never leave you alone."

Sarlona threw her gaze at the stars and ducked from the Northlander's grasp.

Dagmar took a long breath. "Benton thinks you're bearing his children if you both become human."

Heat splashed across Sarlona's cheeks. Her heart swelled while her guts hollowed. "I know."

Dagmar went to the railing, hitching over to fold her arms on it. "Have them." Her voice cracked. "Have a whole litter."

Sarlona couldn't be hearing those words from Dagmar.

"He holds a lot of Marrow," the Northlander went on.

The catwalk fell out from under Sarlona.

Dagmar cleared her throat. "When I'm ready, I'll take your eldest daughter."

Sarlona shook her head. "You can't think I'd do that to one of *my children*."

"They'll know me, Sarlona. Their whole lives. It doesn't have to be difficult..." She tried to stop Sarlona from spinning away but didn't have the strength. "Raise a daughter to be a lorkai. Tell her she's born for it. Don't teach her magic."

Sarlona clenched her jaw on the verge of snorting like a bull.

"Or you can return to me."

Sarlona let out another mirthless laugh.

"You'll have at least twenty years to live the life you wanted."

Not the life she'd wanted. That was gone. But if everything went according to plan, she could have her magic. She could have Benton. And she could see her family.

"You know I can't." Cold enveloped Sarlona like she was bleeding out. "You know it's about more than that."

She was meant to be part of nature. Not exist outside it. She was born to heal: people, animals, and the land when need be. To protect the wild places and fix the things humanity and their relatives broke.

"You've already died, Sarlona. You'll get to be a mother. So you'll never be the crone?" Dagmar shrugged. "At forty, you'll feel your age. And you'll still gain the wisdom of years. Of *millennia*." Dagmar's voice picked up volume and momentum like a snowball rolling downhill. "Rule Ashmore as a human, fuck your sword-wielding pet, have your children, help the people here, and protect the lands."

For someone who'd lost the power to read minds, Dagmar did a hells of a job at it.

"Then take my quick. And keep doing it. Just do it with the power of a lorkai instead of a druid."

Sarlona stared into the black between the stars.

Dagmar's voice softened. "I'll be here to help you through it all." Drawing close, her heat coated Sarlona's side. "You were meant for this, Sarlona. If the Gods didn't want this for you, my father and I would never have learned of you... They would've saved you from us on the beach... They would've taken you when you begged them to... They would have taken me instead of Glaucus."

Sarlona couldn't bear to contemplate her words.

Dagmar squeezed her arms. "You haven't killed anyone yet...You're only going to gain *more* control."

No, by the grace of the Gods she hadn't. But at any moment, the raging monster inside would consume her and anyone else within reach. Even now, it begged her to take Dagmar's hands, then every droplet of her life force...

Dagmar pressed her thumbs into the tight muscles between Sarlona's shoulder blades—wonderful, steadying. But they no longer had the power to steal Sarlona's fight or make her swoon on command.

"It gets easier..." Dagmar whispered in Sarlona's ear like getting the words nearer might make them more believable. "Why would I want the lorkai quick back if it was a curse?"

"Because you're a villain, Dagmar."

"And what will you be... If you choose to end my people?"

Guilt nibbled at Sarlona's chest. She wondered for the thousandth time if protecting herself was reason enough to doom a species. However often her ruthless, indiscriminate hunger reminded her that the lorkai quick came with an evil void, extinction was extreme.

But not all her motives were selfish. "If I change you back into a lorkai, you'll be vulnerable to the Council..."

Dagmar enveloped Sarlona in her iron embrace: brazen, fearless, tender... "Sweet of you to worry." The kiss to her hair sent a shiver sweeping over Sarlona's shoulders. "They've threatened me with imprisonment before and seldom followed through... But make sure you have those children... In case I need to settle for your descendants."

Gods knew why the thought of Dagmar imprisoned for decades sent eels slithering around Sarlona's stomach.

"Let me help you in Zelule. Let me guide you while you and Benton remain lorkai."

Sarlona leaned into the embrace without understanding why.

Dagmar squeezed, and a swell of warmth and safety washed over Sarlona, echoes of the sensations Dagmar had so often inflicted upon her.

"You might believe you're not meant to be a lorkai..." Dagmar kissed her hair again. "But you must believe that I am."

Sarlona couldn't deny it. A human Dagmar felt wrong.

"You and Benton won't survive Zelule alone," Dagmar said again. "Please don't make me live without you."

Sarlona plucked the huge, rough hands from her hips and ducked out of the Northlander's arms. Twenty years was a long time. Perhaps long enough to convince Dagmar to seek a willing daughter or devise some magical means to prevent the lorkai quick from taking hold. "Twenty years from the day I become human," Sarlona said, spearing Dagmar with her gaze.

"Agreed," the Northlander answered.

That wasn't enough. Crushing Dagmar's wrist, Sarlona tapped into her Marrow and rushed her mind. The Northlander didn't struggle, in body or brain. Instead, she held it all out front. Her hope that the Council couldn't help... The worry that she wouldn't be strong enough to turn Sarlona back if they did... And her resolve not to try until Sarlona reached forty.

Then there was the nagging fear that her daughter would never live that long.

They'd all die in Zelule.

Or Sarlona's mentor would attack her again, and she'd be too sentimental to protect herself. The Council was up to something. Kyran would find another way to kill Sarlona if Zelule didn't do the trick.

Sarlona's guard wilted, and she withdrew from Dagmar's mind. As much as the Northlander had victimized and manipulated her, the love and concern were real. She forgot that sometimes. "All right," she said, releasing Dagmar's wrist.

"Thank you." Dagmar sat, resting against the steep roof. "Do it now."

Before Sarlona changed her mind.

Warmth flashed into Sarlona's cheeks, and a cold claw dug into her chest as she recalled what making a lorkai involved. "What if...you don't survive?"

Dagmar smiled. "Then I'll watch over you from the heavens."

Sarlona doubted that's where Dagmar would dwell if things went awry. Maybe that was her version of a joke.

"I survived the first time. I'm built for it." She gestured for Sarlona to sit beside her. "Anyway, you're powerful. Your quick will take."

Sarlona knelt before Dagmar. "Isn't this supposed to be a process?"

"Ideally." The Northlander shrugged. "But we don't have much time, and I don't want you wasting much quick on me. Just give me a dose, kill me, then give me another dose.

"What about the altar? The dagger and burial?" Images of the most terrifying moments of her life flashed in her memories.

"Pomp. Quit stalling, Sarlona." She grinned. "Kiss me."

Dagmar and Glaucus had demanded so many kisses from her. Compelled her to give them away. And hijacked her physiology to make each feel magical.

Steeling herself, she leaned in and took Dagmar by the head. Her lips met the Northlander's, and, for the hundredth time, Sarlona marveled at how soft they were for such a hard woman. Then she focused on her intention like Glaucus had taught her to do through his memories. She imagined her quick rising up, spilling into Dagmar, and transforming the Northlander's body into a lorkai's.

A second later, her abdomen clenched like a vise, and an etheric fluid burned its way up her throat. Her muscles tightened so stiff her bones ached, but she opened her mouth, and the evanescent liquid rushed into Dagmar.

A scream fought the quick for space in the Northlander's throat after the first swallow, and her every fiber tensed, vibrating like a bee upon a windowpane.

Sarlona took Dagmar's reins and paralyzed her gag reflex to help her drink. A minute of shared agony passed before she fell on her haunches, muscles quivering.

Dagmar's eyes blazed manna-blue as she shrieked with clenched teeth. Her back arched, limbs convulsing against the cedar shingles. The scent of urine scorched the air. Then she stilled, unconscious.

Wiping her mouth, Sarlona stood over the crumpled Northlander.

The kiss and quick had been the easy part. It was piercing Dagmar's heart that she dreaded.

It shouldn't be so difficult to kill the woman who'd killed her first.

But the image of Dagmar split head to hip by Sarlona's claw still haunted her. The blood and roars leaked into her nightmares with all the other terrible things she'd experienced in the past couple of months.

This time, Dagmar wasn't immortal. She could die.

Sarlona didn't want to be the one to send her to the next world, whether this one would be better for it or not.

After a deep breath and a prayer that placed Dagmar's fate in the hands of whichever Gods had dominion over Northland lorkai, Sarlona growled and ejected one carpal blade. She pictured Dagmar standing over her naked body with a dagger raised, poised to fill her chest with agony and steal her life forever. The Northlander deserved whatever happened to her. The Gods would decide.

Screaming, Sarlona struck. The shrill cry of a terrified young woman shrouded in the bellow of a demon echoed through the damp air as she skewered Dagmar's heart. Neither sound muffled the wet thunk or the crack of bone. She ripped her serrated claw out with a curse, and blood gurgled from the wound.

Dagmar's slack face paled to bone white while scarlet stained and matted her fur-lined vest. Blood rivulets formed from the saturated clothing, running down the shingles and racing for the gaps in the boards beneath them. It dripped from the overhang to the ground with a rain-like patter.

As many times as Sarlona had helped gut fish, butcher livestock, and clean game, it didn't compare to watching blood spew from a person. She prayed it never would.

Once the last thread of Dagmar's body had gone silent and still, Sarlona knelt beside her. The Northlander would have appeared lovely if her face hadn't been blanched with death. Serene, without the taught jaw or fiery glare, no harsh lines etched her features.

Sarlona tilted Dagmar's head and parted her lips. "Please work. Please come back," she prayed, hoping whatever power governed lorkai would hear.

Pressing her lips to Dagmar's icy ones, she envisioned the Northlander waking, made new by her corrupted Marrow. She relaxed her throat and told the universe that she wanted her quick to fill the mortal vessel in her grasp. That she burned to share her power with another and needed Dagmar to face eternity.

After a moment of faking it, the drive gripped Sarlona in earnest—some primordial instinct in her depths demanded she procreate. A feverish heat raced over her, and she grabbed Dagmar's head, crushing their faces together. Her whole being caught fire as something thrummed and built in her core, far more electric than when she'd spilled her quick into Dagmar a few minutes ago.

Shaking, she straddled Dagmar, adjusted her grip, and tried to force the fluid up from wherever it came. Instead, the bizarre substance raged behind Sarlona's solar plexus, tensed her abdomen to granite, and pricked her limbs with pins and needles. Panic rose in place of her quick. What if she couldn't summon it? What if the concentrated lorkai Marrow burst from her chest, tearing her apart?

But just as the roiling energy threatened to sear a hole through her torso, something snapped. With a shot of pleasure that made her eyes roll, the electric fluid drained from her core and rushed into the base of her throat. Every muscle tightened when her quick rose. Her being knitted into Dagmar's body without a thought. Ribs cracked painlessly while pure power spilled from her on a wave of ecstasy that left a devastating weakness in its wake.

Despite losing control of her own body, Sarlona made Dagmar's drink until the flow of her essence dried to a trickle. Then she slid down Dagmar's front, unable to lift her head from the Northlander's gory chest.

Nothing happened.

Shouldn't Dagmar have expelled an inhuman scream or gulped for breath by now? Surely, her oversized heart should have started beating again...

The widow's walk crumbled beneath Sarlona. The sky expanded into a cold, starless void, and a wagon rolled over her chest. Another ancient entity gone—because of her.

But as the tears pooled in her eyes, something warm tugged on her insides. An invisible rope dragged her nearer to Dagmar, and ethereal strands weaved them together. That familial bond they'd shared returned.

This time, gilded with a sense of responsibility.

Dagmar gasped, and her heart thundered to life. Her scent shifted into a lorkai's.

Sore and breathless, Sarlona hauled herself up using the railing and peered at the stars. She hoped she'd done the right thing. Or that the Gods would forgive her if she hadn't.

Relief wore into irritation when she turned her gaze to the Northlander slumped along the roof. Dagmar could have warned her how intense spawning another monster would be. Knives stabbed Sarlona's sides with each breath, and weakness weighed on her limbs.

She gave up trying to breathe and wiped the blood from her cheek, staring at Dagmar. Soaked in blood and piss, the Northland lorkai looked like the last one to fall on a battlefield.

Sarlona supposed she should clean her up if she could summon the strength to lift her. Dagmar and Glaucus had granted her that kindness. Bathing her and putting her in a new dress... Before burying her alive for some perverse tradition.

A growl too low for human hearing snuck from between Sarlona's teeth as the memories leaked to the front of her thoughts. After abducting, imprisoning, and feeding on her, the two monsters had stripped her naked in a dark, underground chamber. They'd impelled her onto an altar stone, cutting and scarring her. Then they'd murdered her and poured their corrupted Marrow down her throat, stealing her magic and humanity, and cursing her with a wicked hunger her body would kill to satisfy.

Never mind that they'd bathed her without permission. That was a thread in the tapestry of offenses they'd woven to shatter her privacy and autonomy.

Dagmar could sleep in her cold blood and piss.

Sarlona had better warn the guards, anyway. The newborn lorkai would be hungry when she woke.

CHAPTER NINE

If there was any place worse in all the realms for a Northlander lorkai than the Pits of Zelule, Dagmar couldn't think of it. Wandering amid the pools and streams of glowing rock with the henchman wearing her father's face, she might as well have strolled into Kraknar's hell.

The barren, ocher landscape blended with the red-orange sky. Between them, the air wavered, its heat and noxious fumes seeking to drive her eyes shut. The smells of burnt earth and the strange gases it released with scalding steam mingled with the scent of cooking skin. She would have roasted had her ability to heal been much slower. As it was, the ambient temperature only made her skin pink and sore.

"Holy cockin' shit." Benton wiped his brow with his bare forearm for all the good it did. "It's cockin' *hot*."

Dagmar didn't bother taking a breath of lung-scorching air to agree. Wilting, she rested her forehead on the frosty steel of her freshly enchanted axe.

He puffed. "Think we're gettin' close?"

She breathed against her axe blade, relishing the cooling inhale. "Yes." The ground had grown warmer in the last half hour, softening the leather of her boots and molding them to her feet. She imagined rivers of bubbling magma or boiling water running just beneath them. "I hope you're ready."

The red light flashed brighter to her left as he drew his blade. "I'm ready to get this shit over with."

He had none of the heaviness upon him that she bore. The heat didn't seem to bother him like it did her. He had discarded his cloak and shirt but kept Glaucus's breastplate buckled over his otherwise naked chest. If the scorching air reddened his skin, its deep brown tones hid the flush. His spell-swallowing blade rested in his fingers, and Glaucus's long sword was sheathed down his back.

Returning the glance, he flipped his sword around his hand. "Ready as I can be for a fire-throwin' demon bitch."

Glaucus's voice forming Benton's words sent spiky crustaceans skittering up Dagmar's spine. Trying to shut his mouth with her fist wouldn't end well for her, though. Made from Sarlona's quick, she was strong but not like she'd been before Amenduil had ripped the lorkai out of her. Her body was a newborn's, and the one Benton occupied was ancient.

She settled for a sneer. "*Nazarale Bastatep* isn't really a demon." That was the title given to her by the mortals on the Rashivic border. "She's a lich, an ancient one, and not of her own making."

Benton shrugged. "Same difference."

It wasn't. "Nazarale was an *angel* and a gifted pyromancer. Like many of the immortals who fell near the end of the First Wizard War, her body was thrown into the Pits." That was well before Dagmar's time, but Laelia, Glaucus's mother, had told many war stories. "Unlike the others, Nazarale wasn't destroyed."

Who knew why? Maybe when the flames consumed her flesh after centuries of study and worship, the bodily sacrifice induced spiritual unity with the fire deities? Perhaps baptism by flame advanced the understanding necessary to achieve oneness with it?

Dagmar pressed icy steel to her forehead again. "She remains one-part charred corpse and one-part fire spirit."

Benton cocked an eyebrow at her. "And that shit scares you now, huh?"

She hated how well he'd learned to read her lorkai scent in just a few days. "It's not so much fear as foreboding." That none of them would leave the Pits alive. "The assignment to destroy the Demon of Zelule was meant to end the lorkai, not Nazarale."

They parted around an obsidian boulder, but she couldn't let him escape with the hope that he and Sarlona would be allowed to live happy human lives. "There's no reason to destroy Nazarale. She only ventures from the Pits every few years to demand prayers from some poor soul traveling too close."

His knuckles whitened on his grip. "Then why wouldn't the Council just help make us human?"

She brushed her wild hair from her face. "Because this is a lot cheaper and easier. And it absolves those councilors less eager to wipe out a humanoid species of the direct responsibility for our extinction."

His steps and scent grew heavier but not fearful. "Sar knows what she's doin'. And she's a good shot."

She was. That's why she'd agreed to hang back with the enchanted bow and ice arrows. Dagmar had scarcely ever fired a projectile. If her prey's or enemy's blood couldn't splatter across her face, it wasn't real engagement. And Benton had only wielded a bow when his blade had failed to coax enough bread or coin from travelers. Sarlona, however, had used arrows to feed herself and her family often, always choosing them over her spells out of 'fairness' to the game.

"She may know how to set and activate the stones, but she doesn't have a clue what she's doing with the Council." Dagmar growled at the thought of her daughter tossing away eternal life. "She wouldn't know an enemy if the word was carved into his forehead."

He snorted. "Heh. Well, don't tell her I said it, but she ain't always real smart for someone who's done nothin' but learn her whole life."

Dagmar didn't equate intelligence with the instinct for self-preservation like Benton did, but she didn't disagree. "She's beyond naïve." And infuriatingly willing to look for the best in people or to give them the benefit of the doubt. It was her most irritating trait.

But without it, she wouldn't have had anything to do with Benton or Dagmar.

"Benton..." Now wasn't the best time to poke at his bruises, but she had him alone. "If you love her, you won't let her risk *everything* because she misses her magic."

His eyes flared red, matching the skyline. "Cock off."

She pushed. "It's your selfish dream you're supporting, not what's best for her." Setting her jaw, she grabbed his arm. "You want your body back without her domination over it."

He wheeled on her. "That ain't how it is, and you know it." His voice cracked. "She's sufferin', Dagmar. It ain't just missin' her magic or home." He stood on his toes to get in her face. "She feels like you cut her hands off. Never mind this cockin' hunger."

Dagmar didn't retreat an inch. "It takes time to adjust." Decades, but she'd keep the timeline to herself. "You learn to manage it like a mortal need." Without forgetting for a second who lurked behind the face staring up at her, she gripped his inner shoulders and brushed her thumbs along the underside of his jaw. "Then you learn to appreciate satisfying it. Like a good meal, drink, or lay."

He broke their eye contact with a snort.

"She loved your taste, Benton." Dagmar warped her voice into something silky and sensual. "That's what drew her to you. She couldn't get enough of you..." His muscles softened beneath her hands. "She fell in love with you through drinking your Marrow."

He gazed at the blazing horizon.

"Was it an evil thing when you were in her grasp? Or was it divine?"

His words came out as a benign growl. "She almost killed me..."

"You wanted to bed the human girl," Dagmar continued, redoubling her grip. "But *lorkai* Sarlona won your heart."

A sigh leaked out of him like steam from a kettle.

"Remember how deep your bond was..." Instead of letting him go when he tried to shrug her away, she ran her hands down his arms and interlocked her fingers with his.

He stared at her hands like they'd come from another world.

"Remember how sweet it was to feel her in you..." she purred. "To brim with such purpose?"

He met her gaze for a second, eyes cooling to a dim yellow. "I love her just how she is, and I'd be happy to be her Bound again, but this ain't what she—" A blue spark reflected in his eyes, and he yanked his fingers free. "That's the signal. She's got the stones laid."

Dagmar's shoulders slumped when he marched toward the vast pool of molten rock in the distance. Nazarale was said to be tied to the most expansive and central pit into which she'd been thrown. The time had come to face her.

"C'mon, Daggy." He glanced back with a shit-eating grin. "This is gonna work. Even the elves said so."

She prayed he was right. The weapon they intended to destroy Nazarale with was no more than four enchanted aquamarine stones and a scroll to activate them. The Elves of August had designed it in exchange for the Lord of Ashmore's petition to have an elven prisoner freed in Wolfboro. Sarlona only had to set the spell off around the primary lava pit. It would freeze over, forever entombing the Demon of Zelule. Of course, they had to ensure Nazarale was in the fiery basin and immobilized before springing the trap.

Dagmar caught up in a few strides. "The key to surviving a pyromancer is to keep moving and never come at one head-on." Gods knew why she should try to keep Benton alive. "Few spells burn hot enough to instantly destroy a mature lorkai. So, if you feel flame, no matter the agony, move." Of course, that was easier said than done when one's muscles were half incinerated.

He tightened his jaw and wagged his spell-eating blade before jogging for the pit's edge. Squinting, he shielded his face with his arm. "Think she's home?"

"We're about to find out." Spinning, Dagmar peered into the wavering landscape for Sarlona. While she couldn't spot the young woman, she sensed her near, and her scent carried over the cooking rock. She hid behind a large boulder not far to the south, one of the few that dotted the otherwise flat terrain. Hopefully, she'd stick to the plan and stay there, providing cover with the bow rather than joining the fray.

After a deep, uncomfortable breath, Dagmar gestured to the pit. "All right. Offer a prayer for her to steal."

He choked on his laugh. "You offer a cockin' prayer. I don't even know any."

Dagmar put her hands on her hips. "Don't worry, Benton, your words can't reach the Gods from this hell."

His irises turned pink, and he spat at the ground. Staring at the sizzling saliva, he crossed his arms.

She ground her heel into the ochre dirt. "Fine."

First, she silently prayed that her next prayer wouldn't summon Nazarale from the fiery lake. However much she longed to get their task over with and leave Zelule, doing so brought her closer to losing Sarlona to the mortal world.

Assuming she didn't lose her to the next realm or travel there herself.

Though the heat tried to drive her back and force her eyes shut, she stepped to the lava's edge. "Frodavar, Mother of Wisdom, please grant my companions the sense to embrace immortality and avoid immolation today and everyday hereafter." She caught Benton's glare in the corner of her eye and waited, scanning the molten rock as the fine hairs on her raised forearms singed off.

Nothing happened.

"Now what?" Benton asked.

"Piss her off, I guess." She snatched the flask of Silsorian holy water on her belt. Before she could think better of it, she threw it at the pool's center. The metal floated atop the molten earth before spreading outward with a hiss in beads and tendrils.

A moment later, a puff of thin flames appeared above the lava. They danced across the whole of its surface ten feet high.

"I think that did it," Benton said as they retreated.

In the center of the pit, a blackened humanoid husk rose from the melted rock until it hovered above the pool, flames licking at the charred bones of its feet. Nothing remained of the clothes, but an untouched amber amulet hung around a skeletal neck. Its eye sockets lacked their orbs, but fire roared from them and the mouth. The flare of the pelvic bones beneath the crusty, sable membrane that stretched over them gave the fiend away as female.

Nazarale's head swung like a lizard's in Dagmar's direction, the rest of her body following a moment later. The lich's flaming gaze fixed on her.

A green halo encroached on Dagmar's vision when she loosed the glow in her eyes to show Nazarale what she was. She leaned on her axe as though bored, refusing to allow an ounce of fear onto her face. Only Benton and Sarlona could smell it.

As the lich floated nearer, the flame in her orbits burned blue and condensed into ovals. A white-yellow blaze erupted from the charcoal remnants of her skin and muscle, shifting over her skeletal body until it formed the shape of a woman's flesh and concealed the husk beneath. With an upward swipe of her feminine hand, she gathered up the orange flame below her and spread it over her body like a dazzling silk robe. Some of it alighted atop her head and flowed over her shoulders to form a fiery mane.

A beautiful, blinding, fire goddess hovered before them.

Benton cursed under his breath.

Nazarale seemed to smile, though the brilliance of her 'skin' blurred her features. *What lorkai dare enter my realm?* The roar of a blaze and the pop and crackle of burning debris came from her mouth, but the voice in Dagmar's head was a sultry echo. Without waiting for an answer, she struck at Dagmar's mental defenses.

Dagmar flinched, but if the assault was an earnest one, Nazarale wouldn't get through.

Benton winced next, grabbing his head with his offhand. "*Cock.*"

Dagmar locked her luminescent gaze with his. His mental barrier had held, too.

Nazarale was physiologically weak for an immortal so ancient. That didn't mean her magic would be, though. Her spells were what made her dangerous.

"Greetings, Nazarale. I'm Dagmar." She projected her words both aloud and telepathically. "We've come to free you."

Nazarale laughed—the hiss of green wood on the fire.

Why would a lorkai wish to free me? None fought on the side *of reason. I killed several of you in the war.* Her feet touched down on the pit's edge, and the baked earth blackened to soot beneath her.

Dagmar stood her ground. "The war ended over a thousand years ago." True enough, even if another had come and gone and the two magical ideologies squabbled into present times. "You have no enemies and no allies. This is a labor of mercy."

Can it truly have been so long?

"Too long to dwell in Zelule," said Dagmar. "Even for a pyromancer."

And how will you free me, Dagmar? Nazarale's fiery fingertips alighted on Dagmar's axe head. *With frosted steel?*

The axe glowed red hot despite the frost enchantment, and Dagmar had to drop it, though she refused to so much as grimace. "The Elves of August designed a spell to end your torment."

Frozen in the rock, if Nazarale didn't die, she'd at least sleep; a fate less agonizing than imprisonment where one of the hells leaked into the realm of the living.

Not that Dagmar cared either way. "Return to the pit, and I'll enact it."

I have a better idea. Nazarale extended her fingers toward Dagmar's cheek.

Refusing to backpedal, Dagmar turned her head, and the lich's hand alighted on her shoulder. She growled when the fingers seared her shirt to her skin, sidestepping out from under them. The time for talk was done. She scooped up her axe.

I will set *you free.* Nazarale burned so bright that gazing at her was like staring at the sun. *Release you both from your fleshy prisons into the earth and sky.* She held out her hands, and wispy flames sprang into her palms. *All that power trapped in blood and bone... I'll transform you into something pure—light and heat.* Divine *energy...*

Benton bristled to the left, and his blade gleamed when he raised it.

Dagmar grinned. Instead of intensifying her fear, the threats vaporized it. Battle lust drowned her worries. "Your lack of blood won't keep me from trying to spill it, lich."

On you, Dagmar, I will use a slow burn. So that you might keep me company in the pit for a time. The flames in her hands snapped forward like whips.

Dagmar dodged beneath the first, and Benton's sword flashed, eating a second. Before the third struck, she dashed to Nazarale's side.

Dagmar swung her axe, cutting through flame but missing the husk beneath. *Move,* she warned Benton telepathically, the soles of her boots growing hotter. She flipped backward, and a font of fire exploded from the earth where she'd stood not a moment ago. Juking their way forward to avoid the succession of fiery explosions Nazarale sent from the ground, they ran at her.

In close, Dagmar brought her axe back and under, coming up at Nazarale. Just as it hit fire, flames blasted Dagmar rearward. She landed on one knee, singed and smoking.

Benton bobbed and twisted amid fiery tendrils, his blade weaving with him and sucking down every flame it touched.

On her feet in a blink, Dagmar charged in. This time, Nazarale drove her backward with a conjured flock of flaming swallows—a trick Sarlona had used once. The bird-shaped fire swirled over her, dive-bombing two or three at a time. Dagmar ducked and dodged, but a few left blistering trails across her arms and shoulders, keeping her at bay.

The enchantment on Dagmar's axe was less effective than she'd hoped. And while Benton protected himself with his sword, she doubted it could drain enough of Nazarale's power to exhaust her. They couldn't drive the lich into the magma themselves. Not before one of them caught fire.

Dagmar glanced up for that boulder to the south and spotted Sarlona atop a nearby rock, still as a statue. Transparent, the glow from the pit penetrated her body, clothes, and even the bow she trained on Nazarale as if they were flawless glass. The demon hadn't noticed her. And she wouldn't until Sarlona loosed an arrow.

Do it, Dagmar screamed at her daughter.

Sarlona let fly and planted an arrow dead center in Nazarale's chest.

The fiery birds vanished in puffs of smoke as the lich screeched like steam from a kettle. Nazarale lurched, and her fires momentarily died to reveal her blackened bones.

Lunging low, Benton drove his blade at her gut, forcing her to concentrate on reviving her flames there. Dagmar swung over him for her head. Taken off guard, the pyromancer threw up her arm instead of a fresh spell.

A skeletal hand fell to the ground, and a raspy scream pierced their ears.

The missing appendage didn't prevent Nazarale from casting. She called up a blaze around her, pushing Dagmar and Benton to retreat. Both lorkai waited for her to make a move, unable to spot her engulfed in the fire.

Before the flames died, Nazarale launched a fireball in the boulder's direction. Sarlona jumped behind the stone, and the fire smashed into the front of the rock, no more than licking its far side.

With Nazarale open, Dagmar and Benton dove in. His dancing blade kept the fire out of Dagmar's face, and before long, they had the lich on her heels, close to the pool. Nazarale lifted her hand, aiming at Dagmar's head, but three arrows, rapid-fire, pounded into her chest. The flames of her flesh died back again, and before she could recover, Dagmar slammed her axe down, rending the demon's ribcage.

Nazarale reeled, her chest split wide. With a fiery hiss, she plunged into the pool.

"Now," Dagmar yelled.

Sarlona dropped her cloaking with the bow and snatched the scroll from between her teeth without missing a beat. Pronouncing every syllable flawlessly, she read the ancient elven script aloud. The parchment disintegrated in her hands while icy bolts shot up from the four stones surrounding the pit. Streams of pulsing ice magic met above the pool's center and descended into the fire and molten rock. The spell spread from the core of the pit outward, smothering the flames, and the lava's glow dimmed. But the pool didn't solidify as fast as Dagmar had hoped. Seconds dragged by, and the cooling rock remained soft.

Dagmar's chest tightened when the center of the pit began to roil. If the magic was too slow and Nazarale escaped, they had no other way to bind or destroy her. When the lich's skull breached the surface, eyes burning, Dagmar's heart skipped a beat.

Nazarale struggled, flailing like she drowned in a vat of porridge, and didn't rise more than waist-high before the frozen magma held her fast. The fires in her eye sockets died, and she stilled. An obsidian skeleton, half-encased in stone, remained.

Dagmar rested her axe on her shoulder as Benton shoved his blade into its sheath. "Wait here."

She had to be sure Nazarale was gone. After poking the pit's surface and finding it solid, she ventured onto the porous stone.

The lich appeared like a fossil embedded in the rock; no sign of life. Dagmar stretched her mind toward Nazarale's, hesitant to tread into pure, flaming madness, but found only the faintest of slumbering consciousnesses. The former angel would sleep forever rather than burn. Withdrawing, she concluded the lich was dead enough.

The Demon of Zelule was no more.

Satisfied, Dagmar turned. She made it about a quarter of the way back before Sarlona screamed. "Run."

Dagmar should have done just that, but she glanced over her shoulder. Nazarale's eyes flared to life with blue fire and the amulet glowed red-hot through the stone encasing her.

Dagmar pivoted into a sprint as the basalt exploded from Nazarale's bones. The searing heat bore down on her back, and the rock bled red beneath her boots. She dove for the pit's edge when the stone softened below her. Her torso hit solid ground, but her legs landed in the swirling flame and lava. Dagmar roared in unison with Sarlona's next cry of warning while blistering agony ravaged her. Digging her fingers into the scalding earth, she crawled forward.

Blade in hand, Benton grabbed her wrist and dragged her from the fire. She flipped over the second he let go. Her legs were gone from the mid-thigh down. So much for dodging the pyromancer's spells.

This time, Nazarale didn't bother to shape herself into a woman and clothe herself in flame. She hovered before them as the charred husk, her fire racing across the ground for Dagmar.

Benton scooped up the flames with his blade and stood over her. "Quit tryin' to leave me out, you blazin' bitch."

Nazarale hissed, raining molten rocks on them that Benton caught with a swirl of his sword. He skipped left, and Dagmar rolled right when the ground heated and a flaming geyser exploded from the earth. A massive, fiery serpent shot from its core, slithering after him at a dizzying speed. While he fought it off, the lich grabbed the charred tatters of Dagmar's hide pants with a smoldering hand.

Hollering again as the skin on her thigh blistered and burned, Dagmar planted her carpal blades into the ground. The hide disintegrated into ash, and Nazarale reached to take a firmer hold.

Another ice arrow collided with the pyromancer's chest, knocking her rearward.

Sarlona advanced with her bowstring drawn, her next arrow trained on Nazarale's chest. Only one remained in her quiver.

The amulet blazed while the ice melted and sizzled from Nazarale's torso. Perhaps her mastery of flame wasn't intrinsic after all.

The amulet, Dagmar shouted into her daughter's mind as she wriggled backward, and flames erupted from the lich's remaining hand.

Time slowed.

Benton slammed down on top of her, slapping his blade to his back and Sarlona fired.

The arrow missed the pendant but severed the chain above it. Nazarale's amulet plummeted, and the flames cut out.

The lich roared like a blaze and scrambled to retrieve the trinket, but Sarlona's last arrow blasted into her chest and knocked her into the pit. She shrieked when the fire enveloped her, incinerating her desiccated flesh to expose her charred bones. Her eyes died, blue fire extinguished, and she crumbled, the last scraps of her connective tissue disintegrating. The ebony pieces of her flaming skeleton sank into the lava.

Sarlona snatched the lich's severed hand and tossed it into the pool after her.

With her teeth bared, Dagmar frothed and writhed beneath Benton. "Gods, get off me."

He climbed to his feet with a groan, back smoking. "A 'thanks' would be nice, Dags."

The pain consumed any gratefulness, and she growled at him.

Sarlona crept near, her face the picture of concern. "You'll be okay."

"I know!" Dagmar snapped and pounded the ground. The blackened stumps of her lower limbs oozed, and above, nearly to her genitals, had begun to blister. It was going to be a long trip home. "Give me a few minutes," she said through gritted teeth. Much as she didn't want to stay in Zelule another second, she couldn't tolerate being carried at that moment.

Sarlona knelt behind Dagmar. After smoothing her hair, she propped Dagmar's head on her lap.

"I lost my best axe," Dagmar said, shutting her eyes.

Sarlona snorted. "We'll get you another one." Prying open Dagmar's balled fists, she snatched her fingers. "Take what you need."

The warmth in Dagmar's chest dulled the burning in her legs. Sarlona cared. Dagmar couldn't take any more from her daughter, though. "You can't afford it after making me," she said, wrenching her hands free.

Instead of arguing, Sarlona eyed her pet. "Benton..."

He laughed and crossed his arms.

Sarlona gestured to Dagmar's legs. "She can't travel like this... You don't need your strength when you're going to Gulway..."

He sucked in his lips and ground his heel into the hot dirt. "Gods dammit." After sheathing his blade with a grumble, he joined Sarlona on his knees. "You'd better remember this shit when I'm human."

Dagmar took his hands and tapped into his Marrow without hesitation. The familiar taste of her father's energies flooded her with relief. The redness and the blistering high up on her thighs disappeared, and the blinding pain where her legs ended faded to a more bearable ache.

He gave her his stupid grin. "That's doin' it for you, huh?"

"Yes," she said, drawing harder on him. He grimaced but endured it for another minute before tearing his hands away. Dagmar lifted her head a few inches. "Is she gone?"

"Looks like it." He sauntered to the edge of the smoldering pool with a blistered back and snatched Nazarale's amulet. After peering at the small amber pendant with a furrowed brow, he started.

"*Shit.*" He skipped to Sarlona and handed her the necklace.

She stared at it before starting herself. "It's a fire demon *prince.*" She held the amulet for Dagmar to see, and a hideous face, wreathed in flame, flashed below the gem's surface. "Trapped inside... This is... A rare thing. It must be powerful."

"I don't care..." Dagmar groaned. "So long as the bitch has found an Otherrealm hell to burn in."

Sarlona wound up to throw the amulet into the pit after its owner.

Dagmar sat. "Don't."

Sarlona froze.

She snatched the trinket from her daughter before offering it back to her. "Wear it."

Sarlona scrunched her face. "No. I don't want a demon whispering into my heart all day."

Dagmar shoved it at her. "Can it protect you from fire?"

"Well..." Sarlona gazed at the burning sky. "Yeah, to a degree, but—"

Dagmar roared louder than she intended, "Then fucking *wear* it."

"But—" Sarlona snatched it from her. "Fine." After squeezing the broken link together, she slung it over her head.

Benton glared at them. "Done cockin' around?"

"Yeah," Dagmar said and took a deep breath when he grabbed her. She growled again as he took hold of her arm and hauled her into the air. Sarlona ducked under her other arm, and they both held her aloft.

It was excruciating, but she was alive. They all were, for now.

CHAPTER TEN

The closer he trod to Gulway, the heavier Benton's boots became. With each step, the baron's promise sounded more like a trick. Benton didn't get happy endings. Why did he believe the most terrifying monster he'd ever encountered would give him one? And it had been *Dagmar's* idea to get his help; the woman who'd once fed him a healing potion, vial and all, after shattering his grin.

His dread deepened with the shadows. By the time he reached the city, darkness had fallen. The thought of facing the baron at night hung like a noose around his neck.

He'd have to wait until morning. Then he could better distinguish nightmares from reality.

Making his way along the outside of Gulway's double-curtained wall, he searched for an overhang. He had to feed, and his years on the road told him that some troublemaker would be sheltering from the cold mist beyond the gates.

Sure enough, beneath the protrusion of the second tower, the light of a tiny fire flickered. He approached with his hood drawn back and his hand uncomfortably far from his hilt. The scent wafting from the makeshift camp told him two young elf-humans huddled by the fire with a human man who didn't share their blood. The man's odor brimmed with Marrow.

"Well met," he called before they noticed him.

The mage ruffled the second Benton intruded into the light. His knuckles whitened on his staff, and he scanned Benton from underneath his cowl. "Keep moving, old man."

The reminder that Benton was trapped behind a sixty-some-thing-year-old's face struck him like a blow every time. "Can't make room for a weary traveler?" He did his best impression of Glaucus's charming smile and grandfatherly tone.

"Get lost." But the Marrow-rich man continued to eye Benton, his hazel gaze drifting over the tailored clothes and one-of-a-kind sword to settle on his belt pouch. "Unless you're willing to toss down some coin."

Benton glanced at the children whose amber stares were fixed on the flames. Their bare heads bore black braids and pointed ears that seemed in danger of freezing with a fire so small. "How 'bout a silver half-piece?"

"A whole one," the mage countered.

"Fine." Benton fished a silver coin from his purse and dropped it into the man's fingerless glove. Flashing the girl a smile she probably didn't see, Benton sat beside her. He guessed she was the elven equivalent of a fifteen or sixteen-year-old and the boy a bit younger. Both reeked with anxiety.

The man threw a spruce branchlet on the fire, and its short needles glowed orange before curling in a hiss of thick smoke. "You could rent a room for a silver..."

Benton held his hands toward the fire as if they needed warming. "I don't wanna be seen tonight."

After staring for a minute, the mage laid his plain oak staff across his lap. "For another silver, you can use the girl."

Vinegar stung Benton's nostrils, and the young elf peeked at him. Her heartbeat doubled its pace. He rested his hand on her spine, rubbing the muscles that tightened like bowstrings on either side. "How much for both?"

The boy's heart and scent mimicked his sister's.

"Two," the man answered after a pause. "If I have to heal them afterward, that's extra."

Gut twisting, Benton fished the coins from his belt pouch. "Deal. But I don't like an audience."

The caster climbed to his feet once Benton passed him the silvers. "I'll give you half an hour."

"Good enough," Benton agreed as the man left the campfire's light to melt into the gloom. Neither child twitched while he waited for the mage to get beyond human earshot. Both jolted when he stood. "Stay put. Unless you wanna watch him die."

Sliding into the shadows, Benton let whatever wicked thing governed lorkai bodies have its way. He didn't sneak up on the man or say a word.

There was no splicing of energies and gentle draw. He exploded through the umbra and hit the mage head-on like a lightning bolt. The hand that grabbed bare flesh to tap into his Marrow broke the man's neck in the same motion. He drove into the dying man's energies like a pike and sucked them down like that first ale of the night.

After recovering his silver and the man's coppers, Benton returned to the dwindling fire and the children. "Go get a room." He passed the coins into the girl's shaking hands. If he'd been more adept, he might have made them stay, warming their bones, easing the ache in their bellies, and erasing whatever horrors lurked in their minds. He didn't trust himself not to break something or drain them dry.

"Go on." He plopped against the wall beside the girl. "Or stay... But he ain't comin' back, and I ain't good with kids." He tilted his head to the sky and shut his eyes as he leaned on the stone.

The girl whispered to her brother, and they slunk away. Listening to them scurry across saturated grass and moss, he told himself they'd be fine, then tried to forget they existed.

The thing that came for him never made a sound.

For a second, he thought the wall had collapsed on top of him. Then he opened his eyes to find Aldamon standing over him, icy gaze crushing him like tons of cold rock. A freezing puff of wind quashed the fire, plunging him into a dark too deep for even a lorkai.

The baron frowned. "What are you doing out here, Benton? Reliving your youth?"

No words. Benton forgot them all. He couldn't make a sound anyway.

"Come." The vampire hauled Benton up by his coat. "I'm ready for you."

After a few seconds of being dragged along at a disorienting speed, a warm room lit by braziers and thick candles appeared. Its tall stone walls encircled them except where three arched windows let in the night. In the center of the ceiling, a stained-glass, circular portal patterned in Gulway's seal hung partway open by a chain. Shelves filled with books, bottles, jars, and apparatuses Benton couldn't guess the purposes of lined the chamber.

The baron squeezed between two heavy oak tables in the middle of the room and sprinkled a black powder that smelled like seaweed atop one. "Are you certain you want to return to your mortal body?"

Benton had to find a way to answer—take a breath to make a noise, nod, something...

The vampire fixed him with that glacial stare. "You've gained some mastery over Glaucus's, and the Abyssal Lord may not let yours go unscathed."

"Yes," Benton croaked on the third try.

Aldamon traded the jar of onyx dust for a vial of red fluid—Benton's blood—and dipped a fine-tipped paintbrush inside. "Good." Bringing the brush up under his nose, he inhaled. His eyes half closed in a horrifyingly sensuous expression. "I do prefer your aesthetics. Your scent. And, despite its delicate nature in comparison to a lorkai's..." He touched his tongue to the tip of the brush, and his lashes kissed. "Mmm... Your *taste*."

A cold claw crushed Benton's throat while a warm hand gripped him low.

Three nights. He'd never survive that long.

Frozen, he watched the baron paint a series of sigils on the table without a breath. The vampire whispered a monologue over them in a bowel-shaking foreign language, then lit a red candle in each of the cardinal directions.

He produced a large jar, this too filled with blood. "You'll have to disrobe."

The scent of a large canine predator wafted from the vessel when the vampire cracked it. From a warg, Benton guessed. He fumbled with his sword belt as the baron poured the blood in a macabre circle around the table.

While the vampire ringed the blood in pink salt, Benton managed to disarm himself of his cherished blade and Glaucus's long sword, then fought his way out of Glaucus's coat.

Staring at him, Aldamon bit his own hand. The ambrosial scent that hit the air made Benton lurch. The baron winked as he held his hand aloft over the blood-smeared table, letting it drip onto the surface below and saturating the air with the sweet, bewitching odor.

Benton spun to untie his shirt and rip it over his head. As soon as the cloth cleared his eyes, he gazed into Aldamon's face. Every inch of him tensed to stone when the vampire's fingers alighted on his waist.

"Allow my assistance..."

Benton did his best to ignore the warmth conjured by deft fingers as the baron unlaced his pants. His breath hitched with the yank that brought the leather down just below his hips.

"That should do." Mercifully, Aldamon stepped away. "On the clean table now."

Benton crept to the table and lifted himself onto the quilted wood. Gentle hands pressed on his chest and supported the back of his head to lay him down.

Pulling a plum-sized glass orb from the pocket of his coat, the vampire swiveled to the other table. The crystalline ball swirled with black smoke when he released it above the makeshift altar, hanging it in the air.

"This won't take long," he said, retrieving the vial of Benton's blood. After a dab into the vial, he turned the brush on Benton.

Benton shivered with Aldamon bent over him, their faces inches apart while the monster painted an intricate design on his forehead. Some of his tension faded as the brush strokes shifted to his chest, but it returned with a vengeance when the silky bristles tickled his lower abdomen.

Finally, the baron set aside his grisly palette. "There." He snatched the floating marble and shattered it, showering the table below in dark smoke and flecks that sparkled like mica. With a whoosh that sucked the air from Benton's lungs and sputtered the candles, a shadowy vortex opened in the table. "We just need a little help for this last part."

Aldamon vanished, returning seconds later grasping the back of a young man's neck. His shove thrust the dirty, half-naked teenager onto his knees in the narrow space between the tables.

The boy's acrid terror struck Benton in the throat.

"What—" Benton raised himself on his elbows, but a mere look from the vampire laid him down. "Wait, *don't*—"

Benton never saw the baron draw the dagger, only drive it through the young man's sternum. And wrench it up to the boy's mandible with a stomach-twisting crack, rip, and slurp. Charcoal mist bellowed from the gaping wound. Blood spilled across the floor.

Benton shook his head as the latter rose in a mist, coalescing into floating scarlet tendrils that intertwined with the wisps of inky fog. All at once, the nightmarish vapors dove into the howling black hole in the other table, and the young man hit the floor with a thud.

"Cockin' robes..." Benton grumbled.

Holding the dagger with a devilish smile, the vampire went to Benton's side. "Ready?"

Benton gaped at the blade he was sure was about to enter him. *No.* "Yeah..."

Aldamon drew the dagger across his own palm, speaking again in terrible, foreign words that shook the chamber. Its echoes, no doubt reverberating into or out of the Abyss, brought the bile into Benton's throat. He couldn't help recoiling when drops of primeval blood splattered a few inches above his navel.

The vampire tossed the dagger as raven smoke weaved between the fingers of his bleeding hand. "Brace yourself." Pinning Benton by the shoulder with his clean palm, he slapped his smoking, bloody one on the center of Benton's chest.

Soul-rending pain split Benton's ribcage and shot him into oblivion.

CHAPTER ELEVEN

S arlona set the vial of manna on the nightstand beside Dagmar's bed. "Is there anything else you need?"

Dagmar looked her dead in the eyes. "For you to wait until I'm well enough to go with you."

Sarlona broke their stare. "I have to face Sylvanus alone."

"You don't. You just want to. Because you know I'll kill him if he attacks you again."

Sarlona peeked under the sheets she'd wrapped the weeping bone of Dagmar's lengthening femurs in not fifteen minutes ago. "You know me so well." A fact almost as upsetting as the gore she hid beneath the blankets.

"Stop fretting, Sarlona." Dagmar put her hands behind her head and leaned back like she was lounging and not growing new legs. "The guards will see to me." She all but shouted so Gorgil, whose heavy footfalls sounded in the hall, would hear.

"That's right." He smiled just enough to show his tusks when he entered the chamber with a bundle of fresh linens and laid them atop the chest at the foot of the bed. "This isn't the first time a lorkai has lost a limb in Ashmore."

Dagmar narrowed her eyes at Sarlona. "Or a head, for that matter."

Sarlona sneered, refusing to feel another twinge of guilt about bisecting or decapitating Dagmar. The memory horrified her, but that didn't mean she'd been in the wrong. She turned to Gorgil. "Just don't forget that she's hungrier than she used to be."

His somber brown stare told her he understood.

"I started a bunch of healing potions in the cellar, but Cyr will have to finish them." Without her magic, she couldn't.

"They won't help much," Dagmar said.

That was another fun thing Sarlona had learned about being a lorkai. Just like any other spell or concoction, the effects of healing magic and potions were weak on lorkai. "Whatever you do, don't send him up here for anything." Cyr wasn't much of a caster, but he had enough Marrow to trigger a lorkai's prey response.

"I won't, Sarlona." His huge grayish-green hands swallowed hers. "We'll be fine."

His willingness to touch her bare fingers didn't bode well. Didn't he understand that each minute among mortals was a struggle not to take from them? That every naked touch was an invitation to...

It *was* an invitation. Ashmore's guard captain had lived his whole life with two lorkai, including the one she was worried about. The one whom he loved like she was family.

"Okay..." Sarlona retracted her hands. "Save your strength for Dagmar."

"Are you—"

"*I'm* fine," she said. With a wave toward the door, she dismissed him.

He squeezed her shoulder before leaving. "Be careful."

Dagmar adjusted her position with a grimace. "Stop fretting. I won't kill anyone." A grin leaked into her eyes. "Just make sure you return before Benton does."

Sarlona ground her heel into the scuffed plank beneath it. "Fine. I won't fret. Don't you either."

Dagmar leaned forward. "Well, that's impossible with you." Face hardening, she pointed like she was chastising a child. "I know that you *can* handle that druid. If you're set on doing this, promise me you *will*."

"I will." Sarlona wouldn't let Sylvanus hurt her again. Her whole life, she'd done everything he'd asked to the best of her ability, and he'd betrayed her when she needed him most. He'd stolen her childhood and her normalcy, and when he'd lost control of her, he tried to kill her. Sick as the thought made her, she'd drain him and take over his mind if it came to that. She could apologize later, once she was human. "I promise."

Dagmar lay back. "If I have to scrape up your ashes, no caster in the history of this realm will suffer as much as him."

"You won't." If Sylvanus wouldn't listen, she'd make him. He would help her this time, whether he liked it or not.

CHAPTER TWELVE

B enton groaned in the darkness, bones aching, struggling for breath. Vorakor's ebony tentacles waved before him, stretching into eternity.

Aldamon had put him in his body, but it was still in the Abyss. And this time, the waters weren't warm and numbing. They were crushing. Everything hurt.

"Open your eyes."

The sweet, melodic voice sounded distant. Muffled. Familiar, but he didn't recognize it.

"Open your eyes, Benton."

He obeyed, and blessed light greeted him, forcing him to squint. But Vorakor's inky tendrils danced on the edge of his vision. The world was a blur. He couldn't see. "Cock..." Groaning again, he tried to move, but his limbs were lead.

"Be still." That beautiful voice. Masculine, but smooth and gentle. "Just breathe, and look at me."

A shape hovered above him, glowing in the flickering orange light. Humanoid. Gradually, a pale, flawless face solidified. Its sparkling, ice-blue eyes held him spellbound. Aldamon.

No wonder Benton felt like he was being crushed to death.

"You lived as an immortal for weeks." The vampire took Benton by the chin. "You're bound to feel sick and weak in this vessel for a time." He turned Benton's head one way, then the other. "It is dying, after all."

Aldamon's overwhelming aura, which all but ground Benton into the table, didn't help. But the sensations of his body became more recognizable by the second.

"Your eye is scarred." The vampire traced a diagonal line across Benton's face with a gentle fingertip. "It won't take a healing spell."

Benton shivered. "I can still see the Abyss..." Traces of it, anyway. Tentacles slithering into the clouded vision of his right eye.

Aldamon raised his brow and gingerly pried open Benton's lids. "I...see it, too."

Benton saw the watery realm a hells of a lot better when it exploded out of his eye, writhing black tendrils shooting for the baron's throat.

The vampire recoiled, catching the tentacles around his forearm. More burst at him from the side, but he snagged those in his other hand.

Benton screamed. Horror-fueled adrenaline stabbed his thighs and chest as silky extensions of Vorakor slid out of his head. The Abyss was in him, erupting from his eye into this world to drag him to hell. He tried scrambling backward on the table, away from the nightmarish thing of which he was the source.

"Calm down." Struggling against the tendrils, Aldamon hollered in another language. Light spilled from his hands at the reverberating words. The tentacles withered and retreated as he grabbed at them with burning fingers and shouted what had to be holy phrases. A little at a time, he fought them into the Abyss.

Into Benton.

Aldamon grabbed Benton's head, clapping a blinding palm over his right eye until the squiggling in Benton's skull stopped and his skin itched so much he wanted to rip it off. The tendrils faded from his vision, and a white-yellow glow replaced them.

The vampire inched his hand from Benton's face. "Let's...keep that eye closed for now."

Benton shut it tight while he gasped for breath. A sob slipped from him without warning. "Gods..." He should ask them for help. Or mercy. Beg. But they'd never listened before.

"I'll find a solution." Aldamon squeezed his hand. *His.* And wiped a strand of his raven hair out of his face. Black. Not gray. His skin was bronze rather than deep brown.

Benton turned his head. Aldamon's face was soul-trembling enough without pity painted all over it. Never mind that Benton couldn't bear to stare into another man's eyes while he wept.

Glaucus's body still rested on the other table. Eyes shut and face slack, he seemed to slumber. The sight didn't do much to stem Benton's tears.

Aldamon swiped more of Benton's hair from his face. "Complications aside, it must feel good to be free of the lorkai hunger."

With the Abyss trying to open a portal through his face, Benton hadn't noticed. But that all-consuming thirst was gone. The relentless, gnawing ache had left him.

A trickle of relief trailed down his vertebrae. "Yeah..."

The vampire snaked his hand beneath the back of Benton's neck and nudged him into a sitting position. "And to be bound to your mistress once again."

Benton hadn't noticed that either. It entered his cognizance with a flood of warmth. Sarlona was with him, embedded in his being. The connection was rooted so much deeper than the familial blood bond in Glaucus's body. He sensed her out there, loving him, and her general distance and soundness.

"Yeah." Skipping his gaze over the pale corpse between the tables, he met the baron's stare. Those eyes were a whole other kind of abyss. A bright, crystalline cold one that sucked Benton into it in an instant.

The more he reoriented and the horror of the actual Abyss faded, the more terrifying the creature hovering over him became. Aldamon seemed to be suppressing the raging, godlike power that paralyzed ancient immortals but wasn't hiding it far below the surface. Why the vampire had done him this favor, he couldn't imagine, but he hadn't forgotten that it came with a price—three nights. Of what?

"Can you stand?" With a hand on Benton's shoulder, the baron urged him to try.

Shaking, Benton threw his legs over the side of the table. His head pounded, and his back ached, but his limbs obeyed. Groaning, he put his weight on his bare feet. Half to his surprise, his legs held.

Aldamon looked him up and down. His clothes were in tatters.

"It seems you need a bath." A sultriness crept into the vampire's voice that prickled Benton's skin. "But I think a drink is in order first."

"Thank the glowin' gods." A drink would help. But then Benton's blood froze. The drink might not be for him. It might *be* him.

Aldamon smiled, placing his hand on Benton's spine. "Let's see what I have in the cellars."

Some of the ice in Benton's veins thawed, but as he snatched his sword from the bench, he caught the empty eyes of the dead boy. The vampire had split his breast and throat without a moment's hesitation.

Aldamon beckoned with a curled finger, and dread settled across Benton's shoulders like a cloak. In wary silence, he followed the vampire down one dim, winding stairway and long, empty hall after another.

Torches roared to life as the two descended the stairs to the cellars, revealing an enormous chamber of bottles stacked on racks from floor to ceiling, holding glass vessels of every conceivable shape and color. A wall of kegs and barrels transected its middle. It may have been the most beautiful room Benton had ever seen.

Aldamon swept a hand around the cellar. "Pick whatever you'd like."

Benton had no idea where to begin, his gaze roving over one dusty rack after another. "For a man who can't drink, you got a lotta booze."

Hand on his chin, Aldamon perused the shelves himself. "Well, it would be indecent of me if I had nothing to offer guests." He homed in on a shelf with a thick layer of dust and wiped a few jugs to reveal the labels. "And I've found an ancient bottle or two lubricates negotiations with other leaders."

Benton would have supposed the primordial monster had more effective tricks for that.

"Ah." Aldamon's arm disappeared into the back of a shelf. "This..." he said, drawing out a squat bottle, "is called dark swallow." He wiped the dust clear to reveal black glass, then pulled the cork with his fingertips and handed the vessel to Benton. "A dwarven concoction brewed with ingredients that are never exposed to the sun." His smile widened while Benton sniffed the murky fluid. "But at the proper dose, it's sure to lighten your heart."

Benton dragged off the bottle, filling his mouth with the thin, aromatic liquid. Earth, metal, and things he didn't recognize danced on his tongue. The fluid burned like fire on the way down, but it warmed his insides the second it hit his stomach. A fuzziness like he'd drunk three or four pints enveloped him. "Shit."

The vampire set the bottle's cork atop one of the barrels that split the room. "Pleasing, yes?"

It was, but Benton couldn't believe things would stay pleasant. Aldamon was sure to want a drink as well. The notion of being in the vampire's arms with fangs at his throat drove the sweat from Benton's pores.

"Thank you. For all of it." He cleared his throat. "I wasn't gonna make it." Given what had tried to tear its way out of him, he still might not.

Aldamon took the bottle, placing it beside the cork. "You would have." He dug into the pocket of his long, gold-embroidered coat and fished out a handkerchief. "But it's my pleasure, Benton." After folding the cloth lengthwise, he reached for Benton's face. "I like you better this way."

Benton fought to keep from shrinking while the vampire tied the handkerchief around his head, covering the right eye. Not having to hold his lid shut was an instant relief.

Aldamon traced a finger across Benton's stubbly cheek. "I've missed this face."

Though Benton wanted to back away, his feet stayed nailed to the stone floor. "You—I really knew you already?"

"Yes." The baron picked up the dark swallow again. "Glaucus asked me to hone your skills with a blade, so you stayed in Gulway for a time." He sat on a crate and gestured for Benton to do the same.

Benton perched as close to the end of the box as he could.

"But he thought it would be less complicated if you forgot everything except the techniques you learned." His smile didn't leak into his eyes this time. "I tend to leave a mark on people. Especially if I tire of condensing myself."

For a split second, the vampire unwound a thread of his terrible power, and the weight of the castle landed on Benton.

Scare the ever-loving shit out of people better characterized the baron's effect.

"It grows wearisome," Aldamon said with a sigh and set the bottle between them. "Like holding in one's gut all day, I imagine." He gestured to the bottle. "Please."

Benton took another sip. A pleasant tingling radiated out from his stomach and worked the tension from his muscles. All the better if he was drunk. He wanted to be good and gone before he ended up in Aldamon's grasp.

His next swallow was a big one and provoked the baron's grin. Feeling like he'd slipped into a warm bath, he relaxed enough to ask his question. "Why am I stayin' here? What do you want from me?"

"What do I want from you?" Aldamon vanished in Benton's blink. "Oh, Benton..." The whisper came from behind, hot and penetrating on his throat. "*Everything.*"

Shaking, Benton reached for the bottle.

Aldamon's hand caught his, stopping it short.

So much for getting blackout drunk. The alabaster fingers crept up Benton's arm, and Aldamon's other hand alighted on his opposite shoulder. A groan slipped out of him when the vampire massaged tender muscles.

"As for why you must stay..." Aldamon's smooth, melodic voice caressed Benton's ears. "Simply to give you time to readjust to your mortal body."

Benton didn't understand why he couldn't adjust in Ashmore with Sarlona.

The vampire squeezed before releasing his grip. "I'm going to look after you... So very carefully..."

Benton might have prayed to hear someone say that a decade ago. Now, it caused his skin to crawl. As did the warm breath on the back of his neck.

"You are adjusting, yes? Feeling better?"

Besides the bone-rattling terror that demon tentacles could shoot out of his eye and a primeval vampire would take him to bed that night, he was. His pains had faded, or he no longer noticed them. He was shaky, never mind half blind with his vision narrowed, hearing muffled, and sense of smell deadened to uselessness, but the excision of that screaming, all-consuming need to grab people and rip the life out of them more than made up for it. The warm buzz of the dark swallow didn't hurt either. "Yeah..."

Aldamon reappeared before him and corked the bottle Benton thirsted for more of. "Then let's have some dinner, shall we?" He seized Benton's hand and tugged him to his feet.

Benton dragged his heels through the dust but couldn't slow their momentum. "I'm the dinner, ain't I?"

The baron smiled wide enough to show his fangs. "My cook is preparing you a meal. Surely, you've missed food?"

Not as much as he'd missed drinking, but food would be good too, and the dark swallow in Aldamon's free hand heartened him.

Instead of the kitchen, the vampire led Benton to a bathing chamber, where a large basin recessed in the mosaic tile waited, steaming.

The baron hooked his fingers into Benton's sword belt and urged him close. "Let's get you bathed."

Benton froze solid while Aldamon worked at the knot that hung just to the inside of his hipbone. "Can I... wash myself?"

His stomach tumbled into his bowel. Sarlona must have felt this way during her first weeks in Ashmore—captive and powerless, almost every shred of autonomy stripped away. Except she'd had *two* monsters and a house full of ruffians to contend with. None worse than him. And she'd thought she'd been given a life sentence, not three nights.

Gods... He shouldn't have been such an asshole.

"If you like." Aldamon didn't sound happy about it, though. "I'll fetch clean clothes." He took Benton's belt and blade, heading for the door. "I think your eye will behave in the short term, but try to keep it closed when you bathe, just in case."

However much Benton hated for his sword and drink to go, a boulder-like weight lifted the second Aldamon went out the door.

Benton groaned into his hands and rubbed the sides of his head. "Oh, cockin' hells."

But this was good. He had his body, and the maddening thirst was gone. So he was in rough shape and had the full attention of a catastrophic hurricane pretending to be a man? That was temporary. He could go home to Sarlona in a few days. And once she got her magic back, she could help him with his cursed eye.

With the baron gone, Benton was happy to tear off his tattered clothes and hop into the bath. He scrubbed himself with the lavender-scented bar left on the pool's ledge, then lay back. Savoring the hot water's embrace, he surveyed the mosaics that coated the chamber and pulsed in the flickering torchlight. Blue and white tiles swirled along the floor like the sea, while greens and browns rose on three walls in the shape of trees. The wall across from him sported more blues, transected by lines of yellow from the sun in the top left corner. He usually washed in a big half barrel inside a room with bare wood walls.

But as the bath cooled, it reminded him of other water. Of depths alive with ebony tentacles that ensnared his limbs and dragged him from the woman he loved to eternal solitude.

The tiling was too dark. There were too many shadows. His breath caught when something brushed against the back of his calf. He jerked, recoiling, but couldn't see anything except his leg. With the unsteady light and the midnight blue of the tiles below him, anything could escape his compromised vision. Rattled, he popped up. His adrenaline surged at the obsidian snake that shot across the bath's surface between ripples. He scrambled from the basin, cursing the absence of his sword, and crashed right into Aldamon.

Spinning, he retreated into the vampire, ready to try and fight the tentacles that were coiled to strike.

"It's all right, Benton. You're all right." The baron wrapped him in a large towel.

Benton gesticulated at the pool. "There's—It's...cockin' Vorakor's horseshit." Nothing seemed to rise from the water after him, but he couldn't see well.

"There's nothing there, Benton." Aldamon held him tight around the waist. "You're safe."

Could the tendrils have been his imagination? Was he losing his mind? All but naked and trapped in the baron's embrace, Benton couldn't catch his breath. "I want my sword."

The vampire loosened his arms, pausing for Benton to take over his grip on the towel before retreating. "It's right there." He waved at the stack of clothes folded on a bench against the far wall. Benton's sword lay atop it. "You might consider pants first, but the choice is yours."

Pants. Pants were critical. Maybe more so than his sword.

Benton put his back to the vampire and bath, telling himself that neither would bother him while he dressed, or one would take care of the other. He half-dried himself before pulling on the underclothes and leather breeches the baron had brought him. The pants fit too well, as though they'd been tailored. Tying on his sword belt, he pivoted to keep his eye on the vampire and the water.

Melodic whispers on his breath and blinding light skipping across his fingers, Aldamon busied himself with some magic in the corner while Benton finished dressing.

The vampire had brought him a crisp linen tunic, a leather jerkin like the one he'd torn, stockings, and boots in his size. Having yet to view his reflection, Benton sidled to the full-length mirror on the other side of the door. A pang of dread hit him behind the sternum as he peeked at the mirror, half afraid he'd see some shadow-corrupted corpse.

It vanished the second he caught a glimpse of himself. His familiar visage—straight nose, strong cheekbones, and square jaw made him smile with bright teeth. All in a coppery skin tone, framed by messy black hair. He was human.

He was him.

Mostly.

The ragged scar running from the right corner of his brow, through his eye, and hugging his nose to tail off across his lips made him look like a veteran of battles lost.

Then there was the strange white-yellow glow leaking between the lashes of his damaged eye...

Benton's grin wilted altogether when Aldamon floated toward him from behind.

The shadows hugged the vampire, and his irises flashed a demonic yellow. "Open your eye if you want."

Benton did. His whole eye beamed with holy light. Of all the people for light to shine from... Grimacing, he shut it. "What—"

"It won't last." The baron passed him the item he'd been fiddling with—an eyepatch. "You'll have to wear this to keep the Abyss at bay. Until I can figure out something permanent."

Benton rubbed the supple leather between his fingers and inspected the patch's underside. A circle of small, elegant symbols etched into it glowed with a faint, golden light. Wards, maybe. He didn't love the idea of holy magic pressed to his skull, but better than it beaming from his eye. Or worse, the hells spilling from him.

Tying on the eyepatch, he snuffed out the light and stared at the mirror. The man peering back was familiar but different from the one dragged into the Abyssal Waters.

He always would be.

But he held out hope that Sarlona would be able to heal him one day. That the Abyss would only haunt his nightmares, not his body.

And that his vision would improve. He wouldn't be able to fight well like this... His right side would be vulnerable, and his depth perception was off... Again, a pit opened in his gut. Sarlona had been devastated when she lost her magic. Having the talent that she believed defined her stolen away...

The hand on his shoulder ripped Benton's attention from the mirror with the weightiness of millennia.

The vampire squeezed. "Let's get you something to eat. Then you should rest."

Benton followed him to a small dining room off the main hall where an impressive spread of fancy food waited. Though he didn't have much of an appetite, he tried most of it, stalling more than anything. Mercifully, the bottle of dark swallow was returned to him. It quelled the storming fear that the baron's intense gaze stirred.

But once Aldamon tired of watching Benton pick at his food and decided it was time to retire, the drink did less to take the edge off than interfere with Benton's ability to walk. He stumbled near the top of the stairs and would've broken his teeth on the marble had Aldamon not caught him under the arm.

Knowing damn well he was about to lose some blood in the baron's arms, Benton's heart pounded to the point of aching as the vampire coaxed him into the same bedroom he'd spent a night in. He shivered when the door shut behind them.

Aldamon floated closer. "If you need anything, just ask."

Benton's throat went too dry to answer.

"I'll put you to sleep once I've finished," the vampire said, snatching his hand.

Benton went cold. The baron might have to search for his blood on the floor. It had surely drained out of him.

Aldamon tugged him nearer until they were a hair's breadth apart. "It won't be so different from when Sarlona feeds."

Benton wasn't sure if fear or some spell pinned him still like a dead bug on display.

The baron took his other hand, then ran his fingers up Benton's shoulders. "On the bed or standing?"

Benton's vision swirled for a second, and he feared he'd lose the opportunity to choose. On his third try, he rasped an answer, "Standin'."

One of Aldamon's arms snaked around his waist, and Benton's vision narrowed even further. Maybe he'd pass out before the vampire even got started.

"Just a little blood tonight..." Aldamon tilted Benton's head by the jaw to expose his throat. "A soft kiss and a dreamless sleep," he whispered.

The heat of Aldamon's breath on his skin passed through Benton, melting the ice in his veins. "Shit..." His voice broke when the vampire kissed his throat, and a coziness enveloped him like the one Sarlona so often swaddled him in.

Benton winced, anticipating the sting of fangs, but the pain never came. The baron only inflicted a gentle draw and a fluttering warmth that Benton's body begged him to sink into.

After a minute, he had no choice. His knees gave out, and he collapsed backward. The vampire held him tighter, leaning over him. Benton wanted to scream at him to make it hurt, to stop the tenderness pulsing in his solar plexus. Instead, he whimpered. Staring at the arched ceiling, he fought to keep the feeling from consuming his entire being.

We're almost done, Aldamon whispered into his head. *Just close your eyes.*

Benton obeyed, but the sweet sensation intensified. It *was* like when Sarlona fed. When she plucked each pleasing string inside him to smother the drain on his energy and make his body sing. Just as it neared the crescendo, his exhaustion swelled. Every muscle relaxed, and he spun into oblivion.

Gods, I've missed your taste...

CHAPTER THIRTEEN

With scant patches of snow lingering only in the darkest shadows around Mast Landing, and the mud soft where the sun shone, the timing was perfect for planting field peas and oilseed without plowing. Sylvanus would be out blessing fields from sunup to sundown.

Sure enough, Sarlona found the old druid in the Cario's easternmost field just before sunset. The sky blackened with the evening and angry clouds as she approached. A perfect metaphor for the storm in her heart. Transforming herself into crystalline waters, she skipped from one overlooked rock to the next without marring the mud or making a sound.

Before letting the pigmentation flood back into her body, she reminded herself how close her former mentor had come to killing the man she loved. She conjured the image of Benton bleeding out on the cobblestone, organs punctured by branches.

"Sylvanus."

He spun but didn't jump. If she'd surprised him, he didn't show it. His face was timeworn and stoic as always. "Sarlona... I thought it might be you."

No doubt he'd put up wards of warning.

She matched the indifference in his expression. "I've been sent by the Council."

He dabbed spirium-imbued river water on the last harvest stone, then offered a few words of prayer to Verdethion, Agria, and the Mother of All. "I don't belong to the SPS. I have no business with the Council."

She forced irritation into her voice. "That's the problem. They want you to join and tasked me with convincing you."

He corked his consecrated water skin and tied his golden sickle to his belt. "You know that I won't."

She did. "It's the only way they'll try to turn me human. I'm running out of time, Sylvanus."

Rather than meet her eyes, he packed up his satchel. Pouches of herbs, crystals, and his athame went into the bag. "It's too late, Sarlona. It was too late the instant you swallowed that monster's defiled Marrow."

"It's not." A growl slipped out. "I've seen it done... I have to try. And you're going to help me this time. You owe me that."

His emerald gaze, flecked with brown, locked on hers as he straightened. "It's not my fault you were too weak in your magic and faith to save yourself."

Weak. She'd been an unsuspecting girl thrown up against ancient monsters and hardened men. All on her own. "I did *everything* I could to stop them." Her voice cracked.

"Not...everything." He tightened his grip on his staff. "If you couldn't flee in this realm, you should have escaped to the next."

She'd tried. But tears would leak into her voice if she told him that.

A few lines in his wizened face smoothed, and his tone mellowed. "I can help you escape now."

The black, hungry thing inside exploded from the depths. Her claws ejected of their own accord, and the fire burning behind her eyes tinted her vision red. "You're the fucking monster, Sylvanus." The words tangled in her roar.

"You shouldn't have returned." The ozone thickened, pricking her nostrils. "I can't allow things that drain the life and magic from this land to haunt them."

If he refused to see the girl she'd been, she'd be the lorkai for him. "I'm not weak *now*. And I don't intend to drain the life and magic from the *land*." Her muscles twitched, ready to move the instant lightning started to form.

"You can't frighten me, Sarlona." A bolt rocketed from the gnarled apex of his staff.

Sarlona skipped clear, dodging the tendrils like they were lobbed balls, and skidded to a stop behind him. "No. I suppose not. I doubt you've felt anything for a century."

He whipped his hand in a swirling motion, and she hopped left when flames twisted up from the ground in a fiery tornado. It roared after her, driving her back with its blistering heat and raining embers across the field. Devastating as the spell would have been had it sucked her in, it couldn't catch her.

She circled toward him, forcing him to end the spell or burn with her. "If you don't want me haunting this place, help undo what's been done to me."

His green robes whipped in the burgeoning wind, and lightning cracked overhead, illuminating his cold stare. "Carapace." The air surrounding him glowed as his shielding snapped into place.

He made a fist over the end of his staff, then opened his hand, splaying his fingers.

Four huge sheets of crackling energy floated from the clouds, cupping to shape electric canopies. From them, static lightning bolts sprouted like tendrils, forming thick curtains. The giant, electrified jellyfish swam at her from each cardinal direction.

She ducked and weaved through the tentacles, gritting her teeth against the sharp jolt each time a thin tendril of electricity split off to zap her nerves.

"You'll never be rid of me, Sylvanus." After darting free of the tentacles, she turned on one, twirling it around her carpal blade. Static pricked along her arm, but she drew in using the claw as if she'd plunged it into the ground and lapped at the magical energy. The massive, electrified jellyfish shriveled, blinking and flashing when its bell crashed upon his shielding. Though not exactly Marrow, the influx of power hummed through her.

She caught the next jellyfish's tentacle on her blade and whipped it down on his shield. "The Gods cursed you with me."

He'd never outright called her a curse, but he'd made her feel like one. And if his claim that the Gods had charged him with her education was true, there had to be a reason.

"It's up to you whether we're enemies or allies, Sylvanus. Whether I'm in your hair as a human or a monster."

He dismissed the remaining jellyfish with a wave of his hand, and for a second, the ice in his expression melted.

Then, the ground parted beneath her feet. Her stomach plummeted when the soil gave way, opening into a great black chasm. She scrambled up the avalanche of loose dirt and rock, stabbing her claws into the side of the pit before it could entomb her under tons of earth. Using the blades to climb, she skittered free from the hole.

As he lifted his hand again, she charged in, hacking at his protective barrier, sapping a bit of its strength with every strike. A fiery burst blasted her back, and he followed it with a fireball that exploded inches behind her.

Blistering heat licked her hamstrings while vines and roots carved across the ground to grab for her. She'd be in trouble if they held her in place long enough for Sylvanus to hit her with an extended stream of fire. Nazarale's amulet could only do so much. Legs pumping, she ripped them from the ground each time they snagged her and sliced them almost as fast as they sprouted. Once she slowed under the burden of too many woody fetters, she knelt, driving her blades into the ground.

As Sylvanus wound up with what would be an inferno, she drew in with all her might, sucking the Marrow from the earth. The tendrils withered and died, drained of life like the small patch of land around her. She peered into his eyes while she did it.

The instant he unleashed his spell, she zipped clear of the flames.

He gazed at the spot where she'd been for a second, that patch of scorched earth atop gray, barren dirt.

She hit his barrier from behind, getting a dozen strikes in before he spun, arms raised.

A swarm rose with his hands. Raven, thread-waisted wasps—whelk wings.

They descended upon her like a cloud, spindly legs seeking bare skin to alight on. She waved them out of her face with one hand and trusted her immortal blood would overwhelm their paralyzing venom and dissolve any eggs they laid in her flesh before the larvae could hatch to eat at her. The burning pain as their overlong abdomens curled and probed her nape, ears, and arms twisted her lips into a snarl but fueled the rage in her strikes.

He snapped off a freeze spell. To her it descended like fog. The air dried and condensed before the brunt of the cold arrived. Instinct widened her veins and shunted blood to her legs.

She sprinted away while the wasps fell, twisted inky snowflakes on the breeze. Frost grabbed at her feet but failed to impede her. With the ground hardened, she only gained traction.

He wheeled, but she darted behind him faster than he could turn, and she hit his barrier another ten times before he sent a starburst radiating from his chest to sweep her back.

Dodging each successive blast of fire that came her way, a familiar sensation swept over her, like adrenaline infused with elation. Power. Strength and skill wielded by her, or at least *with* her, not by wicked hunger. Her muscles hummed with it. And her former mentor was losing steam.

His gesticulations grew courser, and his spells sputtered. Flames that should have melted rock merely charred it. His barrier wavered.

With a flood of bizarre nostalgia washing over her, she paused in her onslaught. The memory of being on the other side of that barrier, exhausted with two calm and confident lorkai wearing through her shielding, flashed into her vision. "Are you done?" Grimacing, he glared at her. In the fifteen years she'd known him, she'd never seen that wild look in his eyes.

Desperation. She smelled it.

Holding his hands flat, he lowered them. "*Crawl.*"

A massive weight smashed her from above, driving her into the mud on her hands and knees.

With a raspy breath, he shook his head and raised his arms. The dark clouds above blackened, and the air buzzed. Static pricked at her skin, lifting her hair. The wavering sheen of his barrier dissolved as he sacrificed it for extra offensive power.

She growled against the crushing weight, her every fiber straining to make her rise, to dig into the dirt and squirm clear of her impending doom.

With an atmosphere-rending blast, the huge lightning bolt cracked into being. The world blanched, an expanse of white-blue, while the air and ground shook in a deafening boom.

He stared at the sooty patch of smoldering earth and bubbling glass where she'd knelt.

Between the flash and her speed, he hadn't seen her scramble clear and circle him. Brimming with adrenaline and indignation, her heart and mind emptied of all else. She speared him from behind on one carpal blade.

Regret slapped her with his first choking gurgle.

She caught him when she slipped her blade free, guilt spreading over her with his blood. Lowering to her knees, she cursed herself for running through the old man who'd helped rear her. His chest heaved, and his robes stained wine red as she rested his head on her lap and her hand on his jaw.

Weaving her will into his body, she sealed the wound. "I could never kill you, Sylvanus." His right lung was the only organ she'd hit. The blood vessels, muscles, and tendons were simple enough to reconnect. Repairing the lung tissue required more focus, knitting the delicate membranes together and sealing them in place. But she'd been studying and practicing, working to heal Ashmore's sick and injured, whether the Silsorian peasants wanted treatment from a heathen or not.

After hacking up blood for a minute, he took raw, grating breaths. He'd live.

She bore down on his adamantine mental protections. It didn't matter how strong they were. He couldn't keep her out of his brain while she was in physical contact with him. Gut twisting, she forced her way in. "I need your help. Don't make me *take* it."

She let him taste the threat. Contrived sentiment and loyalty burgeoned in his heart with the slightest unraveling of his thoughts.

Her stomach roiled with disgust as she tugged on the strings of his inner workings, but none of this had been her idea. She hadn't asked to be made a lorkai. Or to be so devastatingly betrayed. He could have helped her in the first place, like a mentor should.

After sucking out what sweet, thin vapors of Marrow she could find left in him, she lifted her fingers from his flesh. "Please... Do this one thing for me, and I'll never darken your door again."

He clenched his jaw and shut his eyes. "I'll join," he said, rasping. "You have my word."

CHAPTER FOURTEEN

A ldamon pressed closer. "Just relax, my love."

Benton shrank into the headboard. Shoving at the vampire to no avail, he shook his head. He couldn't do it again already. Half a dozen times that day, he'd been drawn into the baron's embrace and sucked on. Now, taken to the creature's bed and given a sickening new epithet, he was sure Aldamon intended to put more than fangs in him. "Wait..."

The vampire forced Benton's chin up and kissed his throat.

"Pl—" Benton's plea melted into a groan at the tingling, bone-deep flush of the baron's bite. "Gods, ain't you full yet?" Everything fluttered when Aldamon pulled him down and lay atop him. The evil kiss intensified, and a tender heat bloomed in Benton's core. It swallowed him until he lost himself and arched his back, driving his hips into the monster. "Dammit... You're makin' it feel too—" He whined as the storm inside swelled, threatening to drown him. It would break him into a million pieces. Little shards that would belong to Aldamon instead of Sarlona. "*Stop.*"

The vampire withdrew from Benton's throat and lifted some of his weight but didn't climb off or ease the throbbing warmth. "Your taste brings me such bliss, Benton... It would be selfish of me not to reciprocate."

As those cold eyes bore into him, Benton remembered what he was dealing with. There was nothing human left in the thing on top of him. He should have kept his mouth shut and thanked the gods that the vampire wasn't eating him alive.

Unable to stand another second of Aldamon's stare, Benton focused on the wine-red canopy shifting in the cold breeze from the cracked balcony door. "I'm Sar's, I don't wanna…"

The vampire dipped, licking the blood from Benton's throat before it trickled onto the sheets. "Allow me to fetch her. She can watch while I teach you what true pleasure is." His fangs, tinged pink with Benton's blood, peeked from his grin.

The room swirled. Every fiber of Benton's being tensed.

"Then I'll instruct *her*." Aldamon's expression grew still more devilish. "I have so been longing to taste her… Ever since Glaucus confessed her existence." The nauseating ache in the vampire's voice scorched Benton's veins. "A lorkai so powerful… She'll sate me for centuries."

Benton punched him in the kidney before good sense could intervene. *So. Incredibly. Stupid.*

A slight wince wrinkled the vampire's alabaster visage, but a smile leaked into his eyes, intensifying their sparkle. "Does that mean you want me all to yourself?" His smile brightened in Benton's silence. "Just imagine…Sarlona and me devouring you at once…"

Benton shoved the thought away. His heart would give out.

"Then, the two of us taking her together… One invading her—"

"Keep *away* from her," Benton spat, words like sandpaper scratching over itself.

The baron raised his brow. "As the Lady of Ashmore, she'll have to meet me eventually."

Benton cleared his throat and returned his gaze to the dancing silk above them. "Will she have to fuck you eventually?"

"No…" Aldamon shrugged. "Most women desperately want to, though—and I delight in indulging them."

Benton took a deep breath. "Do *I* have to?"

"Of course, you don't *have* to." The words offered little relief when Aldamon leaned in and whispered in Benton's ear, "But after you've *begged* for the privilege, I'll relish indulging you, too." The vampire patted his cheek and rose.

Benton shook his head as if that could dislodge the creature's words or undo the hot breath that had caressed his ear.

Aldamon touched two fingers to Benton's wound, healing it like all the other holes that'd been put in him that day. After licking his fingertips, he shut the balcony door.

Benton squirmed while some unseen critter slithered up and down his spine "Well, I don't— I..." Telling the monster that he didn't want anything to do with him might not be the smartest idea. Aldamon had suppressed his panic-inducing aura so far, but that godlike power lurked just below the surface.

"It's all right, Benton." The baron smiled, eyes laughing as he straightened his coat. "I have some business tomorrow, so you'll be happy to learn I won't vex you during the day."

Benton did his best to stifle his sigh of relief.

"But there is something I want you to do for me."

"What...?" Swallowing hard, Benton tried to rise. His head swam, and he collapsed on the mattress.

Aldamon yanked off Benton's boots, one in each hand. "Tomorrow, go to the library and pick a book to read."

Benton snorted.

"You can tell me about it after dinner." Aldamon set the boots by the door.

"You're givin' me homework?" Sarlona had been making Benton practice, but he still couldn't read well. Why the vampire would want him to, he couldn't imagine.

"I have a small children's section," Aldamon said with a grin, then vanished.

Benton didn't dare contemplate why.

CHAPTER FIFTEEN

The nightmare was always the same. Black tendrils wound around Benton's limbs and ripped him away from Sarlona. Every night, they dragged him deeper into the never-ending darkness. Farther from her and closer to some massive, unseen cloud of pure doom that hungered for him. Waking from it brought no relief now that he was in his own body. His eye opened to a different nightmare. One where he was trapped with a blood-sucking tornado and ebony tendrils still danced on the edge of his vision.

All that was just an epilogue to his traditional nightmares of flames, crispy corpses, and the big, accusatory eyes of his dead kid brother.

Benton staggered to his boots after tossing about in Aldamon's bed, following what couldn't have been more than two hours of sleep. Still woozy, he leaned against the wall to get them on. Though he was sure the vampire had stripped him of it in the dining room, his sword belt hung on a hook by the door. Tying it about his hips lightened his burden despite the extra weight.

He crept down the dim, empty halls, fearing his footfalls might call the vampire and provoke another intimate embrace or bloody kiss. If Aldamon was home, though, he let Benton reach the cellars unmolested.

After grabbing two bottles at random near the cellar door, he headed for the library, cringing each time he clinked the stolen vessels together. He might as well get his assignment over with. Pointless though the task seemed, he wasn't about to invite the baron's irritation with stubbornness.

The enormous, two-level chamber lined with bookcases twice Benton's height surely rivaled any library in Aven. Unlike the gloomy corridors, it glowed with soft starlight, magical lanterns twinkling from hangers along the shelves, and twin chandeliers sparkling above. He wandered around the imposing archive, sipping at a bottle of what he guessed was elven birch spirit until he found a corner brimming with thin, colorful spines and picked a book full of illustrations.

After settling into an overstuffed chair, he went to work. But the words didn't string together like they had for Glaucus's brain. His thoughts drifted from fairytales to Sarlona within minutes, then sank to inky tentacles and what Aldamon might have in store for him on his final night in Gulway. The pages tired him, at least. He fell asleep before finishing a quarter of the book.

The sun spilled throughout much of the library when Benton woke with a start—a stark and welcome contrast to the lightless motif of his Abyssal nightmares.

A tray of tiny, sticky cakes sat on the small table before him, garnished with unfamiliar fruit, and a glass of milk of all things. His book waited beside it, shut but marked with a ribbon inside. After a few bites of sugar and spice that he washed down with whiskey from his second bottle, he slalomed to the three arching, ten-foot-tall windows that loomed front and center of the chamber.

Savoring the warmth from the midday sun beating in, he stretched his stiff neck. The city below was clean and bright—opposite of the few he'd known. Temple steeples towered above their neighbors without crumbling stones. The roofs of shops formed tidy bands, scarcely a shingle out of place. Tiered, multilevel residences stood in neat rows along the hillside, not one with a shattered window or broken shutter. Colorful banners bearing Gulway's golden stag hung across swept, cobbled streets.

But however lovely the city was, Benton's gaze fixed on the distant gate and the hill beyond the wall. Sarlona was out there, waiting for him. And if the baron was true to his word, Benton could go home to her tomorrow. He just had to endure one more night…

After retrieving his book, he wandered. He found a sunny spot, read a page or two, then moved on. Eventually, a double-paned glass door lured him onto an ancient patio overlooking the sea. Aldamon hadn't forbade him from going outside. So once Benton grew too cold in the shade of the castle's shadow, he followed a narrow path that wound down the cliff to a small, sheltered beach. He nestled into the sun-warmed sand, tucking himself between two rocks to break the brisk spring breeze, then returned to the book.

The sun sank well behind the cliffs before he could finish it, and the shadows grew long. However much he wanted the book over with before Aldamon arrived, he'd have to find a warmer, brighter spot to suffer the last few pages.

He closed his book and gazed at the sea, wondering if he should throw a prayer out to it like Sarlona would, for her sake.

Eels wriggled in his gut as a dark, serpentine shape slithered along a cresting wave. A strand of kelp, caught in the current, he hoped. But more stringy shadows appeared with the next rising swell, and they swam for shore with familiar undulations.

Blood turning colder than the spring seawater, he dropped the book and bolted for the narrow, surf-battered path on the far side of the beach. His boots sank too deep as he tried to power himself across the soft, dry sand, thighs burning. Three otherworldly tentacles shot in front of him. He drew his blade and severed their ends with a roundabout swipe. The sky and sea darkened to imitate the lightless Abyss while more tendrils bore down on him. One caught his ankle just as he reached the rocky path, slamming him into the stone. Panic throbbed through his muscles, but he flipped around and sliced the tentacle with a quick slash before scrambling to his feet. The path blurred ahead. His compromised depth perception cost him a slip in the dim light, and he smashed again into the rock.

He got his arms under him, but his sword went flying, and his face hit his hand, knocking his eyepatch onto his forehead. Vorakor's wicked tentacles burst from his skull with a cold rush.

Doubling back, the tendrils spun him and slithered toward the black sea. Abyssal goo wept from his open scar and filled his mouth, garbling his screams. The bitter tar was too thick to spit out, and he didn't dare swallow. It stuck to his front and caked him in sand as he slid over it like a slug, dragged by the nightmarish appendages.

He tried to push himself backward, straining with all his might, and dug the toes of his boots into the sand. But little by little, the horrific tentacles towed him nearer to their larger fellows, the serpentine sentinels that towered over the waves.

He should've known he couldn't escape the Abyss. Only wet, eternal damnation lay ahead.

Until a blinding white light blew up in his face.

The tendrils hissed and shrank as Aldamon's presence crashed into Benton like a tidal wave. His sword flashed in the vampire's hand, pruning the hellish vines. The baron hauled Benton by the waist with one arm and crushed him to his side. After tossing the sword, Aldamon grabbed the fresh tentacles sprouting from Benton's eye with a glowing hand. They writhed, shrieking in Benton's skull—and sluggishly sucked back inside.

With a palm full of holy light clapped over the corrupted eye, Aldamon chanted unfamiliar words in Benton's ear. The melodic, accented song sent the silky tendrils tingling down Benton's throat and into whatever portal to the Abyss lay in his center.

He choked on the last of the vile molasses. "The water..." Staring at the sea of towering tentacles, he pressed into the vampire. He might as well have tried to retreat into an iron wall.

"It's all right," Aldamon said, breaking his chant. "There's nothing in the water..."

Benton blinked, and the tendrils vanished. A peaceful expanse of gray-blue stretched for miles to meet a pink-tinged sky in the late afternoon light. The only things interrupting the horizon were a few sails drifting in the distance.

"But that's interesting." Tilting his head at the slime that had spilled from Benton's wound, Aldamon drew him backward.

The vile liquid thinned and ran across the sand in trickles, coalescing in a crystalline pool of thin shadows.

Benton recognized that puddle. Its placid, glassy surface belied its infinite depth and the endless black tendrils inhabiting it—the Abyssal Waters.

He wasn't in them anymore. They were in him.

Aldamon twisted, spinning Benton away to collapse in a heap. "I've never seen them appear this way..."

He crept closer to the hellish portal, fingers flashing with blinding light while he uttered foreign phrases. Benton's skin itched like a poison ivy rash with every word, but as the vampire drew his hands together, the pool condensed, then vaporized.

Chest heaving, Benton gaped at the sand where it'd been. His wrists hurt, and his left ankle throbbed. He was pretty sure he'd pissed himself.

Aldamon scooped him up, and the world blurred. A second later, they appeared in his bedchamber.

Benton's eyes watered as the baron set him on the edge of the bed. Removed from the vampire's arms, a chill settled over him. What would he do when Aldamon wasn't there to save him?

"Did you enjoy it?" the vampire asked, retying Benton's eyepatch in place.

For a second, Benton thought he meant having Vorakor's tendrils explode from his face. Then he noticed the book of fairytales on the bed beside him.

He snorted. "No."

Aldamon coaxed Benton's arms out of his jerkin, then pulled his shirt over his head. "What didn't you like about it?"

Wiping the tear hanging in his good eye with a sandy palm, Benton answered, "That it's a book."

The vampire unknotted Benton's sword belt next. "Which words didn't you know?"

"Are you cockin' serious?" Benton twitched when Aldamon undid his pants, but he was almost grateful for the touch. The vampire was warm. And it seemed Vorakor couldn't rip him from Aldamon's grasp. For now, Benton was safe.

A smile reached the baron's eyes. "I am."

Benton picked up the book and flipped through it while the vampire yanked off his boots and stockings. "This one."

"Conscience," Aldamon said, glancing at the page. His smile brightened. "Do you know what it means?"

Benton snorted again, and a grin crept onto his face. "You wouldn't think so, but yeah."

"Any others?"

Benton opened to another page and pointed.

Aldamon hauled him to his feet. "Mischievous. I'm certain you're familiar with that one." He tugged Benton's pants at the hip. "Everything off."

Heart pounding, Benton stripped. It would be okay. Anything was better than drowning in the Abyss.

"Lie down while I excuse myself for a moment." Aldamon vanished.

Benton obeyed, and the instant his head touched the pillow, the baron reappeared with a vial of manna.

"Holy magic does not come naturally to me." Aldamon shot back the potion. "But...I think I'd better have a closer look, regardless."

Benton shrank against the bed when the vampire laid one hand on his forehead and the other on his abdomen. Both tingled as a serene, golden light leaked from the monster's palms.

"I'm afraid this will be rather invasive..." Aldamon's eyes flared yellow, and he lifted his hands a hair's breadth. The golden light washed over Benton, cooling and burning his skin like mint oil. "I'll make it pleasant, if I can."

"Just get this Abyssal shit outta me. I don't care how you do it." Anything to keep the lightless hell from tearing out of his face and trying to drag him into it. Or worse—Sarlona.

But a deep yank seemed to pull on Benton's very soul, and dread flooded him.

He grunted with the second draw on his being. The third ripped him into another plane with an awful snap. The chamber went black, and everything but Aldamon disappeared.

Benton lay in a dark void with the vampire at his side. Nothing was beneath him, nor above. The only light came from Aldamon's hands and eyes and Benton's golden, glowing skin. He couldn't move.

The vampire brushed his consciousness. "You'll have to open for me, Benton." Aldamon pressed on his stomach while wrenching at something deep within.

How his mental protections didn't dissolve at the primeval immortal's lightest touch, Benton didn't know. But as much as he wanted whatever this was to be over and the squirming obsidian snakes out of him, he couldn't lower his barrier. Some instinct wouldn't allow it, warning of utter ruin. "Just bust in."

"I might break you." He stroked Benton's forehead and stomach. "Let me in, my love..."

The pressure on Benton's mind built, and something swelled in his chest, longing to spill out. Innate terror wrestled with sweet sensations until the tender caress on his consciousness won. He groaned, and the weakest section of his wall crumbled. The monster seeped inside.

Benton's thoughts slowed like a half-frozen river. Aldamon's paralyzing presence made him cower in the corner of his own mind.

"Deeper now..." The vampire's fingers slid into Benton's hair, holding his head steady as his other hand kneaded the spot where the two halves of his ribcage met.

Benton arched, straining against the palm that spilled heat into the space below his sternum. His core trembled when something rose in his chest and sent blood to his cheeks. He was going to shatter. Into what, he didn't know.

"Succumb..." the vampire purred.

Benton balled his fists and tightened his thighs, whining. Then, in a rush of elation, he cracked down the middle. Electricity and light shot out of his chest, and his body burned away.

In an instant, there was nothing left of him but golden bones. He wasn't even a whole skeleton. Just a shattered ribcage and a sparkling yellow light glowing in its center.

But somehow, Benton felt it, saw it. His flesh and blood were gone, yet warmth and adrenaline coursed through him. Aldamon still hovered over him, fingers buried in his soft light.

"What're you doin' to me?" His voice sounded thin, ethereal, and miles in the distance. How he made any sound at all, he couldn't imagine.

The vampire hooked strands of Benton's light in his fingers and drew them from the gilded bones. "Consider it spiritual dissection."

As the baron plucked free a thread of Benton's light to examine, heat raced up and down it. Benton wished he could shut his nonexistent eyes and tried to will away the sensation. Instead, he gawked in horror while Aldamon sifted through him, unraveling bits of him like tangled yarn, each tug on his light accompanied by a warm flush.

"You gotta stop. Gods, you gotta put me back together..."

"Don't fuss, Benton." Tilting his head, Aldamon peered into the light. He pinched something that made Benton vibrate. "Here we are."

This strand was black and coiled tightly in response to Aldamon's attempts to draw it out. Rooted deep, it rebounded each time he hauled on it. Finally, he grabbed hold and ripped.

Benton screamed, pain exploding in his bones, eye, and soul. Ice water poured over him as the inky wisp grew and solidified. Rearing up to strike, it split into a dozen strands, lengthening and writhing.

Blinding light shot from Aldamon's hands while he wrestled with Vorakor's tendrils. His melodic voice deepened into a boom that shook the darkness. But for each tentacle that hissed and withered in his glowing grasp, another sprouted, winding upward until a mass of ebony vines towered above them like an animated tree.

As they whipped at his face, Aldamon changed tactics, blasting them with streams of light. He shoved them, one by one, stuffing them into the golden glow in Benton's center.

Aldamon's face resembled pale stone as he stared with hollow eyes into the illumination.

Minutes passed before he sucked his teeth and ran his fingers through his hair. "I can't extract Vorakor's curse." He set his hands on each side of Benton's glow. "Even if I put you in Glaucus's body..." He shook his head, expression dour. "He has you, Benton... But...you're not damned yet..."

Benton didn't believe him. When the vampire drew in and wisps of light wafted from the fluorescing orb in his center to Aldamon's lips, dread hit Benton like a sledgehammer.

"What—" Benton's thoughts slipped away. Then, they sloshed back, ebbing and flowing. Aldamon wasn't moving, yet he grew closer. Bits of those golden bones turned to dust, and the vampire breathed them in. "Stop..." Benton's very essence thinned and emptied. Existential terror flooded in to replace it. His next words weren't words.

"It's okay." With Aldamon's deep inhale, the world blinked out, then back. "I'll keep you safe."

Benton whined. A warmth inside swelled and released with the flickering of the light.

"Don't struggle." The vampire's luminescent eyes rolled back. "Let yourself go."

Bliss tried to swallow Benton along with Aldamon. He sputtered out before fading back to a dimmer light. "Gods dammit, *no*, Aldamon... You cockin' monster!" His consciousness shrieked in the void. "You're a cockin' soul-eater?" All the crushing horror exuded by Aldamon's aura, all his elemental dreadfulness, made perfect sense.

Some of the hideous nirvana left the monster's face. "No. I..." He sipped at the last of the golden dust that had been Benton's ribs. "I'll keep you from the Abyss. I'll hold you in sweetness until the end of time."

Benton's panic smashed against the thought-breaking euphoria of absorption into a higher being—the end of all worldly concern—judgments, loneliness, individualism... "You soul-suckin' son-of-a-bitch. I ain't ready to go anywhere." Despite the tender ache begging him to dissolve into Aldamon, he put every ounce of will and intention toward holding himself into being. "Gods, please don't do this to me, Aldamon..."

"You won't cease to be." The monster drew in again, and they groaned together as he ate more of Benton's soul. "It will be like flitting in and out of a pleasant dream." His eyes shut with the next draught.

Static prickled through Benton's consciousness, numbing his thoughts for a minute. "Gods, you never meant to help me..." How could Benton have believed that? "You just wanted '*everything.*'" He was about to get it. "You wanted my cockin' *soul* this whole time..."

The monster must have needed Benton to open first. To *let* him sink claws into his being. Then he could really feed. And Benton had fallen for it.

"No, Benton..." Aldamon's voice was everywhere. It was everything. "It's okay... It's almost over..."

The monster seemed all around him, impossibly close. Benton's light cooled to the glow of a few lightning bugs with Aldamon's breath.

"You soul-cockin' bastard... *Stop.*" Benton panted despite a lack of lungs, on the verge of splintering. Once he did, his pieces would never come back together. "You said you'd help, and you're gonna murder me and take my soul?" Benton was cracking, breaking, ending... He'd never reunite with Sarlona. "I wanna go home to Sar." He'd beg. He'd do anything. "Don't take me from her. Please, Aldamon, don't do this. Please... *Please...*"

Instead of bursting into nothingness and being absorbed into a primordial black hole disguised as a man, Benton slammed into his body. He blinked, unsure if he really lay on a bed in Gulway or if he only existed inside Aldamon.

"I'm sorry." The monster half sat on the edge of the bed and squeezed Benton's hand. "I... With you... Perhaps I wasn't thinking straight. Too pessimistically, I am certain."

The pain in Benton's ankle convinced him that he truly existed in his physical form. He couldn't contemplate the alternative. Nothing had taken his soul. Two horrifying entities had tried, but he still owned it—for now.

As the adrenaline of near obliteration ebbed, tears leaked from his eyes.

Aldamon frowned. "And I've terrified you..."

Shaking, Benton fumbled with the blanket to cover his lap. He was okay. Alive with his soul. "Can I please go home?"

Aldamon scooted to the foot of the bed and cradled Benton's sprained ankle. "In the morning." A green light leaked from the vampire's fingers, and the pain evaporated.

Morning couldn't come fast enough. "I need a drink..."

Aldamon vanished only to reappear a few seconds later with an uncorked bottle. "Benton... No one can clear that curse from your eye except the man who put it there."

He was doomed then. If he ever saw Amenduil again, it would be to stick a blade in him, not beg him to undo what he'd done. Sitting up, Benton took the drink and chugged, not bothering to inspect the label or even sniff the contents. Earthy, metallic liquid coated his tongue and sent warm shivers through his limbs the instant it hit his stomach—dark swallow.

"I can put you in Glaucus's body if you wish." Aldamon sat beside him. "It won't hide your soul from Vorakor, but at least the Abyss wouldn't slither out of you."

"No." As nightmarish as the Abyssal curse was, unlike the lorkai's unrelenting hunger, it seemed to strike intermittently. Sarlona might not be able to cure it, but she'd have ideas for managing it.

"Then I'll add a holy enchant to your sword before you go, in case you must turn it on yourself," Aldamon said.

Imagining falling face-first onto his blade to repel Amenduil's curse, Benton rubbed his jaw.

The monster grasped Benton's shoulder. "Have Sarlona give you another dose or two of her quick before she returns to the Council."

Benton grimaced and narrowed his eye, stomach flipping. Swallowing lorkai vomit wasn't something he wanted to reexperience. The wicked secretion had all but ripped him apart the last time. Never mind that drinking it seemed like a good way to get made back into a lorkai.

Aldamon dragged his fingertips across Benton's throat, tipping his head to the side. "I doubt it will do much to fight off the Abyss, but it will improve your senses. Perhaps that will compensate for your visual impairment."

With Aldamon so close, Benton couldn't worry about his new disadvantage or the evil tendrils lurking in his soul. He contorted to take a sip of the dark swallow as the vampire leaned nearer and whispered against his throat.

"And...it will make you taste even more divine for when we next meet."

Aldamon's lips touched his skin, and a warm flutter started in his core. Benton shut his eye, shuddering as the vampire fell upon him. Dark dread bubbled through the thrumming pleasure that raced along his nerves. Even if he survived until morning with some blood left and his soul intact, there was no escaping Aldamon.

CHAPTER SIXTEEN

The sight of Benton trudging down the muddy road warmed Sarlona more than the afternoon sun filtering through the canopy. He wore the face she'd fallen in love with and the body she'd bound.

"Darlin'…" His low, gruff voice caressed her ears, and his lips twisted into his beautiful grin. The cool breeze delivered his delightful scent, rousing every type of hunger. "Couldn't wait to get your hands on me, huh?"

She rushed to him, crushing him in a hug. He groaned as he squeezed her back. That sound… The scent of him, the beat of his heart, his muscular thighs, the perpetual stubble lining his square jaw, and that stupid grin all lightened her heart and burned her face with a smile. He was him again. He was perfect.

It took all her control not to slip her hands under his shirt and taste him. "Thank the Gods you're all right."

His arms trembled as they tightened so hard she couldn't draw breath, and he rested his cheek on her head. "I am now, sweetheart…"

But beneath the scent of solace lurked anxiety, and his muscles stayed tense when he should have melted in her embrace. No. He wasn't all right.

The oppressive aroma of a primordial immortal was all over him. Then there was the eyepatch.

Despite his attempt to keep her clasped to his chest, she lifted her head to search his face. "You lost your eye…"

The reagents would cost a small fortune, but she could fashion him a magical replacement. Once she could cast.

The delicate, aromatic scent of bliss gave way to a puff of dread as she snaked her arm between them, fingers seeking his cheekbone.

His heart jumped, and his spine went rigid. "I... It's still there. It..." He turned his head.

With a frown, she rested her fingertips on his throat and tapped into his energies. A second later, she seeped into his consciousness.

He softened, groaning, but when she set her mind on his memories of the last few days, his pulse quickened, and he fumbled to screen off that part of himself. "Sar, wait..."

As adept as he'd become at fortifying his mental defenses in Glaucus's body, he couldn't block her in his own. Not with her quick fused to his bones and her touch governing his physiology.

"What's..." Determined, she pushed through the fog. Only to slam into black adamantine and the mental image of a pair of icy blue eyes. Eyes that saw into her and sent a shock to her solar plexus. She started, recoiling in mind and body. The haunting eyes echoed in her vision like she'd peered at the sun beyond the bursting buds above rather than into Benton's being.

He winced. "I don't want you lookin' there." His voice cracked. "Neither does he, I guess."

"That's the baron?" She sank into Benton, refusing to be driven from her own Bound. "What did he..."

"Yeah. I don't..." His voice trailed into a whisper. "He... He ain't just a vampire... He's a soul-eater."

She stiffened and lifted her head from his chest. "Soul-eaters are cosmic, they're not—"

"I know what he tried to— I know what I saw, Sar." His heart raced, and his breaths shallowed. "Just...*know* that. In case he comes knockin'." He stared at branches that had only just begun to come to life. "But I don't wanna talk about it more than that."

Her guts hollowed out at what might have happened to him. About what might be so awful that he'd fear sharing it with her. "I'm sorry, Benton..." She stroked his cheek and manipulated the right levers to flood him with warmth and calm. His uncovered eye rolled, and she held him aloft to keep him from sinking into the cold mud. "It's okay."

It wasn't. But maybe it would be before long. "Can I peek at your eye?" she asked as he regained his feet. "Maybe I can heal it."

He grabbed her wrist before her fingers met supple leather. "You can't. Amen had some nasty magic on that knife." More anger than fear etched itself into his face. "It's cockin' cursed. Abyssal tendrils come out of it."

"Of your *eye*?" She gritted her teeth while the monster inside thrashed. If there'd been anyone to unleash it on other than Benton, she might have let it go. He was *her* Bound, carrying her quick. Yet both Vorakor and the Baron of Gulway thought they could leave their marks in him. She balled her fists, and a scarlet glow encircled her field of view when her eyes flared red.

They had no right.

The monster didn't care how absurd that sounded. How wrong. "I have to see it," she said, fighting to keep the growl out of her voice. "I need to know how bad it is." She couldn't use spells to read whatever magic had embedded in his face, but she might get some hint of what she was dealing with.

"It's pretty cockin' bad, Sar." His hand drifted to his hilt. Whether his instincts were to fight her off or the curse, it didn't matter. He wasn't capable of either. "I ain't lettin' Abyssal bullshit squirm outta me to drag us *both* into the Waters."

"I'm not afraid, Benton." She should have been. But Vorakor had passed on the opportunity to swallow her in the Abyss when he'd stolen Benton. Or maybe he couldn't take her. Maybe her faith or species prevented it.

He dropped his hand. "Well, I am."

Another spike of rage tried to release the demon within. "No one is taking you from me again."

He snorted, but some of the tension left his shoulders. No threat laced his movements as he pulled his blade. "It's got a holy enchant on it now." he said and passed her the sword.

The hilt burned in her grip, tingling like her hand had fallen asleep. She didn't dare contemplate what that meant.

"I got Silsorian holy water, too," he said, digging into his belt pouch.

The vial of luminescent fluid added to the prickling in her hand when she tucked it between her palm and the sword grip.

He stiffened but didn't recoil when her fingertips alighted on his cheekbone. Gingerly, she slid the patch up on his brow, exposing his cursed eye.

He blinked, then held it open while she peered into it.

The electric blue that had captivated her on so many occasions mingled with milky swirls, but the eye was whole. And enchanting as ever—in an otherworldly, haunted way.

She forced a small smile. "You're still beautiful, you know."

He grinned. "I know. That ain't my concern."

She stroked his thick lashes with one fingertip, then pried his scarred lids wider with her thumb and forefinger.

If the injury exuded an Abyssal aura, she couldn't sense it. But after a few seconds of inspecting the eye, something stirred behind it. Between the clouded swirls, the remains of his iris and pupil grew deeper. Like she could be sucked into them. Then, a black shadow swam out of the center, crossing the white. Another shot after it. Little ebony worms wriggled just beneath the surface.

He grabbed her wrist but couldn't dislodge her hand. "They're gonna come out..." His voice shook with the rest of him.

"Is it painful?"

"No...not 'til they started tryin' t—" His breath caught as one of the tiny tendrils phased through his cornea.

It stretched toward her, thickening to the size of a small snake. Three more, thinner and shorter, emerged a second later.

Frozen with horror and fascination, she didn't retract her hand, even while the three smaller tendrils wound around her wrist and crept onto her forearm. The fourth grazed its tip along her cheek in a silky caress.

His heart thundered, and his rapid, shallow breaths rocked his body. But if the tendrils weren't hurting him...

She twisted her hand to run the inky tentacles between her fingers. The smaller snakes rubbed her knuckles, and the larger nuzzled her jaw.

"They seem...friendly." Whether they displayed Benton's affection or Vorakor's, she wasn't sure.

Had the prayer she'd offered, begging the Abyss for Benton's soul, stained hers? Could the lorkai quick have done the same?

He cursed under his breath. "They ain't."

Furrowing her brow, she nudged the tendrils at his eye. "Try to draw them in."

He swore again. "I can't."

"Try." She had a hunch.

After cursing a third time, he shut his good eye. Whether he tried or not, the tendrils remained.

"Gods cockin' dammit, Sar, *help* me." He opened his eye, glaring. "Gimme the holy water."

She hid his blade and vial behind her. "Not yet."

Amenduil's terrible tendrils were under his control. And when she'd channeled the Abyssal Lord in one of her darkest moments, she'd commanded the tentacles that burst from her. Granted, they'd sprouted from her back, not her eye, but Benton's shouldn't be so different. And she wasn't convinced that a cursed dagger alone could have done this to him.

The kind of communion that might occur after soaking in the realm of a god for weeks, though... *That* could imbue someone with an extension of the deity who dwelled in it. Such a link would be harder to dislodge than even the most stubborn curse. But an individual could attune with it to some degree. After all, much of her mastery over the waves had come from being buffeted by them.

She ran her fingers through the horrifying appendages and retreated. They kissed her curled fingertips as she gestured for Benton to follow, straightening after her but not striking. "Come on."

Taking his hand, she led him off the road to the base of an ancient oak that called to her. She tossed the sword and holy water into last year's browned and grayed leaves.

"What're you doin'?" He lunged for his weapon, but she stopped him short.

"I want to try something." She clasped her other hand over the one she'd trapped. "But I need to take control."

He puffed. "Do what you gotta do."

Weaving herself into his body, she grabbed the helm.

He jerked and raged on the inside, every fiber railing against the alien influence.

Buried where voluntary and involuntary met, she found something dark. Something she could touch—a black well of magic fed by the Abyss. It churned excitedly as she peered at it—roiled with glee while she dipped her fingers into it.

Though slow to obey, the tendrils went limp at her command. They straightened, stiffening like lances to either side of her head when she demanded, then coiled up her arm.

She withdrew, releasing him. "They're...yours, Benton. You have to control them."

A pungent mix of terror and fury bloomed in the air. His lips curled into a snarl. "I *can't*," he yelled, shaking out his arms as if trying to get something off him. "If I could, why'd they try and drag me into the damned Abyss?"

She took a deep breath. In his heart, he knew the answer. "Because you think you belong there."

His jaw locked, and he stared past her.

"It'll be all right, Benton. We'll figure it out." She snuck her hand under the tendrils to cradle his cheek and snaked the other around his lower back to pull him near.

His gaze sought hers, and he softened in her arms. "I just…" He slumped. "What if they try to hurt *you*?"

"They won't. They can't harm lorkai." Fueled by Marrow, they couldn't endure her grip once her fingertips glowed blue. She smiled. "It's okay."

It had to be. And she had to prove it to him.

Ignoring the awful protrusions from his scarred but beautiful eye, she craned her neck and kissed him.

His arms enveloped her like a trap, and his obsidian tentacles mimicked them, snaring her waist and shoulders to hug her tight.

Suppressing a shiver, she flicked her tongue to part his lips. He tasted sweeter than ever.

More tendrils slid from his eye as he drove against her with hungry need, each lengthening and thickening. One wound itself through her fingers. Another loosely encircled her throat. A third slipped beneath her collar and down her spine. She stiffened when it curved across her side to rest in the hollow of her hipbone.

He withdrew his kiss just far enough to speak. "Sar…"

That one word begged her for everything—permission, help, relief. And his body screamed so loudly, she didn't have to breach his mind to know his thoughts and feelings. She did anyway, to get as close to him as two beings could be.

Without treading into his memories, she sunk into his thoughts and drew him into hers. Everything would be fine. They were in love, and they were together. He was free of the lorkai thirst, and she might soon be, too.

She held all her affection up for him to see, shared the comfort of his steadying arms, and let her hunger for him leach into his heart.

He crushed her to him and devoured her in a deeper kiss than they'd achieved when he'd occupied Glaucus's body. His rabid desire spilled from his being to swallow her whole, and tender aching exploded into a torturous longing.

Sweeping her back, he pinned her to the mossy oak, his rough stubble scratching one cheek in contrast to the smooth tendril pressed into the other. He tore at the buckles that held on her leather chest piece until he could rip the thing free, then rent the thin linen of her shirt. Keeping her tight to the tree with his hips, he withdrew his kiss and stared at her chest. He moaned and cupped one breast with a callused hand, cradling the side of her face with the other.

His next kiss was softer, but the tentacles tightened. The one that had slithered over her hip descended into her underclothes. Its silky caress slid across her sensitive flesh, and her breath hitched. It squirmed as she snatched his belt, lighting a fire.

Burning, she ripped at the lacing of his pants. The tentacle threatened to dip into her before she could get them open, teasing her entrance. Her thighs ached to welcome it into her depths, but the dark appendage seemed too menacing to invite in. "No..." Mercifully, it nestled just outside of her.

It didn't stay merciful. Once Benton yanked her pants down, the ebony tendril hummed against her like a rattlesnake's tail. "Oh, *Gods*." She writhed, grinding her back into the bark. Waves of heat numbed her mind and weakened her muscles, consuming the strength in both to feed taller flames.

He kissed her hard, plunging his tongue into her mouth as he pulled himself from his pants.

On fire, she tore her lips away. "Gods, Benton... Please... Before—" He drove into her, and she cried out, arching with the deep ridges of the oak's bark digging into her shoulders.

For a moment, she saw the black horror spilling from the face of the man she loved. Nightmarish appendages stretching from another world, entangling them.

But cognizance evaporated an instant after it arrived. His ravenous hands, kisses, and undulations, along with the silky tendrils sliding and buzzing across her, melted her into hot desire.

"I missed you, darlin'," he whispered beside her cheek. The tremor in his voice and the shake in his grip contrasted with the determined power in his hips.

She threw her arms around his neck. "I missed y—"

His thrust broke her words. More tendrils snuck behind her, lashing her thighs to his and cushioning her screaming spine.

"And I missed your *taste*." As she squeezed him from inside and coaxed out a moan, she snaked fingers through his hair to his nape. Tapping into him, she weaved her fathomless thirst into his teeming net of Marrow.

The sweetest cry slipped out of him as she drew in, one that begged the predator in her core to tear him apart. Instead, she plucked the threads that made him hum, enveloping him in an ecstasy she alone could provide.

The tender sensations overwhelmed the pleasure he took between her legs, tempering his thrusts into subdued rocking.

She floundered in her own nirvana as his divine Marrow spilled into her, flooding her with a euphoria only lorkai experienced.

Whatever had happened to him, whatever was in him now, hadn't tainted the magical energies that flowed through him. His Marrow was perfect. And begging to be consumed.

She looked in his beautiful electric eye, ignoring the monstrosity that jutted from the other. "No one tastes like you."

He groaned, slamming himself deeper.

She withdrew all but two fingertips as sparks danced in her vision, afraid one burning need would melt into the other, and she'd take all he had. "No one feels like you."

The tentacles shifted and snared her wrists, cutting off the heavenly flow of Marrow.

"That's right, darlin'," he growled in her ear when his extra appendages spread her arms above her head and plastered her wrists to the tree. They helped him grab her hips and lift her, pinning her aloft. "And you're gonna feel every inch." His urge to devour her leaked from his mind, more demanding than her yearning to swallow him.

She played helpless as though a flick of her wrist couldn't sever the living bonds, and she writhed against the trunk while he drove.

"Gods, Sar. Take it. Take everything..." His words turned into a moan, and his good eye rolled. Spasming, he spilled into her, then slowed to a gentle sway.

She wouldn't take everything, but she'd steal more than given. With a twist of her hand, she grabbed one of the tendrils that fettered her and tapped into his Marrow. Through the awful ebony vein, it came sparkling and thick—him but tinged with something dark like she'd tasted in Amenduil.

He thrust a final time as his rich Marrow flowed into her, and she burst. Each muscle tightened and nerve thrummed. Her high, breathy cry pierced the peaceful forest, chasing a black tide of ecstasy.

When it evaporated, she saw the nightmare again. No hunger clouded her view of Vorakor's wicked tentacles protruding from Benton's face to wrap around her bare flesh. Still woven in his mind, body, and energies, the Abyssal magic pulsed through them both.

She drew hard on the tendril in her grasp. His breath hitched, and his legs wobbled as the ebony ropes shrank and receded with his dwindling Marrow. The thinner tentacles vaporized into obsidian smoke.

She left enough magic that the thicker tendrils, though weak and wilted, didn't wither to nothing. Taking his body from him, she groped for the tentacles' slippery reins. A warmth sloshed into her like hot water the instant she grabbed them, and an intense gaze fixed on her. Not the icy eyes that repelled her from his recent memories. This stare came from an infinite, inky void that tried to draw her in.

Nothing had peered from a realm beyond when she'd taken control of the tendrils earlier...

"Maybe they're not *all* you," she said, voice cracking.

Hot dread trickled through her limbs at the notion she might have been fooled, but she retracted the tendrils that still entangled them without difficulty. The snake that rested against her front slithered away first; then the ropes binding them at the waist and thighs slackened. She reeled them all in, her heart aching at the horror that saturated his mind and permeated his expression while the tendrils receded into his face. He stifled a whimper when she made them phase through his neck and upper chest and melt into his solar plexus with a pleasant tingle.

Releasing her hold on his body, she withdrew from his mind and coaxed him out of hers.

Then she let the guilt wash in. Regret hit her like a ton of bricks.

This wouldn't have happened to him if not for her poor decisions. If she hadn't run from the lorkai and had just accepted her terrible fate...

He never would have drowned in the Abyssal Waters or endured the other traumas of the last several weeks. His beautiful eyes would remain intact without Vorakor's realm lurking behind them. Glaucus would still be alive. Dagmar wouldn't be lying in bed, regrowing her legs.

The only person to suffer would have been her.

Benton frowned as he yanked up his pants. "You okay?"

She clasped her elbows. "This is my fault." Maybe saying it aloud should have triggered tears, but they didn't flow like they used to.

He puffed. "Knock that shit off."

She slunk from between him and the oak and scooped up a few of its old, bronzed leaves from the ground. "Glaucus would still be alive. You'd never have been dragged into the Waters."

"You don't know that," he said while she turned to wipe herself off. "You can't know what Amen was plannin'."

She tossed the soiled leaves, and her heart tumbled into her bowel when she spotted their ebony glaze.

No kids. That was that. Gods knew what Abyssal creature their union would grow if she allowed that black seed to take. And without the promise of children, Dagmar would be more of a problem... She smoothed her hair. No sense getting ahead of herself.

Spinning to him, she muffled the whispers of her panic before they could shout and fastened her pants. "Maybe you're right." She flashed a smile, then slid his eyepatch to cover the orb he'd clamped shut.

If Benton had noticed the second horror he'd expelled, he gave no sign as he fixed his pants. After wrapping the sides of her torn shirt over her chest, he tucked them into her waistband to hold them closed. "You're the best thing that ever happened to me, Sar. You know that."

She knew he believed it. But she couldn't be sure that her quick didn't force him to.

"And the lorkai knew what they were gettin' into."

Whether that was true or not, they had been the ones to bring Amenduil into all their lives. She'd never given Vorakor a second thought before the lorkai had imprisoned her with the help of the Abyssal Lord's most powerful devotee.

"Yeah. Well, Sylvanus agreed to join the SPS." She focused on the scent of damp earth, old leaves, buck urine, and Benton to skip her thoughts over the memory of running her old mentor through. "I want to get to Apogee before Dagmar heals."

Benton snatched his blade and stuck the vial of holy water into his belt pouch. "I'm comin' with you."

Retrieving her chest protection, she smiled. He'd slow her down, but she couldn't bear to part ways with him again so soon. And maybe the councilors would have some insight into whatever dark magic he'd been infected with.

He grinned. "But we're gonna need to stop at the tavern."

CHAPTER SEVENTEEN

The weight of Apogee's wards didn't slam down on Benton's shoulders the second time he entered the SPS's lair. Nor did Jasper or the tower guards appear to notice his existence as he and Sarlona trod up the countless stairs to the councilors' offices. Their watchful gazes were all fixed on her. To them, he was little more than a well-behaved dog tagging along with his deadly master.

Good. Let the casters forget about Benton's spell-swallowing sword and the years he'd wielded it. Let them remain oblivious to the lorkai quick burning in his veins, hotter than ever now that Sarlona had given him a second dose.

Aldamon had been right about that—the extra quick made up for the visual impairment. Probably. Benton hadn't been tested yet, but his muscles hummed with strength and energy. Whispers had become shouts. The charged metallic particles from the magical weapons carried by the guards danced on his tongue. And while his field of view remained narrow, he saw far more through one eye than he ever had with two.

At the moment, it couldn't help but notice how tension knotted Sarlona's spine and her legs strained with every step.

The oppressive, anti-lorkai wards weren't all that weighed on her. A prickle along their bond told him that something was wrong.

He wished she'd whisper into his mind to tell him what.

Once they finally reached Apogee's ninth floor, Jasper led them to the most ornate central door—Kyran's—and knocked.

Sarlona retreated into Benton as it opened, tugging him behind her like she could shield him.

Midnight blue robes flowed from the gap. When a hyper-intelligent, aquamarine gaze locked on Sarlona, Benton's blade didn't wait for him to catch up. Hopping around her, he stabbed at Amenduil before his thoughts had formed the enemy's name.

Benton's blade hit dead center, sinking too easily into the dark mage's gut.

Amen glanced down as though the sword was only a mild violation of his personal space. The asshole had made himself incorporeal. He was a damned ghost.

"Back to your old self, I see." Amenduil scanned Benton, then fixed his stare on Sarlona. "You're looking lovely as ever, my dear."

Rage boiled through Benton while he followed his blade in. Let the shadowy shit stay a specter. Amen wasn't getting his tendrils on Sarlona. Neither would Benton let him put a barrier up.

Amenduil peered into Benton's good eye without retreating an inch, their faces a hand's breadth apart. "This is going to be awkward when I solidify..." He peeked at where part of his gut and robes drifted into Benton's abdomen.

Enough mages stood by that Benton figured someone could sort out that type of accident. "I wanna be close enough to get my hands on your cock-swallowin' throat the second you do."

The smile in Amen's eyes threatened to crack Benton's teeth. "I suppose I can't expect a man like you to understand that I've given him eternal rest..."

Never had Benton longed so deeply for hot blood to spill down his blade's fuller. He grabbed for the mage's ghostly neck, knowing he would grasp only mist.

Amenduil ignored the gesture. "I've given you a *home*, Benton. Doesn't that bring you peace?" The mage ran an ethereal finger across Benton's cheek, and a tingling chill chased it. "Knowing that when you inevitably drown in your own vomitus, warm waters and loving tentacles await you?"

Benton did everything possible to block out the sensation of floating in the Abyss, tangled in Vorakor's whips. And to keep from acknowledging that the only pain there had been knowing that he'd never see light—or Sarlona—again.

He opened his mouth, unsure what profanity or threat would spill out, but the sudden squirming below his diaphragm cut off both. "*No...*"

Amenduil's eyes flooded with tar, and he smiled, retreating to solidify as Benton hitched over.

With no regard for the enchanted eyepatch—or his commands—silk ribbons slipped up Benton's throat, into his nasal cavity, and burst from his eye.

He lunged, half-blind, when the same tendrils exploded from Amenduil's back, and black static crackled in the air around them. His sword sliced at the dark energy rolling toward him, but the ebony lightning danced up the blade and hit Benton dead center. Instead of burning him to a crisp and locking up his limbs, it heated him like a strong drink and left his muscles soft and sluggish.

"Cock you," he growled as the thick tentacles spilling from his eye reached for Amenduil's. The mirrored appendages faced off like two dogs reuniting after months apart—half excited and half defensive.

Sarlona dashed between them before they could touch, snatching a tendril from each man. Benton jerked as she grabbed his reins. The animal in him screamed in protest, unable to tolerate losing all control of his body. But she only sucked his tendrils into the Abyss, returning his autonomy the second they disappeared.

Amenduil she held longer, paralyzed.

Benton couldn't understand why the Abyssal mage didn't collapse into a pool of liquified tissue. Why didn't she kill him?

Fingers and eyes ablaze, Sarlona took Marrow when she should have taken his life. As the sable static faded and the tendrils withered, the ink left Amen's eyes and appeared in Sarlona's.

The guards, slow to react, pointed their weapons at her. Their expressions... They may have feared or despised Amenduil... How could they not? But for them, Sarlona was the true horror. The monster.

"That's illegal." The booming voice tugged everyone's attention to the chamber from which Amen had emerged. Kyran stood in the gap with his arms folded over his chest, glowering at Sarlona.

Her grip on the charcoal snake loosened. The shadows floated from her eyes, and the glow extinguished from her fingertips. "As is Abyssal magic, I was told." She retreated, her gaze fixed on Amenduil's hands.

"Your people are forbidden from feeding on mine," Kyran said from behind Amenduil as the Abyssal mage's tendrils turned to smoke, and the light flooded into his eyes. "There are consequences for it."

Sarlona scowled. "They're not m—"

"It's quite all right, Kyran," Amen said. "Sarlona is dear to me."

His wink made Benton's blade twitch, but Sarlona's sidelong glare stilled it.

Amenduil straightened his robes. "She always has my consent."

She should have held his extracted balls in her palm, but Amen knew as well as Benton that she didn't think that way, even now. Given Kyran's scowl, that was probably a good thing.

The council leader cleared his throat and beckoned. "I don't have much time, Sarlona."

She sidestepped Amenduil with a flash of red in her eyes, but he only leaned in and whispered something in her ear.

Benton glowered at the Abyssal mage, his muscles shaking as he followed her into Kyran's office.

"Isn't there a king's bounty on him?" Sarlona asked, voice quavering. Her face flushed. "Hasn't he violated a hundred SPS laws?"

Kyran glanced at Benton. "Close the door."

Benton shrugged and obeyed, surprised the guards weren't joining them.

"Amenduil's working with us to right some of his wrongs." Kyran sat behind his gigantic desk. "He'll be a valuable asset if he can separate his magic from his spiritual beliefs."

"He *can't*," Sarlona spat.

"Regardless, that's no concern of yours." He gestured toward the ornate chair set before his desk.

Sarlona grabbed the back of it rather than sit. "He killed Glaucus. He sent Benton to the Abyss."

Kyran tented his hands. "So, he freed you from your captors?"

A knife twisted in Benton's gut.

"Perhaps you should thank him." Kyran raised his brow. "Or are you not the victim you led me to believe?"

Benton supposed that running through the second-most politically powerful man in Aven wasn't the smartest move and sheathed his blade to dull the temptation.

Stiffly, Sarlona circled the chair and plopped down. "I've done as the Council asked."

"Yes, I've heard." Kyran reclined in his chair, hands locked behind his head. "You made short work of it all, too."

"Then, you'll change me back now?" Her voice cracked, and Benton's heart broke with it.

Kyran frowned. "Our preparations didn't go as intended..." He dropped his arms and tilted forward. "It doesn't seem we can help you after all. I'm sorry, Sarlona."

Her shoulders slumped, and for a second, Benton worried she'd hit the floor. "We had an agreement..."

Kyran's gaze bounced around the chamber. "I know. And I apologize. But upon deeper investigation... There's no non-sacrificial way. Perhaps, with more of your quick, I can keep experimenting with a few ideas..." He opened his hands on the dark wood of the desk. "But I think you'll have to search beyond Aven for a solution. I'm sorry."

She hung her head.

"We'll apply your recent accomplishments to your Society dues."

She took a deep breath and hitched over, resting her face on her forefingers.

"I can't imagine how terrible this must be for you personally." He rapped his fingers on the desk, and Benton couldn't help but imagine breaking them. "But perhaps, big picture, it's not the worst thing..."

Fluorescent pink spilled from Sarlona's palms, illuminated by her eyes.

Kyran glanced at Benton. "Since he found his answer, you're the last of the lorkai." Shrugging, he went on, "And you have a unique perspective. Unlike your predecessors, you understand the horror of feeding from and turning casters. You can teach your children to behave themselves."

She rose. "I'm not making more. I—"

"Just a couple of males," Kyran interrupted. "To preserve the species."

Benton's blood burned at the notion of Sar putting her quick in other men, then froze, supposing she might decide to keep *him* forever.

"I've already remade Dagmar," she said, glowering. "Talk to *her* if you want more."

Kyran raised his eyebrows. "I see... You shouldn't have done that."

She paled. Benton had a good idea why.

"That puts me in a difficult position," Kyran said, pushing his chair out.

Benton doubted it. In the council leader's sharky eyes, he caught a glimmer of delight.

Kyran sauntered from behind the desk, gaze locked on Sarlona's face. "The Council will have to pursue punitive measures."

Benton eyed the mage's hands and lips for any sign he meant to cast.

"We didn't have the jurisdiction while she was mortal." Kyran crept toward Sarlona. "But now... Execution seems the best course of action."

An invisible hand tightened around Benton's throat.

"Councilor, *please...*" Her voice shook like a wagon on a rocky road. "I don't want that."

His tone softened. "Your capacity for forgiveness is admirable, Sarlona." He grasped her elbows, and every hair on Benton's body stood on end. "But the elder councilors have known Dagmar for decades—she's cruel, unruly, and has committed the gravest crime against you—against us all—that her kind can perpetrate."

In other words, the Council couldn't control Dagmar. But they thought they could control Sarlona.

Kyran ran his hands up to her shoulders, drawing her gaze. "She murdered you, Sarlona. That monster stole everything you had and everything that you were." As Kyran drew one hand up to her cheek, it took all Benton's willpower to stand sentinel rather than pull his blade. "And I'm sure I can't imagine what other torments you endured when you were her prisoner. But you didn't deserve any of them."

Sarlona's eyes watered, and the sounds of her pleading, screaming, and moaning on the other side of her chamber door echoed in Benton's memory.

"You know, it's not uncommon for traumatized captives to develop empathy for their abductors." Kyran patted her arm. "And with lorkai, it's impossible for us to know if they altered your mind to *make* you feel it. It's impossible for *you* to know."

Sarlona blinked without allowing a tear to fall. "I suppose I should make some arrangements, then."

Benton knew damn well that meant go warn Dagmar and help her escape execution.

So did Kyran. "I want you to stay here with us for a time, Sarlona." He gestured at the wall abutting the hallway, and it broke in two places, a guard emerging like an insect from a pupa in each crack in the obsidian blocks.

Benton grabbed his hilt, but neither guard raised their fingers nor a weapon. If their appearance startled Sarlona, it didn't show.

Instead, she turned from them all and gazed at the window.

"It's unbreakable, Sarlona." Kyran cleared his throat. "Even if it wasn't, how would you get your friend down alive?"

She went to the window anyway and peeked out.

Benton didn't need to look out to know how high they were. It took a lot of stairs to steal his breath, and he'd almost run out by the time they'd arrived at the council leader's office.

She spoke into the enchanted glass. "So...I have a new captor?"

"Of course not." As if to prove he didn't mean any harm, Kyran shoved his hands into his pockets. "Listen... Almost every other caster in Aven went through the University. But you were kept in the forest. Then you were held prisoner by lorkai..."

Her eyes glowed yellow, piercing the bright gray-white light of the window that coated her face. Watery, they appeared like twin suns reflecting off a still lake.

"Take some time to be around normal people. Catch your breath." His voice took on such a soothing tone that it made Benton want to retch. "We might not be able to cure you, Sarlona, but we can heal you. And there may be ways we can help mitigate your hunger."

She spun. "My hunger is exactly why I shouldn't be here." The humanity had left her face and voice.

Benton hated that.

Her eyes shifted to match the glow of the amulet that burned between her breasts. "No one wants me here." She gestured at the guards. "Despite all the cantrips you have working to stifle me, I can smell their fear."

It hadn't shown on the guard's stoney faces until that moment, but Benton saw it clear as day.

"And yours." Her countenance calmed, and she swiveled to the window.

Benton didn't doubt her, but the lines in Kyran's face displayed irritation, not fear.

"Let the dust settle." The edge had seeped back into his voice. "Then you can return to Ashmore and plot your path."

"You mean let Dagmar's ashes cool," Sarlona accused the windowpanes.

"Yes," Kyran replied.

The conversation was so ridiculous Benton chuckled. "Just let the bitch burn, Sar."

She and Kyran pivoted to stare at him.

"She ain't done anything but torture you." He shrugged. "And I've lost track of how many times she's knocked my teeth out. Cock 'er."

A hint of a smile crept into Kyran's expression. "Wise for a hired sword. In sentiment, anyhow."

Sarlona gaped.

Benton usually let his weapon make his points for him, but this time, he raised his voice instead of his blade. "He's right, Sar. Dagmar was cockin' with your head before, and she'd still be cockin' with it if she could." Picturing the time Dagmar had broken his jaw and stuffed her long fingers into his mouth, threatening to rip out his tongue, he growled. "And if you manage to undo what she's done, she's gonna do it again." His voice cracked. "I ain't gonna let that happen."

Sarlona swallowed hard. "Benton—"

"It ain't like with you, Sar. She ain't a woman with a curse or a monster inside." Years of frustration spilled into his words. "She *is* the cockin' monster."

Sarlona crossed her arms and peered out the window.

Kyran's gaze followed her. "Well, there you have it..." His dark stare drifted to Benton after a few seconds. "You're a man with talent, I hear."

Benton shrugged, glancing at Sarlona, whose demon-red eyes searched the sky like they tracked a circling bird of prey. "Ain't done me much good."

"It could," Kyran said. "The Council can always use someone who knows how to get things done without quibbling."

Benton glanced at Sarlona, who'd stopped breathing if her stillness was any indication. "I got a job."

Kyran snorted. "I assure you the Council can do more for you than Ashmore. Both of you."

Benton loosened his sword as he approached her. "See, Sar? We don't need Ashmore. And we don't need cockin' Dagmar."

She spun on him and tilted her head.

What are you—

"We're doin' things my way this time, darlin'." Ignoring the whisper in his head, he drew his blade. "You're gonna listen to the smart man."

Kyran cleared his throat. "That's not necessary."

Benton advanced anyway, with his sword point aimed at her sternum.

She retreated against the window, jaw tight and eyes narrowed. "Who's messing with *your* head right now?" Pinching the blade between her fingers, she pushed it to the right, where it aligned more with her shoulder than her chest.

That was fine. Better. His sword had absorbed a lot of Amen's spell, the incorporeal magic humming in his grip. Hopefully, it would be enough to work on a lorkai.

I love you, Sar, he projected from his mind as he stabbed her shoulder and kicked her in the gut. He loosed the stored spell in the blade the second she hit the window and let go.

She disappeared like a ghost through the wall along with his sword.

Hanging his head, Benton turned around. He'd shoved the woman he loved out a nine-story window for a chance to save a monster who despised him. And left himself helpless with a mage he'd probably just infuriated.

The guards ran out. Kyran regarded him for a moment, nostrils flaring. "Pray she comes marching up those stairs of her own accord." Spinning on his heel, he headed for the door. He paused on his way out and glanced back. "Otherwise—you've killed her."

CHAPTER EIGHTEEN

Sarlona floated from the tower window, unsure whether she'd slip through the earth to be entombed deep within it or if the spell would give out and shatter her atop it. Either way, she flipped to greet the meadow feet first.

The maneuver separated her from Benton's blade, and she plummeted as she solidified. Cold wind tore at her hair, and fresh pain exploded in her shoulder. The ground wasn't so distant now, though.

She hit the earth with a sickening crack. Agony exploded up her leg, but she rolled and grabbed Benton's sword. Shifting into her transparent form, she crawled for the distant woods. She could contemplate her next move once she was beyond the range of the tower.

Four guards manifested on the muddy plain, two men and two women. Powerful ones. The average caster wouldn't have the energy left after teleporting to dare face a lorkai.

She had to get up. The soppy earth and matted, brown grass would give her away if she didn't choose her steps well. Strangling a shriek, she hopped to her feet and tried to shut out the pain. Hot anguish radiated from her outer ankle with each shift of weight onto her right leg, but the limb held.

Seconds into her shambling race for the woods, the mages started casting.

A wave of fog from the nearest woman parted around Sarlona, announcing her location. An instant later, a fireball shot from the same direction. She absorbed it with Benton's sword, then powered forward. The forest wasn't far, not for a lorkai.

Familiar words warned of the crush spell before it hit, and she angled the blade over her head. Benton's sword cut through it, drinking it up. Still, the thick, heavy air slowed her as she waded on, blade first. Once she popped out the other side of the affected area, she took off.

But the man who had cast the spell appeared in the tree line ahead of her.

He was good, and he had a big reserve. That wasn't surprising, given his scent. He smelled like a Khalorini—no doubt one of Councilor Talvianna's sons. If Sarlona hurt him, she'd make things a lot worse.

Green light shone from his pupils and fell on her—some clever spell for seeing her. She flicked Benton's blade at him before he could fire anything else off. The crush spell hammered down on his shielding, giving her the second she needed to dart past him.

Her feet tingled, and the scent of ozone flooded the air ahead of his next spell. Plunging the magic-eating sword into the ground, she threw her legs toward the treetops and balanced in a handstand on the hilt. Benton's blade swallowed the burning blue tendrils that raced along the ground.

She dropped as the last spark faded and yanked the sword from the earth. Flinging the spell back at him, she bolted.

And again, he appeared in front of her—too close for his own good. Frustrated, she hacked at his barrier, every slash weakening it ten times more than regular steel. "Don't make me touch you. Stay out of the way."

The young man was powerful, but he was no Sylvanus. No Amenduil.

"Just come back," he said, shooting glowing ropes at her that she easily dodged. "You're not in any trouble. Yet."

She zipped off, but he followed, manifesting before her.

He clapped his hands, then opened them by hinging at the wrists, a motion she recognized as the start of a trap spell.

She ejected her left claw and stabbed the tip into the earth, drawing in before he could finish casting.

The young Khalorini jerked, emerald eyes wide as she drained the life force from the earth.

And from him.

The maneuver was reckless. Dangerous for her, given who he was. Had she not just taken Amenduil's potent Marrow, she wouldn't have dared test her control.

The glow left the Khalorini's eyes, and his barrier collapsed before she yanked her carpal blade free—fighting every longing in her body. He crumpled, hair grayed and skin ashen. With no trace of light in his opened eyes, he looked dead.

She thanked the Gods he wasn't. Taking his limp, wrinkly hand in hers, she tapped him without drinking. She fought her instincts to draw in his life force and impelled a draught of her reserves into the network of energies that powered the man's magic and existence.

Her Marrow flowed like molasses, thick, sticky, and defiant, but a glimmer returned to his eyes. His skin flushed and filled out, and his hair darkened to jet black. A soft groan passed his lips.

She squeezed his hand. "I'm sorry for that." Using her touch, she put him to sleep.

Ankle still screaming, she jogged deeper into the forest. Her heart raged against leaving Benton with the SPS, but she didn't believe they'd hurt him.

Right now, Dagmar's was the life in danger. Sarlona prayed she could get to Ashmore in time to save it. Quick as she was, she'd be lagging while her ankle healed. And a good mage could teleport in an instant.

CHAPTER NINETEEN

B enton waited about ten seconds after Kyran stormed out before ri-
fling through his things in search of a spare robe or cloak—anything
to make himself appear like he belonged there. If he could blend in, he
might escape on his own. With the tower out in the middle of nowhere,
the mages had to have a teleporting station and a caster working it for less
talented individuals. They might take him to one of Ashmore's neighboring towns if he could keep from looking too suspicious.

Of course, Kyran was the one mage in Aven without half a dozen spare
robes strewn about.

Giving up, Benton skidded into the hallway. He assumed the whole
ninth floor consisted of council member offices—not the people he most
wanted to steal from—but one of them had to have left an extra robe on a
hook.

With no guards in sight, he pounded on the nearest door. Silence answered. Perfect. He yanked on the ornate handle, but it didn't budge. As
he scanned the heavy oak for a lock to pick, Kyran's words echoed in his
mind.

You've killed her.

Benton hadn't even considered how Sarlona would land. Maybe she had
hit the ground like a snowball and splattered. What if she'd sunk a quarter
mile into the earth before solidifying and was trapped and fused with the
dirt? How many days of agony would it take before her body spit out

enough pieces of gravel for her to fight her way to the surface? What if she wasn't strong enough to get out on her own?

No, the spell couldn't work that way. Amenduil would've sunk through the floor...

Cock.

Amen might still be skulking about, waiting to do something terrible.

Benton's pulse thundered in his ears. He'd risked everything... So *Dagmar* wouldn't burn?

Gods, he was an idiot.

Giving up on the magically locked door, he jogged up the hall.

No. He'd done it for Sar, not Dagmar. Sarlona would hate herself if a slip of her tongue got Dagmar executed. But more than that, Benton couldn't watch Sarlona be imprisoned again. Even temporarily.

He banged on the next door. No one answered. This one opened when he yanked. Hoping for better luck, he burst into the room.

As he headed for the trunk by the far wall, a gruff voice stopped him dead. "Who are you?"

"Cock." Benton pivoted to find Maliculius sitting behind a desk, quill in hand. Gods knew why the old man hadn't responded to the knock. Maybe he couldn't hear well. "Benton," he all but shouted, unable to concoct a decent lie. "I'm the one who was stuck in Glaucus's body."

"Good to see you found a solution." The old wizard set down his quill. "I take it Kyran's plan to keep Sarlona here didn't go well, then?"

Kyran's plan.

"She got out." Benton shrugged. This councilor didn't seem to have any interest in going after her. "You're really gonna *execute* Dagmar?" He should rejoice at the thought. Instead, the notion put his chest in a vise.

Maliculius pushed his spectacles higher up his nose. "Sarlona remade her, did she?"

"Seems like overkill," Benton said. "To burn her."

Maliculius surveyed him with a cool, gray stare. "Given that she's half the population, I tend to agree. But I'm only one vote."

Benton rested his hand on his empty sheath. Nothing about Maliculius's demeanor screamed threatening, but without his blade, he was at the mercy of any respectable caster. Vulnerable. "Kyran can't keep me here, right? Since I don't throw spells or suck 'em?"

The old man reclined and smoothed his beard. "He shouldn't anyway." He flashed a thin-lipped smile. "I'll take you home."

Benton whistled. "Thank you."

"In a few hours," Maliculius added, retrieving his quill.

Benton's heart sank, but it was a hells of a lot better than walking for days or being kept hostage.

"No doubt Kyran will send men to pick up Dagmar before Sarlona can interfere." The wizard dipped his quill. "Let's not get in the way."

Getting in the way was Benton's job, but he didn't argue. He couldn't do much to combat SPS forces without his blade, and he wasn't about to throw himself in front of a fireball for Dagmar as a mortal man.

Wandering to the large window, he scanned the expansive clearing. Last year's browned grasses stretched to a sea of conifers uninterrupted but for a few meandering tower guards. No blood. One scorch mark.

His heart told him Sarlona had slipped away. The ethereal tether binding them was lengthening. She felt a bit more distant by the second.

Still, something in his gut squirmed. "Kyran said if Sar didn't come back on her own, she was dead." Close enough to what he'd said, anyway.

Long seconds ticked by before Maliculius responded. "The lorkai have always been a concern for the SPS and the caster organizations that preceded us. Especially when they were numerous."

Benton didn't need the history lesson, but as the sinking in his stomach deepened, he listened attentively.

"Under Kyran, the Council has become more hostile to them," the old man continued. "Not *just* the lorkai, but..."

Benton pivoted to meet the councilor's gaze.

"He wants them carefully managed." Maliculius scratched his chin. "Dagmar couldn't have picked a worse time to break the terms of our treaty."

Benton sought his hilt again for comfort, but his fingers closed on empty air.

"Making Sarlona wasn't just illegal... Some of the councilors view it as a threat." His heavy tone became graver still. "And *her* as a threat..."

A hand squeezed Benton's throat. "Sar don't wanna hurt anyone or control anything." Cobwebs filled his mouth. "She just wants to be human. And let be."

"That's the impression I get," Maliculius said. But some of the other councilors don't want to take the chance."

The room seemed to grow colder and darker. Benton wanted to scream, run, fight, something...

"The SPS has a name for casters turned into lorkai—abominations," the old wizard said. "As a mercy—and a disincentive to choosing caster children—they're supposed to be destroyed."

Benton exploded. "How 'bout you just cockin' turn her back?"

Maliculius held up a hand. "I know. But Abyssal or blood—the magic to do so is sacrificial. We couldn't find another way."

"Then use a gods-damned convict." Someone sentenced to death—someone like him.

"It isn't that simple," the councilor said, patting the air for Benton to lower his voice.

Benton didn't quiet. "Amen made it look pretty cockin' simple."

Maliculius scowled. "If it was, do you think we'd be discussing executions?"

"If you hate them that cockin' much. Yeah." Benton balled his fists, arms shaking. "You robes are all cockin' lunatics... I can't predict what the shit you'd do."

The old man just stared for a moment, then gave a long exhale. "It's been weeks... I doubt it's even possible now..." He smoothed his beard. "And some think she's more dangerous as a mortal. No one's supposed to have that much raw power... I've only seen anything like it once in my lifetime."

In Amenduil.

Benton rubbed his temples and ground his teeth. The urge to punch someone was so strong he shook. Too bad the only person there could turn him to dust. "Dagmar was *centuries* old, and Amen managed it."

"I haven't a clue how." Maliculius rubbed his forehead. "The Council will probably spare Sarlona to preserve the species and execute Dagmar for her crimes..." Bits of his beard fluttered with his exhale. "But Kyran doesn't care which of them is more deserving of mercy. He cares about who is more of a threat to the magical community and who can be *managed*. If Sarlona isn't willing to become one of his pawns, she should leave Aven until his term is up. Just to be safe."

CHAPTER TWENTY

Dagmar's legs stung as she hiked the tree line surrounding Ashmore, but the movement and the fresh air, alive with damp earth and new growth, lightened her mood.

All the scents and sounds distracted her from her worry that her blood bond with Sarlona would break at any moment.

And she'd be all alone.

Not that she minded solitude so much. Or that she'd ever let Sarlona get too far from her. But to be the last of her species...

That seemed a heavy burden. So would knowing that everything she and her father had worked for had been erased.

But both paled in comparison to the prospect of watching her daughter waste away as a mere human because... *Why*? Feeding on mortals was wrong? Sarlona knew better than most how sustaining one life required the sacrifice of many others. Humans constantly preyed on each other anyway.

Her daughter's reasons—moral, religious, and other—were shortsighted, if not stupid. None were good enough to discard eternity and ignore destiny.

Dagmar drifted into the forest, snapping twigs and rustling leaves more than usual. Try as she might to concentrate on the patter of cold rain, her thoughts dipped into what she could have done differently.

She should have ripped all Sarlona's rebelliousness from her brain. But sentimentality had won out. Neither Dagmar nor Glaucus had wanted to take anything from the young woman that made her who she was. Stealing her magic was awful enough.

Dagmar wouldn't make that mistake again. Her species couldn't end because she was too soft with her daughter. If she had to make Sarlona twice, she'd ensure the young woman believed it'd been her own idea. She'd make her forget her magic, her family, whatever it took.

Stepping from rock to root, Dagmar sagged. Hopefully, it wouldn't come to that. The Council was just as likely to pat Sarlona on the head and send her home with a list of rogue mages to kill.

Lorkai resisted magic after all. Turning them back into mortals wasn't a thing. If Dagmar hadn't experienced it, she wouldn't have believed it possible...

Her hike wasn't working. The forest had refreshed her all it could. Maybe feeding would make a better distraction than the woods. Playing with Cyr awhile might amuse her. Better to stir fear in another than dwell on her own. She almost wished Benton was around.

Wary of the slick coating left by the icy rain, she hopped from smooth bark to worn basalt toward home.

But an unfamiliar scent wafted across the meadow as she was about to break through the trees. Freezing, she turned transparent. She knew the smell of every villager and regular merchant. This belonged to none of them. And the man smelled clean—a hint of lavender soap mingled with a tinge of sweat and musk. He wasn't a traveler. No shouts at horses straining to drag wagon wheels down Ashmore's muddy road had announced a stranger's arrival. No, whoever this was, he'd teleported in.

Staying low, she crept to the meadow edge and scanned the damp, dead grass leading up to the palisade. The intruder lay prone about fifty feet from the wall, covered in a cloak that blended with the gold, brown, and gray of the meadow.

An SPS spy who'd forgotten to mask his scent, no doubt. She swept her wild, drizzle-coated hair from her face. His presence meant the Council was moving on her. Sarlona must have told them what she'd done.

But just what the Council's intentions were was difficult to say. If left up to Kyran, she had little doubt she'd burn, but most of the other councilors were far less radical. Maybe the man they'd sent to survey Ashmore's defenses would know.

She slunk toward the naughty mage, longing for his screams. But before she got too close, she caught sight of another camouflaged figure, this one feminine and slender.

Scowling, Dagmar retreated the way she'd come. It seemed she had some reconnaissance of her own to conduct.

She picked a tall, sturdy ash near the tree line and climbed for the gray sky, wondering if her human father looked down from it—and if she might be joining him and her brothers far sooner than she planned. Squeezing the diamond-shaped ridges in the bark, she shimmied higher until the ash swayed with her weight, and she had a good view of the manse.

Five figures lay in the grass, but Dagmar guessed there were a couple more on the east side of the palisade where she couldn't see. She cursed under her breath. They had Ashmore surrounded.

Not that it mattered much. The SPS was there to take her, and they weren't about to succeed when she wasn't home. Regardless, she didn't like it—prey invading her territory and Sarlona's lands. As she clung to the vertical branch by her thighs and shielded her eyes from a gust of freezing rain, she again contemplated snatching one of the trespassers. The extra Marrow would do her good, and she wanted answers. Did they intend to execute her, imprison her, or just make a spectacle of an arrest to please constituents? In the old days, she'd been taken into custody a few times only for the Council to hem and haw and ultimately do no more than issue fines and a stern warning. But that was long before Kyran.

Just as she resolved to grab the nearest mage and wring some information out of him, two more appeared on the road, teleporting in. A man and a woman. They strode for Ashmore's gate. Tall and broad-shouldered (for a southerner) with long black hair and a sword strapped to his back, Dagmar recognized the man—Kyran himself.

She dug her nails into the bark. With him there, tearing the Marrow and thoughts from an SPS soldier was almost out of the question. He'd have a fit if he saw it, and she should probably avoid making the situation worse.

As she slid down the ash and dropped the last ten feet, Glaucus's voice sounded in her head. It warned her to fade into the forest.

But the thud of a telekinetic slam against wood echoed off the trees, and the crack of timber followed. A fist of rage lodged in her gut. The mages were breaking through her family's door.

She picked her way into the field and circled the ring of mages stationed outside the wall until she found one with a rabbit's heartbeat. He was terrified.

That meant one of two things—he was weak or smart. Hopefully, the former. Or both.

She strode at him, expecting full well to trigger whatever spell the caster had laid to protect himself and prevent her from escaping Ashmore. It hit her like a sledgehammer, a crushing increase in gravity meant to slow and weaken her, but she gritted her teeth and powered onward, core and thighs burning. Discarding her near invisibility, she ejected her claws and forced red fire into her irises. When the mage flipped over, she snarled and raised one carpal blade as if to skewer him.

He screamed, throwing his hands up and putting everything into his barrier. No longer hindered by his spell, Dagmar zipped to the palisade. She scaled the wall before the frightened mage's nearest friend even got a spell off. By the time the crack of frost magic cut through the wet air and a sheet of ice hit the wall, she was halfway to the gate.

Gorgil braced the heavy iron bar in the massive pair of double doors with his body, toes digging into the gravel as the next spell slammed into the gate. Cyr stood to the side, hands up with palms parallel to the doors and with a matching yellow glow. The doors shook and groaned but held.

"That's enough." Dagmar jerked her head in a gesture for the men to move. *Just cover me.* She spoke into their minds, as well as Lita's, who jogged from behind the house with a throwing knife in hand. And in Gupson's, who swiveled with his bow to aim at the gate from the roof.

"Hold on a second," Dagmar growled. After a deep breath, she tossed the iron bar and threw open the doors. "Can I help you, Council Leader?"

Kyran sneered, pulling a scroll from his belt. "Yes. You can surrender yourself into Council custody."

She took the scroll without slicing his arm off like she wanted to and glanced at the paper. "Charges? Feeding from the magical... Imprisoning the magical... Turning the magical... Assault on the magical... Body snatching for purposes other than feeding... Mental invasion, mind control... *Rape*? Failure to register progeny..."

Shrugging, she tossed the scroll into the mud. "I remember when most of that was legal."

He twisted his face and shook his head. "Well, like a reasonable monster, your grandmother signed the treaty along with the other lorkai families."

Dagmar folded her arms in front of her chest. "*I* never signed anything." Her gaze stayed locked on Kyran's hands. The Marrow radiating from him told her he was ten times more dangerous than any other mage there. But she wasn't about to ignore the others. The young, brunette woman at Kyran's side, his apprentice, Eseld, was flush with Marrow, too. As were a few of the other intruders. But the shuffle of their boots in the grass and swish of their robes painted their every move for her. Two circled toward the gate. The rest kept their positions.

"Neither did I," Kyran replied. "Yet we're both bound to it."

Dagmar took a deep breath. Before Amenduil, she might have prevailed in a situation like this. With her father's help? Certainly. Now, she wasn't sure she could escape, never mind defend Ashmore. "The Council's probable sentence?"

The air shifted behind her, and Jasper's familiar scent flooded her nostrils. A twang from Gupson's bowstring preceded the click of an arrow skipping off a magical barrier, then a clack as it hit gravel. The chime of a throwing knife striking Jasper's carapace spell rang next. Gorgil drew his great sword.

Not yet, Dagmar told them.

Kyran met her stare. "Death."

She widened her stance. "You won't make Sarlona human, then? Or have you decided on genocide?"

He snorted. "That type of magic can take years off your life, even with a sacrifice." His nose wrinkled. "Anyway, a compliant lorkai might prove useful."

The shade of relief that washed over Dagmar as she realized the lorkai wouldn't die with her didn't thin the shadows closing in. She couldn't leave her daughter all alone. "The first century is hard. Sarlona is supposed to remain in my custody."

Kyran smirked. "She fed from a mage when she scampered off, so that will put her in mine." His eyes shone, and he lowered his voice. "Don't worry though, Dagmar. I think she'll take to a leash, and I have no reason to hurt a bitch who obeys."

CHAPTER TWENTY-ONE

Dagmar's jaw ached from her clenched teeth, and a fiery haze coated her vision. Kyran didn't have Sarlona, then... But he wanted something from her. "What if we left Aven?"

He glanced at the sky and shoved his hands in his pockets. Brazen. "So that you can terrorize sorcerers in other kingdoms and reproduce unregulated?" His lips curled. "Your kind is a scourge on this world. I won't risk a horde of your descendants returning in a century."

Dagmar hefted her subpar replacement axe. "Fine. Be that way." *Run. Fight. I don't care*, she told Ashmore's guards. "You'll have to burn me here," she said to Kyran. "I won't be made into a spectacle." Charging, she slammed her axe on his shoulder with a vicious chop. His carapace spell turned it aside.

Gorgil swung at Jasper as another arrow bounced off the mage's back. Cyr sent a telekinetic blast at Eseld, which Lita followed up with a knife aimed at her larynx. Neither did anything.

Kyran's hands filled with fire, and the flames ran up the steel of his black blade as he pulled it. At the same time, an inferno roared to life beyond the palisade, towering higher than the manse. Unable to peek beyond the flames, Dagmar guessed it was too wide to sprint through without serious injury.

She forced a grin. "Are you sure you want to be trapped in here with me?" He could teleport to safety but not without dropping his barrier.

She sidestepped the stream of fire that served as his response.

Three against five. At her best, those would've been good odds. Now? She might be able to take down Kyran, but with Jasper and Eseld to help... And Ashmore's remaining guards were ill-equipped to handle the spellpower leveled at them.

Dagmar rushed in, swiping at the apprentice, then pivoted to smash Kyran in the spine. He rocked forward, but his barrier held, and he twirled, blade flashing fire in her face. She hopped clear, smacking into Eseld, who started fashioning glowing ropes out of thin air.

As Kyran spun on Dagmar, she leaped, winding up, and hammered her axe down on his shoulder with everything she had. The axe-head shattered, but his barrier didn't. The spike of adrenaline in the air and grimace on his face told her it'd hurt, though.

Ejecting her carpal blades, Dagmar sliced the magical snare Eseld threw. Her natural weapons were more effective anyway. If she could stay between the casters so that they had to limit their zone spells *and* keep them on the defensive so they couldn't come up with anything too creative, she might survive this.

With a ferocity that even a Northlander could admire, Gorgil swung his great sword, cracking it on Jasper's barrier. "Cyr, keep them pinched there." He jerked his head toward Kyran and the young woman. "The rest of you on Jasper."

Arrows and knives joined the guard captain's blade against the mage's shield.

Jasper raised his manicured hands and made claws, then drove his fingers forward. The end of the stable behind him collapsed as its nails shot from the beams and hurtled at his assailants. The iron projectiles peppered Gorgil and Lita.

Both guards put their backs to the stable and made themselves small, protecting their heads with their hands before the nails sunk in.

They still screamed as iron pegs sunk into their hands, arms, and hindquarters. Their padded leather vests shielded their torsos.

Neither let up, though. Gorgil melted from the reserved half-orc captain to a rabid berserker. Lita drew her cudgel and battered Jasper's shield like she was trying to pound him into the ground. Her blood splattered across his barrier.

Dagmar growled at Cyr after his telekinetic push failed to sweep Kyran or his apprentice back an inch. "*Heal.*"

A wave of Cyr's hand engulfed Gorgil and Lita in green light, dislodging the nails and closing their wounds. He was good for that, at least.

Dagmar slashed Kyran's shielding as he spat dragon fire. Ducking and weaving, she left burnt fur from her armor and singed hair to poison the air in her wake. With each strike of her claw, she licked away some of the barrier's energy.

A scream like a banshee's knocked Dagmar sideways and stabbed her deep in her left ear. The world quieted, making it harder to discern what Jasper and the guards were doing. She swiveled to Eseld, whose hands rested on her throat and was inhaling to scream again. Before the terrible shriek tore across the yard, Dagmar darted behind the apprentice with a flurry of magic-eroding blades.

The young woman spun wide-eyed, swiping her palms in front of her to reinforce her shields.

Blood trickling from her ear, Dagmar snarled. "I'm going to rip Kyran's head off when I break through his shield." A panicked mage was a sloppy mage. One that burned themselves out quickly. "But you, little girl... I intend to play with you and Jasper for *hours.*"

The woman retreated just beyond the gate, and Dagmar's boots caught as she tried to pursue.

Quicksand sucked her legs down to the knees. Growling, she ripped her feet free from her tall boots and rolled aside as a wave of fire melted the sand to bubbling glass.

She popped up and slammed one of the massive gate doors, knocking Eseld rearward. In another blink, she'd locked the woman out.

Dagmar dove in, hacking at Kyran's barrier, but he swept her back with a stream of fire. A second later, flames flanked her from both sides.

She retreated when two massive, cat-shaped blazes tried to pinch her between them. They pounced together, leaving a small inferno where she'd stood an instant earlier. Zipping backward, she put some distance between them, but they circled out, two fiery lions stalking their prey.

"Is that you, Jasper?" Dagmar rushed the mage, who worked his fingers furiously while crouched with weapons hitting him from three directions. He still appeared put together.

Kyran, Dagmar ordered.

Gorgil charged the more powerful mage with arrows, knives, and bolstering spells following him in.

Dagmar focused on Jasper as the lions wiggled their hindquarters in anticipation of their attack. "Dismiss your cats and carapace if you want me to be gentle with you."

Jasper gritted his perfect teeth against her heavy blow and made the cats leap. Fire exploded behind her as she vaulted over him, enwreathing his barrier. He rose, spinning and bringing his fingers around to make the cats circle.

Dagmar slammed her carpal blades across the carapace over his face with all her strength behind it. "I'm going to drink your Marrow while I crush your fucking balls, Jasper."

He rocked with the blow, light brown features twisted as the cats jumped again. "This isn't *personal*."

As if Dagmar gave a fuck. She juked, and the lions crashed together in another blaze. The scorching heat forced her eyes shut, but the flames only licked at her armor.

He waggled his fingers, firming up his fiery cats. "It's just *justice*." Sweat glazed his hairline. "You decimated that poor girl's life." His voice cracked. "Maybe her soul."

Dagmar leaped, slamming her claws on his shielding. The cats decayed into embers. "I took her life to give her an infinitely more valuable one. Why can none of you see that?" She rammed her claw at his chest, and his carapace trembled.

Whispering, he knitted with his fingers. A glowing net fell over her, each of its strands aflame. Her skin hissed when it alighted atop her and sizzled on her armor. Roaring, she tore through the trap, her claws dissolving every magical string they cut into.

Dagmar hammered on his carapace with both blades, and it gave. His big, chestnut eyes went wide. He hollered as her claw sunk into his thigh—a beautiful sound.

Catching him by the neck, she settled for his throat instead of his balls and didn't crush it all that hard. She tapped into his energies, lifting him close to her face so she could drink his fear with his Marrow.

Kyran ruined it. "Enough!"

Dagmar glanced from Jasper's darkening face and bulging eyes in time for Gorgil's smash into the palisade and Lita to roll a dozen times across the yard before sliding to a stop.

"You dare put your hands on an emissary of the Council?" Kyran boomed.

She did. But after sucking out his reserves and prodding his brain into a coma, she tossed Jasper to the ground.

As she faced Kyran, his apprentice levitated over the wall. Gupson met Eseld with an arrow but screamed when she shot an arm in his direction.

A groan followed a heavy thump behind Dagmar and the crack of bone. She shook her head as a plume of sawdust wafted over her shoulder. That old man and his fragile bones.

Gorgil looked even worse than Gup sounded. Unconscious and slumped against the palisade, blood streamed from the back of his head and mouth. One of his short tusks had punctured his bottom lip. Fortunately, his heart still beat.

Dagmar whispered in Lita's and Cyr's heads. *Take them and get out.* Her chances would diminish without the guards as distractions, but she cared about Gorgil. Glaucus had loved him like a son. And she was fond of Lita. The guardswoman had warmed Dagmar's bed enough times to earn the chance to survive.

Cyr engulfed Gorgil in a green glow, and Lita sprinted for Gupson.

Kyran strode toward Dagmar as his apprentice touched down at his side. "I'm done playing, lorkai."

Dagmar frowned. "You're toys, that's all you're for." She met his hateful gaze through a red lens, her eyes burning with nightmarish fire. "I'm going to cut you open and feed from your insides while your pretty apprentice watches. Then the real fun starts." Swiveling her head, she stared into Eseld's eyes. "I'm going to bind her like a dog, and who knows, maybe once I've got her trained well enough, I'll make a sister for Sarlona."

Kyran flushed so intensely he could've leaked blood. "You spell-sucking cunt. Who the fuck do you think you are to threaten a Society member that way?" He made his hand into a claw and drew it across the air.

Dagmar skipped sideways, and the spell rent the back of her vest instead of her chest.

"You're not Sarlona," he said, swiping both hands this time. "You're nothing special."

She should have sprinted straight instead of right. The spell hit wide and caught her left arm. It took far more sleeve than flesh though, leaving her arm bare but with little more than bloody streaks down it.

His face twisted at her. "You're not even your father, who at least had some intelligence and dignity for a monster."

No, she wasn't. That didn't matter as the guards slipped into the house. Hopefully, Kyran didn't know about the tunnels beneath Ashmore. She didn't see how he could. But now, she had nowhere to retreat to. Not without leading him to the mortals she'd deigned to spare.

A curtain of flame sprang up behind her anyway.

He crept nearer as the scent of the drizzle changed to burn her nostrils. Something caustic brewed in the air. "You're a wild boar, who was granted immortality as a joke." Spittle ejected with his words. "Your trickster god probably whispered in Glaucus's ear to make him choose you."

She wished she'd worn her helm when the first sizzling droplets stung the ridges of her ears. "Lorkai don't need to be special to make sure a robe can never cast another cantrip."

He gazed at the sky, acid raining on the carapace a quarter inch from his face. "You should've given more thought to your words and actions here today." Lowering his stare to meet hers, he smiled. "Because after your ashes have cooled, your daughter will still be here, under my rule."

Dagmar glanced at Jasper, who lay motionless in a muddy, steaming heap. "You know, he's going to melt long before I do."

Eseld raised her hand flat, and a translucent yellow rectangle appeared over Jasper. Dagmar had the feeling Kyran wouldn't have bothered.

The councilor's voice sweetened. "And you don't have to be a lorkai to control minds and manipulate bodies. There are spells for that."

Illegal spells.

Sacrificing the back of her hand, Dagmar shielded her face to keep the burning rain out of her eyes. The sting made her growl, but she clenched her jaw to keep the sound within. Let him keep talking, building her rage. Anger didn't make her sloppy, it made her leave a bigger mess.

He must have held unparalleled confidence in his shielding because he edged in, suicidally close. "*Sarlona* is a beautiful beast. Making her scream will be a pleasant distraction."

Dagmar glanced at Eseld, who swallowed hard. Smart girl.

Kyran wasn't about to let his apprentice's discomfort stop him. "Of course, whether it's for mercy or for more will depend on my mood and her obedience."

Dagmar let the reins on her wrath go and exploded at Kyran, walloping his barrier with both claws. The force of her blows rocked him against his carapace, but one sweep of his hand blasted her through the wall of fire and across the gravel yard.

Smoking and raw, Dagmar jumped to her feet. She scurried clear just as the roof of the manse's awning collapsed and the front door area caved in.

Charging through the spray of ice and frost, she lunged at Eseld. The girl had to be the source of the rain blistering her skin and leaving her vision blurry. The apprentice's shield blinked amid Dagmar's pummeling, and sure enough, the horrific rain stopped.

Eseld retreated, digging into the pouch on her belt, but Dagmar stayed on her. If she could take the young mage down, she had a decent chance with Kyran one-on-one.

Two, maybe three more solid hits would do it. But the earth surrounding the girl softened, liquifying into molten rock and boiling glass. Dagmar skipped rearward, skin ripping from her bare feet as the burning ground seared her soles.

She turned on Kyran, helpless to prevent Eseld from shooting a manna potion. Ignoring the screaming pain of blistered and blackened skin, ulcerated corneas, and a burst eardrum, Dagmar threw herself at him, hacking away. He slashed too, albeit sluggishly, obsidian blade spitting fire and shooting embers in her face.

Meanwhile, the wind whipped up, and every loose bit of debris lifted into the air—nails, splintered wood, rocks, broken glass, arrows, and throwing knives. All zipped in a cyclone, pelting the mages' shields and crashing into Dagmar.

She dodged only the debris that threatened to crack her skull or skewer her organs. Letting up meant Kyran might get a potion down. But more than a few objects embedded in her back or cracked against her bones, and each weakened or slowed her by a sliver of a second.

Still, she just needed to keep hammering and stay in one piece until she got her hands on him.

Easier said than done with two powerful mages throwing fire. And it became even more difficult after Eseld caught her breath. "Vaporize," the woman shouted for extra oomph, spreading her fingers.

Dagmar jumped, flipping over Kyran to use his barrier as her shield. His carapace hissed and rippled. Maybe she could get his apprentice to break through for her.

"How are we going to burn vapors? Use your head, girl," Kyran growled at his apprentice.

Dagmar tried to lop his off, but her claws bounced back at her.

Eseld set her jaw, her expression steely as she circled to get a clear shot at Dagmar. Hinging her fingers at the middle joint, she whispered, "Decay."

Dagmar crow-hopped, trying to keep Kyran between them. Again, his barrier flickered. This spell had a wider spread, though, and grazed her. When she next swiped at Kyran, a strip of putrid flesh slipped off her aching forearm and plopped to the ground. Her left ear followed it.

Shit.

Eseld's eyes widened, and she clutched the front of her robe. If she'd been lighter-featured and fifteen times as powerful, she could've been human-Sarlona's twin—a girl with more Marrow than was good for her and a stomach too weak to take full advantage of it.

"Better," Kyran grumbled, making a fist. Invisible fingers nicked Dagmar's throat as she ducked clear.

The apprentice's face lit up with a devious twinkle in her eye, and she gestured furiously, her stare fixed on Dagmar.

Maybe not so much like Sarlona.

Dagmar didn't see or hear the spell go off. The agony beneath her skin told her she'd been hit. She gritted her teeth against the gnawing pain and spun on Eseld. "Don't make me leave you without hands." Ignoring the wriggling shapes and scraping mandibles in her flesh, Dagmar ducked beneath Kyran's fireball and hacked at the young woman. As though performing a fire dance, she skipped around Eseld, a whirl of carpal blades, dodging bursts of flame.

Until the bugs chewed their way out of her skin.

Dagmar screamed, bent at the waist while a hundred insects burst out of her. The big bugs leapt lazily into the air, wings straining under the weight of their hideous jaws.

Ready to collapse, she plopped to her knees and drove one claw into the ground.

Eseld had been weakened enough that she shouldn't have to stay down long. She couldn't afford to keep still—moving was the only way to survive.

Drawing in, Dagmar ripped what little Marrow lingered in the packed earth itself, then started on the sweet, rich energies of the young mage standing too close.

Eseld squealed, contorting as her shielding flickered, and she fumbled to get off a spell. Flames sputtered like sparks from a defective firecracker.

"Sever," Kyran hollered, reaching for Dagmar from a distance.

She leapt, getting her body clear of the spell, but it clipped her claw. Roaring as half her carpal blade hit the ground in a spurt of blood, she retreated from the apprentice.

Eseld collapsed. Conscious but drained, she dug her fingers into the gravel and crawled toward the palisade.

"Inversion," Kyran growled, stalking for Dagmar as she stumbled clear.

The spell shot just past her head and hit a rain barrel by the front of the house. Sucking inward before bursting out with a spray of water, the staves turned inside out, rendering the barrel a mangled bundle of kindling.

Dagmar juked and reversed direction, charging at Kyran. Fireballs exploded on either side of her, forcing her to come straight on.

"Paralyze."

Dagmar leaped, trying to get above the spell, and slashed his carapace on the way by. It blinked and sputtered. Just a couple more hits could take it down—take *him* down. For good. But she tripped when she pivoted, her right foot numb and useless.

He put his fists together, pulling them apart as she dove aside. "Disarticulate."

Mind-rending pain tore through Dagmar's legs. She bellowed like one of the great white bears of her homeland. Using her arms, she dragged herself to her knees but couldn't stand. Her legs wouldn't hold together, never mind support her weight.

Kyran sauntered to her, sword raised.

She blocked his first swipe. Second. Third. But she was fading. Exhausted. Agonized.

He punched at her with some spell that rocked her skull and made the sky spin in a swirl of flames and gray.

His next slash took off both her hands.

"That's better." Kyran smiled at her and sheathed his blade.

Bleeding out from her wrists and dozens of tiny wounds, skin blistered and burnt, pieces of her strewn about, and legs dislocated, without even the ability to feed, Dagmar was done. Her core muscles trembled to keep her upright.

Kyran helped, taking her by the chin to stop her from slumping over. "Come," he called to his ragged apprentice. "Look at the toothless bear."

Dagmar still had her teeth but doubted she possessed enough strength to gnaw off his hand.

Shuffling, Eseld crept nearer. She stopped well behind him, peering pale-faced over his shoulder. "Can I tell them to take the fire down?"

Dagmar hadn't noticed the heat until that moment.

"Sure. Then get some rest." Kyran smoothed Dagmar's hair. "I can scrape up her pieces myself." Yanking her head back, he made her look in his face. "And I want to have some fun before we return to Apogee."

The apprentice limped away without another word.

The red tinge in Dagmar's vision faded as the fire in her eyes died. She saved some for her voice, though. "I swear to every God below, if you unfasten your pants, I'll bite it off."

Kyran leaned in. "One wave of my hand, and you'll do whatever I desire." He shuddered. "But don't flatter yourself."

One nightmare averted.

He stroked her stinging cheek. "I just wanted to admire you like this for a few moments. On your knees."

Dagmar gave him a toothy smile. "Every second you don't incinerate me is a risk you shouldn't take."

Kyran patted her hair again. "Oh, I don't know... I might keep you. I can't have two female lorkai running about...that's true." Glancing down, he kicked the severed hand and claw that Dagmar had twitched. "And Sarlona suits my needs far better than you."

Dagmar cringed, sure that whatever he desired would be horrifying.

"But she's far more dangerous than you are. Isn't she? Potentially, at least—*eventually*..." He drew his blade and used it to flick her other severed appendage to a safe distance. "And this..." Flipping his blade so he held it upside down, he smashed her across the face with the hilt.

Silvery flecks danced in her vision. She spit blood onto his boot.

"*This* might just be too amusing to give up." He grabbed her hair and yanked her head up to grin in her face. The hint of manna on his breath made her depths scream for sustenance she had no way to take. "Yet not half as entertaining as watching you thrash in chains while your daughter burns in front of you."

He let go, and she slumped forward. Her heart thundered, but instead of giving her the strength to shoulder him in the groin and smother him to death, the boost of adrenaline made her head swim. With her back too weak to hold her up and no hands to catch herself with, she collapsed against his front.

He squeezed her head to his navel and ruffled her hair, laughing. "Don't leave me now, Dagmar. I haven't even started hurting you yet."

She tried to growl, but it came out a wet groan as blood dribbled out of her mouth. Wilting further, her face slid distressingly close to his crotch. Maybe she could at least rupture his balls with a head butt... But he turned so her cheek rested on his hip before she could summon the strength.

"I thought you lorkai stayed conscious unless your brain was damaged..." he said, patting her head again.

Not always—but far too often.

"How disappointing, if untrue."

Biting her lip, she resolved to get her face farther from his genitals if it took her last drop of vigor but caught a rare scent with her next inhalation. Amid the much more potent odors of sweat, pheromones, shit, urine, cum, and Eseld around Kyran's belt, came the scent of the potions hanging in his thin leather pouch. Manna and healing potions, of course... Bolstering and resistance potions. And one that only men of means carried because they cost a small fortune.

"I've wondered for years, just where in their bodies lorkai hold their quick..." Kyran went on as she edged her face toward the belt pouch. "Do you know?"

She took a deep breath. One chance.

"Let's open you up and find out."

Biting the purse, she ripped it from his belt. As she smashed herself face-first into the gravel, she wished for a distant land.

CHAPTER TWENTY-TWO

Ashmore's yard vanished in a metallic flash. Round, river-worn stones replaced the packed dirt. The gentle sound of water lapping at sand and smooth pebbles swallowed Kyran's shout. He was gone.

She was gone.

Unclenching her jaw, Dagmar lifted her face off the gray rocks and the liquids from Kyran's shattered vials pooled on the ice between them. Among the bright colors leaking from the leather pouch trickled mercury—a potion of transportation. Laughing and wishing she could have seen the look on Kyran's face as she disappeared, she flipped onto her back. Blue sky and scrubby pitch pine hovered over her. Familiar peaks loomed to the west. A blacksmith's hammer rang in the distance.

She twisted her head to view the still river, and an eider thrashed its wings, taking off from the water's surface. Her laughter melted into tears when the pain of her mangled body caught up to her, and she realized where she'd landed herself.

Though the trees were different, and the river was higher, she'd arrived at that exact spot once before. Her brother's longboat had groaned and lurched as it struck the beach a few feet to her left.

She'd hopped off and helped haul up the boat, scraping its hull over the pebbles. Then she'd accompanied two of her siblings to the Imperial village just a short hike away. There, they'd broken down the patrician's door—and found a rugged old man with rich brown skin, neat silvery hair, and haunting, storm-gray eyes. Eyes that had glowed after he'd bested and restrained her, staring into her soul.

In her time of greatest need, her subconscious had brought her to where she'd met her lorkai father. Her real father.

Water ran down her cheeks. The pain of missing Glaucus swelled to match the agony in her body and fear for her daughter. She dipped her head, touching her lips to the stone, and lapped at the spilled potions. Hopefully, the healing and manna potions would help her recover enough to get to Sarlona before Kyran could.

CHAPTER TWENTY-THREE

Maliculius left Benton in Baleford so he could avoid Kyran and meet Sarlona on the road. From there, Benton ran his stolen horse northwest, his insides thrumming stronger with every mile that closed between them until she was near.

The horse reared and whinnied as she materialized ahead like an apparition.

"Benton!" Her smile spread ear to ear, then jumped from her face onto his.

He slid off the horse and scooped her up, squeezing her a lot harder than he would a mortal woman.

"I was worried you wouldn't be able to get home." She crushed him back. "That you'd be in trouble..."

"Kyran weren't happy, believe me." He slipped his sword from her belt and pushed her to arm's length so he could see her face. "Maliculius brought me to Baleford. Sorry, I stabbed you and shoved you outta a tower."

She snorted. "I'm pretty much okay now." Taking his shoulders, she moved him aside. "Anyway, I have to warn Dagmar."

He held on tight when she tried to pivot. "*No.* You can't." His stomach sank, but he couldn't let her go.

"What are you—"

He shifted so she didn't topple him. "It's too late, Sar."

Her gaze drifted to the horizon. "No—"

"Kyran took a bunch of mages into Ashmore right after you left." He dug his fingers into her so she couldn't slip his grip.

"She's *alive*, Benton."

He didn't doubt that. Sarlona could probably feel it. "Good." Gods, he meant it. "But it don't matter, Sar."

She clenched her jaw and tried to sidestep him, but he wouldn't loosen his hold.

"There ain't anything to be done. She got away, or she didn't." The notion of abandoning Dagmar ate at his gut against all reason, but he couldn't endanger Sarlona over it. He tugged her from the road, leaving the horse. "We gotta go. West."

"West?" She peered down the road toward Ashmore. "They're going to *kill* her, Benton."

A chill swept over him, but he channeled the iciness into his voice. "Better her than you."

She paused, lips parted as if to ask a question that never formed.

Benton sheathed his blade. "Maliculius said Kyran don't care which of you lives. Long as he gets to have the other on a leash."

Blanching, she shrank. "But why—"

"Never mind why." He dragged her farther into the forest, from the fence row and freshly plowed fields. "And never mind Dagmar." Gods, why did that kill him to say? "We just gotta get outta Aven."

She glared at him in silence for what seemed like minutes. "If the Council has her, I can't just leave her..."

"Gods *dammit*, Sar." He ignored the claw scratching in his chest and yanked on her arm. This time she didn't budge. "Of course, you can... Not everything I said in Apogee was bullshit. She ain't your responsibility. All she's done is hurt you." His voice cracked, but it was true.

Sarlona rubbed her nose, gazing at her boots.

He grabbed her by the sides of her face and stared into her eyes. "I need you to trust me, darlin'. I'm tellin' you we gotta leave Aven, and we gotta go now." Fear crept up on him, tightening his throat and shaking his voice. He couldn't lose her. "Okay?"

She took his hands from her head and squeezed them. "Okay."

He hugged her. "We'll be okay, darlin'."

She kept her gaze on the forest floor. Half-afraid she'd melt into the woods, he snatched her hand and held on tight as she picked her way deeper into the forest.

"So, this is it?" she said, voice cracking. "I'm a monster..."

"The prettiest monster I've seen." He grinned. "It's a big world, sweetheart... There's gotta be someone else out there other than cockin' Amen who can turn you back. Maybe we can find 'em. Just not in Aven."

The shadows swallowed her as she slipped between hemlock boughs, tugging him behind her.

"When that darkness bubbles up, Benton..." She tilted her face at the ground. A splash of red hit her cheeks. "You're my pet. My food."

"As long as I'm yours, Sar." He meant that. "And the darkness don't mind me fuckin' it."

She glared at him side long. "You know what the hunger was like...You're in danger with me."

No. Not since she'd given him her quick and bound him. He sensed that in his soul. Killing him would be like murdering part of herself. It wouldn't happen just because she was hungry. Not now.

"No, I ain't, Sar." A smile warmed his cheeks. "You ain't gonna drain me to death any more than I'm gonna drag you to the Abyss." Every time he recalled what lurked behind his eye, a pit opened in his stomach. But since she'd first controlled those nightmarish tendrils, he'd had little fear that they'd harm *her*. "Maybe that's why we're meant for each other, darlin'... That black stuff we got inside—the other one of us ain't afraid to face it."

CHAPTER TWENTY-FOUR

It took almost a fortnight to reach the first Westveldish town with lodging. That long in the wilderness without supplies had Benton ready to collapse. So, after two pints, potato pie, and a slow fuck, he passed out in their bed at the Boarderline Inn with the sun still in the sky.

All light had bled from the realm when a dagger drove through his chest, tearing him from sleep.

He grabbed for the hilt, but his fingers closed around empty air, and the weight of a wagon crushed his torso. Flailing for Sarlona, he patted only a vacant spot on the narrow mattress beside him. "Sar?"

No answer.

With a vise clamped on his chest, he rolled onto his side.

His floundering heart plopped to the floor.

She hung unconscious in another man's arms, the pale moonlight spilling in from the window to highlight her exposed throat and parted lips.

The eerie shadow, who'd captured her, shifted, and Aldamon's low, melodic song caressed Benton's ears. "She *is* enchanting." Sweet and haunting, even-toned and hypnotic, with just a tinge of an unidentifiable accent, the familiar voice whispered into Benton's soul. "And I'm not under her spell..."

No. But she was under his, half-naked and unconscious in his clutches.

Aldamon gazed at her with a sad smile, curling long fingers upward to stroke her cheek.

Terrified that the soul-eating vampire would vanish with her at any moment, Benton wrenched his muscles from their paralysis. Not even Aldamon had the right to keep them apart. He dragged himself from the bed, collapsing under the weight of the creature's aura, and crawled toward Sarlona like sandbags were tied to his limbs.

"A little dramatic, don't you think?" The hint of disappointment in his tone made Benton wish he could recede into the cracks between the cold floorboards. "You still find me so awful?"

Benton choked on his words before uttering a syllable.

"All right..." Aldamon wrinkled his nose. "I'll condense myself."

A second later, the atmosphere thinned. The chains constricting Benton's chest broke, and he sucked in a deep breath as the crushing gravity fled from the room. A flame danced to life on the candlestick sitting atop the bedside table.

Benton lay prostrate beneath something akin to an ancient dragon rather than a primeval, soul-devouring void.

"That is better, yes?"

Benton climbed to his feet and tottered at them. "Give her here."

"And just like that, he commands me?" Aldamon's tone and eyes laughed as he glanced at Sarlona. "With such a smoky drawl. Exquisitely masculine, no?"

"Please..." Benton cleared his throat. He'd beg if he had to. "What do you want?"

Aldamon shrugged, still regarding Sarlona as if she were a puzzle to solve. "Do *you* not want something?" He spun away when Benton reached for her and smiled. "You were dreaming of me."

Ice replaced the blood in Benton's veins. "I'm...sorry."

"Don't be. I'm delighted." With a sparkling smile at Benton, Aldamon threw Sarlona over his shoulder.

"Aldamon..." Benton almost gagged on the name, terrified the soul-eater was about to teleport to Gulway with all his heart and purpose. "Please put her down..."

"My, you do revel it in, don't you?" Stalking nearer, Aldamon peered into Benton's eyes.

Frozen, Benton stared into those pale, spellbinding irises. Gods, he'd never escape them...

The vampire cocked his head. "You love the feeling of her collar tightening around your neck."

Benton swallowed hard. "I've had one asshole or another yankin' on my lead my whole life." His comfortable grin crept onto his face. "She's the only one to pet me good and let me sleep in the bed."

Aldamon broke their gaze. "A man as empty as you have been... I suppose all he ever wants is to be filled."

Eyeing the sword belt that hung on the bedpost, Benton hoped he wasn't dumb enough to go for his blade. "Please, put her down," he repeated.

"I came a great distance." Aldamon's fangs peeked from his smile. "Aren't you going to offer me a drink?"

A chill clawed up Benton's spine. He prayed the vampire just thirsted for blood. "You got the only taste of my soul you're gettin'."

"How long will you hold that against me?" Aldamon asked, manifesting behind him. Warm breath spread over Benton's nape.

Shivering again, he ducked. By the time he swiveled, the vampire hovered over Sarlona on the bed, fangs bared.

Benton's heart jumped into his throat. "Don't. Fine, you can have *me*."

Aldamon paused, arctic eyes laughing.

"My blood," Benton clarified.

"Arousing..." The vampire straightened, mercifully distancing his fangs from Sarlona's throat. "But why should I not have you both?"

Benton's heart pounded so hard that he twitched with each beat.

"Relax, Benton." Aldamon sat on the edge of the bed beside Sarlona. "I'm only teasing you."

Cocking *why*? "What do you want, Aldamon?" Benton asked, dreading the answer. "Really."

The vampire scooted back on the bed and patted the spot on the other side of Sarlona. "To make you an offer."

Benton was sure he didn't want whatever Aldamon had come to sell but sat where bidden.

"I want to offer you both a home." The vampire brushed the hair from her face, then trailed his fingers from Sarlona's scalp to her throat. "Come stay with me in Gulway—forever."

Benton's heart plummeted into his gut. Swallowing, he groped for a diplomatic reply. "We can't go to Aven. The Council might execute Sar."

"Benton..." Aldamon's tone tugged Benton's gaze from Sarlona's face to his. Every trace of amusement left it. "She's not safe here. They'll come to Westveld. They'll go to Northland or Rashiva. Kyran's reach is long, and she made the magical world nervous before she could drain it."

Dragon talons closed around Benton's chest.

"There are far worse things they could do than execute her." Aldamon's words struck as quiet and deadly as an assassin's blade.

Benton would break if he tried to contemplate them.

"But she'll be safe under my roof," the vampire said.

Safe from *one* threat. Maybe. Benton searched the monster's eyes. They reminded him of Sarlona's. Not because of their color. Aldamon's eyes were the pale blue of a Northland glacier, not the deep blue of the Avenian Sea. But their luster was similar. They possessed some otherworldly brilliance, like those first rays of sunlight to penetrate the clouds after days of rain and gray. Some alluring magic that drew Benton in and made sweet promises...

He broke their stare. Those eyes were made for deception. He would never see the truth in them. "Not safe from you."

The slightest smile seeped into Aldamon's expression. He cocked his head with a slow blink. "No."

Desperate for light, Benton focused on the drop of it flickering atop the candle. "If you want us safe, just kill Kyran."

The vampire chuckled. "You ask me to assassinate the leader of the magical world?"

"Yeah, why not?" Benton asked the candle, knowing damn well that the price for that favor would be a lot higher than he could pay.

The vampire leaned toward him over Sarlona. "For good or ill, that would have ramifications throughout this realm. Can you imagine if I meddled in the world's affairs?"

Shuddering, Benton wasn't about to try. Aldamon could probably conquer a continent in an afternoon if he wanted.

"I've kept to my corner of Aven for millennia..." The vampire rested a hand on Sarlona's leg as he gazed out the window. "Do you think I'm not tempted to spread beyond it? Who could stop me should I decide that all the little ants are no longer fit to rule themselves?"

Only a god, if any existed. "Worth a shot." Stiffening, Benton watched, helpless, while the vampire kneaded Sarlona's thigh. Aldamon would make her prey again. Despite her supernatural strength, he'd hold her down and drink from her, just like Dagmar and Glaucus had. He'd fuck her. And for all Benton knew, the monster would take her soul before the end.

"I don't wanna be your toy, Aldamon." Benton gulped, afraid the ancient being would take offense. "And I sure as cock can't watch Sar be one."

The vampire pressed his mouth into a thin line and raised his eyebrows. "Disappointing...but understandable."

Benton's nerves itched when Aldamon ran fingertips from her leg to her cheek. Though her face appeared peaceful, he imagined the vampire's every caress put a new nightmare in her head.

"She would grow to incredible power with my Marrow and tutelage."

Benton imagined her enthralled with her hands on Aldamon's bare flesh, and a spike of jealousy pricked his gut. "What're you tellin' *me* for? Wake her up and ask her if she wants to go with you." But even as the suggestion passed his lips, he hoped the vampire wouldn't rouse her. He didn't want to subject her to Aldamon. Once she was awake with her heart pounding and terror in her eyes, the monster might not be able to help himself. Like a fox in a henhouse, he might go on a rampage.

Aldamon stared at the floor, silence stretching out between them. Then, "Once...I interfere with her, there's no going back... Do you understand?"

"No."

The vampire's eyes narrowed. "When I peer into her future..." He reached out tentatively and swirled his hands as though trying to clear smoke that wasn't there. "Where I should see all her possible paths, I see nothing."

Benton's blood skimmed over with ice. "Does that mean she don't have one?

Aldamon furrowed his brow. "Perhaps... It could also mean she destroys them all."

A derisive snort slipped from Benton before he could stop it. "The cock she does."

"Something Sarlona touches has devastating consequences for this realm." His voice grew even more haunting. Dire. "I fear it will be me."

Benton would put his last coin on Aldamon being correct. Assuming *anything* he said was true.

"But..." Slack faced, the monster's gaze appeared milky, as if some fog ahead were reflecting in his eyes. "I'd hate for the lorkai to die out so soon. Or be enslaved." He tipped Sarlona's head back. "Glaucus was the great-great-great-grandson of a cherished consort. I've looked after his line for millennia."

Benton couldn't care less about the fate of the lorkai species or what the creature beside him was going through. All he could see was how exposed Sarlona's throat was with a soul-sucking vampire hovering over her.

"Opening my doors to his beloved granddaughter and her handsome companion isn't *too* meddlesome, is it?" With his attention fixed on Sarlona, the monster seemed to ask her. "Even if we feed each other's power..." The vampire leaned nearer her throat.

In his mind's eye, Benton saw the two monsters intertwined again. He imagined Sarlona mad with energy she had no outlet for—and shaped by a creature whose humanity had been lost before the first stone tower breached the horizon. While Aldamon used her as a font to increase his own godlike power.

Defying every instinct, he grabbed Aldamon's shoulder. "It's a shitty idea." The words barely escaped his tightening throat. "You'll just rile each other up."

The vampire straightened. With a slight smile, he met Benton's stare. "You see? That's why I asked you."

Benton shrank when Aldamon floated a hand near his face.

After missing Benton's cheek, the vampire's fingers alighted on Sarlona's. She took a deeper breath and arched with a wispy moan.

"It's too bad, though. We would have enjoyed each other's company." He traced the side of her face, then her lips. His fingers blurred with a red-orange glint.

Frost prickled Benton's skin. "What was *that*?"

"What was what, my love?" Aldamon's gaze lingered on Sarlona. He trailed a finger down her throat.

She swallowed.

"Gods dammit. You put somethin' in her mouth," Benton said as the vampire rose. "That wasn't your blood, was it?"

Seconds dragged like minutes as Aldamon watched him. He may have avoided the vampire's fangs so far this visit, but those glacial eyes drank him in. An icy chill swept over his skin while a warm tremor rattled his bones.

"Goodbye, Benton..." Aldamon's melodic voice grew more haunting and sounded miles away. Sweet and entrancing, it pulled on Benton's insides—a siren song that begged him to follow. "May you both find peace..."

For the next heartbeat, peace seemed to dwell in Aldamon's embrace. The gentlest smile tugged the monster's lips but didn't enter his eyes. "*However* it comes."

The claw in Benton's chest let go. Aldamon vanished in a blink.

Sarlona shot upright, ejecting her carpal blades. One almost grazed Benton's ear. "What the hells was that?"

His heart still pounded, but he forced calm into his voice. "That was Aldamon, sweetheart."

Her eyes widened, and she gulped for air. "Are you okay? What did he want?"

Benton didn't really know. To keep her as a powerful elixir? "To warn us, I think..." He smeared the fresh beads of sweat into his hairline, then inspected her. "Do you feel okay? He..." Gods knew what Aldamon had done, but Benton didn't want to worry her. "He was holdin' you when I woke up."

Her pale features contorted. "Yeah. Just...startled." She folded her claws in and rubbed her arms as though chilled. "What was the warning?"

He wasn't sure about that either. That she might destroy the world somehow? Aldamon's every word, gaze, and touch felt laced with a lie. But one thing he'd said rang true—Kyran's reach was long. "That we've gotta get farther from the border."

CHAPTER TWENTY-FIVE

W aves roared from the far end of the island but only lapped at the small cove where Sarlona had taken to offering her sunset prayers. The tiny pebbles tinkled with each animate ridge that met its end atop them with a fizz of protest. She'd never know if the sea sounded the same in southwestern Northland as it did home in Mast Landing. Though it had rumbled in the distance when she'd confronted Sylvanus—needlessly, it turned out—she hadn't sat with it there. Her home had never spoken to her while she listened with lorkai ears. But she reminded herself that it was the same sea. Tydras still ruled it. And despite the fresh doubt that He cared for her, offering Him her love twice a day granted her a sense of peace and normalcy that had been missing from her existence for months.

There was a familiarity to life with Benton on their little island, even though she experienced the sights, smells, and sensations in new ways. The open air and expanse of blue that sliced across the sky like the edge of a blade far in the distance... The salt, the stone... And the quiet.

It reminded her of the many days and nights spent on the beach or camping deep in the forest with Sylvanus. But now her companion loved her as deeply as anyone ever could, and her chores were centered on caring for someone instead of the rigorous spell work and physical torments meant to hone her discipline.

She'd never be at peace while a Marrow-devouring void yawned in her depths, but contentedness no longer hid in another realm. Cuddled in their hut with their minds touching and his taste on her fingertips, joy seeped into her heart.

And Benton was happier than he'd ever been. Loved, fed, and with no one near who might stab him in the back, life had light in it, no matter the darkness lurking in them both.

He came around the corner of the island, passing between two boulders, just as the last sliver of sun sunk into the sea, and she disbanded her divine circle. They'd only been there a few weeks, but he'd already worn a trail along the island's perimeter. He patrolled it when bored, just like he'd walked along Ashmore's palisade.

"You done, darlin'?"

She rose, brushing the grit from her pants. "Yep."

He swatted her backside a few times, pretending to help. "Wanna take me into town?"

She shoved his hands at him. "Am I going to have to carry you home?"

He grinned bright as ever, teeth glowing in the dusk against skin that had tanned from coastal sunshine. "I'll be good."

She doubted it. "Sure. It's calm enough." Their dinghy, a wreck she'd patched with birch bark and sealskin, was barely seaworthy. "I should feed anyway."

That was their arrangement—they'd go into Roknur every few days so Sarlona could feed and Benton could drink. However much she hated stealing magical energy from strangers, he wasn't quite enough to keep her sated on his own. And she wouldn't risk allowing herself to become so hungry that she lost control.

While she fed on whichever unfortunate villager wandered off into the shadows alone, Benton would hock what she'd managed to scrounge up in the last few days—fish, meat, pelts, pearls, or trinkets recovered from the sea floor. Then he'd buy whatever they needed to supplement what she couldn't hunt or forage. The night would end in a tavern with either their last coin or when Benton couldn't walk straight.

"Great." He hauled the dinghy into the water as she snatched fish from their makeshift live well—a barrel she'd set into the ground to keep them cool—and loaded them into a big basket.

"You know, you could save yourself a lotta effort if you just pocket a few coins from everyone you feel up," he said, setting the oars in their locks.

Sarlona sneered. They had the same argument each time they left the island. Why couldn't they just rob folks? Why couldn't they take mercenary work from every hooded figure who sat in the shadiest corner of Roknur's seediest tavern? "Because losing a few coins makes their lives more difficult, Benton."

He gave her that shit-eating grin she'd missed so much when he'd been wearing Glaucus's skin. "But it makes *ours* easier."

Hers was easy enough. Now that she couldn't freeze, Sarlona never tired of wandering the woods and waves. "Afraid of a little hard work all of a sudden?" she asked, setting the basket of gasping fish in the boat.

His smile faltered, and his brow wrinkled as his gaze strayed from her face to somewhere over her right shoulder.

She spun. "What?" In the distance, a yellow light cruised up the coast in their direction.

"What the cock is that?"

Whatever it was, its warm glow illuminated the waters while it bobbed along, pausing or veering off here and there. It reminded her of a will-o-wisp, but the color was wrong, and she'd never seen one rove over open seawater. It didn't make a sound, and she couldn't smell it. "I think it's a spell."

With a whisper of steel on leather, he drew his blade. "What kinda spell?"

She didn't answer, but the light's features sharpened as it neared. A strand trailed the central orb like a lost eye with the nerve still attached, skimming the water. Her heart jumped. That's exactly what it was—an eye the size of a dinner plate, complete with iris and pupil etched in a whiter light at the front. "A search spell? It's scanning for something..."

As it drew nearer, she prayed it sought anything but them. "Put your sword away." She turned her body and clothes transparent, all but disappearing, and crouched behind the dinghy. It might be too late, depending on the spell's range. "Pretend to be a fisherman or something."

Benton snorted and shoved his blade back into his belt. Bending over the boat, he fiddled with its contents.

The eye drifted closer, its iris and pupil scanning side to side while its dangling nerve left a rippling wake. Sarlona peeked around the dinghy's stern as it cruised by their small island.

"We shoulda kept goin' west," Benton said under his breath. "Not doubled back and up the coast."

He was probably right. But Kyran would've expected them to flee to Westveld in search of someone who could make her human. Few talented casters resided in Northland. Besides, the SPS had less influence there.

With the magic eye almost past the island, Benton straightened. As if on cue, it pivoted and shot at him. Cursing, he tore his blade from its sheath. The eye impaled itself on the end of his sword and dissolved.

Sarlona's shoulders sagged, weariness seeping in. Living as a monster was bad enough without being hunted like one. "I guess it's t—"

The cacophony of heartbeats stole her voice, and a dozen humanoid scents flooded her nasal cavity. She faced Kyran and the SPS mages, who'd appeared behind her in a semicircle.

"Dagmar's still alive," she said, conjuring the pigments into her flesh. Gods knew why that was the first thing out of her mouth.

Charcoal eyes narrowing, Kyran's lips twisted into a snarl. "She fled. Which is why I've had to track you down." He smoothed his features to appear amiable. "The magical world can't have two female lorkai running about ungoverned."

"*You* can't have two at all." She hadn't forgotten that, however reasonable he attempted to sound.

"No," he agreed. "One female and a few males. Just enough to preserve the species."

The muscles in her arms itched to eject her blades. "So, you manage immortals like the king's herd?"

"Yes. Surely a former druid can understand that concept," Kyran said as he approached.

Former. "Can't I just be left alone, Councilor?" She glanced about, seeking a second of solace in the gates of Tydras's realm, where faint pink clashed with umbral waters. Without Benton, she could have disappeared into the sea. She couldn't stand to abandon him with Kyran again, though. "I'm not bothering anyone here. I won't make any children unless you ask me to." Her stomach flipped. "And I'll pay my SPS dues in whatever tasks the Council deems appropriate."

Kyran's smile might have appeared warm had it touched his eyes. "That's why I like you, Sarlona. You're reasonable. Diplomatic." He stretched a gloved hand toward her. "But, no, we can't leave you alone. You're an *abomination.*" Now, the simper hit his stare as if he delighted in telling her that. "Come along, and perhaps you can convince me that I should wait for Dagmar to turn up rather than have you humanely destroyed."

Dread squeezed Sarlona's throat while the monster roared inside. Benton's heart thundered above the beats of the rest. Pure rage leaked from his pores. He'd never let her go without a fight. Neither would the black thing that Dagmar had left in her depths.

She backed away. Compliance and 'convincing' might keep her alive, but she doubted she could trade Dagmar's life for her own anyway. Complicated as her nightmarish bond with her mother-daughter was, it was strong.

"You expect me to go quietly when you might decide to incinerate me?" She let the monster flood her eyes with red light.

"Euthanize," he whispered. "You wouldn't be aware of it. But I have a feeling Dagmar will surrender herself if you're in custody."

Sensing that every chain of restraint in Benton was about to break, she shouted telepathically for him to keep still.

Kyran crept closer—so near she could have snapped his neck had she not been sure that he'd already shielded himself. "You can't tell me you haven't wished for death after having such tremendous magic ripped from you and replaced by hunger?"

No, she couldn't. "Not any longer." Since she and Benton had settled on the island, she'd come to believe she could endure as a lorkai. With him at her side, the thirst—the darkness—was bearable.

Kyran shrugged. "Good. We'd much rather be rid of Dagmar. But I need you to draw her out. And given what you did to Talvianna's son upon your departure from Apogee, you're destined to spend a little time in a dungeon cell, anyway."

She hadn't forgotten the young mage she'd dropped in the woods near the tower. In fact, with her attention drawn to him, she smelled him nearby. "He looks well to me," she said, staring past Kyran at the green-eyed guard. "I was careful not to hurt him."

"You drained him. You fed from a caster against his will." Kyran's words passed through clenched teeth. "A *person*. Do you not understand that?"

She understood. Not just what she'd done but what she was dealing with. Realization settled on her like a blanket of foreboding snow. "Of course I do. *Everyone* I feed from is a person."

"Yes. Well, it's a particularly heinous thing to do to a caster." He cleared his throat. "Which is why it's *illegal*. Time to face the consequences."

She swept her gaze over the tiny beach, scanning also with her ears and olfaction. Ten casters, including Kyran, had come to collect her.

Benton could take a couple of the weaker ones if he could keep them in front of him. Based on the reek and hum of his Marrow alone, Kyran might be as difficult to defeat as Sylvanus. The man standing beside the mage she'd drained, an older Khalorini brother by the scent, wasn't much weaker. And the power of the young woman nearest Kyran wasn't anything to sneeze at.

Even if Sarlona and Benton could defeat them... Even if they killed Kyran... Then what? It would probably piss off the rest of the Council. "I want your promise that Benton will be allowed to go free."

Benton snorted like a bull.

"Fine," Kyran said. "Magicless sell-swords don't concern me."

She fixed her gaze on the younger Khalorini again. Maybe she'd wronged him. Perhaps she'd shown him mercy. Either way... He'd felt trustworthy when she'd grazed his mind. And he was a skilled teleporter. "If he takes Benton to Rashiva *now,* I'll go with you."

"Fine." Kyran gestured from the younger Khalorini brother to Benton.

Benton raised his sword point higher as the young man neared. "I ain't cockin' goin' anywhere, and neither is Sar."

"Bent—"

But he lunged at the teleporter, ending her negotiations.

The caster blasted him back, and the older brother, a man decked out in the leather and steel of a dedicated warcaster, elevated his hand with lightning dancing between his fingers.

Sarlona was on him before he could point them, hacking at his carapace.

The island exploded.

Flames, lightning, ice, acid, rocks, whirling gadgets, and rotating blades flew in every direction. Gaping cracks in the earth roared as they sucked up the sea, opening between razor-sharp spikes that burst upward from the rock. Vampiric mists melded with dissolving fogs. Zones of crushing gravity splattered areas of gelled atmospheres.

Sarlona slipped through it all like each spell was a branch in the forest. Flitting from behind one mage to the next, she lapped at their shielding with her slashing claws. Hopefully, the casters would burn themselves out, or their zone spells would wear down each other's protections enough for her to break them.

Periodically, she paused, appearing farther into the island's interior to draw them farther from Benton and keep him clear of the zone spells. He worked on the casters at the edge of the fray, darting in and stabbing at their backs each time Sarlona hit them and zipped off. They'd fire something to repel him, which he'd catch on his blade and return to them.

Finally, after one of Kyran's molten lead balls grazed Sarlona's arm and hit an older woman dead on, she saw her first opportunity.

Spinning along the woman's side to her back, she pivoted and drove both claws at the old sorceress's shoulders. The ivory swords popped through the last of the mage's carapace. Sarlona relented before her carpal blades hit bone and grabbed the woman by the nape. The sorceress collapsed as Sarlona yanked out the last vapors of her Marrow and forced her into a coma for good measure. Another woman rushed in, throwing a glowing shield over the fallen sorceress while marble-sized meteors rained from above.

Glancing at the beach as Sarlona sprinted for the crumbling forest, she spotted Benton standing over a heavy-set man, who struggled to cast a sputtering healing spell on his bleeding thigh.

With a swipe that seemed quick even to a lorkai, Benton caught twin balls of purple flame that tried to flank him on the edge of his blade and whipped the spell back at the man who'd thrown it. A violet fireball shot at the caster, splitting midway and crashing into his sides before coating his carapace in a burning purple net.

But Benton's blade couldn't absorb the wall of water that was rising perpendicular to the surf behind him.

Sarlona's bones ached beneath her tightened muscles. How dare they use the *sea* against her? To harm her Bound...

She zipped in, grabbing Benton about the waist and dragging him clear when the wave crested. The younger Khalorini appeared, snatching the husky mage in the nick of time. The water thundered as it pummeled the beach and receded with a roar, taking the sand with it.

Impressive, but nothing like the wave Sarlona had conjured in her last-ditch effort to escape the lorkai in Mast Landing. She ground her teeth, itching to show the SPS mages real mastery of the sea.

As she spun Benton away from a roaring steam of fire, it occurred to her that she might just be able to.

Snatching him by the wrist, she took his reins. He jerked and raged internally as she made him shove his sword into his scabbard. Stepping behind him, she rested her palm along his jaw and released his wrist to free up his other arm. Then she called his Marrow to his fingertips instead of hers.

At her command, he raised hands as though to cover his face, swooped them back and shouted, "Scutum."

Translucent, adamantine plates snapped in place around them a second before a boulder shot for them from the rocky waterline. It bounced off the shielding like a stick off ice.

Benton's unuttered curses fell silent in Sarlona's head, and the hum of magic echoed along his nerves. Stunned, he stared in horrified awe while she lifted his hands, palms facing the sky. A proper wave rose in line with the surf, coming from the deeper sea.

He wasn't the only one. For a few seconds, all the mages gawked, some wide-eyed, others squinting as though what they were seeing couldn't be right. Whether that was due to sheer surprise at Benton's sudden con-version or abject horror at a lorkai's appropriation of another's inborn capacity for magic, she didn't know. Or care. It allowed her to build the wave that much higher.

Though she called the sea with all her soul, the wall of water grew to about three-quarters of what she intended. However Marrow-rich Benton was, he didn't possess half the reserve of her human body. His muscles shook, and his heart galloped. His every fiber burned with awakened Mar-row. Needing his focus and intent for a decent spell, she silenced his racing thoughts.

She made him whisper "anchor," and the mages shouted it themselves an instant before the thundering crash of the wave drowned all other sounds. Benton's adrenaline surged with the raging waters, but neither their scutum nor anchor was in danger of failing.

The same couldn't be said for the casters. She scanned the island as the waters receded to find the younger Khalorini brother, the injured man, the unconscious woman, and one other gone. Teleported home at the last second, Sarlona hoped.

She released Benton, rushing Kyran and the remaining Khalorini before either could shoot anything at Benton. Neither seemed the least bit worse for wear. Nor did the young woman.

Sweat dripped from the brows of the other three mages, though. Their hands shook, and their chests heaved as they reinforced their carapaces.

Sarlona went for the weakest—a blond man relying on a wand to empower his ice spells—while Kyran and the girl conjured hulking steel warriors to keep Benton busy.

In a blink, Sarlona struck the mage's carapace a dozen times. Once it flickered, she punched through and snapped the wand between her fingers. In the same motion, she grabbed his hand and ripped out his remaining rivulets of Marrow. As he collapsed, she tugged the threads in his brain that would keep him unconscious.

She flipped rearward over the spinning, flame-belching blade that shot for her spine and dodged a pillar of lightning that melted the ground to glass. Looping back, she picked her path through sluggish explosions and lobbed projectiles.

The dank scent and eerie tingle of Abyssal magic hit the air behind her.

She didn't have to pivot to know who manifested at her back. The familiar, steady heartbeat and alluring odor told her who was there. Never mind the overpowering thrum of Marrow.

"You're late," Kyran growled as he whipped his obsidian blade in Sarlona's direction, shooting a fifty-foot stream of flame at her.

She skipped out of its way.

Amenduil shrugged. "I'm a busy man."

Before the dread could crush her heart, Benton's curse drew her attention. As the second conjured warrior collapsed at his feet, Abyssal tendrils burst from his eye, heedless of the enchanted patch. He swiped at them with his blade, but they regrew instantly, thicker and longer.

Sarlona zipped to his side and caught him when he lost his balance, struggling against the unholy appendages. Cupping his jaw from behind, she took control and snapped a carapace in place before three fireballs crashed into them. The flames rolled over it, doing no more than warming their skin.

She stilled his mind, stifling his panic, and coaxed the tendrils back while she used his free hand to grab the water. Sharp tangles of coral flew from the sea with a flick of his wrist and collided with the nearest mage, knocking him over, carapace and all.

But she couldn't hope to use Benton to match Amenduil's magic. He didn't have that kind of Marrow. No one did. And she couldn't connect his body with the great expanse of sapphire on the dim horizon like she had her own.

He'd die there on that island, and she'd either burn or be imprisoned.

As she threw another wall of water at the mages in frustration, Benton's tentacles wiggled in his core, begging to be let out.

She tried to ignore them as she sheathed his blade and called every strand of beachbind kelp to slither from the rocks and drag the mages to the depths. But maybe Vorakor's tentacles weren't so different from the kelp—smooth cords sliding out from the dark to wrap around wayward limbs and drag victims into the watery deep.

The tendrils writhed harder, sending a pleasant tremor through Benton that she could have sworn permeated her body, too. Behind them loomed a swell of power—black but warm—on the order she'd once known.

Though Benton's body couldn't connect with the sea, it was joined inextricably with another god's realm.

Sarlona released her hold on Vorakor's tentacles, and they slipped free in a euphoric burst. He cried out as she called that shadowy swell to roil up.

"*Cock.* What are you doin', Sar? *Don't,*" he growled, fighting for control he couldn't win.

She didn't know the best words or gestures for any Abyssal spells, so she went by instinct, winding up with both hands and letting them fill with the raging umbra from below. Benton shook while the dark magic built until he was bursting with it, onyx static crackling around them.

"Cock, fuck, *cock.*" He whined through gritted teeth.

CHAPTER TWENTY-SIX

B enton fought Sarlona and the Abyss with all his might, but he was just a tool, wielded by far more powerful entities. The world plunged into darkness as she swept his hands forward, spreading his fingers wide. Waves of living shadow tore out of him like obsidian flame, scorching his veins and racking his muscles on the way out. Despite that and the horror of unleashing hell through his being, elation rivaled the dread. He surged, eyes wide and heart pounding with adrenaline like when a man who'd lunged at him just slipped off his bloodied blade.

"*Cock...*" he said as the raven fire raged on. It must have spilled from him for a full minute. When it sputtered out, the only thing left standing was Amenduil, perched atop the island's tallest boulder, which now resembled lava rock instead of granite.

The Abyssal mage had blackened—skin, robes...down to the whites of the eyes and teeth he bared in a devilish grin.

Smooth and glassy water sparkled in the brightening moonlight with flashes of squirming onyx tendrils everywhere the ground dipped. A few tentacles breached their hell puddles, winding closer to the fallen mages.

Kyran rose from his knees, shooting a manna potion. He glared at Amenduil as Sarlona wound up with Benton's hand. "*Stop* her!"

Amen chuckled.

Kyran refreshed his carapace just before an inky ball shot from Benton's palm. The ebony glob splattered across the councilor's front, obscuring his face and hissing while it ate at the shielding. The young, green-eyed warcaster followed Kyran's example, staggering to his feet and throwing back a potion. A man in brown robes, who crouched over the fallen blond, vomited tar. Once he finished spewing the nightmarish exudate, he grabbed the downed mage and vanished. A scrawny, middle-aged man with tendrils wrapping around his legs disappeared a second later.

Kyran shook his head as the young woman glanced from where the man had vanished to the council leader. "Don't you fucking dare."

Shakily, the girl, whose veins had turned jet black, shot a healing potion, then a vial of manna. Of course, Benton's demands to obliterate the young woman before she could do either went unheeded.

At least Sarlona fired shadowy lightning at Kyran. The asshole caught it on a glowing white shield that expanded from his hand, though.

"Vorakor has truly blessed you both." Amenduil's smile resembled that of a proud father.

Benton would've done just about anything to punch it off him.

"Does this mean you two are ready to join me and the Embrace?" the Abyssal mage all but sang, his color returning.

Benton tried to respond with the most violent and obscene refusal he could conjure, but Sarlona held him silent as she met the green-eyed mage's blue lightning with a charcoal bolt.

Kyran looked like he'd explode. "We had an agreement!"

Amenduil hovered out from his perch before touching down in front of them. "We still might, depending on Sarlona's stubbornness," he replied, eyeing her over Benton's shoulder. "What do you say, my dear? Would you prefer to go to the councilor's dungeon or with me to Port Brummit?"

Benton would try to take off her head and flee with it if she chose either.

"How could we ever trust you after what you did?" She forced sun beams to erupt from Benton's palms, illuminating Amenduil's shielding and scorching the earth beneath his feet.

Benton ignored how unnatural it felt compared to the Abyssal magic. And how much Sarlona struggled to reel in his tendrils this time.

"Have a little faith, my dear." Amenduil retreated from the bleached ground with a grimace like he'd stepped in horse shit. "The blacker, the better."

"I won't abandon my gods," she said, raising the scattered sand with Benton's arms. "I won't pray to darkness." The coarse grains blasted against the carapaces of the four remaining mages.

Amenduil pouted as his protections deflected the sand. "Then don't be so flirtatious with it, Sarlona." His tone grew sickening, and he shook his head. "You've given me and our Abyssal Lord the wrong idea by dabbling with his magic just now." Wagging a finger at her in a manner that made Benton yearn to snap it off, he went on, "And the ways you've let Him touch you when He's reached out of Benton..." Amenduil closed a fist over his shoulder, quashing the rock-melting fireball Kyran sent in their direction. "I have to admit, they've made me blush."

Benton wasn't sure whether Sarlona's hands went cold, his face flushed with rage, or both. The notion of Amenduil spying on them...

Golden light spilled from Benton's palms as his arms shot out toward the Abyssal mage. It rushed at Amenduil in a stream but parted around him, breaking on his shielding.

"Why can't I be left alone?" Sarlona snarled. "*Why?*" She sent a radiant blast from Benton's core that knocked everyone except Amenduil onto their asses.

The light magic struggled on its way out, though. His insides thinned. Sarlona couldn't use him for much longer.

"Because you're not meant to be hidden away in the forest like your old mentor insisted, my dear." With a pointed stare at the glowing fluid before him, it turned to obsidian. "Vorakor has big plans for you. They started with the lorkai." He glanced at Kyran, who had fists full of flame. "Come with me, and you can skip *that* whole part."

Kyran unleashed, and this time, Amenduil let the blast by. The fireball burst into an inferno across Benton's shielding, its flames raging so hot Benton tried to shrink into Sarlona. His core emptied into a dusty hollow. He wanted to glance down to make sure his organs hadn't fallen out. Instinct told him he couldn't take another blast.

Clapping her palm over his good eye, Sarlona swept his hand out and made him shout a Wildman phrase. His eyelids flashed red beneath the patch and her palm. An instant later, she let go—of everything. He pulled his blade as he opened bleary eyes and darted left. Sarlona was already hacking at Kyran's barrier, who had his fingers over his eyes with green light spilling from them. Squinting, the two young mages cast to heal themselves too.

Of course, Amen had seen the spell coming or avoided it somehow. Tendrils burst from his back and shot for Benton.

He sliced off the first shadowy snake before it touched him and hacked through the second when it caught his ankle. The third went for his throat, splitting along his blade, and the fourth grabbed his off-hand wrist for a split second before he sliced it free.

"You know I'm just toying with you, my friend." Amenduil's eyes dimmed to pitch, and he lifted into the air. "I could rip you apart from within."

Benton didn't doubt him as those wicked tentacles thrashed in his solar plexus. But he hadn't forgotten the hefty holy enchantment that Aldamon had added to his blade, either. It might just do more damage than Amen expected. And if he had to use the sword on himself... Well, that's what it was for.

Amen whipped his tendrils down, grabbing for Benton's weapon. "How can you not accept Vorakor as your father, having rested in His warm waters?"

Benton dodged to the side and chopped downward, severing the ebony snakes.

Black static danced between Amenduil's fingertips. "Having felt His power flow through you?"

Benton caught the crackling shadow Amenduil flung on his sword, but the blade didn't swallow it. Instead, the Abyssal magic swept across the steel and up his arm. The sensation of warm water coating his skin and silky tendrils cradling his limbs washed over him. A swell of euphoria, like Sarlona played with his insides, almost brought a groan to his lips. The Abyssal Waters lapped at him from within, begging to devour him.

"How?" Amenduil asked with a sickening grin. "When He's gazed into your heart, seen everything that you are, and implored you so personally to be His."

Benton raged against whatever warm thing tried to fill him. There'd been so many cold, empty years before Ashmore. Any honey-toned entity could have patched his wounds and coaxed him into submission. *Anything* could have answered his prayers in childhood, and he would have fallen to his knees. But nothing had reached out to him when he'd needed it. The universe had left him bleeding and alone.

Only now that Sarlona had already given Benton what he'd desperately required did he pose the slightest interest to something higher than himself. "Cause he's just a big cockin' Otherrealm monster who eats souls like every other asshole who claims to be a god."

Amenduil frowned. "I can't wait to show you how wrong you are."

Benton lunged at him, but the blade deflected.

"Come with me. Sarlona will follow, and you can save her from the agony that awaits her beyond our Abyssal Lord's domain."

Amen just wanted Sar. Vorakor did, too. Benton didn't blame them. He was an afterthought. But the dusk darkened with Amenduil's stare, and the same heat Benton experienced with Sarlona in his arms blossomed in his chest. It took all his concentration not to let the ethereal tendrils fluttering in his core burst free.

Amenduil cocked his head, floating nearer over the charred and desiccated ground while spells flew in the background. "You still don't *hear* Him, do you?"

Benton couldn't hear anything. Not the crack of spells or pounding of surf. Just Amenduil's voice, lower and sweeter than usual, but muffled as though Benton was underwater.

And with his limbs sluggish and heavy like warm tendrils ensnared them, he could barely move.

It would have been easy to keep standing there, letting Amenduil creep closer and do gods knew what to him. But a flash of blonde, carpal blades, and fire to his right reminded him that Sarlona needed help. And it sure as cock didn't lie in the Abyss.

"I just hear a lotta bullshit." Benton softened his knees and raised the tip of his blade. "Stop cockin' around."

Amenduil shrugged, then, without missing a beat, wound up with a ball of inky flame. Benton ducked and jabbed, catching the shadowy inferno on his blade and flicking it sideways at the female mage. When he popped up to rush forward and ram his holy enchant into Amen's shielding, black lightning sundered the air. He got his blade on the thick bolt that came toward him, too big for his sword to swallow, but the other branches exploded close by, sending painful jolts that threatened to drive him to his knees.

The shock slowed him enough for one of Amenduil's tendrils to snatch his wrist.

The Abyssal mage ripped him through the air with a yank that dislocated his sword arm and seemed to tear him out of existence. He broke across a boulder the size of a horse, spine cracking along its arch and skull smashing against jagged granite in an explosion of pain. His sword clanged to the ground. As he tried to reach for it, the sky spun in a blue-gray, faint pink, and starry swirl. He couldn't lift his arm. Or feel it. Everything but his aching skull went dead and numb.

That was it.

Amenduil's face congealed above him. "Go home, my friend. Down into the Abyss." With a storm of glittering black flecks whirling between his fingers, the Abyssal mage stretched a hand toward him.

Benton prayed the only darkness waiting for him was oblivion when the sparkling, ebony dust spilled into his chest. The world plunged into the deepest night, and he fell—farther and faster than ever.

But he crashed to a stop, frozen as the pale light of dusk blanketed his failing vision. A pair of glowing red eyes pierced it. Sarlona stood over him, roaring like a dragon and slashing so ferociously that she put Amenduil on his heels.

She crouched, grabbing a hand he couldn't feel, but there wasn't time to heal him. She couldn't stay still, or one of the mages would hit her. They'd both go up in a fireball. Too breathless to demand aloud that she run, he screamed it in his head.

But she scooped up his sword and sliced at the first blast of flame, absorbing it and spitting it back. Spells and his blade flashed as she knelt beside him with a firm grip on his hand and tears streaming from her burning eyes.

He begged her to leave. She couldn't fix him while catching spells from four directions. But instead of fleeing, she bent, damn her, for a kiss. She hitched, no doubt trying to get her quick into him to save his life as she had once before. But with her head down, she couldn't defend herself. A second passed before she crumpled half atop him and rolled onto her side.

Her head was twisted wrong, and her arms and feet faced rearward. Her eyes cooled and peered into his. He strained to keep them open, to gaze into her enchanting blue for a few more seconds before its beauty was snatched from him forever. When his lashes fluttered, she smiled and flopped her mangled arm to land her hand across his throat.

Knowing he'd never feel her sweet fingertips again, their warmth brought tears. The pain in his head numbed as her energies wove into his, but she had to realize he was empty. He had nothing left to give her, no matter how willing.

His heart lurched, and he sucked in half a rattling breath as she shoved a trickle of Marrow into him instead of the other way around. It was a good idea. But how she could use his body to heal either of them when it couldn't even wiggle a finger or form a word, he couldn't imagine.

Then she swept into his head and turned his thoughts toward Gulway. *Cock.* No.

His mind raced along the route to the city until he slammed into Aldamon's haunting stare and adamantine block at the castle's inner gate. *No, Sar. Don't.*

Tears collected in one corner of her smile. *Be good, Benton.*

He screamed in protest, fighting to put her face in his mind's eye rather than Gulway's gate. But soon, it was all he saw—his only focus. He wanted to be there. His insides jumped, and his thoughts reached for that spot, forgetting anywhere else existed. His stomach flipped as his every particle bound with partners a world away. Then he was racing for them through a maze of night, forest, and field, all blending.

He slammed into the ground. His mind was free, but his body was broken. Men shouted nearby. Tall, familiar doors loomed over him, splashed orange with the torchlight. Glowing gold armor took their place, and the face of a raven-haired woman solidified in front of him for a second. *Wrenwyn.*

"Get the baron," she hollered over her shoulder, then leaned closer.

She vanished between Benton's lids as he tripped into a world of fangs, tendrils, and utter despair.

CHAPTER TWENTY-SEVEN

Sarlona woke with a splitting headache and another set of eyes staring into hers. Or through hers. The hazel orbs a few inches from her own seemed not to see. It took her a second to register why... They weren't in a head. Instead, they rested upon a little wooden block, pulled out on taut nerves from an excised brain.

She shot up and almost tumbled from the table she'd been lain on—a blood-stained slab nicked in a thousand places from knives and scalpels.

Hands clutched her shoulders, steadying her. "Do you like it?" Kyran whispered in her ear. "It took me weeks to first lay out..." He kneaded cold, aching muscles. "And it requires quite a bit of maintenance... But scientifically—*artistically*—it's a masterpiece, wouldn't you agree?"

'It', she guessed by the scent, was a male vampire—something humanoid and immortal. But the smell was the only clue to the creature's identity. It had no face, no skin at all.

It was a landscape sculpted out of flesh.

The unfortunate vampire's parts had been dissected and pinned or placed on a small hook for display. He'd been spread over half the table, onto the floor, up an entire wall, and across the ceiling in grotesque magnificence. The blood vessels formed an appalling spiderweb tapestry with the heart at its center. The intestines hung like garland around the room, and the stomach had been turned out to reveal the texture within. Muscles had been teased apart into fascicles and stretched every which way. And the two bean-shaped kidneys hung with the bladder in a grisly trinity. If 'it' had been a cadaver, dead of natural causes, it would've been extraordinary. But the immortal would still be walking about if not for Kyran.

'It' was still alive.

"Come." Kyran took her elbow and beckoned her.

She rose, shaking and with joints screaming where his magic had twisted her bones apart. Her feet were bound together by a faery silk cord too short to let her leap from the table. Or run. Using his grip to steady herself, she hopped down, careful not to upset his 'masterpiece.'

"I'd heard you have an inquisitive mind. So, I knew you'd appreciate this..." He made a sweeping gesture at the vivisection. "I'm sure you're familiar with the parts, from helping on the farm, cleaning game, and perhaps your studies?"

Transfixed and unable to catch her breath, she only nodded.

"Never seen the insides of a humanoid though, have you?"

She shook her head.

Not like that. *No one* had seen anything that resembled what was laid out before her now.

Kyran guided her closer to the wall of horrors.

"These are the lungs." He pointed to what resembled two small bushes without leaves. "The vasculature anyway."

Much as she wanted to run, she couldn't get her feet to do more than shuffle. She didn't suppose she'd get very far. Her throbbing hands wouldn't move in the contraption that bound them, and the suffocating scent of dirt and rock told her she was deep underground.

He gestured to her left. "Those are the genitals over there."

She didn't look, keeping her stare fixed on the small network of blood vessels before her.

"The liver, the spleen. That's the appendix," he said.

Afraid to ignore him, she bobbed her head again. She understood the threat but couldn't make her voice work well enough to tell him she'd seen enough. To express her gratitude that he hadn't already burned her or left her decorating the wall opposite the unlucky vampire.

Taking her upper arm, he led her to the table. "That's the inside of the ears." He pointed next to two small, coiled masses that he had climbing over the brain like snails. "I destroyed the bones and the integument. They just didn't fit with the piece." His tone suggested that he spoke only of an art installation. "Of course, I have to keep scraping off bits of the skin and plucking out the seeds of cartilage that grow back..."

He took a small bottle of human blood and a pipette from the table.

"And parts do tend to migrate over time, despite the pins. But I've developed some cantrips to help with that."

Sarlona scanned the room for an exit while he drew blood into the pipette. None were visible. Any door leading from that chamber was concealed well enough that she couldn't detect a draft.

"I took special care to leave as many nerves intact as possible." With his free hand on her back, he guided her nearer the table until her hips hit it. "All the major ones are still attached to the spinal cord and that to the brain, of course."

She'd expected to wake up dead or not at all after she'd made Benton teleport to Gulway, and Kyran had rammed his sword point through the side of her head.

This was so much worse...

And Benton—she couldn't feel him. That hit harder than the horror before her. But she couldn't contemplate what that might mean now. She'd break.

"And I encourage as many to grow back as I can." Kyran pressed on her spine to hinge her down for a better view. "Faalhid's punishment for accusing me of magical crimes. To denounce the Council and slander me in such a way..." He scowled at what remained of the anatomized man. "That kind of insubordination can't be taken lightly." His hand slid up from her back, and he patted her head. "Wouldn't you agree?"

She froze, torn between a monster's rage and a little girl's terror.

Weaving his fingers into her hair, he yanked her close and whispered in her ear. "Watch." He let the droplets of blood drain from the pipette onto the brain's surface.

The hazel eyes on the table roared to life. They didn't move—with no muscle attached, they couldn't—but the pupils shrank to the size of pinholes.

Then the wretched vampire wailed into her mind—the most pitiful, heartrending 'sound' she'd ever known. A perfect manifestation of agony and despair, grating on her soul.

The noise faded, and the torture chamber went dark.

Both reappeared when Kyran tapped her cheek. He propped her up from behind. "We'll have to work on that faint heart." Chuckling, he steadied her while she got her feet beneath her. "Imagine a lorkai so delicate."

She barely registered his words. The sound of the vivisected vampire's agony drowned out her very thoughts.

"Come, I can see you've had enough." He guided her to the room's bare wall, lagging to accommodate her short, faery-silk-hindered stride. After he slapped his free palm to the stone, a section of wall faded, and he tugged her along. When the rocks solidified behind them, the wailing and reek of suffering grew fainter. The vise in her chest loosened.

"Immortals make perfect test subjects," he said, leaning on a bare table. "The opportunities you provide for experimentation are endless." A small smile crept onto his face. "Any strong study requires replication, after all."

She should have gone with Amenduil. He might have ruined her soul, but warm water and eternal dark seemed a sweet mercy when compared to illimitable vivisection.

"But I think you might be useful in other capacities." His tone was light and inviting, as though he was interviewing her for an apprenticeship instead of threatening her with decades of unmitigated torture. "Let's talk, shall we?"

She scanned the room for any new horrors. This chamber was barren except for a large tub, an iron hook that hung from the ceiling by a chain, and the battered table. It reeked of mortal blood and Marrow. This room had a door at least, but if she could trust the scents wafting from beneath it, it led to more suffering.

He patted the table beside him. "Sit."

With the table higher than her hips and her hands bound, she had to hop up backward to get onto it.

"I apologize for the discomfort of the lorkai cuffs. It's the only method we've found for binding your kind."

She gazed at her throbbing hands, bound by a sharply toothed pair of metal jaws, like one of the leg-hold traps used by furriers but with much longer teeth. The enchanted mithril spikes penetrated her hands and wrists, clasping them in an angry bite. She couldn't wrench them apart, not without ripping her hands off. And ejecting her carpal blades from that position would sever her forearms.

"Though, honestly, I hadn't believed you'd require them." He sounded disappointed in her. "You shouldn't have run from me, Sarlona."

She shouldn't have. Now, he was pissed off, and the last person she wanted irritated with her, given what he was capable of.

She cleared her throat, determined to gather enough courage to speak. "Why aren't I dead?"

He craned his neck to look into her downturned face, though she didn't want him staring at the fear it no doubt displayed. "Your overgrown maker surrendered herself once she learned we had you."

Her heart skipped a beat. Dagmar would suffer, too. Or burn in her place. The thought of either sent a rush of cold water across her skin. She supposed she was lucky she hadn't been shown Dagmar as a wall hanging.

He tipped her face up by the chin. "So, we're back to choosing which of you to put out of your misery."

"It should be me," she said, cringing. Her offer wasn't one of self-sacrifice to save Dagmar. It was to escape that dungeon, even if it meant death. "I didn't want this life. I tried to kill myself to escape it," she admitted, choking on the words. "They wouldn't let me die."

He frowned and cupped her jaw as if he gave a shit. "But perhaps that's why it should be you who lives. You're not a monster..."

She could've sworn he'd called her one before.

"Not...in heart and soul. Just in body and, perhaps, mind."

He was, though. One far worse than Dagmar. Or even Amenduil.

He shrugged, then pointed to the wall they'd come through. "*That*...is for my enemies." He smiled and raised the pitch of his voice as if talking to a young child. "You're not my enemy, are you, Sarlona?"

She shook her head. Best not to declare it, anyway.

"Of course not." He stroked her hair again. The touching had to be a test to assess what she'd tolerate. Not a trace of affection or attraction perfumed his scent.

"In fact, you could be an ally." He took her trapped hands in his and whispered over them. The warmth of his skin caught her by surprise. No thin, invisible armor coated his body. Another test. This one to see if she'd try to contort her hands to get a finger pad on him. Or bite out his throat.

She wasn't rash enough to attempt either.

Anyway, the green light that leaked from his palms numbed her aching hands. "Thank you, Councilor."

His smile touched his dark gaze, appearing more genuine. "Being my ally has advantages, Sarlona. It will get you places. Out of my laboratories for a start."

She cleared her throat "I'm sure if the Council decides I should live, I can be helpful to you." Whatever it took to keep her from being spread across a dungeon wall. Unless...he made her smear someone else across it.

"Good. Then I'll be upfront with you, Sarlona." He landed two fingers in the hollow of her throat, and she froze. As he drew them down the front of her tattered shirt between her breasts, she reminded herself that he likely had a spell for every violent act, trauma, and violation imaginable. A soft touch was the last thing she had to fear from him.

"I want..." Smiling, he kneaded the tip of her sternum where her ribcage came together. "Your quick."

She stared at his hand, trying to imagine why, but came up empty. "For what?" Her voice was little more than a whisper.

"A project I've been working on for quite some time. I've finally made some advancements thanks to what you left us."

She held in a sigh when he headed for the door.

"I'll show you. Wait here."

After a prayer to Tydras for strength, she circled the room, sniffing for any path out but where Kyran had gone. If there was one, she couldn't sense it.

He returned after just a few minutes anyway, wearing a strange contraption over one hand and forearm and prodding a haggard man in front of him.

"Who's this?" she asked, dread tightening its noose around her throat. Clad in filthy rags for pants with his hands bound in front of him, the human man was a prisoner.

Kyran dragged him to the tub and hook. "Seventeen."

"What are you going to do?" the man asked once he climbed into the basin. He reeked of fear as Kyran attached the large iron hook to his fetters.

"Nothing you could understand. Keep quiet, and I won't dissolve your jaw first." Kyran went to the winch and cranked up the clanking chain, lifting the man's thin arms above his greasy, disheveled hair. He balanced on his toes to avoid hanging, with his bare, hollow chest heaving.

She tried to raise her voice to speaking volume. "What *are* you going to do?" Not that there was much she could do to stop him. Her only option was to try to body slam Kyran to death before he got a shield up.

If he hadn't put one up already.

He centered himself in front of the prisoner and aimed his bedecked arm at the man. "Watch."

She squinted at the contraption that resembled a steel gauntlet but for the empty vial set into the underside of the wrist and the jointed metal tubing that ran from the vial to the fingertips.

"*Drain*," Kyran whispered, and her heart sunk into the grimy stone floor.

The center of the prisoner's torso lit up manna-blue an instant before Kyran's metal hand did. The man grimaced and hollered through gritted teeth as branching tendrils illuminated along his torso like rivers drawn on a map. A second later, a fluorescing, blue mist wound from the brightest point in his chest toward Kyran's bizarre gauntlet. The sweet scent of pure Marrow saturated the air.

Her compassion and monstrous hunger screamed alongside the man. "You're going to kill him." She shouldered Kyran's outstretched arm.

He scowled and blasted her back with a telekinetic burst from his free palm.

Hands bound and feet tethered, she hit the wall with bone-cracking force and fell on her ass.

Marrow flowed from the writhing prisoner until, with a sudden, wet snap, the veiny network of Marrow-bearing threads ripped out of the prisoner's torso. The delicate netting dulled and cracked, breaking into dusty shards and falling like ashes into the tub.

The man slumped forward, dead.

Kyran turned from him without a second glance and beckoned Sarlona with a curled finger. "Look."

She rose, spine throbbing as he removed the gauntlet and set it on the table. Carefully, he unscrewed the vial and held it for her to see.

Two drops. A man had died in agony for a trickle of Marrow.

She hated herself for wishing she could grab the vial and drink it. "What good is it to you?"

With a glowing smile, he corked the tiny glass bottle. "It's essentially concentrated manna."

The Abyss opened beneath her.

"Imagine a world where the faeries no longer monopolize it." Holding up the vial, he glanced at the ceiling as if it were the open sky filled with endless possibilities. "Where mages aren't shackled by their whims."

She imagined a world where men like him had unbridled access to fonts of power torn from those without it. "A *life* for...a few drops?"

He waved her off. "A wretched, magicless life. Don't pretend you wouldn't do the same on a bad day, lorkai." With a shrug, he traded the vial for the gauntlet. "Anyway, this is a prototype. Improving upon it is what you and your progeny are for." He waved it near her face. "You're quick powered the enchants. With more of it—and enough experimenta- tion—I'm sure I can make it much more effective."

So not only had she failed to save the unfortunate man, she'd helped kill him. How did her every decision consistently worsen each situation? "And make it less deadly, I hope."

He shrugged again. "Ideally. Those with a high capacity for magic who never bothered to master it would be worth milking repeatedly."

People like Benton.

Kyran shot a glare at the corpse hanging in the tub. "Not like *that* waste of bread and water."

Indignation clawed for space among the fear in her gut. The monster stirred. "Why not 'milk' those who have mastered it, too?"

Kyran sneered. "Because that would make me a lorkai. A spellcasting one, but still." Sitting on the table, he reclined toward her, almost playfully. "I can see you have a bleeding heart for the simpleminded primitives, but think about it, Sarlona..." He lowered his voice as though telling her a secret. "Before Dagmar mutilated you...did you really view the half-wits in your little town who couldn't cast a cantrip as your equals?"

No. She'd always felt less than them for her freakish power and reclusive lifestyle. They'd made sure of that.

Angling nearer to him and into the darkness within, she whispered, "Every day, I fight to keep myself from ripping the last vapor of Marrow from weaker beings to sustain myself... But I'm the monster? You're *work- ing* to do so for no better reason than to empower yourself. And think, what? That you're a visionary?"

He smiled wider. "The Gods blessed us with some of their power so that *we* could rule, not the cave folk." Rapping his knuckles on the table, he went on, "I'm going to change the world, lorkai. And you're going to help me." His dead eyes flickered as he grabbed her chin and stared into hers. "Or you can spend the next fifty years limbless and impaled on an acid-secreting pike, the practice target for my new spells." He leaned in until she tasted his breath. "And believe me, I have a flair for the creative." Withdrawing, he patted her cheek and lightened his tone. "Starting now."

CHAPTER TWENTY-EIGHT

Having taken one sniff around to find there were bigger, badder monsters about, the black thing inside slipped into its murky swamp like a serpent. Sarlona slid from the table and followed Kyran through a ghostly door.

Finding the room was no more than an office, she thanked the Gods. A preponderance of books, glassware, tools, and apparatuses filled the shelves lining much of the chamber. Kyran went for the big, cluttered desk in the corner and turned the captain-style chair in her direction. She kept an eye fixed on him when she crept to it, fearing a trap.

He just plucked a flask off the nearest shelf and plopped it on the desk.

Staring at the empty glass as though it were the Abyss, she tried to come up with some way to avoid helping Kyran commit crimes against humanity or becoming a gruesome tapestry or practice dummy.

She drew a blank.

"Listen..." he puffed. "You already steal Marrow. And you restored Dagmar's ability to do so, too. This isn't any different. Not if you work on ways of devising a more efficient and less lethal device." He squeezed her shoulder. "I don't *want* to rip the life force out of people. It's the side effect of a thorough extraction."

Shaking, she leaned over the flask. What choice did she have? If the opportunity to escape or stop him presented itself later, she'd take it. For now...

She focused on the ethereal hum in her bones and her core and called the strange energy to gather in her stomach. It came to her like leeches slithering across dry ground. Once she had enough to expel, she imagined it rising, trying to feel it in her throat. Before long, her stomach hitched, and every muscle tightened to the point of pain. The quick slid up her throat like molasses pouring from a jar, resisting every inch of progress. It had never been this hard. When it at last crawled into her mouth, she spat it into the flask, gagging on the strings that still hung in her throat. The blinding blue liquid barely covered the bottom of the glass.

"I'm sorry. I'm weak," she said, breathless.

To her surprise, he patted her back, fingers lingering to rub her aching ribs. "That's all right, lorkai. That's a start."

She wiped her mouth on her shoulder. "When do you decide which of us...?"

"The Council votes tomorrow night," he replied, corking the flask. "I didn't mean to make you wish for death... Perhaps I shouldn't have shown you Faalhid. I just needed you to understand what it means to oppose me."

She hugged her trapped hands to her chest.

"I plan to advocate for Dagmar's execution, not yours," he said, placing the flask on the shelf.

That might have been the worst news she'd ever heard. She wiped her tears with her forearm. "I'm going to need Marrow after a couple days. Or I'll lose all control." She half hoped she would. If the monster rose and swallowed her, she wouldn't have to endure any of this.

He came up behind her and laid his hands on her shoulders. "I'll make certain you're fed."

She tried to ignore the tingling along her spine while he massaged her knotted muscles. It wasn't difficult with the Abyss stretching out before her.

Until a pleasant shiver accompanied the fingertip that he slid up her throat. He was working some magic on her. "If you do what I ask, you'll be just fine, Sarlona. You might even be rewarded."

She jerked with the flush of pleasure that washed over her, not so unlike the sensation that Glaucus's touch had conjured when she'd done as she'd been told. Except Glaucus had emanated warmth and affection. Kyran poisoned the very air around him.

The rawhide lacing slithered the rest of the way out of her tattered shirt while his fingers caressed her throat. A fire roared to life between her legs even as her stomach did nauseating flips. "That isn't necessary, Councilor." Her voice cracked.

The hands left her, but the tingling and fire didn't as he leaned on the desk and peered into her face. "Given your isolation, I don't imagine you've been with a caster. Or did Sylvanus..."

Her heart leapt so far into her throat that she choked. "*No*," she replied after he tilted his head and raised his brow.

He stared into her eyes with the slightest smile, an expression that was probably meant to be seductive but made her want to retch. "I can't wait to show you what you've been missing."

He was testing her again.

She tried not to shake as his gaze opened her shirt. Drawing closer, he grinned. "And to see the look on Dagmar's face when I tell her I've fucked you senseless... Right before she burns."

Sarlona's cheeks caught fire and the rest of her grew cold. "I'm..." Rejecting him seemed a sure way to get herself strewn across the walls. She just didn't think she could live with herself if she went along with what he seemed to have planned. "I'm very much in love with Benton."

Kyran snorted. "You're 'in love' with that miscreant?" He folded his arms. "Well, unless you teleported him to the feet of an extraordinary healer, he's quite dead."

She prayed that was exactly what she'd done. But something in her gut told her she'd failed.

Kyran angled nearer. "Anyway... This has nothing to do with affection."

Her back arched, and she almost slipped from the chair as a bolt of ecstasy tore through her. "*Gods...*"

He hovered over her and tipped her chin, so she'd gaze into his empty eyes. "It's about power and obedience. You can obey me, can't you, Sarlona?"

She didn't know. Her heart screamed in disgust, but her pragmatism begged for compliance and her body burned for him to work his magic. She shuddered to imagine how easily his spell would have brought her to her knees had she been human—and how horrific the consequences might be if she resisted.

Unable to catch her breath, her answer was a soft hiss, "Yes."

"Good," he said, patting her cheek. "Now, relax." He reclined and leered as the binding that had concealed her breasts disintegrated.

She couldn't keep her chest from heaving. Her skin heated and prickled with gooseflesh at once.

After laying aside his black sword, he patted the space on the desk beside him. "Come. Bend over for me."

The cold mist in her heart battled the inferno down low. She yelped when something buzzed against her front, driving her to stand. Before she'd willed a step, her thighs pushed into the desk.

"The magic will make you feel me inside." His wave had her hinging over, breasts and abdomen flattened to the cold, smooth wood. She opened her stance as wide as the tether allowed. A warm current pulsed through her, forcing a moan from her lips.

"And I'll feel myself in you..." He ran his fingers up her spine. "But we won't fornicate in a true, physical sense. I would never debase myself with a monster that way."

If it brought relief and ended quickly, she no longer cared what they did. The fire in her core was unbearable. She'd burn up.

"You're a pretty girl, Sarlona... And you had so much potential. It's a terrible shame Dagmar ruined you with her filthy quick."

She rested her cheek on her forearms while he reached into his pants with a whisper. Invisible hands grasped her hips a second later. Non-existent fingers explored her flesh beneath her saturated underclothes. Something thick and warm prodded at her entrance. Every fiber of her body pleaded for it to thrust into her.

The rest of her thrashed in protest.

He patted her head. "Your thirst for magic must be much deeper than the average spell-drinker's... Yearning for your own on top of the aberrant hunger..."

The need between her thighs obliterated both.

"The emptiness must be unbearable..."

It was. It would devour her if she couldn't alleviate it.

"But my magic will fill you in ways you've never imagined." He trailed fingertips down her cheek and brushed her lips. "Not even a lorkai could conjure the sensations you're about to experience."

She bit her wrist, moaning.

Bending, he whispered in her ear, "I think I'll fuck you across the ceiling. You're going to come so hard that you fall to your knees and pray to me afterward."

"Oh, Gods..." Her organs jolted like they were trying to escape. His magic had already threaded through her.

"Now ask me to take you."

"Please, Councilor..." She panted when rigid heat pressed into her, parting but not quite penetrating. Gods, the worst monster in Aven was about to ravish her, and she'd scream with relief.

With a self-satisfied smile, he stared into her eyes. "*Beg me* to fuck you, lorkai."

She should have. Instead, she popped up and slammed her mithril-bound fists into the side of his head.

But Kyran didn't crumple to the floor with a shattered skull. Instead, the chamber inverted, and the blue light of magical torches whirled. She crashed on the dungeon floor with her head throbbing. He had a harm reflection spell in place. Of course, he did.

"Oh, Sarlona..." He cracked his knuckles as she scrambled to flip herself over. "It seems you require some training after all."

An extra brick-load of weight crashed on her shoulders, and an electrified whip strangled her before the room stopped spinning.

She screamed with the shock from the noose scorching her neck and zapping her nerves. Until its strangling grip cut off her shrieks. Then, she contorted against the stone silently.

"I don't think you'll take long to break in, though." He retracted his lightning whip and raised a hand, smashing her into the ceiling and pinning her there. "What can I start with that won't be too much for you... Ah." Reaching toward her, he made a pinching motion.

With a crack, something in her chest gave, and agony exploded through her torso. She writhed, screaming past gritted teeth, which only intensified the pain. When he pinched the air again, two more ribs snapped.

He waited for her to stop wriggling before lining his finger up with his torso and drawing down.

Her abdomen split along the center as though sliced by a blade, and her intestines rained in a shower of blood like a bundle of rope dropped from the mast of a ship. Oblivion rushed up to take her before they hit the floor.

When she came to, magic pinned her to the wall, and her guts were where they belonged.

Kyran loomed too close, with her blood splattered up the black leather of his boots and pants. "You don't like gore..." He flashed a smile. "That's okay. I can punish you without it."

She shrieked when he twisted his fingers, and her insides knotted in agony. "But if you really misbehave... I'll take you apart piece by piece, and make sure you stay hyperconscious." He waited for her to run out of screams before relaxing his fingers. "There."

She slumped forward, shaking and gasping for breath.

He drew nearer, stooping so she saw his face. "You'll be good for me this time, won't you?"

She tried to nod but wasn't sure she twitched. Her voice wouldn't work.

"Wonderful." He smiled with all the light of a demon.

She could have sworn she caught a flicker of hellfire in his eyes.

But it was just the reflection of the rest of her shirt burning off.

Wincing, she shook her shoulders to displace the flaming tatters before they seared her flesh. The smell of scorched cloth, skin, and hair joined in the effort to make her vomit.

"Where were we?" With one hand on his chin, he lowered the other.

Her pants ripped open and slid over her hips. As he dipped his hand into his trousers with a whisper the second time, she tried to picture the sea. She imagined floating in its cooling waters.

Claws bit into her thighs with his grasping motion. "I'm afraid I'm much less inclined to make this pleasant for you now."

She shut her eyes and reminded herself that all things end. All things but her, perhaps. Kyran would die in fifty or so years, though. And whoever found her in his dungeon had to be less horrible.

"Rather unseemly behavior for an esteemed councilor, isn't this, Kyran?"

Her eyes snapped open at the familiar voice. She'd never been half as happy to see Amenduil.

Kyran jumped and spun with a sneer. "How could you possibly have gotten down here?"

Amen smiled. "*Skill*, Councilor." Leaning around Kyran, he peeked at her. "I require a private word with Sarlona."

"Later."

Amen shrugged and folded his hands in front of him. "It's pressing."

Glaring at the floor, Kyran growled. "Fine... *Fine.*" He straightened and put a finger in Amenduil's face. "But if you find a way to take her from here, your shadow-worshipping brethren will never be safe crawling from their holes again."

Amen lifted his arm and jangled the three delicate bangles that encircled his wrist—anchor cuffs. "That would be quite a trick, even for me."

Kyran snorted and headed for the wall. "Don't be long." The stone faded in the shape of a doorway as he placed his hands on it. He glanced at her before stepping through. "I *am* going to fuck you tonight, Sarlona. With a dragon's cock."

Amenduil stared at her while the rock solidified. Then he sucked his teeth and let his breath out with a puff. "He's going to do worse than that, I'm afraid."

Cold sunk deeper into her bones than ever. "Can you get me out of here?" she asked with little hope.

He cocked an eyebrow. "Our Abyssal Lord's loving tendrils are looking more appealing, are they?" After peering into her eyes for a moment, he frowned. "No, I'm sorry, my dear." His gaze drifted over her body before he raised a hand.

Her pants slid up her hips and fastened themselves. A gossamer covering appeared over her torso, just enough to blur the curved lines where creamy white met salmon pink. Good enough. If she'd had the mental energy to care what he saw, she'd have used it to make herself transparent.

"I could break these given some time..." he said, glancing at the anchor cuffs. "But they confiscated my potions and made me burn myself out before letting me into Apogee." He scratched his nose. "You know how difficult teleporting with a lorkai is."

Impossible. Yet she'd seen him do it twice.

"Then why have you come?"

He rested his hand on her cheek and smiled. Unlike Kyran, he radiated a warmth that made it easy to forget what he was. "To say goodbye. And urge you to pray to Vorakor in your darkest hours." He slid his hand onto her shoulder and squeezed. "I can't help you, but *He* might. He is a god, after all. The one who loves you."

She hadn't expected Amenduil, of all people, to be her knight in shining armor, of course. But having the splinter of hope that had lodged in her when he'd appeared torn out devastated her. She wanted to hurt him.

"Do you ever wonder, Amen..." she said, meeting his gaze. "If the threat of you gets one Silsorian to pray a bit harder before bed... Gets just one to mean it when they kneel... If you don't actually do Silsor's work?"

"No," he answered after a moment. "I do as I'm meant to do." But the smile left his eyes, and irritation was etched into his features. "Just because a soul runs to Silsor doesn't mean He'll save it. Ask any priest. They'll give you a list of indiscretions the length of a dragon's tail for which Silsor will cast his imperfect faithful into the Abyss."

"The will of a god and the words of a priest are two different things, I think," she told him.

"I agree." Amenduil leaned closer and stroked the side of her face. "It isn't important to me that all souls go to Vorakor, my dear. Only that those who are meant for Him do."

If all her prayers to Tydras had landed her in a place darker than the Abyss, perhaps she did belong to Vorakor. She couldn't bear to worship him, though.

"Amen..." she said as one light-smothering thought led to another. She fought to keep the tears in. "I can't feel Benton anymore."

He stared at her blankly for a moment. "Well... I did try to kill him. I don't often fail."

"You were watching us..." She took a deep breath. "Can you see him now?"

Amenduil exhaled through his nose, and his eyes blackened. "No..."

"Does that mean he's..."

"Probably. But not in the Abyss... How disappointing." Amenduil screwed up his features. "And *surprising*."

Maybe Benton's soul was someplace better. Or maybe Aldamon had devoured it, just like Benton had feared.

"I could have forgiven you everything but taking him." A tear trickled down her cheek and hung from her jaw.

"I know... And you still don't truly hate me. Do you?" He wiped the tear with a caress of his thumb. "No. You're just about incapable of it..." He glanced toward the wall where Kyran had disappeared. "Down here, you'll learn."

Her gaze sunk to the blood-splotched floor. "Goodbye, Amen."

Frowning, he retreated but didn't leave. Instead, he stared, head cocked. She narrowed her eyes. "What?"

"I'm torn." He stroked his short beard. "The more you suffer, the faster you'll turn to Vorakor. But I confess... I abhor the thought of Kyran doing things to you that I wouldn't even inflict upon a Silsorian templar."

"Kill me, then." Her voice warbled, but she looked him dead in the eye.

He met her stare with a subdued smile. "I'm sorry, my dear." Stepping closer, he took her face in his hands. "You tried so hard not to hurt people. It's a shame they want nothing more than to hurt you." He took a deep breath. "This should get you through tonight, anyway."

Something shot into her brain like a painless spike, scrambling her vision. She couldn't remember where she was or how she'd come to be there. Someone spoke in words she didn't understand. Her body was numb, but it seemed to obey her. Sluggishly. It didn't matter anyway. Nothing did. Her thoughts swirled and sloshed like everything else: scents, sounds, and colors, ebbing and flowing but never solidifying enough to make sense of.

CHAPTER TWENTY-NINE

Benton opened both eyes to a bright, cerulean sky, with a gut full of dread. His eyepatch was gone, yet no dark tentacles tried to slither out of him.

He curled his fingers, knitting them through tender grass. *Impossible.*

Shaking, he climbed to his feet and glanced around. The lush meadow stretching in all directions didn't appear the least bit familiar. Wasn't he supposed to be in Gulway? Hadn't he seen the gates? Hadn't Sarlona sent him...

Sar.

Gods, he couldn't feel her. And she'd been broken, helpless... At Kyran and Amenduil's mercy...

He grabbed for his hilt, seeking a shred of comfort to combat the mountain of foreboding that loomed overhead. Finding the grip only added to it. He'd lost his powerful blade in Northland...

For a few minutes, he did nothing but peer across the meadow while the warmth of the sun battled his rising gooseflesh. The miragelike horizon wavered as though it was just loose energy molded into a distant tree line.

This was death?

"One version of it."

Aldamon's lilting whisper breezed into Benton's ear and permeated his entire being.

He pivoted, blood skimming over with ice. "Oh *cock*..." His voice cracked. "You ate my soul, didn't you?" Panic scattered his thoughts and made his chest heave. His heart crawled into his throat.

"It's all right, Benton."

"You soul-sucking son of a bitch..." Benton hitched over, unable to catch his breath.

The vampire grabbed his shoulders and nudged him upright. "I'm quite certain I can spit you out."

Benton scrutinized the grass, cursing and trying to keep his heart and lungs in his chest. Not that it mattered where they went now.

Sarlona had been right. He should've picked a deity to worship. One he could beg for help.

"I'm sorry." The smile that so often danced in the monster's eyes was nowhere to be found. "Absorbing your soul was the only way to stop you from slipping into the Abyss."

"Just..." Gods, he couldn't think straight. "Sar's in trouble... Can you help her? *Without* eating her soul."

Amusement seeped into the vampire's expression. "Don't you want her here with you?"

Benton drew his blade, but it turned to smoke before he could swing it.

The light left Aldamon's face as fast as it'd come. "It's not my place."

The hood fell over Benton's head, and a noose wreathed his neck again. The hangman could pull the lever any second.

"Why the cock not?" Benton wasn't sure it had been wise to utter her name. Aldamon wasn't cruel, but he was infinitely more dangerous than Kyran—and eternal.

"I've told you why." Aldamon drove his haunted, ice-blue stare through Benton's core. "The fate to concern yourself with is your own."

The sun brightened. Its blissful rays penetrated Benton's clothes to kiss his skin and melt his gooseflesh.

"You must choose, Benton," Aldamon said, spinning him around.

A quaint cottage rose from the grass on a nearby hill, surrounded by flowers. It beckoned, inviting. So much more so when Sarlona stepped from it, wearing a simple blue dress with her hair up in braids and an empty basket in her arms. The sight punched Benton in the heart. No, she wasn't dead—wasn't there. The doppelgänger tilted her face to the sun, squinting a moment, then disappeared behind the side of the cottage, oblivious to the men watching.

"If you're ready to rest, you can stay here." Aldamon waved at the house. "With her. Safe in my care."

Benton gaped at him. "But... She ain't real. None of it is."

"Reality, Benton, is a myth."

Benton rubbed his temples. The afterlife Aldamon had constructed for him was far better than he deserved, but the real Sarlona needed him. "I ain't ready, Aldamon."

The vampire's eyes darkened. "I've restored your heartbeat, but your sinister friend's magic is profound. Your injuries resist all healing."

Frustration tightened Benton's throat. "You can steal souls, but you can't heal through cockin' Amen's spells?" It didn't surprise him, though. He'd witnessed Amenduil perform impossible spells on multiple occasions.

"His magic is divine. I am not." Annoyance threaded Aldamon's tone. "If not for Sarlona's quick, I wouldn't have been able to reanimate you at all."

Benton examined the tender green grass, lost.

"It will be weeks before you're well, depending on the spell's persistence," the vampire said, calling Benton's focus. "Perhaps much longer."

Lying broken in Gulway with Aldamon while Sarlona was imprisoned or worse in Apogee... Maybe Benton's soul had landed in one of the hells after all.

He met the monster's gaze with lead in his gut and frost coating his tongue. "Can you put me back in Glaucus's body?"

Aldamon flashed a smile, but he shook his head. "I'm afraid I've stored it as bonemeal to prevent it from trying to feed. It would take quite some time to regenerate."

Benton cursed under his breath. "I ain't stayin' here, Aldamon. Not if you're givin' me the choice."

The vampire licked his lips. "This will hurt." His hands clamped on Benton's shoulders and ripped him from his sanctuary.

Excruciating pain exploded up Benton's spine and into his skull. A shriek slipped past his gritted teeth.

"Try to be still." Aldamon placed a palm on his forehead, and Benton relaxed. Despite his screaming mind, his muscles softened, and a pleasant warmth flowed from Aldamon's hand, replacing the pain.

He tried to focus on the familiar satin canopy above him rather than the fanged face that hovered before it. Much as he'd hoped he'd never return, he was in the baron's chamber, more helpless than ever. He couldn't twitch anything below his navel, and his fingers barely curled. At least he could feel the silk sheets on his bare skin.

Aldamon's gaze intensified. "How badly do you want to stand, Benton?"

A fresh dose of uneasiness spilled into Benton's chest. "Gods, what are you playin' at now?" he groaned. "Pretty cockin' bad, Al."

The vampire smiled with sparkling eyes and slid his hand to cradle Benton's face. "I can't mend you with my will alone..." He glanced away for a second, then speared Benton's heart with his otherworldly stare. "But a few sips of my blood will have you strong enough to pull a wagon within moments."

Benton went cold despite the warmth of the creature's hand.

Imagining Aldamon's blood pumping through his veins, Benton shuddered. What if it had the same binding effect as Sarlona's quick? What if it turned him into a vampire? That wasn't any better than a lorkai...

He swallowed hard, trying to wet the cotton that stuffed his mouth. "No."

Aldamon pouted. "There have been few to receive it... It's a tremendous gift."

Benton tried to retreat into the mattress. "Yeah, well... I've used that line. And the first part definitely ain't true."

The vampire's hand slid onto his shoulder and squeezed. "I'm asking you to be my son."

Benton had never wished more to be able to pop up and run. All he could do was tremble. His vocal cords shriveled into paper when he tried to speak. "*No.*"

"All your life, you've longed for a father..." Aldamon's fingers strayed to Benton's neck and traced an artery. "You're finally offered one, and you'll reject him?"

Benton tried to clear his throat, which turned into a coughing fit. His words were quiet rasps. "You're so full of shit."

Aldamon raised his brow. "Am I?"

"You're bored," Benton croaked. "You want someone to cock with..." he said, flinching at his poor choice of words.

The vampire tilted his head like a hawk.

Now that Benton's mouth was running, he couldn't shut it. "I know damn well that every time you've helped me, it's been for your own cockin' amusement. So, you can keep your blood—and your *hands*—to yourself."

Aldamon's smile bled into his eyes, sparking their twinkle.

"Was I really dead, or do you just need my permission to keep my soul down?"

The vampire took Benton by the chin and leaned closer. "If I *needed* your permission for anything, my love—I'd have it."

Benton's chest and throat tightened. Eyes bored into him that seemed to chuckle at everything he was.

Aldamon flashed his fangs and squeezed Benton's leg. His voice dipped dark and low. "You're right, though. I want to have some...*fun*."

Benton gulped. His skin heated and chilled while beads of sweat formed from head to toe.

"Come play with me, Benton."

"N— *No*." As hard as Benton tried to squirm away, he couldn't wiggle below the waist. "I ain't dumb enough to think that drinkin' blood from the king of the cockin' monsters is gonna make anything better."

"Oh, my love..." Aldamon's stare raced around the room. "I'm more like their *god* than their king... They all pretend I don't exist until they're desperate for my aid—or they offend me. Then they beg, cower, and prostrate themselves." The vampire patted his thigh. "My blood will fix your body. It may even purge the curse from your eye." His tone sounded as though the transaction was a done deal.

With great effort, Benton twitched his head. "Please don't do this to me."

Aldamon's lips held his smile, but his eyes didn't. "What else is there to do?"

The tears came out of nowhere, hitting his throat and eyes at the same time. "Sar wants me to be good... I can't do that burnin' for folks' blood." It screamed in him all over again, that terrible hunger he'd experienced in Glaucus's body. Vampires, as far as he knew—the young ones anyway—had even less restraint than lorkai. And he'd be linked to Aldamon for eternity. *Made* of him... "I— All right... Go get her, please. We'll— We'll stay with you if that's what you want..." His insides twisted into knots. He prayed he wasn't selling Sarlona's soul in exchange for her life. "You can do whatever the hells you want with me if you protect her..."

"It's too late for that, Benton. The political fallout from breaking into Apogee and freeing a monster..." Aldamon shook his head with a pout. "You were right before. She's a thread I cannot tug on... What if I unravel it all?" Staring into space, he skimmed his hand up Benton's hip and abdomen to lay it on his chest. "But *you*. You are a thread that would bind me to this realm. Through you, I can understand the mortal and the material."

"If you won't help her, I gotta try." Benton fought harder to sit than he'd ever tried anything. Of course, he couldn't raise an inch. "Cyr will get me healed up eventually." He had to believe that.

Aldamon let out a long sigh. "It's her *quick* that compels you to do so." He patted Benton's stomach. "You don't even have your sword... What will you do?"

Benton had no clue, but he couldn't think straight with Aldamon hovering over him.

"All right... If you wish to return to Ashmore, I'll take you there." Aldamon's gaze drifted from Benton toward the balcony, below which the surf rumbled. "Perhaps the mages will show more compassion than I imagine..." He offered a smile Benton didn't believe. "Perhaps Sarlona will be able to heal you herself."

"Thank you, Aldamon." He prayed the monster wasn't teasing him.

Aldamon flashed another thin-lipped, joyless smile. "I'm going to make you sleep for a time."

Benton meant to protest but slipped into a dream.

CHAPTER THIRTY

S ound solidified first—a child's sobbing from the other side of the wall, footsteps above, rats below, heartbeats... Her sight cleared next—a bare, circular chamber with dark stone walls, a stained floor... Then her sense of smell returned, leading with the reek of her blood. The scent of rodents followed, and Kyran. The stench of three unfamiliar mortal men... Dagmar...

Sarlona shivered as sensation flooded into her body, simultaneous to her memories and thoughts coalescing. Her heart thrashed, naked chest heaving. She hung, suspended magically, just off the floor with her toes grazing the gore-caked stone in the center of an underground cell. Her hands were bound above her head in the lorkai cuffs, and her ankles were still tethered together with the faery silk cord.

She was nude and covered in dried blood, but alone, whole, and—other than where the enchantments on the lorkai cuffs battled her body's effort to heal the wounds they'd caused—uninjured. Whether Kyran had healed her after inflicting his tortures or she'd been left alone long enough to mend herself, she had no idea.

But she couldn't endure them while cognizant. She had to escape.

Or ensure her execution.

The magic field that gripped her allowed only a few inches of movement in any direction, and even that was a struggle. After turning herself glassy, she tried manipulating her body to reject and expel the angry metal fangs of the lorkai cuffs, but the enchanted mithril wouldn't budge. At least an hour passed of alternating panic and despair, interrupted with short meditations to rein in her racing thoughts.

It wasn't until Kyran stepped through the wall opposite her that her desperation formed a plan.

The instant they locked gazes, she struck his mind with everything she had.

He reeled, falling back with a shout, clapping a hand to his head.

She hadn't penetrated, she couldn't. A mage like him had superb protections. Her hope was to scare him.

Face the picture of rage, he snarled, straightening and stalking toward her. "How fucking *dare* you, you little—"

She hit him a second time. Just as hard.

He winced and stumbled, stomping forward. "I'm going to—"

Again, she slammed into the barrier around his mind.

He growled, shooting a hand in her direction while he charged at her with a spell on his lips.

She struck as fire burst from his fingertips. The ball of flames went wide, grazing her ribs. Gritting her teeth against the pain of blistering skin, she smashed into his mental protection.

Swearing, he stumbled, lightning dancing in his palm.

She hit him when he grasped for her and electric tendrils snared her throat. Tuning out the pain and convulsions, she focused on pummeling his barrier.

With a roar, he pulled Benton's sword and shoved it through her eye.

The world vanished in a flash of agony.

***

Kyran's stern features and a splitting headache greeted Sarlona when she next woke. "Listen carefully, now, Sarlona..."

She didn't. Instead, she struck at his mental defenses. He'd have to kill her, keep her unconscious, or leave her alone. Otherwise, she might break into his mind someday.

He grimaced. "You spell-sucking whore. If you th—"

She hit his mind with everything she had.

He grasped his head with both hands. "*Fuck.* If you don't—"

She lashed out in rapid succession.

Dizziness hit her with his outstretched arm, telling her to relax and let her guard down.

She shook it off and slammed into his mental barrier again. Sylvanus had trained her to protect her mind since she was five, and that ability had been amplified by the lorkai quick. At his best, she doubted Kyran could control her that way, never mind when she was hitting back and had him on his heels.

"Fine," he growled through clenched teeth. "If this is your choice. I'll use your mother, instead. And I won't be half as gentle with *her*."

She recognized the beginnings of a projectile spell as he wound up and let him get it off uninterrupted. A thin, red-hot iron spike shot from his palm and hit her between the eyes, delivering sweet oblivion.

CHAPTER THIRTY-ONE

S arlona woke to another aching skull, hands still throbbing over her head. But the light of day greeted her this time. A stiff, cold breeze bit her skin and tugged at her hair.

Bound to an adamantine post on Apogee's rooftop by enchanted chains from ankle to throat, she'd left Kyran's dungeon laboratory hundreds of feet below.

Relief washed in like a blessed wave and receded just as quickly. However much she'd hoped to convince Kyran to kill her, her heart thundered while the tower guards dumped extra firewood beneath her.

Flesh exposed for all to see, except for those narrow bands concealed by the enchanted steel, heat flashed over her cheeks. Trembling, she made herself crystal clear and chafed against the chains, testing the strength of their magic. They only squeezed tighter, burning and itching as they dug into her bare flesh.

Now that her execution was upon her, it didn't bring the solace she'd hoped for. Her heart thrashed, and blood pounded in her ears, knowing she'd be eaten by flames within the hour. Probably while conscious.

The crowd didn't help. Gods forbid she be allowed to scream, cry, and die in relative privacy. Dozens of tower guards lined Apogee's parapet in addition to those preparing for a bonfire. She recognized many from her two trips to the tower and the fight in Northland. In fact, every mage she'd faced on that little island was in attendance. At least that meant she hadn't killed anyone.

The Council had assembled opposite her, each of its nine members seated on a platform high above the other spectators. Between her and them were eight rows of benches, split down the middle by an aisle and dotted with strangers who had come to watch her burn, plus Jasper.

More than fifty faces gawked at her, and she didn't want to see any of them.

None less than 'her' crowd who lined up on the right of the Council. Each made her heart sink lower. Dagmar sat fettered to a heavy chair, her hands trapped in lorkai cuffs and a glowing-red chain strung before her throat, no doubt designed to do something horrible if she attempted to rise.

A few feet to the side of her stood Amenduil, evidently unconcerned that Dagmar would slice him into jerky one strip at a time if given the opportunity. With his beautiful aqua eyes dewy and a slight, sympathetic smile bending his lips, his gaze was perhaps the most obnoxious of them all. Every few minutes, as Kyran led his peers through a litany of bureaucratic bullshit, Amen whispered a fresh prayer to Vorakor on Sarlona's behalf, entreating the dark god to take her gently into the Abyss where she could rest in his loving embrace.

Several paces away from him, Sylvanus offered his quiet prayers to the Wildman gods. His were less specific, asking that the Gods' will be done and Sarlona find peace in the Otherrealms. She was surprised he'd come. And wished he hadn't. His was the last face she wanted to see. It reminded her of all her failures and inadequacies. Not to mention the first life she'd lost, which she'd yet to finish mourning.

So when Sylvanus started toward her during a Silsorian priest's reading of the Evensong, she squirmed in her chains.

He picked his way up the stacked wood without dislodging a single split log. "Have you been praying?"

"Of course." Now he was her mentor again?

Had his scent not confirmed his identity, his gentle expression would have led her to believe he was an imposter. "Think of cool sands and calm waters. You'll be with Tydras soon."

Whatever trembling walls had been keeping her tears at bay broke with the softness of his words. She hoped he couldn't see them trickle down her transparent cheeks.

"It's a difficult road home." He shoved his hands into the pockets of his green robes. "But you *are* going home."

She tried to dip her head, but the chain beneath her chin allowed only the slightest movement.

"I requested your ashes for your parents, but the Council claims they belong to the creature that did this to you." He glanced over his shoulder at Dagmar. "They plan to free her."

A sliver of tension bled from Sarlona's chest.

"They don't believe she'll victimize another caster as she did you…" he whispered, but Sarlona had no doubt that Dagmar heard every word. "Not after this."

Sarlona couldn't care about when or to whom Dagmar might try to pass on her quick. But hearing that the Northlander might escape decorating Kyran's walls loosened the vise on Sarlona's heart.

Sylvanus turned his hazel eyes to the wood beneath their feet. "I…know I was harsh…" Despite her eyes being crystal orbs, he met her gaze. "You were a good kid, Sarlona. I want you to know that I know that…" He cleared his throat, but it did nothing to dislodge the gravel from it. "I never hated you. Only what you might do."

He could have said that years ago.

"I loved you, Sylvanus." Not anymore. She allowed no shred of affection to creep into her voice. "But you shouldn't have made me your apprentice." She'd never had any say in the matter. Her parents hadn't been given a choice either. If Sylvanus hadn't recognized her power and demanded to shape it his way, she might have had a normal life. A longer one.

On the other hand, someone like Kyran or Amenduil might have found her and tried to mold her to their benefit.

Sylvanus's beard bobbed with his head. "I never *wanted* any of this for you…" His expression slackened. "When you wandered off those years ago, and I found you in that grove… I saw…" He gazed at the sky. "I was going to end it there."

Her skin iced over. He would have murdered a five-year-old? Even as she was about to burn, he found ways to hurt her.

"You could have left this world a beloved child instead of a monster." As the sun peeked through the dim slate sky for a second, he met her gaze. "Never knowing evil. Never knowing there was something wrong with you."

She was more certain than ever that everything wrong with her was his doing.

"Instead, the Gods demanded that I teach you the old ways..."

He always blamed the Gods for her apprenticeship. Always made it clear that he hadn't desired an apprentice. But he'd never told her that the Gods had stayed his hand.

He stroked his beard. "It's hard to understand why...when they'd take you before you completed your education..."

It was. Or why they wouldn't answer her prayers after so much of her life had been devoted to them.

He laid his gnarled, chalky hand on her shoulder. "But you can leave knowing you've done whatever they tasked you with. The pains and sorrows they willed for you in this world will soon be gone."

He was right about that much. After its gruesome crescendo, all her suffering—the fear, pain, loneliness—would stay in this world while she ascended to the next. Tydras would take her in his arms and lay her upon his warm sands beside gentle, glittering waves, where she'd feel His love for all time. Or until He sent her to live a new life and learn fresh lessons well-rested.

"*Warm* waters." Amenduil's low whisper drew her attention from the paradise in her mind's eye. "That's the difference between Vorakor's Abyss and a sea god's depths."

No doubt only she and Dagmar heard him.

"Both are dark and full of monsters... But our Abyssal Lord's waters are warm and *always* gentle." His gaze was fixed on Sarlona from across the rooftop, irises swallowed in inky black. "The depths of the sea are liquid ice. They crush bone..."

She tried not to think about that. "Goodbye, Sylvanus."

He dipped as he descended the pile. "Farewell, Sarlona. Perhaps we'll meet in the Otherrealms under happier circumstances."

She'd rather they didn't.

"The Wildmen gods are temperamental, Sarlona. None more so than Tydras." Amenduil's words slithered into her ears like one of Vorakor's tendrils. "His anger wipes cities from maps and sweeps children away so their mothers have no bodies to bury."

Maybe. But Tydras was perfect.

"Do you think you know him, my dear? By playing at his gates? Splashing in his shallows?" His words didn't just ring in her ears, they echoed in her mind. "Sailing atop his periphery? His realm is the unfathomable deep..."

A chill wormed up her spine, grinding it against the post where the Council executed its magical criminals and monsters.

The clouds behind Amenduil, far beyond Apogee's parapet seemed to blacken. "...like the Abyssal Lord's. Perhaps Tydras and Vorakor are two names for the same truth."

No. Amen said himself that the waters were different. One warm and one cold... If the deities were one and the same, it wouldn't make any difference to him whether she prayed to Tydras or Vorakor.

"Or perhaps not... Vorakor would grant you rest. But 'your' gods have yet more to demand of you."

Amen's words, no doubt laced with some spell, seemed to stick to her, and she had no way to brush them off.

"They want more of your suffering, Sarlona—every scream and tear they can wring out. Until you are pain manifest. Only then will they toss your shattered remains to the dark, frozen depths to drift alone."

Dagmar jumped her chair, glaring at him. "Shut your fucking mouth, or I'll drag *you* to the depths and watch the hagfish feed on your bloated corpse."

Sarlona shivered. Dagmar's outburst erased the sensation of Amenduil's whispers crawling over her skin, but some had already lodged in her brain.

"Ask our Abyssal Lord to take you home. He'll help you sweetly to the next realm." He ended his monologue when the Silsorian priest, a young mage who must have had unshakable faith to stand upon the same rooftop as Amenduil, finished with his reading.

The world emptied after that. Only her thundering chest and the smoky sky she was about to join as vapors, ashes, and energy remained. The chains itched and burned with each gulp of air while her ribcage tested their strength. Her breaths and heartbeat made the pole bound to her spine quiver.

Please let me rest with Tydras in the Shimmering Sands. Please, Gods. Please, Tydras. She tried to hold His glittering waves in her thoughts, but her mind drifted to Benton. She imagined she felt him again, in some faraway place. Maybe he wasn't dead after all. Or perhaps as her own passing ticked nearer, the Veil between them grew thinner, allowing her to sense him. *Please let me rest in the Shimmering Sands, and please let Benton stay there with me if he's dead.* How could she be at peace without him?

She shut her eyes. Her glassy eyelids only blurred the terrible world before her. "Please, please, please."

I'm so sorry, Sarlona.

Dagmar.

She reopened her eyes to spy the Northlander's full of tears.

I'm sorry I did this to you.

The lorkai reeked of fear and torment from across the roof. Unable to weather Dagmar's misery atop her own, she didn't answer, trying to stay focused on the next world. Attempting with all her being to go to Tydras before Kyran sent her there.

Dagmar's gaze flared blue. *I love you. I'll love you until the last star falls from the sky.*

Knowing Dagmar's lust for blood and vengeance, the Northlander wouldn't last the week. She'd find herself in Sarlona's place, raging at Kyran or on the receiving end of one of Amenduil's devastating spells.

The tears trailed from the Northlander's eyes with her blink.

And I'll pray every remaining day that the Gods are kind enough to let me visit you in the Shimmering Sands when I'm done.

Sarlona rested her head on cold, hard metal, closed her eyes, muddling the sky, and whispered. "Waves. Sun. Sand. Tydras. Home."

Benton...

She reached out to Dagmar. *If Benton's still alive, look after him.*

Dagmar's reply went unheard in the shadow of Kyran's command. "Light it."

Terror tore through Sarlona like a rabid dog. Where was the angry, hungry predator in her now? Why did the young druidess and farm girl have to bear the brunt of this? She scrunched her eyelids so tight that her face ached, but she still caught a flash from the nearest tower guard. Distorted flames leapt up from the wood below her.

The heat clutched her like a dragon's claw, and she thrashed in the heavy chains. But fire ignited a burst of indignation that shot words ahead of her screams. "Kyran is using my quick to turn stolen Marrow into manna. He's ripping the life force from non-magical prisoners." Maybe outing him could save them. Stop him. Hopefully, it would convince him to put her out. "Check his lab—"

An invisible hand crushed her throat at the moment blistering agony swept over her legs. The warnings she meant to shout into the minds of the assembled crowd crumbled into inhuman shrieks as flames swathed her like a flesh-flaying cloak.

She writhed, racked by thought-breaking pain, cracking bones against the enchanted chains. *Gods, please. Make it stop. Gods, help me.*

Woodsmoke smothered all scent but cooking meat and burnt hair. The crackling of integument and sizzling of fluids filled the space between the snapping and popping of logs. Clear skin blackened when it died, revealing charred flesh that flaked off her body.

Gods, she was really burning alive. *End. End. End. Gods,* please. She screamed into every sentient mind within miles. *Fucking kill me.*

Dagmar's roars rivaled the fire's. Wood cracked, and metal crashed somewhere beyond hell. The Northlander's face and shoulders burst through the demonic light—snarling, bloody, crooked, smoking—only to be sucked away in a swirl of sparks and ashes.

Seconds slowed into minutes as flaming chunks of Sarlona's flesh dripped from her body to join the cinders below. The fire burned like syrup flowed. How long could it take for a lorkai brain to cook? Why wouldn't the heat and flame touch her eyes and erase the horrifying sight of her descent into the hells?

She smashed her head into the adamantine, hoping to knock herself out. With the chain across her throat and her flesh melting around it, she couldn't gain enough momentum.

Her skin numbed as the pain seeped deeper into her being. Muscles thickened into meat.

Her soul was being incinerated. *Kill me. Kill me. Please kill me.*

How could her gods let this happen to her? Make her experience each second of fire eating her body?

Shadows danced just beyond the fire, stretching cool, soothing tendrils toward her. Begging to draw her from the flames into a far gentler hell.

With her flesh withered and charred, fat rendered and bubbling on the glowing wood, the chains weren't so tight. But it was hard to move, cooked. Every twitch tore muscle. Ripped things apart. Still, she slipped out of the chains, leaving long strips of flesh seared to them.

Only to collapse on her hands and knees, deeper into the fire.

She couldn't take it. Things broke inside that should never have been tested. *Yes. All right? Please, Vorakor, help me. Take me from this. I beg you. I'll be yours. Please.*

The agonizing heat faded to warmth as the shadows swept in. Silky, cooling tentacles cradled her wreckage. Just like Amenduil said they would. They drew her down into the soft, sweet darkness, far from the harsh and horrible light. It was over. She was dead. If she'd had tears, she'd have wept with gratitude while her thoughts dissolved to the image of the infinite night swaddling her, and that evil, orange glow above shrinking and fading.

A sweet voice whispered as oblivion took her. *At last. You've come home.*

CHAPTER THIRTY-TWO

D agmar visualized her red-hot anger fading with the pink in the sky—washed out by the soothing blue that deepened above and the waves below. It cooled her just enough to keep her from crushing the wooden box in her trembling hands.

Even the first of the evening's stars were irritating. What sense of self-importance gave them the gall to take their places before the others? Why did they seem to mock her with their cold magnificence? How did they proclaim through their twinkling that they'd had the power to aid her if only they'd cared? What were they, those indifferent lights so ready to be spectators to her misery? The Gods? The ancestors? Or were they merely fires burning in the heavens?

Whatever those hanging beacons were, she wanted to rip them from the sky and dash them on the hard sand until they respected the bleakness of the occasion.

Instead, she knelt in the shallows with a slow inhale, letting the cool water flow around her waistband and boots with the next wave.

Sarlona had loved the sea with such intensity... But its boundless horizon did nothing for Dagmar.

Cold seawater couldn't combat her boiling blood. Pounding surf couldn't drown out her thundering heart. It would take the storm of the millennium for the ocean to match her rage.

She had so many people to kill. To destroy. *Then* kill.

Kyran, most of all. The arrogant prick thought his magic could bind her to the desperate bargain she'd made to spare Sarlona more torture and compel her to provide quick on demand. He believed the enchanted stone embedded in her brain would stop her from slicing him open and using his entrails to strangle his apprentice in front of him. But she'd find a way to break his spells. Then he'd suffer more than anyone who had ever lived. For now, she'd have to hurt him from afar.

A wave a little taller than the rest collided with her abdomen, splashing salty water onto her lips and sending cool trickles down her shirt.

She should be thinking about Sarlona, not revenge.

But each time she did, she saw her daughter's beautiful face charred and bubbling. She endured the young woman's agonized shrieks as she begged to die. And she remembered Sarlona's blank look and incoherent babbling when Kyran turned her inside out a little at a time.

Then Dagmar's anger would spike, and guilt would tighten a noose encircling her throat.

She'd failed her daughter in so many ways. Failed her *species*. Despite shredding her hands and nearly taking her own head off, she hadn't even been able to end her daughter's torment. She'd fought through poison-tipped arrows and lightning bolts to reach the girl, just to be ripped backward by half a dozen spells the instant she'd breached the flames. Smoking and bloody, she'd lain broken, watching her daughter's husk tear itself off the adamantine stake and collapse.

Even in the open air, the smell of burning hair and meat had been suffocating. The roaring fire and the sizzling and popping of flesh and bone had swallowed every sound but Sarlona's telepathic scream for Vorakor's aid. And Dagmar had looked on, poison and spells holding her still, as Amenduil hit Sarlona with a black fireball. Not only had the conflagration incinerated her skeleton, it had melted the adamantine pole and cracked the stone parapet behind it.

Dagmar's soul had shattered in that moment, and a piece slipped out to leave a gaping hole. Then despair washed in to permeate her entire being.

Of all the terrible things she had seen over the centuries, her daughter's death was the worst. She doubted she'd ever view so much as a candle flame without reliving it.

Another wave hit higher, this one slapping her chest and pouring into her shirt. The sky had darkened, and the tide had risen noticeably.

She took a deep breath and gazed at the wooden vessel in her hands.

Her daughter was in a little oak box...

It took all Dagmar's focus to picture the young woman as anything but a burning, shrieking husk. To see her face, soft and smiling, eyes sparkling like the sea. Dagmar had taken so many smiles from her. Starting when she'd revealed herself to the young woman on that very beach. That had been so fun, though. Fighting her, testing her, touching her for the first time while she was awake, tasting her... Taking her home.

'My blood is in these sands,' Sarlona had said. 'My bones are destined to become them.'

Despite how sure Dagmar and her father had been that Sarlona would live for millennia among her many children and their descendants, the girl had been right.

Dagmar opened the box. "I'm sorry, Sarlona." Praying to Tydras and her own sea god—Myrnir—for her daughter's peace, she sprinkled the ashes between waves. The dust blended with the foam and the swirling silt. "Go. Be your sands. And be at peace."

The next wave rumbled by, and Sarlona was gone.

Dagmar closed her eyes, adding a few tears to the endless sea, then rose.

Much as she never wanted to set foot in Ashmore again, she had to get home. She had to transfer Ashmore's rule to Gorgil, beg Aldamon to lift Kyran's spells when she'd never hated him more, fuck up the SPS's world, and disappear. But first, she had to prod Benton into existence and tell him the only good thing he'd ever had was gone forever. She had to take care of him.

Like she'd promised.

CHAPTER THIRTY-THREE

Dagmar lurked in the doorway of her dead father's room where her dead daughter's pet lay broken. The journey to his bedside seemed too harrowing to complete.

Beneath the adrenaline-triggering stench of Aldamon, Benton still reeked of Sarlona. The smell of her wasn't just on him. It was *in* him. And much stronger than when his body had entered the Abyssal Waters. Sarlona must have given him more of her quick—a high dose.

As if he didn't annoy Dagmar enough, now his very aroma would torment her. She couldn't avoid him any longer, though. He'd been lying unconscious in that bed for days. Cyr's healing spells hadn't scraped whatever was wrong with him. Neither had potions. But Dagmar could patch up almost anything with enough effort.

Of course, that might require hours by his side, touching him. Invading and manipulating his body—an unpleasant enough experience without the sight and smell of him relentlessly reminding her of everything she'd lost.

She rubbed her face when she reached his bedside, then stared at him. A leather patch covered his right eye but only partially concealed the ragged scar across his face. Everything else looked intact, whole. She peeked beneath the sheet Gorgil had placed over his lower body to make sure. Nothing appeared amiss, but he smelled injured. The sickly-sweet odor of corrupted tissue and the body's healing leaked from him with traces of still less appealing substances.

With a sigh, she sat on the bed and clapped a hand over his clammy forearm. Dread tightened her chest. Much as it amused her to vex him, his sorrow and grief would only add to hers.

She seeped into his body, then his mind, sifting through everything that had happened in the weeks since he'd left by himself for Gulway. Aldamon had put blocks up, but she skirted around where she could and assumed she was better off not seeing the rest.

Tears leaked from her at those sweet moments with Sarlona, which flashed by like the illustrations in a book as one flipped the pages.

She took a minute to let her eyes dry and receded to the edge of his thoughts. Smelling and listening to his anguish would be bad enough... She didn't need to experience the brunt of it along with him. After a deep breath, she prodded his brain to consciousness. "Wake up, Benton."

His thick lashes fluttered, and his good eye opened.

A second of confusion as he registered her face. A pulse of terror. His pupil constricted with the agony that exploded up his spine. Burning pain radiated from the black lesion within his shattered vertebrae. A knife stabbed at the back of his head.

Worst, though, was the gaping hole where Sarlona had been. Like the one left in Dagmar's heart, but deeper and with an added sensation like a lost limb. Much as she wanted to recoil and leave him to suffer it alone, she sent a trickle of numbness into his chest to ease his torment.

He hitched and tried to speak, croaking unintelligibly instead. Half sunken into his mind, she understood him.

"She's strewn across the shallows of Mast Landing's beach." How Dagmar answered without her voice cracking, she didn't know. "She's gone."

He knew that. His insides were hollower than they'd been when he'd drifted into the Abyss and he and Sarlona were a realm apart. A sob racked his body, and tears filled his pretty eye.

"I know..." She grabbed a cup of water from the nightstand, careful not to let go of him. "I'll hang them all with their own intestines, eventually..." Hopefully. "If I can get you swinging a sword, you can help me."

"Just—" His words came out a rasp. "Just cockin' kill me, Dagmar."

He meant it, too.

"Benton..." She exhaled as she slid her hand up his arm and behind him. Spreading her fingers to support his neck and shoulders, she lifted him into a reclined position.

A hoarse scream bled past his teeth.

She brought the cup to his lips and poured a sip into his mouth. "When have you known me to be that merciful?"

He half swallowed, half choked, sending his lungs into a spasm that made fresh jolts of excruciation shoot up his back. But the fluid wet his throat, and he got a few drops down.

"Anyway, she told me to look after you." She laid him on the pillow with a gentleness that hurt. "It was all she said to me."

That did nothing to erode his grief or despair.

Dagmar ran her hand to his front as she replaced the cup and delved deeper into the trillions of pieces that comprised his machinery. The fluid and debris pressing on his brain beneath the half-healed crack in his skull was the most immediate threat to his life, but the injury to his back was more extensive. Vertebrae in his neck and lumbar region were broken, with damage to the spinal cord in both places. Dark energy contaminated the injuries, stifling the regrowth of his tissues. It squirmed away like a writhing eel when she tried to catch it. She'd have to hold it at bay while she goaded each particle into resuming its work.

Biting on her tongue, she patted his chest. "I'm going to flip you over." A fresh swell of dread went through him, but she swept the numbness up from below his waist to cover every inch of him.

His breath came out as a relieved moan. A tear trailed down his cheek. He wished he could go to sleep and never wake.

"There's no relief in the next realm for people like us." She rolled him over and slid her hand up into his hair. "You know that." Driving her will at his injury, she staved off the slippery shadows that gnawed at his wounds. Then, one at a time, she demanded a mineral secretion from the particles along the crack in his skull. "But Sarlona's resting now. With her god, in a realm of light." Dagmar had to keep telling herself that. And denying that Sarlona's desperate plea to Vorakor might have landed her elsewhere. "Her whole life was dedicated to that end. Try to take some comfort in that."

He did. A tiny shred of it. That was a start.

Look after him.

Dagmar drifted further into him than she intended while she broke down the clotted blood lodged within his skull. He was dead already; a ghost trapped in the land of the living.

She could relate. What was she, if not a relic? A relict? The last of a creature that shouldn't exist anymore. An accident of time? The loneliness punched into her heart and squeezed, taking the breath out of her. It mangled his insides, too.

But neither of them was entirely alone. They shared something sacred—Sarlona's quick.

She wound her fingers tighter into his hair and kneaded his scalp, careful not to push on the injury. He opened his eye, peeking sidelong at her. Trepidation and confusion fought the tenderness brought by her fingertips. She struggled to be gentle with him, but her daughter's last request echoed ceaselessly in her mind.

"I can't promise I'll never hurt you again, Benton." She sent a warm tremor through as much of his body as he could feel. He needed the reminder that there were still things in the world other than pain. "But I promise, I'll try not to."

He groaned into the sheets with the next tingling flush she generated in his core. The noise both made her stomach flip and roused her hunger.

"You're all I have left..." Having pumped the extra fluid from around his brain and repaired each blood vessel there, she dedicated most of her focus to the bone. "Of her."

But not *just* Sarlona. Her father, too. Benton had shared Glaucus's brain, and echoes of the Lord of Ashmore had since haunted his dreams. They were forever part of the human man. Memories of memories...

She shook her head. "So much of her quick wasted on you." Rubbing his shoulder with her free hand, she drove bone to grow with frustrating slowness while the inky taint fought her. "But, in a strange way, it makes you family..."

She would have ripped the quick from him if she could. So that she wouldn't have to smell it, *feel* it. So it wouldn't tug on her like a child on their mother's arm, drawing her toward him.

"Neither of us is quite as devastatingly alone as we feel."

"It ain't bein' alone..." He cleared his throat but still sounded like a basilisk choking on gravel. "It's thinkin' Sar might be."

"She was devout. The Gods wouldn't allow it." Dagmar had to believe that. If she could have believed her father had been waiting in the next realm to watch over Sarlona, she'd have had a shred of real solace.

"There ain't no cockin' gods, Daggy."

Her father's pet name for her shot fire into her veins, but she resisted the urge to put him out of his misery.

"No good ones. Just things that call themselves that. To lure souls in and use 'em up."

"Figured it all out, did you?" She sneered. "Spend a few minutes dead here and there, and you think you know the ways of the universe?"

He couldn't turn his head, but his gaze veered away from her. "I know that havin' my soul swallowed and sucked on ain't inspired any faith."

After setting another particle to make bone, she moved to the next. Approximately 2500 to go. In the skull injury alone.

"Perhaps, if you'd had some, that wouldn't have happened to you." Softening, she lowered her voice. "*Sarlona* is at peace, Benton..." Dagmar would scream it until he believed it. Until it was true. "But if you die today, you never will be. You'll sink into the Abyss and never see Sarlona again."

He still wouldn't meet her gaze. There wasn't any light in his eye.

"She sent you to Gulway to survive. And she told you to be good so you might join her one day."

That did it. He glanced at her with a flicker of *something* in his eye.

"You're going to do as she wished. Because you're her Bound, and that's your duty." Her gaze drifted to the window, and she shook her head. "Just like my duty is to continue the lorkai species."

She had to see her father's dream of a restored lorkai people realized. More than ever, since Sarlona had been destroyed because of it. If Dagmar decided now that bringing the lorkai back wasn't so important... Then Sarlona had died for no reason at all. Nothing they'd done to her had served any purpose... "And like my duty to look after you."

Realization smashed into her so hard she nearly fell on him.

Oh... Fuck.

She didn't have to wait decades to have another child. Not even years... If she could avoid losing more quick to Kyran, a few months might be enough time.

Fuck, fuck, fuck. Dagmar calmed her heart before it lurched into a sprint and took a deep breath.

Rubbing Benton's head, she sent a wave of exhaustion through him.

She needed time to think... "You should rest more..." Sleep rose and swallowed him a few moments later.

Gods, she didn't want to do it. She flipped him over, and a fresh plume of his scent—Sarlona's scent—wafted into her nostrils. She had to. There was so much of her daughter in him. So much *lorkai* in him. He was half made already—by a female of extraordinary power. And he carried a lot of Marrow without any magical training...

He was *perfect*.

After pulling the sheet up to his chin, she smoothed it around him, trying to see him in a different light... As a... Her stomach did another flip. Covering her face with her hands, she groaned into her palms, then gazed at him again and licked her lips.

She could turn Benton before the year was out. And what better way to look after him than to give him the gift of immortality and keep him at her side eternally?

CHAPTER THIRTY-FOUR

Waking provided no escape from the nightmares. It just added waves of physical agony to the anguish echoing from the chasm in Benton's soul.

The cloudless blue, birdsong, and midmorning sun that splashed through the window mocked him. He'd never trust their lies of light again. All was darkness, however bright the day.

He whined, jaw clenched with white-hot pain radiating from his spine until he couldn't take it anymore. "*Dagmar.*" His shout didn't break this time, ricocheting off the sparsely decorated walls.

She appeared at his bedside an instant later. Once, he'd been terrified anytime a door floated shut behind her, trapping them alone. She'd been the source of so much pain. Now, she was the only thing that stopped it. He couldn't help groaning when she took his hand, and the dagger in his back dissolved.

"Good morning," she grumbled with a sneer, then propped him up to give him a swig of water. After laying him down, she stared into space, presumedly reevaluating his injuries at a depth he couldn't conceive of. "Squeeze my hand."

It took all his effort to close his fingers around hers. He couldn't even ball his other fist in frustration.

Shrugging, she tugged the blanket off his feet. "Move your toes."

With tremendous effort, he bent them halfway.

"Well, it's progress..." She yanked the blanket off him, baring everything, and his face heated.

Mercifully, he lost all sensation as she rolled him onto his stomach. It returned after she'd adjusted his arms to rest in front of him and covered his ass.

"The spell is fading, whatever it is..." Her fingertips trailed down his backbone to the two vertebrae that remained splintered. "And it isn't undoing any of my work."

It didn't matter. She could repair every nerve. He'd just be a walking pile of wreckage. Nothing but broken pieces...

"If I ever catch this slippery black shit," she said, tracing his spine, "I'm going to shove it up Amenduil's ass where it belongs."

Benton snorted. "I got a couple tentacles for him too, but he'd probably like that..." The flicker of amusement faded with the recollection of something she'd mentioned the night before. "Amen..." his voice cracked, "was there? He saw everything?" The notion that Amenduil's face had been among the last Sarlona saw ate at Benton's insides.

Dagmar's fingers froze. "He's the one who ended it." Hissing her exhale, she dug her nails into Benton's skin. "I'd be grateful...if I didn't half suspect he was the culprit dragging it out. And if he hadn't destroyed my father."

Fresh tar oozed into Benton's heart. It stuck to his lungs and caught in his throat. "It—It weren't quick?"

He jolted at the crack of Dagmar splitting the oak headboard with her fist.

"No, Benton, it wasn't *fucking* quick. Lorkai don't burn fucking quick." A growl deeper and louder than a dire wolf's leaked from her. "And someone's magic made it *extra* slow."

He grew frigid as the blood drained out of him. His heart raced, and he couldn't breathe. Water pooled in his eye.

Some of the monster fled her voice. "I don't hate you enough to give you the details." She stroked his spine, sending pleasant heat to melt the ice lodged in his veins.

But there were some aches even a lorkai couldn't deaden. "I just..." Sarlona had suffered *so* much, and he hadn't even been there... "I didn't get to say goodbye..." Tears dampened his eyepatch and dripped into stubble that bordered on a beard. "I didn't tell her I loved her that last time. I weren't there when she needed me."

"Thank the fucking *Gods* you *weren't* there," Dagmar growled, a beast roaring through her. "Whether you believe in them or not." Bending close, she rumbled in his ear. "And thank the lord baron that you were unconscious when it happened..." She twisted his head too far to the side. "Because if you'd heard her begging for death across your bond, neither he nor I would've been able to put your pieces back together."

He decayed into pure pain. A sob shook his broken body.

Her grip softened with a sigh, and she rubbed his vertebrae. "I'm—" Her voice gentled as warm trickles emanated from her hands. "It's good you weren't there, Benton. And not just for you." She worked her fingertips deep into muscles that shivered with relief despite the lead in his gut. "Kyran would have used you to control Sarlona. He would have enslaved her." She shrugged. "I'd be dead, and you'd be a magical experiment... It wasn't quick, but it did end." Dagmar caressed his cheek, breaking the stream of tears in a gesture too tender for the brutal Northlander. "She's dead, not *destroyed*. Nothing would have been worse for her than being molded into a weapon to be wielded by someone like Kyran."

Dagmar was probably right, but he couldn't take comfort in her words.

"She's not suffering anymore..." Her fingertips heated. "That's for us to do..."

He'd been born for it.

"But not all the time..." She tapped into his Marrow, diverting a flow never meant to leave his being.

He jerked, insides tightening as she drew on it. That raw, rough sensation reached down through his core and into his soul.

"Come on, Benton..." A sultry tone tinged her deep voice. "I've been working so hard to make you well. You could offer me a few sips..."

As though she required his permission. She'd get his Marrow regardless. Any resistance was instinctual.

She whispered in his ear as she drew circles on his back. "Or must I coax the Marrow out of you like my daughter did?"

Before he could protest, she drew from his deepest parts and poured warm rain into him. Trembling, he tried to will the wonderful sensation away. "What—" She'd so rarely fed from him, and it'd always hurt. He'd never imagined her touch could be so sweet.

"I forgot how sublime you taste..."

The rain became a downpour. He bit the sheets as the torrent formed pools of ecstasy. "*Cock...*" With each passing second, the urge to fight the terrible pull of her feeding eroded, and he panted into the mattress. "What're you doin'?"

Her groan hit him low. "Playing with my food..." She brushed his mind.

Now, she wanted him to give up his thoughts, too?

Something was off. It couldn't be Dagmar who massaged his back, making every sore muscle fiber loosen with relief. Maybe he was still dreaming.

While the tension drained from his spine, it built in his front. He wanted to grind his hips into the bed, but they still wouldn't obey him. Fortunately. Gods knew what else he would've tried to do with them. "Don't. Just yank it out, Daggy."

Cock. He hadn't meant to call her that this time.

Her hands froze, and he braced for them to turn into claws and wrench a scream out of him. She just squeezed a bit. "Find another name."

The rain intensified into a storm, and he shook from head to toe. "Please... Please..." He forgot what he was begging for.

"We've both known so much pain..." She sighed. Or maybe moaned. Gods damn it, he loved the sound of it. "Maybe it's time for something sweeter."

Her deluge drowned him. Like Sarlona's had. He broke, and the Marrow gushed out of him. "Okay..." He groaned as she lapped up the flow. Something else would spill out of him if she didn't stop. "Fine. *Cock.* Do what you want."

How could *Dagmar* have caught him under a spell so beautiful that it rivaled Sarlona's?

His eyes welled up, and he buried his face in the sheets to hide his tears and muffle his growl. Just as ecstasy threatened to shatter him and scatter his pieces on the winds, it ebbed.

"I want a little taste of you, Benton, that's all." She patted him while she drained the remaining trickles of his magical energy. "And to get a sword in your hand."

He inhaled, catching his breath and savoring the warm but more muted sensation pulsing in his depths. It felt too good to question her motives, but not so heavenly that she'd have to change the sheets, and he'd question the very nature of love and loyalty.

She untangled their energies, and her hands settled over his broken vertebrae. The tender heat flowing from them didn't wane, though. "She asked me to look after you," Dagmar told him again. "So, I will."

Maybe nothing was *wrong*. Perhaps Sarlona's love was so powerful that it had crossed realms to work through Dagmar. Maybe Sarlona's quick had changed the Northlander like it had changed him.

CHAPTER THIRTY-FIVE

Dagmar hovered with her head in her hands outside what had been her father's door for centuries.

Forever.

She would really make that idiot her blood, bonding them for eternity. Her and Benton—family. Dropping her hands, she shook her head.

No. Not for all time. She didn't intend to live another century. Only long enough to secure the future of the lorkai and the man in the next room. That would cement Glaucus's legacy and fulfill her promise to Sarlona. After that, she could start a proper rampage that she was unlikely to survive.

"Okay..." She took a deep breath and threw open the door.

Benton jolted, but the scent that hit the air wasn't pure fear and dread. A tinge of relief wafted from him. It ought to. She took his pain away, after all.

The spicy hint of male excitement that followed—that's what she'd been hoping for. Gods, he was easy to manipulate. Maybe she could even get him to swallow the quick without a fuss.

Much as she wanted to grab him and force it down his throat, Sarlona wouldn't have liked that. And Glaucus had always insisted the making was supposed to be a seduction...

She held in a shiver and sat on the bed.

He rolled over for her without a word amid lots of growling and wincing.

"Good mutt," she said, patting his backside. She couldn't help herself. "I didn't think you knew any tricks."

He stiffened under her hand, but his shitty, crooked grin finally appeared. "I'm almost housebroken, too." He glanced to the opposite side of the bed, below which a chamber pot waited. "I can piss off the edge of the bed."

"Impressive." With a flash of a smile, she skipped her hand from his haunch to the small of his back, then reached into his body. Laying the other on his shoulder, she radiated a tingling heat from her fingertips as she coaxed nerve fibers to grow together, one pair at a time.

She caressed the edge of his mind to test if he'd open. He shuddered, his mental barrier wavering, but he held it in place.

Tapping into him, she drew carefully on his magical energy. His rich, sweet Marrow washed some of the tension from her. Kindness came easiest while tasting him. "You could use a shave." Spreading her fingers, she slid her hand to rest on his hip. "And a bath."

Vinegar scented the air with a hint of something peppery.

"Think you'll float if I dump you in the stream?" With a wicked smile, she rolled him over.

"No, but it'd be a mercy." His breath caught when she tugged his Marrow harder and started a warm tingling deep in his core.

She adjusted the blanket to drape low over his hips. "Well, I've put too much effort into fixing you to drown you at this point." With her hand sprawled on his lower abdomen, she fed, worked on his back, *and* filled his insides with a pleasant static.

Half of his obnoxious grin crept onto his face. "Guess you'll have to give me a sponge bath then." A hint of the old Benton.

She sneered. "I'd hate to tax your cock like that when I've just got it working." But she sent a hot wave through him to do just that.

Cursing, he stared at the ceiling.

"It's all right. You don't have to fight it." She'd trained him early on that his bones broke when he imagined her as something to fuck. Now he had to learn that his every thought was safe with her. She had to teach him that the closer they became, the less he'd hurt.

Easing the draw of Marrow, she savored one drop of him at a time. Then she flooded him with the soft, electric rain Sarlona had used on him. "I know how good I'm making you feel."

He moaned, deep in her thrall within moments. "*Cock*, Dag—Dags."

Tenderly, she stroked his mind. "Let me in so I know exactly what you need." She could read him from his body and scent well enough. But she wanted to test his trust.

He groaned again with a slight shake of his head. "You know what I need. And you can't give it to me. No one can."

She frowned. "No, I suppose not..." But she brought him right to the edge of ecstasy and trapped him there.

He writhed as much as his body allowed. "Gods dammit... *Cock*. Cock..."

She made gentle circles on his stomach, tracing his abdominal muscles and taking slow, deep breaths to catch the nuances of his scent while sipping from him. His chest heaved, and his working muscles tensed to granite as she stretched two fingers down to tickle the hollow of his hip.

Half lost in the fog of his Marrow, she ached to break into his mind and experience his bliss alongside him.

Instead, she pulled him back far enough from the precipice that he could form coherent thoughts.

"Benton... It will take weeks to heal you." Retracting her wayward fingers, she rested her palm just below his navel and patted him. "There's a much easier way..."

His beautiful blue eye widened, shining like Northland's glacial streams.

"I'm strong enough now to spare a little quick." She might as well have dumped ice water on him.

"*Don't*, Dagmar." His voice quavered. "Don't you cockin' do that to me."

She tossed her gaze at the ceiling before spearing his with burning irises. "Relax. I wouldn't *bind* you with it. Do you think I'd want that?"

He turned his head when she reached to stroke his cheek.

She grabbed his shoulder, still drinking, healing, and dumping chemicals into his blood that made him tingle. "A lorkai's quick doesn't automatically bind you. Sarlona did that to you deliberately."

"No." He probably would've folded his arms like a stubborn child if it hadn't been such a monumental effort. "I ain't gonna swallow your cockin' vomit. I don't care what it does."

"Oh, Benton... You'll eat spoonfuls of glass with a gory smile if that's what I decide." She wanted to slam him into the cracked headboard and roar in his face. Instead, she kept her hands and voice gentle. "But I'm trying my damnedest to be good to you."

He wouldn't meet her stare.

"It's all right." She gave him a playful squeeze. "We can do it the hard way, but I'm beginning to think you enjoy my company."

He snorted.

"I *know* you enjoy my touch." Sliding her electric fingers lower, she set off a euphoric cascade that would have had him bucking if he possessed the strength.

"Well, you're *makin'* me..." He whined through his teeth, gasping. "Dammit..."

Chuckling, she hit him with it again. He jerked and made the perfect mewl—the sound of prey. It triggered every hunger and sharpened every sense.

He was the second-best thing she'd ever tasted...

She drew deep for a moment, and that sound slipped from him a second time. Without thinking, she breathed against his throat, drinking in his scent. Sarlona's scent. Her father's. *Her own.* As much as they had been a part of Sarlona.

"Gods, I want to eat you alive." She licked the salt from his throat, tasting his flesh along with his Marrow.

His fingertips alighted on her nape as though he wanted to pull her closer. "You're gonna— *Cock.* Dags, you're gonna make me—" He groaned, red and trembling, leaking terror and desire.

She could do it. Shaking his hand off, she straddled him. She could pour her quick into him. Hells, she could probably fuck him if it would help him go along with it. Resting her hand along his jaw, she caressed his lips with her thumb, trying to coax them open.

His lips parted, and he sucked in a deep breath. "Gods dammit..." He bit her thumb, back trying to arch as she pinned him still. "Holy cock." He growled, his face strained and dewy with sweat. "What... Why're you...?"

Careful not to rest much of her significant weight on his fragile body, she sat on him enough to feel him rock-hard between her legs. "Because it's *fun*, Benton." She grinned. "It's fun to watch you pant and shake and moan and try with all your might not to come for me." Cradling his jaw, she shoved her thumb farther into his mouth. "I *like* it, all right? But I can torture you in more violent ways if you prefer."

"But..." He bit her thumb again, trying to catch his breath. "You don't like *me*."

She leaned down, staring at the delightful squirming prey caught between her thighs and struggled to remember *why*.

He wasn't the same piece of shit Glaucus had saved from the gallows. Or quite the asshole who had swallowed Sarlona's quick. Neither was he exactly the guard who'd gone into the Abyssal Waters or spent weeks using her father's brain...

He was the man who had lost the person he'd loved with all his heart and soul. The man who was the closest thing Dagmar had left to family. And the person who had spent the last weeks of Sarlona's short life making her feel loved.

Dagmar stared into his face. Even with the eyepatch, the ragged scar, and days of grime, he was beautiful. "I don't want to..." She bent lower still, sniffing his throat. He was a part of her and her of him, even if neither liked it. Not Bound but forever linked. She'd *love* him, though, if she gave him her quick. No matter how much she tried to deny it.

"But that's *my* quick in you... My father's... Passed down by my daughter." She wiped the hair from his face. "Look at me."

He did, without being forced.

She sent one last fiery wave through him as she leaned in.

Whimpering, he arched against her.

Her lips and mind brushed his at once.

With a final whine, he opened his mouth and lowered his barrier.

His burning mortal fires collided with her reproductive ones as she flooded into him, and the conflagration consumed her. Trapping him in a tender kiss, she focused on her scant reserve of quick. *For him*. Her soon-to-be new child. She'd make him with care, like she had Sarlona.

The quick rose with little prompting, eager to enter him. Everything contracted—exploded—and she embedded in his mind and body with barbed hooks, compelling him to swallow her quick as it spurted into his mouth. Bone-splitting ecstasy racked her core with each pulse of concentrated Marrow that left her and implanted in him.

He convulsed, trying to scream into her mouth while the quick ravished him and ate the elusive tar that had been hiding in his veins. It knitted his damaged nerves together and summoned cartilage beads to replace irreparable bone. As it shot through his systems, the potent immortal substance bolstered each to prepare them for transformation. It weaved nets to capture Marrow and primed his organs to store more.

"*Cock*." He growled against her lips. His eyes streamed, and the tendrils behind the cursed one shifted. "Gods... It *hurts*..."

As he swallowed the last drop of quick she could summon, she withdrew her kiss and crushed his arms to his sides.

Tendrils erupted from beneath his dislodged eyepatch as pain and pleasure blended to reach a crescendo. Stars exploded in his vision, and a high-pitched whine droned in his ears. He spilled his seed with a muscle-rending spasm, and his unobstructed iris flickered yellow before his eye rolled. The black tendrils flailed, wrapping around her arm and throat as his consciousness unraveled and his mind went dark. His urine let go a second later.

She grabbed the tendril that limply gripped her throat and ripped the last of his Marrow from him. The shadowy snakes withered and retracted.

Shaking, she collapsed on the bed. Her very soul seemed to waver, thin and empty. But that was good. She'd given everything, like a mother should. That was how she'd made Sarlona. How her father had made her. And Benton had taken the quick well. It'd gone to work on him right away.

She stared at him, his face now the picture of peace with his long lashes frozen in a soft kiss and every trace of tension gone from his features. Lovely.

He may not be the child she'd wanted, but he'd make a strong and beautiful son.

CHAPTER THIRTY-SIX

Benton clung to Dagmar's arm with each shaky step. Staying upright made his abdomen burn like he'd done a hundred sit-ups. She'd had to carry him down the stairs.

How he'd made it halfway from the house to the palisade, he didn't know, but that was as far as he was going. The frustration and prickling pain shooting from his lower back was bad enough. He didn't need the humiliation of hobbling around in his underclothes in front of the other guards—and Gorgil, silhouetted by the torchlight, stood near the gate.

"I can't go any farther."

Dagmar stared at him, her stony features impossible to read. "You can make it to the road. I'll carry you from there."

His face ignited to match his stomach. He didn't want to be carried anywhere else. "Where're we goin'?"

She flashed a smile, the type of devious expression she got when she had some terrible task for him. "To get you your bath."

A chill crawled over him despite the hot, humid air. She *was* going to dump him in the stream. The old Dagmar would let him sink and take in a lungful of water before fishing him out. This one... He didn't have a clue.

"Go on." She nudged him forward. "You can make it."

He forced one leg ahead, swaying as he shifted his weight. Her hand landed on his spine, steadying him and numbing the pain.

"Well, look at you," Gorgil said when they approached the gate, tusks gleaming with his wide smile. "On your feet already."

Seven years and Benton still wasn't used to the fact that the guard captain wasn't an asshole. "Yep."

Gorgil opened the doors, and the world became a blur of stars and shadows.

After several disorienting seconds, granite lay under his feet, and trees towered over him. Dagmar held him upright until the pine boughs stopped spinning, and his stomach caught up to him. He swayed at the edge of a woodland pool, fed by a gentle waterfall.

"Where are we?" The stream, obviously, but he didn't recognize the spot. Then again, he'd never done much exploring.

"About three miles north of the house." She guided him onto the sloping boulder to stick his legs into the pool and joined him after yanking off her huge boots. Working her fingers into his quivering back muscles, she leaned close. "I want you to take another dose of my quick tonight."

A chill coated his body like he'd plunged into the pool. The splash of falling water seemed to go silent. "I— I don't want anymore, Dags... Yours—" Instinct told him Dagmar's was far less potent than Sarlona's had been, but it tore through him more violently. "It's...painful."

"But not *just* painful." She mimicked his shit-eating grin.

A pang hit him in the solar plexus. He'd gotten off both times she'd shared her quick with him so far. And pissed himself...

Somehow, swallowing her quick felt like a betrayal of Sarlona.

He tried to focus on the cool, bracing water between his toes rather than the delightful pressure of her fingertips. "Everything feels weird after."

"It's making you well, Benton." Her fingers wandered up his spine. "It made you walk. Another swallow should have you almost back to normal." She pushed on the muscle deep between his shoulder blades until he groaned. "Once you've fully recovered, you'll feel better than ever."

He believed her. And he wanted to do as she asked. She'd been kind to him since they'd returned to Ashmore. Never mind that disobeying Dagmar had always come with severe consequences, and she'd just make him do it anyway. "Don't it seem...wrong? Me takin' yours when I'm supposed to belong to Sar?"

Thinking about it felt like plummeting from a mountaintop—a terrible emptiness flowed into him.

Dagmar's hand froze. She was quiet for a few seconds, then said, "When Glaucus's sister, Idalia, died, she had a Bound..." After a sigh, she went silent again for a moment. "Her quick vaporized from the woman at the instant of her death."

The bond with Sarlona made him experience the loss of her that much more acutely, but the thought of it breaking... That opened a black hole more infinite than the Abyss to swallow him. He thanked the stars that Sarlona's quick hadn't left him.

"If Sarlona's death didn't dissolve your bond... If your connection can stretch between realms..." Dagmar's voice grew as gentle as Benton had ever heard it. "I could never erode what's between you."

She snaked her arm around him and squeezed.

Cocking Dagmar *hugged* him.

Taking his chin in her other hand, she tilted his face to meet her faintly glowing green gaze. "Your relationship with her will never be any less special than when she was here with us. Nothing can change that."

The face he gazed into belonged to a different monster. A new woman from the stony, brutal Northlander he'd cowered from. He still couldn't decide what to make of her.

She ran her thumb across his lips. Gods knew why he wanted to part them for it.

"I have to go to the capital for a few days," she said, dropping her hand. "I want you able to run and defend yourself before then. Just in case."

A sliver of disappointment embedded in his chest. "If I'm better, I could go, too..." Something was wrong with him. He couldn't bear to be parted from *Dagmar*?

"You want to come with me?" She chuckled and patted him. "You do make a fine pet."

He stared at the pool. Watching the edge where it overflowed and spilled down the rocks to coalesce below, he wondered if Dagmar would ever think of him as something more than an animal.

"You can't come with me, Benton." Her touch turned sensual when she dragged one finger down his vertebrae, licking at his Marrow. "I'm going there to cause some trouble. And I don't want you seen outside Ashmore's gates."

He stiffened, both from her words and her finger breaching the waistband of his underclothes. "Why the hells not?"

"Everyone believes you're dead. I want to keep it that way awhile."

He didn't see why anyone would give a shit if he'd survived or not. "For how long?"

She skipped her hand up to support his back as his arms and abs started to shake. "Until I say, Benton." Her voice was forceful but not the monstrous growl she'd always used with him.

Still gazing at the pool, he hoped she remembered how months or years could drag on to a human. After another pat between his shoulders, she retracted her hand, and he almost toppled.

She fished a hunk of soap from her pocket. "Time for your bath." Smiling, she rose and, to his astonishment, slipped out of her fur-lined vest, then unlaced the front of her tunic. He gaped as she pulled her shirt over her head, revealing an iron torso adorned with soft, creamy flesh.

Gulping, he tore his gaze away. She wouldn't have been his type had he been the type to choose one, yet he'd always found her muscular thighs frustratingly alluring. Never more so than when she slid off her hide pants to bare them and stood over him in her underclothes. He tried his damnedest to focus on the sparkles of moonlight dancing with the rippling water. Different Dagmar or not, he still feared that if she caught him picturing her bent over in front of him, she'd re-break his back.

She twisted and hopped into the pool with hardly a splash, muscles flexing. "Come on."

Grabbing him under his knee and by his opposite forearm, she helped him slide down the coarse granite and into the water. The cold sucked the breath out of him for a second, but the pool was far from icy. In fact, the cool, clean water provided instant relief to his hot, grimy skin.

"Close your eye." She slipped his eyepatch off and flung it onto the rock. "Lean back."

Without the strength to resist on his best day, he obeyed, and the cool water flowed around his shoulders and scalp. He stared at the stars and hunted for the constellations Sarlona had shown him while Dagmar ran the soap over his chest. Her thumb and little finger scraped across his skin, sending tender tingles through him. The warm hand that held him at the surface and crushed his left side to her abdomen tugged out his Marrow. Try as he might to keep his attention on the sky, her bare chest was right there, and her soapy hand was all over him.

He couldn't do it. "Do I get to wash you next?"

She glared at him as she ran the soap up to his throat, then rubbed it over his neck and into his scruff. "I can't stress enough how critical it is to your wellbeing that you keep your hands to yourself"

His cheeks puffed out with his exhale. "It ain't fair."

She drew him closer to work the soap into his scalp and hair. "Most things aren't."

"Come on, Dags—" He tried to pull away, but he was a minnow swimming against a tidal wave. This was the test—whether she'd break him or not. He took a deep breath. "You can't put your wet tits in my face while you're feelin' me up and expect me to behave myself."

Her eyes sparkled with the trace of a smile beneath their yellow glow, but it didn't show on her lips. "Hold your breath."

Bracing for her to drown him, he did as commanded.

She dunked him under and tousled his hair to get the soap out. To his surprise, she hauled him up just when his lungs started to itch. "I told you, Benton, I enjoy tormenting you." Grinning, she urged him onto his feet. "Stand still so I can do it in earnest."

Heart pounding, he did his best. He could stand better in the water with less weight on his back, but now his legs wobbled for a different reason.

Slipping behind him, she rested her hands on his waist. Electric heat emanated from her fingers, making his insides hum. She crushed him to her body, smooth and, but for the softness pressed into his shoulders, hard as a marble statue, "Open for me." She breathed the words behind his ear, stroking the outer limit of his mind, and they seemed to pass right into his skull. His barrier dissolved like sugar. She flooded into him—a stream of dominating warmth—and he couldn't remember why he'd ever wanted to be alone there. He groaned as she filled his empty places. With Sarlona gone, there were a lot of them.

Her hands roved his sides, still holding the soap in one. Then she dipped her thumbs into the hollows of his hipbones.

He'd grown thin. Traveling on foot with no more than what he carried on his belt, scavenging for food along the Northland coast, lying for days in a coma... He hadn't eaten regular meals since before he'd gone into the Abyss.

She must have noticed, too. Leaning down, she whispered beside his head. "I'd break you, Benton." Her tongue flicked his earlobe. "You'd never survive the night with me."

Gods, he wanted to try. She wasn't anything like Sarlona, but she was still...cocking *hot*.

"No, I'm not my daughter... I have *centuries* of experience." She hooked her fingers into the waistband of his underclothes, and with a quick yank, tore the threadbare linen free. "Centuries of practice manipulating mortal bodies and dredging up hidden desires..."

"Gods dammit, Dags..." He was so hard it hurt, and his body shook to the point of spasm as she slid the soap over his hips and thighs.

He jerked with a yelp when her teeth nipped his nape, and she reached between his legs.

"You twitch like a mouse beneath a cat's paw." She bit his ear next.

He moaned and jerked again as she rubbed him with soapy fingers.

"Careful..." She growled along his throat. "Those kinds of noises excite me."

His heart beat too fast, and his breaths were too ragged when her left arm locked across his front. A hot hurricane tore from his depths. Her hand was pure, electric pleasure. "Oh, *gods*."

She kissed his shoulder, then ran the soap up and down his length. "You'll meet them where I'm about to send you." Discarding the soap, she wrapped her hand around him and squeezed. Her fingertips heated and tingled as she tapped into his Marrow. "Scream loud for me."

His eyes began to roll, and the stars blinked before her hand even moved. "Wait..." He gasped, fighting to catch his breath while her lips crawled up the side of his neck, and her hands drew on his Marrow. "Wait, Dags..."

Sarlona had only been gone a few weeks.

The kisses turned into nibbles.

"I just..." As much as he burned for Dagmar's touch, guilt gnawed at his gut. "This... Sar..." Gods, he couldn't even speak. He needed Dagmar to devour him, whether remorse would pick at his bones afterward or not.

Her hands stilled, but the sensations they produced didn't. "She'd want you to feel good."

Probably. But on those occasions when that monster inside Sarlona had reared its head, it had made clear that he belonged to *her* in every way imaginable.

"Sarlona's a realm away, in Tydras' arms... But she left *you* in *mine*." Dagmar's grip tightened.

"Gods... Okay, Dags— Just..." He still didn't know what the hells was happening. It didn't seem real. Maybe he *had* died. Dagmar had definitely lost her cocking mind. "I ain't ever gonna feel about anyone like I did Sar."

"No, you're not." She patted his hair. "You *can't*." Her breath on his neck seemed to flow into him. "But you don't have to love me, Benton." She tickled the end of him with enchanted fingers, and he groaned, his entire body vibrating. "You don't even have to like me." Purring in his ear, she crushed him against her and applied smooth, tender strokes that had him bucking. "You just have to come harder than you ever have for me..."

He almost did. "Cock."

She stroked him faster. "Then swallow my quick and come harder still."

"Dags..." He moaned, feeling as though she caressed his whole soul and not just his cock. "Gods dammit... I'm go—"

She slowed and breathed deeply in his ear. "Not yet, though..."

He had to. If he didn't, the fire within would tear him apart. "You gotta..." He tried to beg, but his voice crumbled. "Dags... Please... I can't. I can't take it."

Her low, perfect whisper drifted into his mind like a spell. "You'll take everything I give you."

He *would* break. She'd kill him and have to shove the life back into him. "Gods..." He thrashed, burning for *her* to take something. *Needing* her to. "Let me put it in you."

She laughed beside his head—a deep, sweet sound.

He longed to make other noises come from her. Resolving to do just that, he opened his cursed eye. Sarlona had enjoyed his tendrils. Dagmar might, too.

The black whips shot from him the instant his lids parted with a delightful release that took the edge off his torture. They seemed to sense his intentions, even if he couldn't control them quite like his other appendages. Without much prompting, they curled backward and snared Dagmar's throat and thighs.

"That's a naughty thing to do, Benton." Her voice was quiet and raspy from the snake strangling her, but she spoke clearly in his head.

Another tendril snagged the wrist of the arm that trapped his waist and wrenched it free, twisting her arm up behind her and binding it tightly. He left the hand gripping him free to work. "I'm gonna fuck you, Dags. You're gonna come for me, too."

She laughed, and his ecstasy surged to the point where his mind went blank, and the waterfall muted. Every fiber of his being throbbed. He'd either rip apart or pass out. "No... No, wait..." His knees gave out.

She pulled him from the edge and held him while he got his legs under him. "I love hearing you beg."

"*You're* gonna beg." He tightened his bizarre appendages to choke off her laugh and slid them up her thighs an inch at a time. Fighting each wave of euphoria that threatened to stop his advance, if not his heart, he wormed them into her underclothes.

She stiffened when the end of one tendril slid through her warm folds. Her throat strained under his grasp, and she yanked on the shadowy rope knotted around her arm, shaking as its cohort writhed against her front.

He loosened the Abyssal noose just enough that he could hear her growls.

She ground into his back, and her fingers circled the tip of him, tasting his Marrow and melting him into pure need.

"Please, Dags... You're killin' me."

"You've started trouble, Benton." Panting in his ear, she came as close to begging as he could hope for. "Now you have to finish it."

Lengthening the tendrils that ensnared her throat and arm, he stretched them to join the two that had breached her underclothes. He took a deep breath, half-fearing her wrath when he dipped one inside her. Her granite abdomen tensed into adamantine, and she rocked her hips to drive it deeper. Swirling the tentacle, he obliged until it would go no farther.

Her low, reverberating moan had him thrusting into her hand. She squeezed him tighter as he made the snake twist and thicken, then she thrashed with a growl. "*Fuck* me if you're going to fuck me."

He shot a second tendril up into her, ramming it deep.

"Fuck." Her jerk almost snapped him in half. "That's better. Oh, that's good, Benton..." She writhed with the ebony appendages, moaning and working her hand faster. "*Fuck* me."

He commanded the tentacles to squirm and twist like eels out of water.

"Gods, yes." She gasped. "Hurt me. Fuck me and *hurt me*."

The demand echoed so loud in his skull that he didn't second guess it. He rammed the third, thick tendril into her. "Cockin' *take it*, Dags."

Her buck made pain explode up his back for a split second before she killed it, and he tightened the snare encircling her throat to cut off her deafening roar.

She thrashed, growling as his three wicked tendrils wriggled within her, and the tip of a fourth vibrated against her on the outside. All while she dangled him on the precipice of soul-splitting release, exhausted muscles screaming with tension.

But after just a minute of effort, she cried out in his mind, and her soft insides crushed his tendrils as she convulsed. She wrenched her arm free, rending the black tentacle that had restrained it and grabbed the one around her neck. With a draw that shook his bones, she sucked the Marrow from him until they dissipated into smoke.

Spasms racked his body a second later. Colors he had no names for burst into his vision. His heart thundered in his ears. He felt nothing, then everything. Rapture ripped through his being, and he screamed until his voice ran out. Then there was nothing but bright white light and a warm, wispy sensation like he'd turned into steam.

When he solidified, he floated in cold water, muscles useless with exhaustion and bones throbbing.

She *had* broken him.

"You're okay." Huge hands hauled him upright, and the pain vanished.

He still couldn't stand. His feet kept slipping in the leafy muck.

"You did well." She grinned, pinning him to the granite boulder. "But you're not done yet."

He didn't have a shred of will remaining. When she leaned in, he parted his lips.

She kissed him first, deep and demanding, and he couldn't help kissing her in return. Then, his body was hers. She hitched, spilling her thick, syrupy gin into his mouth. He swallowed, eyes watering as it burned its way down and hit his guts like an explosion. Every inch of him knotted up and caught fire.

She held his convulsing body to the granite and slammed him with the sweet, warm rain that rolled his eyes as he took another swallow. It drowned the pain of her sizzling quick. He moaned and pushed against her while it built into a torrent flooding his recesses. Within seconds, the tender prickling and fiery secretion tore him apart, wresting a hoarse scream out of him. Then, the night went silent. Bright stars, dark trees, and rippling water all spun together. The only things that didn't blur were the demonic red eyes staring into his. Sinking into oblivion, he left those behind, too.

CHAPTER THIRTY-SEVEN

Dagmar stood over the sleeping priest in the gloom of the rectory, her blazing red gaze lighting up his serene, young face. Little did he know it would be the last peaceful moment of his life.

She bent low, twisting her face into an extra menacing snarl, and squeezed his throat tight enough so he couldn't scream and wake his sleeping fellows. Acrid terror hit the air an instant after his blue eyes flew open, then the stench of urine. He jerked as she snatched his reins, then went still except for his quaking bones.

She violated his mind with no regard for how barbarously she penetrated his mental barrier and sifted through him to determine just how horrendous she'd make his death.

Not very, it turned out. Traces of guilt itched in her gut—the young priest wasn't an awful man.

He'd been at Apogee to deliver Sarlona's death sermon because he believed all souls deserved a chance for forgiveness and Silsor's light. Even the souls of monsters. However strong his conviction that dark denizens must be routed to protect the innocent, he hadn't *wanted* her to burn. In fact, the memory of the dying girl ripping herself from the stake and shrieking into his mind had haunted his dreams every night since. He was a genuinely faithful Silsorian who didn't desire anyone's suffering.

Dagmar wilted. When she'd picked her way to the quiet temple on the outskirts of Royal City, she had intended to cut him open and spread his guts about while he was still alive.

Instead, she numbed his fear and filled him with the same warmth Silsor's Light provided him as she drained his Marrow and started on his life force.

His benign thoughts and good intentions wouldn't spare him from a Silsorian's greatest defilement, but they'd earned him a gentle death. Of course, that meant more work for her. He wouldn't make the mess she needed without flailing limbs and a pounding pulse.

She left him unconscious and hovering between life and death while she searched for a jar. The nearest thing she could find in the chamber was a decanter of holy water. After dumping it on the floor, she returned to the priest and slit his wrist. Once her vessel was filled, she healed the wound and stopped his heart. If it looked like an evil spell had collected his blood, all the better.

With the decanter in one hand and his pale, naked corpse over her shoulder, she crept down to the temple. Fortunately, no lost souls sat in the pews seeking forgiveness for the evening's sins. They would've had to add to her display.

With one hand, she dragged the dead priest to the center of the chancel, then pushed the pulpit off to the side so it wouldn't obstruct the circle she intended to create. Or the view. Keeping her ears perked in case anyone came to the temple door or stirred in the rectory, she laid the naked man spread eagle, then poured a ring of blood around him.

The poor priest was destined to become one of Vorakor's Eyes—a murderous offering to the Abyssal Lord made by the most devout of the Nocturnal Embrace's adherents. One said to allow the wicked god to peer into the place of its construction and send his whispers to anyone who passed over the unhallowed ground.

Bullshit. Probably.

Using the balled-up altar cloth, she painted eight bloody tentacles radiating out from the ring, one for each cardinal and ordinal direction, all the while trying not to think about Benton's tendrils and just what they'd done to her. He'd been so fucking proud of himself afterward, too. She'd never been as happy to leave Ashmore.

With the tendrils done, she ejected a carpal blade and punched it through the dead priest's sternum. Careful not to cut into his heart or intestines, she sliced her way to his pubic bone, then peeled him open. His ribs snapped as she wrenched him apart, reminding her of men she'd tortured in Northland centuries ago. Split down the middle, he resembled the cast skin of a dragonfly nymph. Except everything was still in there.

Not for long.

She pulled out his intestines and cut them into eight lengths, laying them to radiate out from his abdominal cavity to the bloody ring like more tendrils. The heart came out next, drooling blood. After she dislocated the priest's jaw to accommodate it with a pop, she stuffed the muscular organ down his throat.

She'd cut out a heart to make the owner swallow it before. And removed genitalia. Sticking them in the cavity where the heart had been was new.

That wasn't the worst of it, either. Vorakor's demented disciples had to go above and beyond all conventional corpse desecration to appease their Abyssal Lord, of course.

She held her breath, then plucked the priest's pale blue eyes out of his head. And grimaced as she shoved them up his ass. "Fucking hells."

The smell of burnt meat drew her gaze upward once she'd finished her task. Sarlona's charred husk glared at her with glowing eyes from the pews. She bore a striking resemblance to the Demon of Zelule.

Dagmar's heart paused for just a second. She knew damned well that the disapproving apparition existed only in her head. If she'd been of sound mind, she wouldn't be doing things like transplanting a priest's eyes to his rectum or stroking Benton's cock while she rode his cursed tentacles.

She ignored the haunting hallucination and replaced the man's right hand with his left foot—the final step in the Eye's creation.

Retreating, she surveyed her handiwork.

Horrific.

But a Vorakor's Eye crafted from a priest in a Silsorian temple would make the Light Guard lose their fucking minds. They'd crusade about, hunting the Nocturnal Embrace with renewed vigor, laying siege to the slums in Port Brummit, and executing anyone in black who wasn't on the way to a funeral.

Amenduil would suspect her, of course. But the evil cult couldn't very well explain to their mortal enemies that a fabled monster had framed them.

Guilt nibbled her insides as she wiped up her oversized boot prints. No doubt there would be collateral damage in the conflict she initiated. Pagans mistaken for Vorakor's Children... Innocent Silsorians taken hostage in retaliation...

She'd made the priest's body unsuitable for burial in consecrated Silsorian ground, too. According to their doctrine, he might never find his way to Silsor's heaven. She shook her head. He could have avoided it by speaking up against Kyran's cruelty or putting Sarlona out of her misery before Amenduil did.

Dagmar fished the cyan-and-sable strip of fabric from her pocket—a scrap she'd torn from a tower guard's uniform. The guard who'd lit Sarlona's pyre. Dagmar had been to his home in the city and hidden the Nocturnal Embrace's paraphernalia there. Hopefully, the Light Guard would take the bait, searching the residences of all the tower guards who lived in or had close ties to the city. They'd find signs of Abyssal worship in two other guards' residences who had been at Apogee the day of Sarlona's execution, as well.

If all went according to Dagmar's plan, the Light Guard would execute three tower guards and a boatload of Amenduil's brethren for her.

Even better, there'd be questions about just what the hells was going on at Apogee. Amenduil had been seen there by dozens of mages, some of whom had to be Silsorian. Kyran had been *working with* him. There'd be more than questions—there'd be an inquisition. The king would get involved. Relations between the Silsorian crown and the SPS would decay.

Hells, maybe she'd start the third wizard war. That would keep the SPS busy. Who knows? Maybe Kyran would get ousted. Talvianna had already initiated an investigation after Sarlona's last-minute accusations.

Dagmar wasn't counting on much of that as she snagged the bit of uniform on a splintery corner of the pulpit, but imagining it was fun.

Of course, flaying half the Council with a rusty spoon would be much more amusing. But that would have to wait. She couldn't risk going toe to toe with any of them until after Benton was made—and had a daughter of his own.

CHAPTER THIRTY-EIGHT

The sun warmed Benton's shoulders in contrast to the cool, wet grass beneath his bare feet. Birdsong spilled from the forest's edge, each warbler competing for the longest trill among the serviceberry blossoms. Had the sweet, smoky scent of burnt timber not filled his nostrils along with a more pungent odor, he might have smelled the delicate blooms.

The blaze had extinguished itself, but dark smoke still billowed into the clear sky from the smoldering pile of charcoal that had been his home. He watched it drift upward with a lightness in his chest.

Until movement drew his gaze to the ground. Something stirred in the rubble. His heart leapt into his throat as a blackened, twisted form sprouted from the ashes, uncurling like a fern from the forest floor.

A man. The fire had claimed his ears, nose, and lips, but Benton recognized the pale green eyes—his stepfather's.

Dale lumbered at him, cooked skin cracking and oozing.

The area of the scorched man's exposed teeth and gums expanded in a grotesque smile. Somehow, despite the disarray of his mouth, he spoke.

"There you are, Ben. We've been waitin' for you." Dry, raspy laughter rattled out of Dale's maw.

Adrenaline raced through Benton's thighs, and rage crawled up his throat. "Lie the cock back down and go back to bein' dead."

"That's how you talk to your elders? After all I did for you?" Dale shambled closer, flakes of charred skin fluttering to the ground.

Benton went for a blade he wasn't carrying. "It's the way to talk to grilled rat shit."

Dale motioned to his blistered body. "And this is your thanks."

"You deserved worse than you got." Benton's voice wavered.

"It's all right, Ben. We forgive you." Dale lunged for him with skeletal hands.

"Cock off." Benton sidestepped him and wound up. "I'll kill you however many times it takes for you to stay dead." His knuckles hit sooty bone, and Dale crumbled into ashes, wafting on the breeze.

"Benny?"

Benton whipped around as another scorched body lumbered toward him, this one bearing his mother's roasted features.

Her skin tightened and cracked over her angular frame with every step. "You're back... And you're all grown up..."

He jumped when she approached too fast, appearing right before him.

Vomit rose in his throat at the acrid reek of her smoldering flesh. His limbs grew too heavy to lift as she reached a shriveled hand at his face. "What have you done to your eye?" Rough, crusty fingers caressed his cheek.

He shook her off, retreating. "Get away from me, bitch."

"Shhh... Come to your mother, Benny." She paused to set her jaw into place when it came unhinged, then opened her skeletal arms. "Come with us so we can be a family."

He gritted his teeth and shoved her. She crumbled to ash between his fingers. Off balance, he stumbled, falling to his hands and knees. He held his breath as the dust of his mother settled over him.

The rubble stirred again.

He knew what came next. Who.

His throat dried to desert sand, and a clamp tightened on his chest. A small, blackened body rose from the debris.

But he blinked, and the husk wasn't his brother. It was too tall, and its beautiful eyes were the color of the Avenian sea.

"Sar?" His heart tumbled past his gut, plummeting into an endless void.

Her bones cracked her dried flesh and popped through at her joints. Despite muscle that had shriveled to jerky, she floated to him with all the grace and fluidity of a lorkai.

His legs wouldn't work. He shook too violently to stand. "No, Sar... No." He was sinking into the Abyss.

Charred skeletal claws that had once been smooth, delicate fingers grabbed the sides of his head. The stench of burnt meat brought the bile into his throat while she bent near. Her beautiful hair, skin, lips, breasts... Fire had taken all of it. Everything but the eyes.

Eyes a few inches from his own, boring into his soul... He closed his lids so he wouldn't have to see them and quaked as she kissed him with crusty, papery flesh.

His scream followed him into the waking world.

He hauled himself to the edge of the bed and retched. Only mucus left his empty stomach.

After a minute of shaking and telling himself the image of Sarlona had just been a nightmare, he rolled from the bed. He prayed his bad dreams wouldn't forever include her among his flame-eaten victims. That torment he couldn't endure, no matter how interesting Dagmar made his evenings.

Drenched in cold sweat, he splashed water on his face from the wash basin. Leaning forward on the bureau, he watched the trickles run down his cheeks and onto his chest in the mirror. He looked skinny and pale.

His strength had returned, though, and then some. Dagmar's quick had healed him like she'd promised. But he still didn't feel right. He was restless and had no appetite. His left forearm oscillated between itching and aching. Maybe she could fix that.

A pang struck his gut. Now that he'd recovered, she might not play with him. Might not touch him... She might never let him touch her back... Then what would he live for?

However mad it sounded, her attention had made existence bearable. It kept him from crumbling into a weeping heap of despair.

Having caught his breath, he wiped the wetness from his cheeks into his hair, careful not to dislodge his eyepatch. His heart stopped when he dropped his hands. Sarlona peered at him from the mirror—blackened to a crisp, lips withered to form a petrified snarl, and all her softness burned away. But her eyes were whole and clear, their deep blue boring into him.

"*Cock.*" He reeled, stumbling from the mirror with adrenaline bursting through his veins. "No, gods dammit." Dragon talons clutched his chest. "*Please*, no."

He shut his eyes, praying to any deity who would listen, that she'd be gone when he opened them.

She wasn't. The blue-eyed demon glared at him from the other side of the glass, still and silent.

Gasping for breath, he tried to gather himself. He was imagining things...losing his mind...

Or she was haunting him. Because he was cocking around with Dagmar...

Or because of their bond. They weren't supposed to be apart. Maybe he was meant to be dead with her...

"Sar?" His voice cracked. He crept closer. If she was real, she'd tell him why she'd come. She'd explain what he had to do so she could rest...

He reached toward the mirror, mesmerized by her gaze. Her perfect blue threatened to spill out and drown him from a shell of pure horror as she extended her arm. He must still be sleeping...trapped in another nightmare.

His fingers collided with cool glass. He lowered his hand, peering deeper into the grisly face. She lowered hers too...

Then he stared into his own eyes—electric blue. *Both* of them. His eyes, in her hellish remains. "What..." He leaned in.

The eyes flickered with yellow light, and he started. He shook his head, backpedaling. She mirrored him. Then she held out her left arm and flicked out her carpal blade. Looking at the serrated ivory sword, she swung it on its hinge.

Benton blinked, and his reflection gawked at him. Chest still heaving, thighs aching with adrenaline, he watched the mirror, fearing its image would change back.

His itching forearm at last drew his gaze away. Squinting, he scratched at his wrist.

Was there something there? A wrinkle? A seam...

Realization hit him like a ton of bricks. He nearly toppled.

Sarlona had come to *warn* him.

He almost sprinted from the chamber in his underclothes, catching himself with his hand on the knob.

"Cock, fuck, cock..."

Spinning, he darted to the bureau and dressed at lightning speed. He'd need a sword too...

"Okay, okay..."

After a few deep breaths, he calmed his expression and strode from the room. Dagmar hadn't returned. He had some time to escape. Maybe another whole day.

Calmly as he could, he went to the barracks.

Gupson glanced up from the stick he was whittling at the table. "What are you doing down here?" He tossed his gray hair. "I thought you were too good for the rabble now."

"Always was..." Benton headed for the weapons rack. "I'm feelin' good. Figured I should start makin' myself useful..." Frowning, he scanned the swords. Nothing rivaled the blade he'd lost in Northland. "Before Dagmar decides I ain't worth keeping."

Gupson set aside his stick to take a drink. "I don't think she will... Me and Lita begged her to let us smother you when you were still pissing the bed."

Grabbing a dead guard's blade, Benton snorted. "Yeah, well, I ain't takin' the chance. I need some fresh air anyhow."

"Don't overdo it." The old chair groaned across the battered floor as Gupson rose. "I've never seen a man half that dead get up again."

Benton shoved the blade into his belt. "I'm just wanderin' around." Without another look at Gupson, he strode for the stairs.

He fast walked for the door with Gupson trailing him. The guards knew. They had orders to keep him there. Lita guarded the gate.

Benton could take them both. But if the ensuing racket drew Gorgil and Cyr, getting out might be a challenge.

"Where do you think *you're* going?" Lita asked with her hands on her wiry hips.

"Out." Benton stalked toward her. "*I* ain't on duty."

"No shit. Your only duty has been in lorkai bedrooms for months." She grinned, bright teeth gleaming from her brown face. "Can you even swing a blade anymore?"

He was ready to draw it in a blink. "Test me, darlin'. I'd love to poke you good."

She pulled her cudgels. "Honey, you've been trying for years and haven't managed it yet."

"You can't leave," Gupson said from behind. "Dagmar doesn't want anyone coming or going while she's gone. You know that."

Benton glanced over his shoulder. The old man had his bow trained on him. "I'm just goin' for a walk."

"*Benton*." Gorgil came jogging from the side of the house and Cyr appeared on Benton's left.

Benton spat at the ground. They were going to try to stop him from leaving.

"You're not allowed beyond the palisade." Gorgil unsheathed his massive blade. "On Dagmar's orders."

Benton loosed his second-rate steel. "Why the cock not?"

Lita and Gorgil closed in. Cyr raised his hands. Gupson drew back his bowstring.

"You know why..." Gorgil's voice was soft for a man his size holding a gigantic blade. So were his russet eyes. "Or you wouldn't be so determined to go."

"I can't do it." Benton tried to hold the panic out of his voice. "Not again. Not forever... You don't know what it's like." The memory of the soul-deep thirst to rip the magic out of everyone he came across, the *life* if they didn't have enough, stole his breath.

"I'm sorry." Gorgil frowned, tusks peeking out like a bulldog's canines.

"You're *all* gonna be sorry if Dagmar gets her way." Benton's heart thundered, and his hands trembled. "Sar ain't here to make sure I behave myself this time." He flashed his grin at Lita, knowing full well that Cyr would be who he couldn't keep his hands from.

"Not as sorry as we'd be defying Dagmar." Gorgil motioned for Benton's blade.

Benton snorted at the captain's hand and pivoted to the gate. An arrow thunked into the wood beside his shoulder when he dipped to heave the iron bar out of its brackets. Lita darted in and swung for Benton's sword arm, but he batted her cudgel away with his blade and spun left toward Cyr. He ducked behind the mage and popped up, sword to the man's throat. His own speed surprised him. He shouldn't have been that fast.

"You're gonna teleport us to Wolfboro."

Cyr struggled, but the scrawny man didn't have a prayer of wrenching free from one bolstered by the quick of two lorkai. "The hells I am."

Benton growled, unsure if Cyr could even teleport two people without a potion. "I'm in just the kinda mood to slit someone's throat." The mage deserved it for not being smart enough to put up a shield.

The man's voice fought to squeeze past the flat of Benton's blade. "Better that than what Dagmar would do to me."

Good point. Benton snatched the knife from Cyr's belt and jabbed it into his hip. The mage howled as Benton shoved him at Lita and lunged at Gorgil.

The guard captain flung his giant sword in front of Benton's just in time to avoid getting skewered. But Benton pushed and, with far more strength than he should have possessed, forced Gorgil's sword arm against his body. Then he drew back much faster than the orc-human swung his blade to the front and rammed his sword through Gorgil's knee. The large man collapsed with a holler, blood gushing from the wound when Benton withdrew his blade.

Benton juked just clear of an arrow and spun to the gate. Throwing his shoulder up under the bar before Gupson could nock another one, he sent it thudding to the ground. Lita swung at him, but he caught one cudgel on his blade and snagged her wrist as she whipped the other at his side. He shoved her, sticking her in the bicep, then retreated. "Sorry, sweetheart, I'll get you good next time."

As he yanked open the gate, though, he hoped they'd never reunite. He slipped through, closing it just when an arrow grazed his arm, stinging him on the way by. It didn't matter now. He was out. Cyr would have to heal himself and his two companions before throwing spells at Benton. He sprinted for the woods. Gorgil and Lita would never catch up to him. Gupson would need a lucky shot to bring him down.

Lungs and thighs burning as he ran, he remembered that Sarlona had made that same desperate race for freedom. He thanked the sky above that he didn't have some alcoholic asshole with an enchanted blade pounding at his heels.

Gupson's next arrow went wide, disappearing into the grass to Benton's right. That was it—Benton had made it. He just had to run to someplace Dagmar could never find him...

He didn't let the hopelessness of that endeavor mire him while he barreled into the woods. Ignoring the voice in his head that declared he only delayed the inevitable, he ran until he collapsed. Then he got up and sprinted again. He kept racing deeper and deeper into the woods until his shaking muscles wouldn't carry him any farther, and exhaustion drove him to the forest floor.

CHAPTER THIRTY-NINE

Dagmar set the bottle of birch spirit on the delicate nightstand beside the low bed as carefully as she could. Everything the elves made was dainty, even in Goldenbark Forest, where the long-lived humanoids were of a wilder and more primitive sort. She'd be astounded if she didn't break all the furniture in the remote cottage within the month.

Squatting farther than was comfortable, she lowered herself onto the bed rather than drop and jolt Benton awake. She'd kept him sedated since finding him passed out, face down in the damp moss after his panicked flight from Ashmore. Now that they were far from home or where anyone would look for them, he needed to wake. The man had to eat, after all.

She didn't want to scare him, though. He'd been frightened enough when he'd figured out what she had planned for him. And broken enough. That he'd dreamed of Sarlona burnt in his nightmares when he'd never seen her like that... And then hallucinated, as Dagmar had...

She had to be careful, or she'd crack him beyond repair.

Gazing at his still and peaceful face with a whisper of warmth in her chest, she laid her large palm on his cheek and caressed his exposed eyelid with her thumb.

It fluttered open, and his eye darted about before his stare locked on her face, and his pupil constricted to the size of a pinprick. Acrid terror burst into the air, and his heart pounded like a warhorse's hoofbeats. He tried to shoot from the bed but only raised a few inches before she pushed him flat by the chest, holding him down with one hand. "Be still. I—"

"*No*, Dagmar..." He writhed beneath her hand. "You can't. You can't do this to me. Not again. I won't—" Gulping for air, he couldn't get another word out.

"It's all right, Benton." Tugging the right threads on his insides, she *made* it all right. A torrent of calm and warmth washed over him.

His body relaxed, and his panicked thoughts stalled. Water leaked into his eye, though. "*Please*, Dags..." His voice was so soft, sweet, and earnest that it played with her heartstrings.

"I'll make it fun, Benton, I promise." She rubbed his stomach. "You fought the monster in Glaucus's body too hard. I'll teach you how to feed your own." Sending shivers through him, she worked her hand lower. "And we can do whatever you need to make life worth living until you get used to it."

A hint of sweet and spicy wafted from him with the pungent scent of fear. "I—"

"*Time*. It just takes time..." She grabbed his hands. "I didn't want to be Glaucus's daughter." Of course, she'd adapted to life as a lorkai quicker than most. Joining the family that had executed two of her brothers and humiliated her was the difficult part. "You take each day as it comes, and the next is easier than the last."

His stomach tightened under her hand as she jolted him with another shot of ecstasy. A warm and tantalizing shock better than anything he could find in a bottle, a warm bath, or a mortal's arms. Something only a lorkai could provide. The instant his muscles relaxed, she hit him with it again. Harder.

He groaned, arching.

"You won't become a lorkai tonight, Benton. Or tomorrow." She let him catch his breath, then sent another pulse through him. "Not next week. Nor the week after."

He scanned the curved ceiling, panting.

"It may take months. So, try to calm yourself. And just survive each day. Like you used to." He'd been so good at that before Sarlona. Even better before Ashmore. "This time, at least you're not alone."

With her caress, a claw of euphoria grabbed his insides. His muscles stiffened, and he arched again. Too many of his ribs showed. He whimpered when she released her grip, the kind of sound that made her want to pounce.

She took a deep breath to stop herself. "Gods, I could do that to you all afternoon...while I drink your Marrow one sip at a time..."

He flushed and hardened, his eye wide and skin dewy. The spicy aroma she'd come to crave from him dominated the air.

She gave him a crooked smile and stroked his cheek instead of the delicate skin beside his hip bone. "Would you like that, Benton?"

The pepper that wafted from him stung her nose. Trembling, he swallowed. "Yeah..." After a big inhale, he met her gaze. "Yeah, I'd like it, Dags. Let's do that."

She grinned, hunger spiking. "Good."

He shoved her hand away. "You gotta let me up, though. Before I piss myself."

She followed him to the door of the one-room cottage, which she'd left ajar to let in the breeze.

He peered out at the small clearing and towering golden wood alive with sparkling flowers, glowing insects, gilded birds, and blond beasts. "Where the hells are we?"

"Goldenbark Forest." She leaned against the doorframe as he passed onto the covered porch. "Was the forest of golden-barked trees not a clue?"

He unfastened his pants at the edge of the porch. "*Why?*"

"So Kyran can't locate me." She folded her arms across her chest. "And so no one finds out about you."

He exhaled as the stench of urine cut through the green and earthy scents that pervaded the outdoors. "How long are we stayin'?"

"Consider it a permanent move."

Glancing back, he grimaced. "Really?"

"Ashmore isn't safe for either of us anymore. Not after the trouble I've stirred up. This is home until I can kill Kyran." She waited for him to finish before grabbing him by the shoulder and drawing him indoors. "Don't worry, I've got everything you need." She gestured to the bottle on the nightstand.

He ripped out the cork and downed a gulp without even sniffing it first. "Thank the glowin' gods." Yawning, he drifted toward the potbelly stove. "Did you..." He peeked inside the cast iron vessel sitting atop it, then screwed his face up at her. "*Cook?*"

She sneered. "I can cook. I had to do it for my father and brothers after my mother died." A fact that still pissed her off some seven hundred years later. "And you're not the first mortal I've had to feed since."

He squinted at the simmering stew. "Is it people, Dags?"

She snorted. "It's *partridge*. And you're going to eat it." Grabbing a bowl from the shelf, she glowered at him. "But it'll be you if you're not careful."

"Heh. No, it won't." He took another drink, then gave her his shittiest grin. "You gotta take good care of me." His voice was sing-song-y. "And you like how I taste too much."

"I've done worse things with my food..." Scooping the stew into the bowl, she skewered him with her glare. "I'm glad your *hysterics* are over with."

After a deep breath, he puffed. "Just takin' a break from 'em..." He snatched the bowl from her and sat at the white wicker table by the window. "I'll try to do like you said. *Today* might be okay..."

"It will be better than okay." She leaned awkwardly on the short counter rather than try to sit near him in a flimsy chair.

He ate, staring out the window at the glittering forest with his uncovered eye watering.

"The Goldenbark elves are second only to the faeries in protecting their territory from outsiders," Dagmar said to fill the silence. To try to distract him from missing Sarlona, dreading his impending transformation, or whatever else was making him hurt. "Even the Council couldn't find us here if they thought to look."

He sniffed and cleared his throat. "How'd *we* get here then?"

"I called in a centuries-old favor with their chieftain." A favor owed more to Glaucus than to her, but the ancient elf had seemed eager to repay it and mess with Kyran. He hadn't taken convincing to provide refuge. "It's more difficult still to get out than in. Even I have trouble with all the illusion and confusion wards..." Much as she didn't want to upset him further by pointing out that there was no chance of escape, he had to understand it.

He took another big drink before glancing at her. "Well, if I can drink and fuck here, Dags, I guess there ain't no reason for me to go anywhere else."

Something squirmed in her gut. Irritation or heat? She *had* told him they could do what he needed...

"So, this is what we're doin'?" He wiped his eye and slicked his hair back. "Playin' house until I sprout claws?"

"I'm weak, Benton. The kind of quick required to reproduce... I don't have anything close to that. So, I need a safe, quiet place. Somewhere I can take my sweet time with you, and we can grow strong together."

He perked up. "Are you sure you can even do it?"

"Not sure, but confident. You have a lot of quick from a *powerful* female in your body..." The first dose, before Sarlona spent herself on Dagmar, had been particularly potent. If she'd put even a trace of the intent to make Benton a lorkai into him, he might have risen from the dead without any help from Aldamon. "My hope is that I can trigger it... You'll be Sarlona's progeny, Benton, not mine." A lie. He'd be some aberrant combination of both, but it would comfort him to think of himself as Sarlona's spawn once he was turned.

A shadow passed over his face while the light flickered in his eye.

"It will happen, Benton." He needed to come to terms with that. "Your body's already adjusting," she said, gesturing to his left arm. Worry gnawed at her heart, though. Usually, a mortal's body gained strength, agility, and heightened senses...primed itself... That was all good. But the change in his arm was bizarre. She'd never heard of a mortal developing more than minor internal changes ahead of the making. Of course, to her knowledge, no one had ever been fed quick as potent as Sarlona's. "But I'm not going to complete the making until I'm *certain* you'll survive it."

His eye glazed over, and he took another swig from his bottle before finishing his soup. "When..." He gulped. "It happens..." After a deep breath, he rose and paced before the door. "What am I supposed to do, hunt elves? The Goldenbark chieftain is fine with us terrorizin' his people?" He narrowed his eye. "What're *you* gonna eat? I ain't enough with you young and spittin' up all your quick into me."

She grinned. "I'll show you." Striding out the door, she motioned for him to follow.

He groaned. "I ain't gonna like this, am I?"

Smiling to herself, she led the way around the side of the cottage. "Well, it's more for me at the moment, but you might still enjoy it."

He hung back as she heaved clear the boulder she'd laid before the cellar door, then unchained the lock.

"If anyone's got pieces missin' or bones goin' the wrong way in there, I ain't in the mood for it," he said from behind.

She threw the door open. "I haven't done any visible damage. Yet."

The man and woman within squinted against the midday sun and shrank into the wall they were chained to. Dagmar let her eyes flare red and grinned. Something about mages fitted with metal collars always made her smile. Now more than ever.

"Hells, Dags, who do you got in there?" Reaching for an absent sword, Benton peeked inside. His gaze settled on the middle-aged woman, and he smiled. "Heh. Don't I know you, darlin'?"

He should. She was one of the three women who had accompanied Kyran to collect Sarlona from Northland. She peered at him with a blank expression.

"They can't speak. I've made modifications to their vocal cords."

Benton gave her a look, but his heartbeat and breaths were steady. If he was horrified, he didn't show it. "Who's this one?" He jerked his chin at the man.

Dagmar hunched over for the low ceiling and descended the two steps into the shallow cellar. The scent of pure terror in the air spiked as she stalked toward her prisoners. She took a deep breath, wanting to answer without tearing the man's face off. "This is Rasteel..." Grabbing the man by the hair, she wrenched his head up to view her fiery eyes and every wisp of malice behind them. The smell of fear intensified, and ammonia followed it. "He's one of the tower guards who...*introduced himself* to Sarlona while she was in Kyran's care."

Benton's nostrils flared, and his skin mottled. Clenching his fists, he advanced toward the man. He glowered at the doomed mage, heart raging, then glanced at Dagmar. "What are you gonna do with 'em?" His voice shook.

"Drain them, mostly." Dagmar wound her fingers tighter into her captive's matted brown hair. "Rasteel here is destined to have his tongue, hands, and cock removed," she said, reveling in the tremble beneath her palm.

He shut his eyes, and a tear trailed down his cheek.

She'd make him fill a river. "But I'm not in any hurry."

After smacking the mage's head on the stone, she turned to Benton. "I plan for them to last, but I'm sure I'll add to our stores in the coming months." She took him by the arm and led him from the dank cellar to the gilded glade. The sweet smell of meadow grass baking in the summer sun replaced the reek of frightened mages as she closed her makeshift dungeon. "Do you understand that you don't need to fret over losing control and draining the life out of innocents?" she asked, patting him on the shoulder. "We'll have a little herd of casters for you to drink from. Mages I would make swallow their own eyes and balls if they weren't feeding you." Squeezing him, she forced a lightness into her voice. "You won't want for Marrow, but if you lose control occasionally, your victims will have earned the death you grant them."

Benton paled and headed up the steps to the porch and into the cottage. Snatching up his birch spirit, he downed the rest of the bottle. "I hope you got more of these."

She handed him a fresh one from the pantry.

It took him three seconds to wrench out the cork and start on it. "Gotta enjoy it while I can."

She stared past him, out the door, at a golden butterfly fluttering between flaxen blooms. Her chest knotted up. Sarlona would have loved it here. If the young woman's magic hadn't been so dangerous, and she hadn't regenerated Marrow so quickly... Dagmar could have taken her someplace like this to make her. Just the two of them. Not locked her in a warded chamber guarded by alcoholic criminals and dark mages. With enough time, warm words, and gentle touches, she might have convinced Sarlona that becoming a lorkai wasn't the worst thing in the world. Like she hoped to do with Benton. "There will be plenty of things to enjoy."

He scrutinized the hardwood plank between his bare feet. "I don't get quite the pleasure outta torturin' folks that you do. Even if they're askin' for it."

As well as she'd come to understand him, she wasn't sure whether he'd visit their two captives before he hungered for them. Or if he'd leave their respective punishments to her. "I don't get off on causing pain," she told him. Fear, on the other hand... Mortals tasted better when flavored with it. "It just doesn't bother me."

"No..." He gave her a dangerous grin. The kind she'd have knocked from his face not long ago. "You kinda get off on receivin' it, though, don't you, Dags?"

Heat smattered her cheeks, and her muscles itched. Gods, she'd never live that down... But she'd take any smile she could get from him. "I'm sure, given a few more centuries, you'll figure out what gets a woman off."

He snorted, reddening. "I made Sar scream every cockin' time."

Dagmar's stomach twisted at the thought of him with Sarlona, even though she could appreciate him in some of the ways her daughter had. He tasted divine and was fun to play with, but Sarlona had been too good for him. "I do seem to remember her hollering for help when you made those first advances."

He folded one arm, drinking with the other, and peeked out the window. "Yeah..." He shrank. "I was an asshole."

Maybe she shouldn't have reminded him of that.

"Gods...this is just what she was feelin'..." he said after a few minutes, rubbing his temple. "Except *worse.*"

That was true. After years of bouncing between bands of highwaymen only to land in a lorkai's barracks, unlike Sarlona, he was well accustomed to violence and monsters of all kinds. He had no family or future to lose. His captor had imprisoned him in an enchanted wood, not a cold, warded room. No large men were drooling over him. He wasn't afraid of being touched. And no one was threatening to take his sword arm. His talents would be enhanced when he turned.

He had only one major fear about becoming a monster—that he'd be fucking great at it. What if he didn't just have ravenous and ruthless moments but became thirst incarnate? A force of soulless depredation.

"It is ironic..." Dagmar said, sweeping her hair back. "You helped me do to her what I'm doing to you."

He angled away, hiding his face as he drank.

"Perhaps this is just what you deserve." She crept closer and rested her hands on his shoulders. "Perhaps it can be your penance."

He peeked at her with a watery eye.

"For everything." She slid her hands over his arms. "You were a monster, so now you have to live as one." Tugging his elbow, she spun him. "*Accept* that. And *let go* of your guilt."

He slumped with his sigh and stared at her knees. "It's that easy, huh?"

She tipped his chin to gaze into his face, but he wouldn't meet her stare. The dread still wafted off him. "It could be. Look at me, Benton."

His electric blue eye locked with hers, and she patted his head. "I won't let you kill a child, all right? That will *never* happen again. I won't allow it." She meant that.

He slunk out from under her hands. "Okay."

Reclining against the counter, he gazed toward the window. "Even if..." He shook his head. "I don't know if I can live another day without her, Dags...never mind...forever."

"I understand..." She parted her lips. *Too well.* She wasn't about to lie down and die, though. And she wouldn't let him do it either. "But if you died today, Benton, you'd still be without her. Our souls can't follow where she's gone." She prayed she was half wrong. That while Sarlona rested in Tydras's heaven, far from the Abyss, she'd be allowed to call her Bound up from the depths when she wanted company. And Dagmar hoped she'd be permitted to leave the halls of her ancestors to visit her daughter.

Benton wilted. He looked like he'd sink into the floorboards.

Sidling up to him, she spoke with the gentlest voice she'd learned to summon. "But maybe, given enough time, you can change that."

A hint of hope infiltrated the scent of despair.

"Meanwhile, you need a purpose." All that kept Dagmar from her own desolation was the duty to continue her species and wreak vengeance on the Council. "How about helping me skin mages alive?"

Benton snorted. "Yeah, *that's* what Sar would've wanted. She told me to be good, Dags."

Dagmar half sat on the counter, too tall to lean on it comfortably, and crossed her arms. "Just because we love her doesn't mean she was right about everything. She was far too forgiving."

"Well, that was one of my favorite things about her." With a slight wince, he bobbed his head. "I wanna do Kyran and that one down there slow," he said, tapping the floor with his foot. "Kick Amen's ass somehow... But I ain't interested in gettin' creative with every robe in Apogee."

Dagmar grumbled. But if he wasn't ready to wage a bloody and terrible war on the people who'd taken the love of his life from him, that was okay. Better that he stayed out of trouble until he was much more challenging to kill. "They don't deserve our mercy, Benton. Not after what they did to Sarlona. None of them."

CHAPTER FORTY

D agmar trailed Benton to the deck when he meandered outside with his bottle and down from the porch to gaze off into the glittering forest. He wouldn't try to run. His panicked scent had shifted to dread and grief, and he couldn't escape the forest.

The bronze of his muscled back melded beautifully with the woods beyond—one more stunning hue in a muted palette of autumnal colors. He looked like a celestial being from behind with flecks of golden bark sparkling as they floated from the trees to land in his hair and stick to his dewy skin.

"Sar woulda liked it here."

A peaceful forest that appeared as enchanting as the magic it radiated? "Yes." She and Glaucus should have brought Sarlona here once she was made. It was the perfect place to raise a lorkai child. To feed from the earth and grow strong together.

Provided one had a few Marrow-rich mortals chained in the cellar.

"Come back up, Benton." She'd fed on her prisoners just a few hours ago, but she couldn't ignore his sweet smell and the sight of so much exposed skin any longer. Her need for Marrow was worse than ever.

Pivoting, he met her hungry stare. Spiciness tinged the breeze while he ascended the steps and set his drink on the whitewashed railing.

She curled her fingers at him, beckoning. Like an obedient dog, he came to her.

His shoulders trembled when she grasped them, but his skin flushed. Peppery pheromones rivaled the reek of alcohol.

Her fingertips glowed fiery blue, and he twitched as she tapped into him. His rich, sugary Marrow flowed to her without any cajoling.

Perfect.

He grabbed her waist. "I wanna fuck you right."

Heat slapped her cheeks, breaking the spell of his ambrosial energy.

She dropped her hands. "It's a fine balance keeping you between despondence and impudence."

His teeth showed with his shitty grin. "I'm complicated."

"You're an idiot." Batting his arms away, she went to the railing, careful not to lean too much on the airy wood. "And drunk." She glanced over her shoulder only to catch his beautiful, electric gaze. "I told you... You couldn't handle it."

He came nearer, so stupidly close. The stench of birch spirit clung to him. "I like it rough, Dags." With brazenness that was hard to comprehend, he rested his palm on her lower back and pressed his hardening cock into her upper hamstring.

He was intoxicated and knew she wouldn't maim him—an obnoxious combination.

"But..." His voice turned sultry as he slid his hand up her spine. "I could go real soft and slow like Glaucus did. If you want..."

She grabbed him by the upper arm and flung him, one-handed, over the rail before she could stop herself. He landed with a thud, skidding on his knees and forearms.

Fuck. Benton *had* seen memories of her while inhabiting Glaucus's brain. She hadn't dared peek into that corner of his mind...

With a hissing sigh through her teeth, she watched him climb to his feet.

After rescuing the bottle that had fallen with him, he brushed the grass off his knees and forearms and tromped up the steps. "Use your words, Dags."

However much she hated Benton holding onto memories of her at her most vulnerable, tearing them out of him seemed too much like erasing bits of Glaucus. "Stay out of intimate moments that don't belong to you."

He flashed half of his grin. "You gotta help me make some new ones, then."

She crossed her arms to keep from tossing him over the rail again.

After another swig, he wandered indoors, tugging her pants at the hip on the way by. "You're gonna take my cock this time."

She sneered, but her pulse jumped, and heat kissed her between the legs. *Fuck*. Her boots brought her into the cottage's threshold without her command.

"And I'm gonna come in you." He flopped onto the bed.

Blood burned her ears. "If you're ready to have some fun, I'm happy to entertain. But *that's* not happening."

He put his arms behind his head. "You're afraid you'll love it."

She wasn't sure what she was afraid of. Letting him play out his dominance fantasy couldn't harm anything but her self-respect.

"Benton, I cherish our playtime." She purred as she drew nearer, just to torture him. "I adore making little cries come out of you." Longing for them seemed dangerous, but her fires ignited regardless. "And I delight in watching you shake and beg." She'd force him to do both. "I even relish it when you scream and contort like I've stuck you with my claw as you explode."

The scent in the air was pure heat. He stared at her with parted lips.

"And I fucking *love* how you taste..." She'd caress every inch of him that night, draining his last vapor of Marrow. Maybe she'd lick him, too. "But I rarely enjoy cock. Especially from mortal men."

"Yeah, Dags... I know..." His grin widened. "But I'm special."

He was, damn him. Something was alluring in him that was difficult to describe. Like a spark. A star on a dreary night that peeked through the clouds. Or a firefly that hid in the grass. Whatever it was, it had made Sarlona love him. A man who, without it, might have repulsed her. It had probably drawn Aldamon to him, too. And it beckoned Dagmar now.

Giving in to it, she plopped down beside him. She couldn't avoid touching and kissing him, even if she wanted to. Not if she was going to turn him. With a burst of lorkai speed, she yanked him onto her lap. "*I* fuck *you*, Benton. That's how this works."

He grunted as she grabbed him over the pants and tapped into his Marrow with the hand on his ribs. "Understand?"

He strained against her palm and groaned when she flooded him with warm rain. "Uh-huh."

Her moan slipped free when the first sips of his Marrow hit her system, humming along her bones. "So keep your eyepatch on." Even as she gave the order, she ached with the memory of his otherworldly tendrils choking her and thrashing...inside. She pushed her hips into him while she pressed on his mental barrier.

He squirmed in her arms as she sent a bolt of pleasure zipping along his nerves. "*Cock.* Okay, okay." Panting, he tried to stand. "Let me taste you, then. I want you to come for me." He threw open his mind, and she tumbled inside, where the image of her roaring with his face between her legs was front and center.

Fire raced through her, but she crushed him tighter to herself. "The only thing you're using that tongue for is lapping up my quick."

He pictured doing just that off her breasts and down her abdomen to the soft flesh between her thighs.

The quick rose to the base of her throat without the intense focus usually required to call it. "Shit." She nudged him off her and spun him. "Kiss me."

He all but tackled her, and she let him shove her shoulders to the wall. His lips grazed hers, teasing them before his stubbly kiss landed on her cheek. He whispered beside her mouth, "If you want a kiss, then y—"

Growling, she nipped his bottom lip. "You take my quick, Benton. Swallow it for me like a good little Bound. Then tell me how nice I feel inside you." The thought of him drinking without having to control his body made her muscles knot and the quick spurt into her mouth.

Kissing her deeply, he swept his tongue between her lips and sucked out the sweet, aromatic fluid. A second after swallowing, he whined, stiffened, and convulsed like he'd been struck with an electric bolt.

She held him tight to her and kept him from tumbling over the edge of bliss while he rode out the storm.

Gasping, he cursed and sat back, legs wide to straddle hers.

Sarlona had never swallowed willingly.

Smiling, she rubbed his thighs. "Good boy. Now, what's it feel like?"

"Like sugar and spice, what else?" Tantalizing her with more kisses along her jaw, he unfastened her vest and tore open her shirt.

She sucked in a sharp breath when his rough hands grasped her breasts.

He groaned. "Cock, you feel good, Dags." Pulling at her sleeve, he coaxed her to slip out of her top.

Her stomach fluttered as she reclined bare chested for him.

He just gawked for a moment. "Someone oughtta carve you outta marble, you know that..." His hands roved up her iron abs to the elaborate scar Glaucus had left her with. Following its lines with his fingertips, he traced the intricate design across her chest to her cleavage. "You look like one of them Rashivic statues."

A rendition of Alinabah that was displayed outside their temples—the Rashivic war goddess.

He squeezed one breast and kissed her throat like she might never allow it again. "I'll swallow every drop you got for me if I can take your pants off."

She hitched as her quick came up with barely a thought. Her reproductive fires ignited, begging her to plunge a claw through his heart and pour herself into him one trickle at a time until he was hers forever.

She couldn't risk it yet.

Mouth full of liquid power, she sought his lips with hers, but he put his fingers between them. "I wanna lick it off you."

The inferno within raged too hot to deny him. She spat the quick onto her chest.

He dipped his fingers into the glowing liquid and painted her with it, coating her nipples with extra care. Its tingling burn and his agile tongue had her throbbing so hard that she untied her pants herself.

His nails dug into her arms, and he growled past clenched teeth, quaking atop her each time he swallowed. Once he'd licked her clean, he unfastened his pants. "How 'bout you swallow something of mine now?" he asked, grinning.

Dagmar snorted and yanked him off her, tossing him flat on the bed. What he truly longed for had her on all fours. She didn't know if she could do that for him either, but she could make him scream himself hoarse. Straddling him, she clapped her hands on his chest and leaned close to his ear. "Oh, I plan to devour you, Benton—every vapor of Marrow." She drew on his energies and sent a jolt of ecstasy crackling through him.

Balling the blanket in his fists, he hollered—the delicious cry of prey caught in her clutches. "Wait, Dags... No..." His chest heaved, and his eye widened.

She sipped rather than drank and dulled the storm she'd conjured in him to a drizzle.

He hooked his fingers into her waistband and tried to tug her pants down. "Come on, Dags... I gotta give it to you."

With him protruding from his open pants and only thin layers of hide and linen between them, the thought became more appealing by the second.

He arched against her. "I drank all your quick. So you're gonna take all my cock." In his mind's eye, she moaned in heat as he tried to split her in half.

She would have put him through a wall for picturing that a few months ago. Now, it made the ache between her legs unbearable.

She hopped off him and slipped out of her pants and boots. "All right..." The thought of him screaming and writhing beneath her, eyes rolled back and bleeding the scent of bliss was too enticing to resist while she throbbed like this. "But I plan to ruin mortal women for you."

For once, he had nothing to say. He just stared with his gaze crawling up and down her naked body.

She shoved him flat when he tried to rise. "*Stay.*" Kneeling on the bed, she yanked his pants down to his ankles, then straddled him again.

His body twitched with his heartbeat. He shook so vigorously when she grasped him that the bed vibrated.

Her heart thundered, and her blood scorched her skin as she lined him up with her entrance. Wispy embers swirled in her recesses, needing to be stamped out. All her being ached to envelop him. Gods, how could she want him this way? *Benton.*

Her chest heaved as he jutted his hips just enough to push his end into her. She held him steady while she lowered herself bit by bit until she was impaled. How many years had it been since she'd last let a mortal man enter her?

Grabbing her hips, he tried to pull her down as he rammed himself up. He hit her deep, jostling too small a noise from her. His spicy scent burned her nose, and his wild, hungry thoughts brought more blood to her face.

Beaming, he thrust, and another shock raced from her core to her fingertips and toes. "Cock, Dags..." His tone was warm and teasing. "You're too soft and sweet inside to be a real monster."

She wrapped a hand around his throat and ripped at his Marrow to remind him of the truth, but his ambrosial taste triggered a moan that just encouraged him. Merciless, he drove, punctuating each pleasure-laden stroke with a pulse of pain that had her close to exploding within seconds.

She tightened on him, but that only made him wilder, and she was too slick for it to temper his fevered thrusts. "Gods, Benton..." Half of her couldn't believe that she'd even let him fill her...never mind that he felt so fucking incredible. His every movement catapulted her nearer to shattering. "Slow down..." Instead, he attacked more voraciously, and she gasped, fighting to keep from unraveling. "Slow down or—" *Too late.* A hurricane tore through her center, arching her back, locking her muscles, and curling her toes. She roared as waves of pleasure crashed on her insides.

Her scream quieted into a moan, but while the ecstasy receded from her, it built in him.

"Cock. *Fuck*, that's good." He frantically slammed himself up, nails digging into her thighs. "I'm gonna come so deep in you that you cockin' taste it."

Once he teetered on the cusp of bliss, she grabbed his hands to keep him from toppling into it. Pinning his wrists above his head, she rested more of her weight on him and stilled his hips. "Didn't I tell you to go slow?" She ground on him a little at a time.

Panting and glistening with sweat, he wriggled beneath her. "I got you good, s—"

His words were devoured by his moan when she sent a jolt of tingling warmth through his bones and drew hard on his magical energy. Heat raced into her with his heavenly taste, seeming to saturate her every fiber. The divine Marrow, combined with the whine he made each time she tightened on him, drove her wild. His feverish longing became her own. She rode him until she'd drained most of his magical energy, and his muscles shook with exhaustion.

Then she let him work his hips again. He pounded into her, a little weaker and jerkier than before. Each thrust still delivered that forceful burst of pain-tinged pleasure she craved.

His beautiful eye held all the wildness of a Northland wolf's as he thrashed beneath her. "Here you go, darlin', I'm gonna fill you up." A sweet scream of ecstasy tore out of him, and he spilled into her. "Fuckin' *take it*, Dags... You take all of it."

She chased the end of his euphoria into her own. Her muscles burned tensing in rapture, and the ceiling bleached while her eyes rolled and flared with white light. For a few seconds, she dissolved into bliss.

When she returned to being, she found Benton gasping beneath her. Contentment fluttered in his chest, but he winced from his throbbing wrist. She'd fractured it in her grip. "Sorry," she said, breaths ragged, and mended the bone.

"That's all right." He closed his eye while she healed his torn muscles for good measure. "Will you lay with me some?"

"In a minute." She rose, breaking their mental connection, and wiped herself off. "There's something I should get over with since we're both topless."

His eye popped open with a raised brow, and he hauled his pants up.

She pointed to the scar on her chest.

Puffing, he shut his eye again. "Great."

She shrugged. "Sorry." *Not really.* Even when other lorkai families still lived, the scars hadn't served much practical purpose. There was no reason to do it other than tradition—and to mark him as hers.

He went limp. "I don't give a cock. That's the least of my cockin' problems."

She flicked out one carpal blade and hinged it at a forty-five-degree angle to point it at her chest. "It'll hurt me more than it's going to hurt you, anyway."

"Why?" He peeked at her just as she rammed the tip of her claw up under her sternum and into her heart, careful not to nick her lungs this time. "What the *cock* are you doin'?" With his eye wide, he shot into a sitting position.

She yanked her blade out with a growl and a gush of blood, pain crushing her chest in a vise. Grimacing, she waved him down with her other arm. "I'm supposed to do it with a claw dipped in my heart's blood."

"*Why?*" He screwed up his face and lay back.

Who knew for certain? But it had been important to Glaucus. She shook her head. Her claw had missed her lung, but expanding her chest enough for the breath to speak was still agony. *Some symbolic bullshit.*

With blood streaming down her front, she grabbed Benton's hand and numbed his chest.

He stared at the ceiling when she began her work. "Thanks, Dags..."

She couldn't imagine what for as she mutilated him.

Squeezing her hand, he glanced at her face and gave her a thin-lipped smile. "I just... Thanks for at least pretendin' you care about me."

She paused the careful slice of her claw through his skin to gaze into his eye. *I'm not pretending, Benton.* Not anymore. *I...* Gods, could she actually say it? It was true, wasn't it? There was too much of her in him to deny it any longer... *I love you.*

Red flooded his cheeks, and his eye brightened, an uncharacteristically earnest grin splitting his face. He was glowing.

"Dags—" Breath stuttering, he strangled her fingers. Dew seeped into his eye and tightened his throat.

He didn't have to say it. His scent reeked of it. Not like it had for Sarlona, but...

He loved her back.

CHAPTER
FORTY-ONE

Benton bolted upright in bed with the image of Sarlona's charred face pursuing him into the waking world and a raspy scream in his throat.

It was the same nightmare. His immolated kid brother morphed into the crispy corpse of the woman he would have died for. Both gone. Burned. Because of him.

In the dim light, it took him a moment to recognize the interior of the tiny bungalow that had become his new home. The delicate, airy, pastel cottage contrasted with Ashmore's crude, shadowy, unpainted rooms.

The brawny arm he'd fallen asleep with no longer crushed him to a broader chest than his own. Dagmar had gone.

After wiping his sweaty hair out of his eye, he stretched for the bottle on the nightstand and froze—someone lurked in the cottage's open doorway, silhouetted by the moonlight. A figure much too small to be Dagmar.

And too dark and emaciated to be anything other than an animated corpse. He prayed for the Demon of Zelule or his mother's carcass. But when the blackened woman turned to glance at him, Sarlona's eyes blazed from the scorched face.

"Sar—" He choked on her name. "I *can't*." His insides tried to rip free of his body.

She disappeared out the door, her spindly hand lingering on the frame and tailing her.

He scrambled from the bed, tangling himself in the elven silk blanket and almost crashing to the floor. Much as he didn't want to see Sarlona like that for another second, he had to chase her. What if she was truly there—*somehow*—having resurrected from the inferno? Or what if she had crossed the Veil to tell him something?

He ran onto the porch to find her below, drifting along the forest edge. "Sar, *wait*."

She twisted again, eyes glowing with blue flame, then kept walking. Blue-gray wisps rose from her sizzling footprints and hung like a smoky trail for him to follow.

"Don't do this to me," he screamed at her back, whatever she was. "*Please*." His voice cracked, and tears stung his eyes.

She didn't slow, desiccated legs propelling her forward one labored step at a time.

He stumbled after her, pursuing her into the ominous shadows of the forest, which wasn't so glittering in the moonlight as beneath the rays of a golden sun. "*Stop*, gods dammit." Catching up to her, he grabbed for her shoulder but didn't quite dare to touch it, afraid his hand would land on crusty, singed flesh—and terrified that it wouldn't. With clenched teeth and a grimace, he hopped in front of her.

She—it—what—whoever was there, stopped short. Her eyes jittered as she surveyed him. And they were *her* eyes— Even squinting against their glow, he recognized the thick rings around her irises and the striations and splotches uniquely hers.

"I'm beggin' you, Sar." His voice broke—his soul—as he gazed at the wreckage of her once beautiful features. "If it's you... *Talk* to me. Talk in my head if you can't speak."

She reached for him, and his pounding heart leapt into his throat. Cracks of blue light appeared at the tips of her skeletal fingers an instant before the cooked appendages grasped his arms.

Cold bone. Meat seared onto a spit. She was real. She had to be... "Sar—"

The leather of her face crinkled as she stared at the spot where her fingers met his skin. She adjusted her grip, and the cracks in her fingers glowed brighter, but there came no draw on his Marrow. The dehydrated meat where lips had been receded, revealing long, smoky teeth. Then she shrieked in his face—this otherworldly sound that reverberated in his bowels and streamed from a mouth that opened too wide.

Benton fell on his haunches, heart thrashing like a wild bird caught in a cage. "Cock."

She spun, marching on.

"*Cock you*," he yelled after her. Croaked. He couldn't take a breath big enough to holler. "You gods-damned demon." Adrenaline shook his legs, making it hard to stand. It took him a few moments to climb to his feet. He staggered after her. The burnt woman might still be her—confused or driven mad. Starving but unable to feed. He felt her. Vaguely. Not, like before, but... "*Hey.*"

He caught up to her at the edge of a glassy pool. She stared at the still, dark water.

Shit.

Shadowy things squirmed at the edges of his right eye's obstructed vision. Tendrils slithered deep in his center, begging to slide out of the Abyss and burst from his face. He told them to calm the cock down.

"Sar... Come this way." Despite knowing he wouldn't be able to budge her, he snatched her wrist. Her black, papery skin crumbled under his grip, giving way to bone.

She pivoted to him, blue eyes blazing as her gaze roved over his body. He froze when she leaned close and sniffed his throat.

"Come with me, darlin'." His voice disintegrated into a whisper. "Dagmar can help you. She'll get you feelin' better."

Peering into his eye, she grabbed his wrist with bony fingers. After flipping over his arm in her hands, she ran rough, dry fingertips up and down his arm. She took his hand and snapped his wrist back. With a pleasant release, a carpal blade shot out of it. He gaped at the razor-sharp ivory claw in terrified disbelief.

Her eyes cooled to the deep, perfect blue he loved. She glared at him hungrily and squeezed his hand as she turned, leaving him to contemplate the aberrant appendage.

He glanced from her back to the blade. If the lorkai quick had put that evil glint in her beautiful eyes, it would transform him into Vorakor himself.

Gentle splashing tore his attention from his arm.

She'd entered the inky pool.

"*No*, Sar. Wait." With a floundering step, he grasped at her as she waded deeper. His fingers clutched air.

She was gone. Not a ripple in the glassy, onyx pool remained.

Alone, carpal blade sticking from his left arm, the Abyss seemed to open in his chest. He couldn't imagine how he'd take the next breath. Gazing into the towering trees, he searched for the stars or even a glimmer in a canopy full of them earlier. All the golden light had melted away like his hope.

He couldn't do this.

Dwelling in his dreams was one thing. But he couldn't cope with Sarlona haunting his reality. Not in the horrific form she'd taken. Something had to be wrong. Worse than her having been stolen from him.

Maybe he wasn't supposed to be fucking Dagmar or becoming a lorkai. Or...

As he stared at the obsidian pool and tentacles swirled in his depths, he felt like he was sinking into them. What if she'd gone down to the Abyss?

Vorakor's darkness had crept into her once when she was still human, desperate to escape the warded chamber the lorkai had imprisoned her in... She'd even prayed to him to save Benton's soul. And with Amenduil there at her death, casting the spell that ended her...

He couldn't live with her being there alone. No matter how much he cared for Dagmar.

The dread and emptiness ate him alive at the very thought. He floated in the Abyss already. Somehow, his soul had made its way back into the endless umbra. The rest of him might as well join it.

Maybe he could find Sarlona there. They could drift together, entangled in Vorakor's tendrils for eternity. That ending seemed far less nightmarish than one where Benton lived forever, and she drifted in shadows with only wicked appendages to keep her company.

They were meant to be together—always.

He ripped off his eyepatch and tossed it on the forest floor. Ethereal tentacles roiled in his core, wriggling in excitement while they slid up his throat and phased through his eye. He grunted with release as they shot outward, manifesting in his physical reality the instant they exited his scarred cornea.

"Just take me. I don't wanna be here anymore."

Tears followed the tendrils, streaming from both eyes. They blackened as they hit the earth and beaded atop it rather than being absorbed. Moving across the leaf litter like droplets of ebony mercury, they ran together, forming globs, then expanded. The puddle swelled until its edge met the pool Sarlona had vanished into.

Despite the gloom, he sensed movement beneath the glassy surface, infinite tentacles with no beginnings but hungry ends, waving in the boundless depths.

He had to enter them. But his legs wouldn't take him into the hellish pool.

"Please... I can't. Help me." He wasn't sure whether he begged the Abyss itself to swallow him or his cursed appendages to drag him into the Waters, but his tentacles responded. They curved toward him, coiling up his thighs and wrists as he collapsed to his knees.

His heart tried to break free of his heaving chest as one silky tendril encircled his throat. But this was the right thing to do.

The tarred ropes constricted, squeezing first, then strangling. Those snaring his wrists slipped into his palms and tightened to hold his hands.

He couldn't help thrashing when the tentacle around his neck crushed his throat closed. His chest spasmed, trying to cough without breath, lungs pulsing in a plea for air but unable to expand. Blood pounded behind his eyes, threatening to pop them from his skull and leak through the pores in his face.

He toppled on his side at the edge of the Abyss, which swelled and crept nearer like a rising tide. His thoughts unraveled while he convulsed in his silky bindings.

He'd be with Sarlona soon.

He would have been. The forest exploded with a terrible blinding white light, and a booming voice formed foreign words that echoed off the trees.

Dagmar towered over him, scraps of burning paper falling through her fingers. "Shit." She shook her smoking hand, and she grabbed him with the other, dragging him away from the shrinking pool. Grasping the tentacle that choked him, she tore the Marrow out of him, turning them into wisps of raven smoke within seconds. He slipped out of her grip and hit the ground with a thud, but she yanked him onto his feet. "Open."

Coughing and fighting for air, he didn't even attempt to keep her out of his mind. Neither did he open it fast enough.

She punctured his shaky barrier with a sharp spike of her will.

"Ah, *cock*." His head throbbed like she'd cracked it on a rock. Everything he'd seen, heard, thought, and felt since he'd awoken played in his mind at dizzying speed.

"You fucking coward." She slammed him against a tree. "You think you're getting out of this?" the Dagmar he'd known for years roared at him.

He choked on his tears, then growled through the agony of his bruised spine. "I can't cockin' do it, Dags. I can't see her like *that*."

"That wasn't *her*. You know her better than that." Gripping his throat and shoving him harder into the tree, she brought her face a few inches from his.

The feeble light from her luminescent eyes swallowed the subtle femininity of her features. The squareness of her jaw, the rigidness of her nose and brow, and the faint glint of her bared canines made her resemble a demon-possessed barbarian warlord.

"Listen to me, Benton." All the frustration of a hungry Northland bear bled into her voice. "You don't *get to* die, understand?" Her irises bore into his, burning red. "If you try to hurt yourself again, I'll give you to Aldamon." She loosened her hold. "Those are your choices: me or Gulway. Not death. I won't break my promise to her."

Benton's heart shot into arrhythmia at the notion. But he couldn't persist with Sarlona's charred visage haunting him. "It's my fault..." Throat swollen and raw, he whispered, "If I hadn't pushed Sar outta the tower... *You'd* be dead, and she'd be alive."

He swung at Dagmar with the jagged malformation sticking from his wrist. Gods knew why. She caught his arm anyway.

"And if it weren't for me, she coulda run and hid, and Kyran never would've found her."

Dagmar's expression softened. "Maybe..." She patted the side of his face, and the pain bled from his back and throat. "The actions of *many* brought us here... But Kyran and his allies are at fault—not you."

Extending his arm to examine the awful weapon jutting from his wrist, she ran her thumb along its edge. "It's not fully formed... I don't think you could feed with this..." Her gaze skipped to his eyes, concern etched in her features. "Fortunately, you don't feel the urge to."

He yanked his arm away and tightened the muscle that folded the strange claw into his forearm. "Yeah."

Thank the gods. Maddening hunger with no ability to feed would've expedited his journey into becoming a mindless, uncontrollable monster.

She shook her head. "I've never heard of someone turning gradually this way…"

"What's it mean?"

She shrugged and snatched his wrist again. "I don't know." Rubbing along the seam where the blade had ejected, she drove out the dull ache. "I wish my father was here…"

He glared at his arm. "Sar told me to be good, Dags…" His transformation was happening too fast. Dagmar had made it sound like he had months left before he became a monster. "I can't do that rippin' the magic outta folks… *She* could barely do it…"

Dagmar skimmed her hand up his arm and squeezed his shoulder. "Of course, you can." Her tone dripped with certainty. "One touch and you can see into a man's heart. See his crimes and intentions… Even change his mind…" Spinning, she scanned the ground before scooping up his eyepatch. "Imagine the injustices you can set right. The ones you can prevent."

He hadn't considered that. His thoughts drifted to the two kids he'd encountered outside Gulway's gate. He'd helped them. *Probably.*

"You'll be able to make people well who could never afford a healer or potion…" She dusted off the eyepatch and tied it to his head. "You know, most of Ashmore's peasants die of old age. Almost all their children get to grow up. You know how rare that is."

All too well.

"Besides, you don't always have to be terrifying when you feed." With a devious grin, she smoothed his hair. "Just keep that beautiful eye blue and put on a clean shirt before you drift into a lonely young woman's bedroom. You'll be the sweetest dream she's ever had."

He couldn't suppress a small smile. "Heh."

She snaked her arm behind him, sweeping him forward. "Let's go."

"Dags…" He dragged his feet and shrugged her off. "*Somethin'* ain't right. I don't know… I seen *somethin'.*"

Her shoulders slumped, and the blue light of her glowing gaze blended with the scant moonbeams that peeked through the leaves as she tilted her head to the canopy. "It's going to be hard for a long time, but—"

His muscles knotted in frustration. "I *felt* her, Dagmar." He rapped his fingers on his chest. "Not right here but...*somewhere*."

She let her arms go limp at her sides and stared at him, forehead wrinkled. Her lips parted like she meant to speak, but nothing left them.

He dug his toes into moist, humusy soil. "What?"

She puffed, glancing around as if there was anything to view but smooth, papery bark and darkness. "I've seen her too..."

He balled his fists.

Her gaze locked on his face. "But she wouldn't want you to hurt yourself, Benton. I am *certain* of that."

It sure as cock seemed like she did. She acted like she wanted him to join her in the Abyss. "She's tryin' to tell me somethin' then, Dags."

Dagmar's shrug made his face burn. "We both carry her quick... This may just be a symptom of it..." She sucked her lips and blinked. "Some echo left of her from a traumatic death that's still bound to us..." Her apathetic tone sent his nails biting into his palms.

He gazed past her to the pool. While still glassy, it didn't appear so black. Instead, it glowed a faint blue in the muted moonlight. Or perhaps it reflected the color of the lightening sky.

"I think... I think..." Gods, he didn't know what the hells he thought. Or felt, for that matter. Other than the pain of missing the woman he loved more than anything. "She's alive. And needs help." Maybe? Some instinct drew him toward her still. Could it really tug on him from an Otherrealm?

Dagmar's pale skin bleached to bone white, but she snorted. "*Nothing* survives that kind of fire, Benton." Her hands went to her granite hips. "I *felt* her die. I collected the ashes myself. There was no living piece left."

He couldn't describe the sensation—this draw on his soul that had grown worse over the past few days, maddening. Restlessness had replaced emptiness. "Just—" Throwing open his mental protections, he grabbed her hand. "*Feel* it."

Moving into him, she did. And cocked an eyebrow. "I know, but...I'm not sure it's anything but the quick itself."

He ripped his hand free, nostrils flaring. "Well, I gotta be sure. Or I'm gonna lose the rest of my cockin' mind." Gulping for air, he shook his head. "I can't live with her burnt-up ghost skulkin' around." Tears hung perilously from his exposed eye. The notion that even a piece of her tormented soul might be trapped in this realm gutted him.

"Calm down." Dagmar half sneered but the irritation fled her voice for her next words. "Sit," she said, motioning to the large tree she'd pinned him to. "If she's alive, you can join with her."

He put his back to the tree and sat, trying to quash the swell of hope in his chest. If it grew too big only to be snatched away, it would destroy him.

"Close your eyes and think of her," Dagmar said, hushed. "Picture her face."

He shut his eyes and imagined Sarlona's, brimming with all the depth and beauty of the sea.

"Exclude everything else." Dagmar made her voice as gentle and soothing as he'd ever heard it. "There is only Sarlona..."

However central she was in his heart and mind, it took him a minute to fight off the barrage of images and ramblings that tended to cycle through his thoughts before her enchanting eyes, soothing voice, and smooth skin were the whole world.

"Feel her quick within you."

He always did. Knowing that it flowed in his veins was his greatest comfort. His insides thrummed, and his skin prickled as he focused on it. A sensation of immense power rolled into him. Part of her was with him. In him.

"Imagine yourself reaching out to her..." Dagmar whispered.

In his mind's eye, his hand hovered near Sarlona's face. He stroked her hair, weaving the silky, sandy waves between his fingers.

Dagmar's voice intruded from another world. "Call to her."

"Sar?"

Dagmar snorted, distant. "*Telepathically*," she said with a hint of exasperation.

Sar, he screamed in his mind, like an idiot, praying with all his soul for an answer. Nothing. But her life-giving smile and captivating eyes held him spellbound. Until they sucked him in. Then she stood there, right in front of him.

"Join with her," some ethereal voice from another realm commanded.

He was trying. Pulling Sarlona into his arms, he squeezed her close. Her warm, lean frame pressed against his chest, kindling a fire in his core. Inhaling beside her soft locks, sun-kissed skin, salt, and soil filled his nostrils—her scent when she'd still been human.

Then, he was yanked forward, spinning and flailing through the nothingness until he collided with another consciousness.

Hers.

He stared using her eyes at the most beautiful light he'd ever seen—light that made him doubt everything. This shattering beacon that stunned him into stillness and triggered a longing for yet another thing he couldn't have.

Crashing waves rumbled over the calls of gulls in the distance. The taste of salt was on Sarlona's lips. Her fingers curled in fine sand. One thought played in her head—she was home.

The blinding light dimmed, and a handsome man peered out of it. His skin glowed, and sunshine poured from his eyes. Warmth and goodness radiated from his upheld hands and into Sarlona, filling her with joy and gentleness that made her eyes water.

It wasn't meant for Benton.

He recoiled before he got caught witnessing something he wasn't supposed to see, and the devastating brightness burned him hollow.

"Benton."

Slamming into himself, he opened his eyes to Dagmar's green ones fluorescing a few inches from his face.

She patted his cheek with her huge palm. "You're...*smoking*." Grimacing, she waved gray wisps from his eyepatch. "Are you okay?"

With the bleached shadow of the blinding light warming his insides, he couldn't help but grin. "I found her."

Dagmar's face slackened, pale as snow. She parted her lips, but a moment passed before she uttered a warbling word. "And?"

"She's..." He blinked, shaking his head. His bond with Sarlona was so strong he could breach the gates of the sea god's realm to reach her. "She's in the Shimmering Sands." He beamed even as he leaked tears. Sarlona would bask in that sweet, angelic glow forever. "Tydras was with her."

Dagmar's eyes cooled to a dull blue and watered. She covered her mouth for a second, then blinked her tears away. "Good." Smiling, she hauled him to his feet and into her arms. "That's what I thought."

It was better than good. Seeing Sarlona in the heaven she'd prayed for with the god she adored made all the difference in the world. And having his face crushed into Dagmar's chest didn't hurt. He hugged her back.

"She's okay." Dagmar stroked the back of his head and loosened her embrace. Stooping, she caught his lips with hers, trapping him in a long, tender kiss. A kiss she receded from without squirting any quick into him.

Warmth bloomed in his gut and spilled through his limbs.

She pointed him in the direction he'd come from, where the light of dawn seeped into the woods, then took his hand. "And we'll be okay, too."

For the moment, at least, Benton believed her.

EPILOGUE

Kael left camp when the first streaks of pink and orange splashed across the sky, forsaking the clanging of pots and grumbling of men for the serenity of the sea. The morning business could wait. Those first rays of dawn were for Silsor. There was no better time to pray than while the light conquered the night each morning.

He cleared his mind as switchgrass changed to dune grass, and the meadowlarks' high-pitched, lilting songs gave way to a cacophony of gulls. By the time his boots dug into white sands, the last of the stars had faded and a sliver of the blazing pink sun peeked from behind dark but dazzling waters.

The clamoring gulls drowned out the rumbling waves by the time he emerged from between sand dunes and trudged onto the beach. Dozens of sable silhouettes cruised, fluttered, and scurried around a massive oblong shadow.

The screeching would make for a less peaceful morning prayer.

Curious, he neared the gigantic carcass, its fishy reek competing with the salty sea air. A whale? But the narrow, crisp lines of a broad, stiff dorsal fin and vertically oriented tail solidified when he approached. He'd never seen a shark so large. The gulls hopped and flapped a couple of yards away when he circled the monstrous fish. A few charged back in and ripped off bits of flesh, then retreated to the crowd of birds, which tried to steal their prizes. The far side of the shark revealed the cause of its death—a gaping wound in its belly.

Except for some fine-tooth marks in the skin, the lacerations were neat. Perhaps the result of an offshore fisherman's blade who'd been hunting a maneater. Or maybe some monster of the deep had caused the wound.

He left the shark and gulls behind, trudging up the beach to drier sand for a place to kneel before the sun escaped the water. The only abominable creatures he had to concern himself with were those that preyed on the people of Aven. And right now, he and his men were hunting the pack of werewolves they'd driven into the nearby cave system, not sea monsters.

But no sooner had he cleared his head than he spotted a pink heap between the piles of seaweed at the high-water mark. For a moment, he imagined the lump was the shark's entrails, but as he strained his eyes in the early morning light, a humanoid shape came into view.

A pit opened in his stomach. Someone had been flayed. A woman. Her pink and white flesh oozed yellowish fluid and drops of blood where her skin should have been. A horrific death.

Armor clanking, he knelt. With a tight throat, he offered a prayer for the unfortunate woman, beseeching Silsor to take pity on her soul and grant her a far more peaceful afterlife than her end had been.

Much as he didn't want a clearer picture of the atrocity before him, he tossed a shining orb over the woman's body to illuminate the scene. Though doubtful, he hoped for some sign of the woman's identity or the fiend responsible for her death. Only a wretched spell could have removed her skin so cleanly. And the villain who had wielded it should be hunted with more enthusiasm than any werecreature.

His stomach knotted as he leaned closer, hovering his hands over her and loosing a scan spell so he might pick up any residue of the awful magic that had done this to her. A jolt of dread gripped his chest when a pitch-black aura engulfing her body popped into his mind's eye.

Abyssal magic. He clenched his jaw. The Nocturnal Embrace had done this to her, then. Or, at the very least, a rogue caster devoted to Vorakor. What they were doing on the Tork'nuk Plains or off their coast was a mystery. One he intended to get to the bottom of.

Silsor would have to forgive him for offering his morning prayers on his feet while he hiked back to camp. He wanted to get his scouts to the beach immediately.

But the slightest movement caught his eye as he reached to snuff out his orb. He feared he imagined it. A trick of the light? Or maybe he'd seen a small fly scuttle along the woman's throat... Squinting, he bent lower.

The faintest twitch shook the blood vessels that wrapped around her like webbing.

Hope speared his chest, and adrenaline burst into his veins. A trace of life remained in her. She wasn't breathing, but she wasn't quite dead. He wasn't too late.

Praying aloud to Silsor, he ripped off his gloves and laid his hands on the center of her cold, wet chest and forehead. Using every scrap of Marrow, he poured Silsor's healing light into her.

Smooth, tanned skin formed over muscle and fascia within seconds, and dirty-blonde waves sprouted from her head. Young. And beautifully proportioned.

A large, decorative scar marred an otherwise exquisite chest. She was a heathen, then. Or perhaps the Embrace had done that to her, too, though he didn't recognize the markings.

"Please, Silsor. Wake her." He kept the healing light flowing, trembling as it roared from his body. Her chest rose with a breath. His heart soared.

A lean abdomen and strong arms sat her up when she opened eyes that were as blue as the sea. Blinking, she shaded her face with one hand. "Tydras?" Her voice cracked, just breaching a whisper.

With a beaming smile and burning cheeks, he killed the light. She *was* a heathen. "I am but a humble paladin of Silsor, I'm afraid." He ripped his long, blue cape from his shoulders and threw it over hers. "Captain Kaelynn Rayne. Of King Maerdeth's Light Guard. Second Division."

She gaped.

"You're safe, I promise." He adjusted the cape to better cover her front.

With a slack expression, she gazed up and down the beach. "But...I'm dead."

God help the poor girl. He could only imagine what she'd been through. "No, milady. You're very much alive." He tucked his gloves into his belt and helped the young woman to her feet. "And you're going to be okay."

Eventually. After he'd purged the terrible darkness from her. He saw it clearly now, this black thing hovering over her, left by Vorakor's wicked children. Pagan or not, he'd drive it away. Silsor had to have delivered the girl to him for a reason.

"What's your name?"

She peered at him like she couldn't remember. "Sa—" Shaking her head, she gazed at the sea before meeting his stare again. "Samara."

~~~

Thanks for reading! If you enjoyed *Blackened*, please spread the word. Nothing brightens an author's day and encourages them to keep writing like a positive review. And stay tuned for *Swallowed*, the third book in the the Seeds and Shadows series.

ABOUT THE AUTHOR

Tucked away in a shadowy wood while creatures of the night and bad guys with blades whisper in her ear, K.W. writes spicy dark fantasy full of monsters, magic, and mayhem. Her background in ecology instilled a fascination with predator-prey relationships, and she thinks fires burn hottest if started between enemies.

When she isn't tormenting her morally gray characters, K.W. enjoys roller skating, skimboarding, and spending time with her husband and daughter.

K.W. loves to hear from readers. Connect with her through her website or social media accounts.

Website: kwbernard.com
Twitter: @KerryWBernard
BlueSky: @kwbernard.bsky.social
Instagram: @k.w.bernard
Facebook: K. W. Bernard - Author

www.ingramcontent.com/pod-product-compliance
Lightning Source LLC
Chambersburg PA
CBHW070636260626
47161CB00007B/2729